M000284323

CLASS III THREAT

Copyright © 2021 by Larry Enmon

All rights reserved.

No part of this book may be reproduced in any form or by any electronic or mechanical means, including information storage and retrieval systems, without written permission from the author, except for the use of brief quotations in a book review.

Cover by Fresh Design

Print ISBN 978-1-945419-89-8

Ebook ISBN 978-1-945519-86-7

LCCN 2021936203

This book is a work of fiction. Names, characters, businesses, places, events, locales, and incidents are either the products of the author's imagination or used in a fictitious manner. Any resemblance to actual persons, living or dead, or actual events is purely coincidental. Brand names are the property of the respective companies; author and publisher hold no claim.

CLASS III THREAT

LARRY ENMON

FAWKES PRESS

This book is dedicated to the men and women of the United States Secret Service, by whose efforts we are guaranteed that The People and not an assassin decides our next president.

AUTHOR'S NOTE

Each U.S. Secret Service field office has a Protective Intelligence (PI) element that investigates threats against individuals the Secret Service protects—most notably the president. The majority of threat cases originate from headquarter referrals and involve persons with some form of mental illness. During my tenure with the Secret Service, I spent years working protective intelligence investigations, and they are by far the most interesting and challenging.

The Service classifies threats against its protectees in order of risk and uses three designations. Recently they changed the name of the designations for all official correspondence, but the experienced men and women who conduct these sensitive investigations still prefer the old names. They're now used only in conversation.

Class I – someone who shows an inappropriate or unusual interest in a protectee and is considered of little danger

Class II – a person who makes a threat, but appears not to have the ability or will to carry it out and is considered potentially dangerous

Class III – an individual who makes a threat, has the will and ability to carry it out, and is considered extremely dangerous

No man is worth his salt who is not ready at all times to risk his well-being, to risk his body, to risk his life, in a great cause.

- Theodore Roosevelt

ONE

Rana Saleem pretended to read the paper while keeping his eyes on the two Federal Investigation Agency agents. If checked, Saleem's papers would pass as genuine, but it was best to not take any chances. He had witnessed Pakistani intelligence agents do some crazy things in the past. Not all were sophisticated, but they were effective. Pick out a likely suspect, escort them to prison, and interrogate them until they confessed to something. Guys with absolute authority could never be counted on to do the expected.

Saleem would have preferred a cold beer, but the café patrons all drank hot tea or coffee, so he did the same. He always did what the locals did: wore the same clothes, spoke the same dialect, ate the same foods. His survival depended on not being noticed. Unlike his coworkers assigned to the embassy, Saleem's status as a CIA non-official cover agent afforded him no diplomatic protection. A NOC lived by his wits. When one disappeared into the deep, ugly morass, they were soon forgotten and replaced.

Saleem's rotation was almost over. He never wanted one to end so much. He hated this dreary country—a dirty, dangerous assignment. In less than a month, he'd be sipping a properly aged Sonoma red at his favorite restaurant while watching the sunset over the Golden Gate Bridge. But today he dressed as one of the gray persons shuffling around in the sweltering heat of Islamabad. The oppressive temperatures of late July generally cleared the streets by this time of day, although the covered café patio offered some shade and relative comfort. A lazy ceiling fan rotated as Saleem sipped his coffee and waited. The thick air hung like a veil over the patrons. Petrol fumes, body odor, and the sweet aroma of grilling lamb both excited and sickened the senses. *It was almost time.* Saleem chanced a quick glance around to see if the asset had arrived.

The two FIA agents stopped some customers near the door and checked their identification. The short one aggressively interrogated a man about some problem with his papers. The tall one looked up at the other customers to see who was staring. Saleem made sure not to make eye contact. That was the fastest way to get interviewed or arrested. He swatted a group of flies circling his cup and checked his watch for the third time. The two small rocks on the corner of the terrace wall were the asset's signal for an urgent meeting, so he expected him soon.

What was so important he thought it necessary to break with the sched-uled meeting time?

Two minutes later, the asset strolled in, late as usual. One of the FIA agents stared his way. The asset meandered to the counter and purchased a pack of cigarettes. He scanned the customers but did not acknowledge Saleem. The second FIA agent also gave the asset a hard gaze.

Saleem held his breath and his jaw clenched. *Do not look back at them, you idiot.*

The asset kept his eyes down, pocketed the cigarettes, and left.

Saleem finished his coffee, dropped some coins on the table, and rose leisurely. He could not appear too anxious to leave. FIA always stopped those who looked in a hurry. Saleem would trail the asset at a discreet distance to ensure the guy was not followed. The Agency's safe house in this area of Islamabad was only a few blocks away.

Ten minutes later, when Saleem stepped through the safe house door, the coolness of the room greeted him—the air conditioner set at a comfortable 22° Celsius. Only the light above the small table was on, leaving the rest of the room in shadows.

The asset, looking like a weasel with a scraggly beard and slits for eyes, relaxed at the table, smoking and drinking a beer. An ugly black mole sat in the center of his forehead.

Saleem walked to the refrigerator. "That was close back at the café."

The asset did not answer, just smoked his cigarette, staring at the ashtray.

Saleem helped himself to a beer and sat at the table across from the guy. "We were not supposed to meet until next week." He took a swallow and studied the swarthy fellow with the gold front tooth. He always had an animal odor about him. In the beginning, the guy most likely believed in all the militant Islamic bullshit. Somewhere along the way, he had switched sides. Saleem never completely trusted an asset who switched sides—could be a double agent.

"What is wrong?" Saleem asked.

The asset leaned back in the chair, rolled the tip of his cigarette in the ashtray, and smirked. "I have news." He took another long drag before saying, "They are going ahead with the plan."

Saleem lowered the bottle and fixed eyes on him. *Oh, shit.* "You said they only talked about it—that it would never happen."

The man shrugged and a grin cracked the corners of his lips. "I miscalculated."

A sudden chill sent goosebumps running up Saleem's arms. "When? Where?"

The asset drew on the cigarette again and showed a relaxed expression. He blew out a slow stream of smoke. "Do not know yet, but soon. It has already gone operational. I just found out."

Saleem stood and walked to the other end of the living area. His mind worked better when he moved. He had already alerted the Agency about the plan, but he had never expected it to actually go forward. Rubbing the back of his neck, he stared at the floor. After a few seconds he looked up. "Did they decide who?"

"Sayed," the asset said.

Saleem took long strides back to the table. "I thought he was indispensable."

"None of us are indispensable." The man flashed a quick smile. "Besides, he begged for the chance."

Saleem bent low and leaned on the table, making eye contact. In a menacing voice he said, "You find out the details and get them to me fast. Understand?"

The man appeared unfazed. He shrugged and again rolled the ash from the cigarette. "I will do the best I can, but if I appear too interested, they may get suspicious."

Saleem snatched him up by his lapels and slammed him against the wall. He leaned to within a few inches of the guy's face. The tobacco breath had a rotten odor. Holding up his index finger in front of the man's eyes, Saleem whispered, "I could kill you and your family with just this. All I have to do is push a few numbers in my phone and you are all dead. You have taken our money for a long time. How long would al-Qaeda let you live if I told them what you had been doing?" Saleem raised his voice and tightened his grip on the man. "I do not care how you do it, or how much danger it puts you in, just get the damn details."

The guy's eyes widened, and he stammered, "I will contact you when I find out more, but understand this, your president is in grave danger."

TWO

ichael Roberts sat at his desk and reread the email for the third time. The first read disappointed him, the second frustrated him, and the third angered him. Passed over for promotion the second year in a row. He reared back in the chair and ran a hand through his hair.

What the hell? He had the highest performance evaluation in the Dallas office—Dick made sure of that. Could other agents have placed that much higher around the country? Not a chance.

The Secret Service had a very subtle way of letting you know when you weren't promotable. Every time you bid for promotion, they passed you over. No explanation, no reason, other than you just didn't make the final cut. Was that the signal headquarters had sent with this email? Now he'd have to wait another year before he could bid on a supervisor position unless something unexpected came up.

Roberts stared at the email and twisted the ring on his finger, a nervous habit he'd recently picked up. *Need to talk this over with someone.* Dick might know something; from his years in headquarters, he knew all the players on the promotion board. He and the Secret Service Director were said to be best friends.

Laughter sounded outside Roberts' door as a group of agents

shared a joke in the hall. He twisted the ring again, thinking about how he'd approach Dick with this.

Roberts stared at his hand—his dad's old army ring. When Roberts was born in 1985, his father was well past middle age. Few World War II veterans were still having kids that late in life. By the time Roberts graduated from high school, his dad was an old man. Roberts realized early he'd been an accident. During his childhood, his mom seemed all worn out—a woman no longer in her prime and tired from raising two older brothers. But his dad saw Michael as one last chance to spend quality time with a son. He lavished attention on him. Not working full time anymore, his father dropped him off at school and was there to pick him up every day. Michael never had a spare minute growing up—baseball, camping and fishing trips, and just hanging out together. The old guy made sure he stayed busy and entertained.

Roberts' mom never understood his desire to enter the military or join the Secret Service. But the old man got it. He'd always been a warrior at heart—a patriot.

Roberts stopped twisting the ring and headed to Dick's office. As supervisor of the Protective Intelligence Squad, Dick didn't leave his desk too often.

Walking down the hall, Roberts brushed past a gaggle of agents working on convention assignments standing in a half-circle, having an impromptu meeting. Everyone had a stack of papers and note-books. Bridget drew her long red hair over her shoulder and discreetly winked as he passed.

"Morning, Michael."

Agent Bridget O'Neil was one of his favorite people in the office, mostly because she shared his hatred of bureaucracy and love of spicy Thai food. They usually did a coffee or break room chat every day, but this morning he was on a mission—no time for chit chat.

"Morning, Bridget," he said, and marched down the hall.

He peeked inside Dick's office and found him in his usual position —leaning back in his chair with his black wingtips resting on the edge of the desk, talking on the phone. His resemblance to a younger Jack Nicholson always made the ladies take a second look. Dick had been known to take advantage of the resemblance.

Dick noticed Roberts at the door and waved him in. From the phone conversation, it sounded like another discussion with his broker. Seemed like he had one every other day. Dick always reserved his harshest criticism for that guy.

"No, hell no. Those shares aren't going anywhere but down. Did you read that article in Barron's last week?" Dick asked. "Well, you should. They're saying it's time to take profits."

Roberts loved Dick's office—the large picture window behind his desk, the wall of plaques, awards, and certificates, the bookshelf of mementos from travels around the world over a thirty-five-year career. Dick's stock trading and gambling profits were legendary. Folks said they netted him more than his salary.

"What?" Dick switched ears with the phone. "Well, if you think they're so damn good, buy them yourself, but get me out." Dick released a long, tired breath. "Okay, call me when you have something better." He dropped the phone back into the cradle and ran both hands back over his thin salt and pepper hair.

As Roberts took a seat, Dick scooted his legs under the desk and pulled the knot in his tie a little snugger. The guy probably spent more on clothes than most agents did on their kid's college fund. A whiff of his new hundred-dollar cologne drifted across the desk. His lips formed into his trademark facial expression, a combination of a grin and a smirk. People in the office called it the "devil smile."

"So, what's on your mind, Ace?"

On the way to the office, Roberts had decided to take the direct approach regarding the email. He held it up. "Have you seen the promotion list?"

The devil smile faded, and Dick looked down, pushing his chair back a couple of feet. "I saw it."

Roberts didn't mince words. "Well, what's the deal? I've been passed over again."

Dick blew out a breath. "Yeah, I know. We need to talk about it this afternoon."

If Dick put him off till the afternoon, there was a good chance something else would come up and they'd end up talking about it tomorrow, or the next day. Roberts leaned closer and said, "If I'm being passed over every year, there must be a reason."

Dick squirmed in the chair, shuffling papers, but didn't meet eyes with him. "There is, but I'm not ready to discuss it just now. Besides, something's come up and I need your help. The promotion email can wait." Dick tapped a piece of paper on his desk. "This just came in."

Roberts' stomach churned with frustration. You couldn't hurry Dick. He was stubborn that way. "Okay, what do you need?"

"I just got a new referral that I want you to handle, personally—sounds screwy. Need you to do the interview."

"Is it a threat?"

Dick hesitated a moment. "In a manner of speaking, but the witnesses are a six-year-old girl and her mother. Talk to them and decide how you want to handle it."

Roberts gave the referral a quick glance. He was still aggravated Dick put him off, but that was Dick's way. He'd get to it in his own time.

"I'll take care of it," Roberts said and slipped the referral into his jacket pocket.

Dick fiddled with his gold cuff links. "We'll talk about promotion boards when you get back."

Roberts strolled toward the door. Dick *did* know something but wouldn't discuss it. That probably meant it wasn't good.

Dick said, "Hey, don't forget to take someone with you. The last thing we need is you interviewing a crazy cat lady by yourself."

"Is there anyone left in the squad?"

Dick shook his head. "Naw, everyone but you is out doing site advances for the damn convention. Grab someone from financial crimes." Dick picked the phone back up. "I'll call the supervisor over there and clear it."

"Okay, thanks." Roberts was still pissed because Dick had deflected the promotion conversation, but wasn't going to let him know. Roberts planned to knock the interview out, write up his report, and still have the promotion conversation with Dick before lunch.

"If I'm not here when you get back, check in with me later. I have a follow-up doctor's appointment about some tests later this morning," Dick said. The devil smile had returned.

"Nothing serious, I trust."

Dick dialed several numbers on the phone. "Naw, but they kinda pissed me off."

Dick didn't suffer fools easily. "What happened?"

"Well, the nurse told me they needed a blood, urine, fecal, and semen sample."

Roberts shrugged. "So?"

Dick put the receiver to his ear and the devil smile became wider. "I told her if I'd known that, I could've just brought in my old underwear from last night." He adjusted his tie knot again and winked. "We'll talk after you get back."

Roberts smiled and shook his head. Dick was the champion of the zinger. No way to stay angry with a guy like that.

Roberts marched down the hall in search of a partner from financial crimes. He was lucky to have Dick as a supervisor. Everyone liked the guy. He was the office fixer. If a foreign dignitary came to town and wanted a private box for his family of six to a sold-out Cowboy's game —call Dick. If a bigwig from DHS rolled in and couldn't get reservations at his favorite restaurant—let Dick know. No matter what the venue or time, Dick always came through. The guy knew everyone. Folks said he made lots of contacts at the horse track and casinos.

Yeah, everyone liked Dick, everybody except the Special Agent in Charge. Rumor said the SAIC and Dick had been friends on the president's detail until that Russian trip. After that, they hardly ever talked. No one knew why.

While Roberts walked down the hall, he studied the referral. As usual, it read like a bad book report:

"Duty Agent received a telephone call from subject (Susan Porter) this date. She indicated she and daughter (Abigail Porter), six years of age, had information regarding a threat to POTUS. Reportee stated she did not wish to discuss the matter over the phone, but would prefer an agent speak to her in person."

When Roberts turned the corner and entered the financial crimes area, his spirits dropped. With over a dozen cubicles, the place should have been buzzing with agents talking on phones, typing, or bullshitting. It wasn't. He searched each cubicle, but the only available agent was Keller.

Oh, crap.

Keller had about a year on the job and a master's degree in accounting. Guy was a CPA and one of the *new breed* the Service wanted. When Roberts hired on, most of the applicants were former police or military. Traveling in a group, they were often mistaken for a professional athletic team. Of course, misbehavior by a few had led to the *new breed* recruiting effort. Fewer athletes, more brainiacs.

Keller got along with everyone, but was a pencil-neck—not your first choice for a backup in a fistfight. There probably wasn't going to be any trouble with this interview, so Keller would be okay. Besides, what choice did Roberts have?

He leaned inside the cubicle. "Hey, want to go on a PI interview?"

Keller slid off his wire-framed glasses, blinked a couple of times, and gave Roberts the *I'm not sure I know what you're talking about* look he was famous for. "Right now?"

This was why Keller was the only guy not out doing fieldwork. His people skills were lacking. Roberts leaned a little closer. "Well, it's a PI investigation. How long do you think we should wait to do it?"

Keller's cheeks blushed. "Sorry. Sure, what do you need me to do?"

"You drive and back me up. Get your jacket, gun, and notebook. Meet you out front in five minutes."

Susan Porter lived just off North MacArthur, about ten minutes from the office. Roberts briefed Keller on the way. The look on his face did not inspire confidence.

They parked in front of the upscale condominium and approached the door. The morning temperatures already tracked above ninety. The heat index today was expected to be over a hundred—another miserable summer day in North Texas.

Keller bit his lower lip. "I've only been on one PI interview before."

"How did it go?" Roberts asked.

Keller fumbled with something in his pocket, pulled out an inhaler, and took a hit. "Kinda made me nervous. My asthma acts up when I'm nervous."

"Great," Roberts mumbled. He removed his sunglasses and rang the doorbell. The sooner they knocked this out, the sooner he'd get an answer to his promotion question. "Just relax, I'll do all the talking. You take notes and fill out the questionnaire. And keep your eyes open. Never know about PI interviews."

That was an understatement. Most interviewees had an underlying mental health issue, which made them as unpredictable as a basket of snakes. Roberts had several who'd broken down, cried, and asked for forgiveness after admitting to threatening the president. And just as many became combative and tried to take a swing at him. The last one threw a carton of buttermilk, missing Roberts' head by inches, before they'd managed to cuff him.

The condo door opened, and an attractive woman studied the pair. She was in her early thirties, with shoulder-length strawberry-blond hair and light blue eyes. The loose green, cotton blouse didn't disguise her figure. Full breasts, trim waist, and round hips.

"Are you Susan Porter?" Roberts asked.

Her forehead furrowed. "Yes?" She gave them the hard look you'd give an unwanted salesman or religious hawker.

"Special Agent Roberts." He displayed his ID.

Keller flopped open his identification.

She examined the credentials a moment. "Oh, yes, Secret Service." Her brow relaxed. "Please, come in."

Roberts stepped inside, taking in the details of the living space, looking for clues about Ms. Porter's mental state. The interior of her condo was clean, open, and airy, and the cool air conditioner gave it a welcoming feel. She had arranged her paintings, rugs, and plants in just the right places to provide a splash of color, catching the morning light that filtered in through the blinds.

This place looks safe enough.

Susan directed them to chairs in the living room. She sat on the sofa next to Roberts, clasped her hands together, and laid them on her lap. "So, could I offer you some refreshments?"

Roberts felt distracted. Couldn't quite put his finger on it, but something wasn't right. He made another scan of the place, making sure he hadn't missed something important. "No, thank you. We'd really like to discuss the threat to the president you called about."

Susan nodded. "Oh, right." She moved closer to the sofa's edge and rubbed her palms against her shorts. "I suppose I should call Abbey. She's the one who knows all about it."

Roberts settled back in the seat. "Who's Abbey?"

Susan's left knee bounced, and she cleared her throat. "My daughter."

Roberts' mind went on alert. Perhaps he'd been mistaken. He stiffened and leaned forward. *A six-year-old who knows all about a presidential threat?* The hair on the back of his neck prickled. "Is she here?"

"Yes, she's in her room." Susan's voice dropped to a more serious tone. "There's one thing you should know before talking to her."

Roberts tilted his head in her direction. "Yes?"

She glanced over Roberts' shoulder down the hall and, in a weak voice, said, "She's an Indigo Child."

Roberts wracked his brain, but got nothing. Keller was no help. He hadn't taken his eyes off the V-neck blouse Susan wore, which revealed more than ample cleavage. If his tongue hung out any longer, it might touch the floor.

Roberts shook his head. "A what?"

"An Indigo Child."

"I'm sorry, but I don't know what that is. Is she a special needs child or something?"

From her pained expression, he had a bad feeling he wasn't going to like her answer.

Susan blushed. "Oh, no, nothing like that. It's just that she has retrocognition and sees auras." She stood. "I'll go get her. Make yourselves comfortable." She walked toward the hall leading to the rear of the residence.

Keller scribbled in his notebook. "What's retrocognition, and how do you spell it?"

Roberts hadn't completely recovered from Susan's last words. *Yup, he'd somehow missed a sign.* This place was far from normal. "It's the paranormal transference of information about an event or object in the past."

Roberts knew about the paranormal. All PI agents received advanced specialized training in psychology to assist them in unraveling the delusions of the mentally ill, and most crazy people thought they possessed some sort of psychic ability. Roberts had even done a little research on people who saw auras. Nothing in the scientific community could prove or disprove aura reading, and Roberts figured it was most likely another mental challenge some folks faced.

Keller finished writing and craned his neck toward the back hall. He winked and whispered, "Did you see the rack she's carrying around? I bet they're store-bought."

Roberts couldn't believe Keller's greatest observation of the interview so far had been Susan's body. He controlled his temper and leaned closer, keeping his voice low. "Don't you understand, if she thinks her daughter possesses retrocognition, they're both messed up?" Roberts looked down the hall. "Just stay alert and watch yourself. No telling what could happen when she drags that kid out."

Keller frowned and mumbled, "What a shame, someone that good looking and nuts."

THREE

Hashem Abdul-Sattar aL-Sayed had slept a restless sleep. His dreams were not peaceful. He lay in bed staring at the ceiling of the dark hotel room, old smells from some previous animal in the room worming their way to his nose. Harsh rays of sun slashed through the small spaces between the cheap blinds, laying stripes on his hands as they drifted over his scars. On his arms, his chest, and the most recent, his abdomen. He remembered each encounter, each sacrifice, each battle. The men he had killed; the men who almost killed him. Sometimes doubts slipped into his thoughts. Had it all been worth it? Had his sacrifices been worth the cost? He wiped the ideas from his mind. Of course, they had.

His only concern today was the loss of his prayer beads. Being raised in a Muslim household, he remained keenly aware of omens. The loss of the beads was a bad one. He tossed and turned, his past memory at last gaining the upper hand.

———

The White Mountains of Eastern Afghanistan near the Khyber Pass. November 29, 2001, before dawn. He and his two companions had begun ascending the mountain to the cave complex of Tora Bora the night before. The temperature had dropped a few degrees every hour, making their wait even more miserable. Blowing snow stung his eyes, and he squinted.

Sayed lay on the cold rocky ground with his bodyguard, rubbing his gloved hands together for warmth that never came. The waiting was difficult because it allowed him too much time to think. There were so many ways this could go wrong. Whatever happened, the plans must be delivered. He chanced a peek over the edge of the ravine that sheltered him and his companion, but the mountain remained dark and covered with snow. Cold wind and ice pellets pelted his face as he shielded his eyes and gazed up.

Black clouds rolled in, filling the sky with swollen gray stains that signaled more snow later today. The ravine offered little protection from the US aircraft, which constantly circled overhead. The popping of stray gunfire in the distance reminded him it was still very much a war zone. At first light, the Americans would renew their bombing attack.

The bodyguard edged closer and pulled the wool wrap from his mouth. "It should not be much longer. He is probably on his way back."

Sayed nodded and blew on his hands. They could not stay here much longer. The ditch offered the minimum amount of protection against the infrared and thermal imaging technology the US warplanes possessed. Day by day, they had systematically destroyed the al-Qaeda redoubt and its defenders. US Special Forces and their Afghan allies had moved like vermin into position on the lower levels of the mountain. Using their hand-held target designators, they painted the mouths of caves with lasers until a plane delivered a bomb or missile. Dozens of brothers had died or been buried alive as a result of this cowardly type of fighting.

Sayed had no guarantee he would make it back to the cave. He tapped his bodyguard on the shoulder. The man turned, his face a mask of dark against the snowy background. Sayed held up the satchel. "If I do not make it, this case must find its way to the sheikh.

There is a map and letter for him." The thought that the satchel could end up in enemy hands was Sayed's greatest fear.

The bodyguard nodded and turned back to the snowy path.

The battle had not gone as expected. Fearing their positions might be overrun, the sheikh had sent Sayed on the most urgent of missions. He had completed the task and could report success. How long since the guide had left? Half an hour, or a little longer?

Running footsteps echoed in the darkness. His bodyguard sprang into a kneeling position, swinging his weapon toward the path as the intruder approached.

"Who is there?" the bodyguard shouted.

"It is me, do not shoot," came the whispered reply.

Out of the darkness, Hassan—the guide—hurried down the ravine toward them.

He motioned with his hand. "All is ready. Come, hurry."

Sayed and his bodyguard scrambled to their feet and followed the guide along the path and up the dark ravine about a quarter of a mile where a ditch with heavily packed snow waited. Hassan advanced and gave the passcode.

"Allah is great."

In the darkness, on the other side of the ditch, a voice answered, "And so is his prophet, Mohammed."

Hassan replied, "Our lives are in their service."

"Advance," the voice said.

Sayed and his companions eased across the ditch filled with ankle-deep snow. He felt the presence of the men on the other side before actually seeing them. Soon, dark outlines of haggard brothers dressed in heavy clothes appeared from the stone outcroppings. Sayed passed through the outer defensive perimeter and exchanged greetings with them. They offered hugs or gave a pat on the back. Their morale appeared high, but the fatigue and worry in their tightly drawn faces bore testimony to the beating they had taken over the weeks.

The first light of day broke through the dense clouds as Sayed entered the second, and last, defensive perimeter. He gazed at the granite cave complex he had followed the sheikh into weeks earlier.

Sayed turned back and thanked his companions. He must now

report the success of his mission, alone. He hugged each one and whispered, "Allah be with you."

Sayed moved through the familiar cave passages and studied the eyes of the men he passed. Who would go, and who would stay and fight a rear-guard action? A heavy rug covered the entrance to the sheikh's chamber. Sayed announced his presence and waited for permission to enter. He hoped to find the sheikh alone.

A voice inside ordered him in, and he found Dr. Ayman-al-Zawahiri and the sheikh sitting together on the carpet-covered stone floor, the remains of a meal of rice and lamb kebabs on their plates. They ate olives and sipped mint tea. The kerosene heater and lanterns lit and warmed the small stone room—giving it a petrochemical odor.

Bin Laden rose, clad in heavy robes with his signature camouflage jacket unbuttoned, and greeted Sayed with an embrace and kiss on each cheek.

"Allah be praised, you have returned safe. Tell us of the outcome."

Sayed sat, and Zawahiri poured him a glass of mint tea. Zawahiri pouring him tea! The man was a near-prophet. With the successful completion of the mission, Sayed's standing with the sheikh and Zawahiri had risen. Sayed accepted the tea with a nod and greedily sipped the sweet brew. Its warmth soothed him as his cold fingers tingled with the sudden heat.

Bin Laden allowed him to enjoy his drink a moment before breaking the silence. "Now, what did you learn? Is the deal struck?"

Sayed wiped his lower lip with his finger. "Yes, Sheikh, it could not have gone better. The plan is arranged, and we should leave as soon as possible. The dogs of the Northern Alliance are closing in. We will be surrounded and cut off soon."

Bin Laden shifted his gaze to Zawahiri, who nodded.

"Where did you meet, and who attended the meeting?" Zawahiri asked. He leaned his large frame on a stack of pillows in the corner. He always wore a suspicious glare.

"At the home of Younus Khalis," Sayed replied.

Bin Laden took a sip of tea and set the glass aside. "And those in attendance?"

"I met with Khalis, Awol Gul, and Mohammed Amin."

"Do you suspect treachery?" Zawahiri asked. His tone and expression were laced with suspicion.

That was just like Zawahiri, always suspecting something, but never offering proof of anything. "No, Doctor, I delivered the sheikh's generous gift to Khalis, and I believe we can count on his loyalty."

Zawahiri leaned forward with a cold glint in his eye. "Count on his loyalty! That old bandit? More like bought three times over."

"Doctor," bin Laden counseled, "our struggle and the jihad has only begun. We'll need friends in this area for many years. Is it not worth a few extra coins to ensure our escape and guarantee loyalties for the future? Besides, Khalis has several commanders who he must share the gift with."

Zawahiri settled back on the pillows. He slipped off his glasses and massaged his eyes with his thumb and index finger. "Of course, excuse my grumblings. I'm very tired." Zawahiri allowed a rare smile, but behind that innocent expression lay the mind of a true politician. He'd staked out his suspicions of Sayed's plan. It was now up to Sayed to either make it work or receive an I told you so from Zawahiri. Ignoring the old pig was the safest bet.

"Now for the details," Sayed said. He pulled out a large map and spread it on the floor. "We should leave after sunset today. With the cloud cover, and snow tonight, our tracks will soon be hidden. This ravine here," Sayed pointed at the map, "will lead us straight to the meeting spot. Where the pine forest begins is the rendezvous location. Gul and his escorts will join us, and we will travel this easterly route"—Sayed's finger squirmed along the map—"through Parachinar to the tribal areas, less than twenty miles away. If we leave tonight, we'll easily be safe before noon tomorrow."

"Excellent. Any questions, Doctor?" Bin Laden passed the map to Zawahiri.

Zawahiri pulled his glasses lower on his nose as he bent forward and examined it, his customary frown firmly in place. He pointed to a couple of spots along the way. "These areas appear to be exceptionally rough going. We'll need the proper equipment."

Sayed gritted his teeth. "Of course, Doctor. I'll instruct the men to pack climbing gear." The old man just had to throw in a comment.

The sheikh rose, and Sayed did the same. Bin Laden approached and held out his hands, palms up. Sayed grasped the hands of his master, not knowing what to expect. They were as cold as his.

"You can lead us to this meeting location, Sayed?" bin Laden asked.

"Yes, Sheikh, all will be as I've explained."

Bin Laden smiled. "Good, then please accept this as a small token of my appreciation." With that, he reached into his jacket and retrieved a set of the most beautiful prayer beads Sayed had ever seen. Thirty-three beads in the string. Every other one a black or white pearl. The last three beads were amber, with a large, gold crescent moon medallion on the end. Inscribed on one side were the words, "God is great." On the opposite side, the inscription, TO MY MOST LOYAL SAYED, FROM THE SHEIKH.

Bin Laden pressed them into Sayed's hands and held tight. "You have served me well and faithfully these many years. Only my most loyal confidantes, advisors, and commanders receive such a tribute." Bin Laden's countenance was warm and reassuring, his eyes sincere.

"Fewer than six of these exist." Zawahiri said, and held up an identical set.

"Go with Allah always, and hold me up in your prayers to him," bin Laden said, embracing Sayed. "Now eat something and rest. We'll leave when it's dark."

"Thank you, Sheikh." Sayed bowed as tears clouded his vision. When he spoke again, he choked on emotion. "I shall cherish these always. You honor me more than I deserve with this gift." Sayed felt like a small child receiving a great reward from his father. The father he always wished he'd had.

"No, it is you who honor me with your loyalty," Bin Laden replied.

———

This last memory shook Sayed awake. He sat up too quickly, and a bolt of sharp pain raced through the recently healed wound in his abdomen. Beads of sweat ran down his cheeks.

A serious mistake of basic operational security, taking the prayer beads on this assignment.

When traveling under an assumed identity, never retain anything that could compromise that identity.

Sayed had written those words years ago when revising the Syrian foreign intelligence protocols, and now he had broken his own rule. But, in his heart of hearts, he understood he would never have left them behind. The beads provided strength and fortified him in his spiritual times of doubt. Since the sheikh's death, they were all he had to remember him. And now they, too, were gone.

He stared again at the filtered light shining into the dingy room. He'd waited a long time for a chance like this. A chance to strike a decisive blow against the infidels. A chance to seek revenge.

This was his time, and no power on earth would stop him.

FOUR

Susan strolled back into the living room holding the child's hand. "Gentlemen, this is my daughter, Abigail."

Roberts and Keller rose.

The young girl stood behind her mother like a small statue. Her long, silky blond hair barely touched her slim shoulders. She closely studied them as if trying to figure out a complicated math problem. Roberts didn't know very much about kids or how tall the average six-year-old should be, but this child was tiny, which made her appear younger. But her size wasn't her most striking feature. It was the eyes. Large, blue eyes—clear and wide. They had an old wisdom look about them. They weren't crazy eyes though, not like people with extreme psychological issues.

Roberts pulled in a breath and a tinge of anxiety ran up his spine. He didn't like the prospect of interviewing her. He bit his lip. Something about that kid gave him the willies.

Roberts smiled at the strange girl with the big blue eyes. "Hi, I'm Michael," he pointed to Keller, "and this is Edward. Mind if we ask you a few questions, Abigail?"

The little girl only stared at him. Roberts glanced at Susan, grinned, and then turned back to Abigail. She continued gazing at him with a blank expression. *Was she non-verbal?* He was about to rephrase the question when she spoke.

"Are Michael and Edward your first or last names?"

He was startled—*weird.* "They're our first names," Roberts replied.

"May I see your identification, please?" she asked in a soft, expressionless tone.

"Certainly." Roberts displayed his Secret Service commission book. "Here you go."

Abigail eyed Keller. "Are you also a Secret Service Agent, or just a friend of Special Agent Roberts?"

Keller quickly presented his credentials.

She held out her small hand. "How do you do. I'm Abigail, but you may call me Abbey if you like."

Roberts did a double-take at the precocious child. *Getting weirder every minute.* "Thank you, Abbey." He shook the child's hand and pointed at the sofa. "Let's sit down for a few minutes and you tell me what you know about this threat against the president."

Roberts kept a close eye on the girl. He still had a bad feeling. Something was seriously odd here, but he couldn't quite figure it out. Keller had his notebook opened and pen at the ready. Should have told him to be more discreet. That kind of pose made PI subjects nervous. Lots clam up at the sight of paper and pen.

Abbey sat with her hands in her lap. "That's what you do, isn't it?"

"What?"

"Protect the president."

"Yes, that's why we're here," Roberts said. "Your mother says you have the ability of retrocognition. Is that true?" Asking this question so early in the interview was a double-edged sword. Roberts wanted to clear the air on the subject before the child went into her account of what happened. If she had psychological issues or just a vivid imagination, this might bring it out early and give him a heads up on how to continue the interview. No use wasting a lot of time. He wanted to wrap this up. Get back to the office and talk to Dick about the promotion email.

Roberts leaned forward in the chair, waiting to see how she

responded. Susan lowered her head and gave her daughter a nervous smile.

Abbey didn't answer immediately. She raked her blond hair out of her eyes and leaned forward, arms resting on her legs. Her eyes met Roberts' in an uncomfortable stare down. "Well, not really retrocognition," she said. "It's more like psychometry."

Roberts eased back a bit and searched his memory. Never interviewed anyone who claimed that particular power. *How the hell does she know about this stuff? The mother—has to be the mother.* He shot another glance at Susan. Her neutral expression gave nothing away.

Roberts nodded. "So, how do you know what psychometry is, Abbey?"

"I read about it."

He again leaned in closer. "Tell me what it is?"

Abbey never took her eyes off his. She recited it as if reading from a text. "It's when a person can tell something about another person by touching an object that belongs to them. Some people call it token-object reading." She allowed a satisfied grin to crack her lips.

Shit—right out of the book.

Keller was feverishly trying to keep up with the notes, his face a mask of confusion and bewilderment. Of course, that was his natural look.

"That's correct," Roberts said. "That's exactly what it is. Your mother also told us you can see people's auras. Is that true?" The way she explained this would give him more insight into her mental state than any other answer.

Abbey sat very still—her shy expression disarming. She dropped her gaze. "Yes," she whispered.

Roberts got the feeling he'd embarrassed her with the question. *Quick, time for a follow-up before she had time to recover.* "Do you see auras around everyone, or just some people?"

Abbey looked up and her blue eyes bore in on his. In a quiet voice she said, "Everyone has an aura, unless they're dead."

Good answer. "Do you see an aura around me right now?"

Abbey nodded. "Uh-huh."

"What color is it?"

She cocked her head from side to side several times and her small brow crinkled. "Kind of a blue color."

Roberts slowly released a breath. "What does that mean to you?"

"It means you're a nice person with nice thoughts."

Apparently, Keller couldn't resist. "Do you see anything around me?" A goofy smile spread across his lips.

Abbey studied his features for a short while. "You're also probably a nice person, but sometimes you have naughty thoughts."

Susan smirked.

Keller's smile drooped.

Roberts held back a snicker. Boy, did she have him pegged. "Abbey, your mother said you know something about a threat against the president. Is that so?"

She didn't answer at first. Finally, she nodded and said, "Yes."

"Tell me about it," Roberts said.

Abbey lowered her eyes again. In a voice just above a whisper, she said, "It happened two days ago in Houston. We were visiting my aunt and uncle. They took us to watch the president arrive in his plane." Abbey paused, gathering her thoughts.

"My brother is with the president's re-election campaign in Houston," Susan spoke up, stroking the child's head. "We get VIP passes to all political events."

Roberts wasn't sure if she was bragging or complaining—he hated political events. But he kept looking at Abbey. People always gave themselves away, if you knew what to look for.

"Okay, tell me about what happened," Roberts said.

"Well," Abbey flashed a shy grin, "we were standing at the airport with the rest of the people, when something fell on my foot. The president had just passed, waving and heading for his car. I glanced down and saw a pretty string of beads lying on the ground. A tall man stood beside me wiping his face with a handkerchief. I figured he'd dropped them. When I looked at him, his color was black."

Roberts was confused. He shifted positions. "Black? He was a Black man?"

Abbey shook her head. "No, his aura."

"I see." Roberts cleared his throat. "What happened, then?"

Abbey stared at the floor in thought. "I bent down and picked them up, because the man probably didn't realize he'd lost them." Her lips puckered like she tasted something bitter. "When I touched them, I experienced the strongest reading I've ever felt. And that's when I had the vision."

"Vision?" Roberts asked. He again studied Susan for a response, but got nothing. He got nothing from Abbey either. She sat perfectly still. Her face couldn't have had a blanker expression. *So much for his great body language reading skills.* "Tell me what you saw," he said.

Abbey's shoulders tensed. "I felt the hate the man had for the president. I think he wants to kill him."

Roberts sat back in the chair. *Just as he thought.* Poor little thing needed serious psychological counseling. "Is that it?"

Abbey reached over and put her small hand on her mother's leg. "Yes, by the time the vision ended the man had disappeared into the crowd."

Roberts turned to Susan. "Do you have these beads?"

She nodded.

Roberts closely eyed Abbey. Did she really believe this, or was it just a stunt to gain attention or publicity? Were these two vying to be on a talk show?

When Susan handed him a white envelope, Roberts opened it and released the contents onto the coffee table. A string of prayer beads, every other one white or black, except for the last three, an amber color. A gold, crescent moon medallion hung from the bottom with Arabic writing on each side.

Roberts used his pen and lifted the beads for a closer examination. He cut his stare back to Abbey. "Have you ever seen this man before?"

She shook her head. "No."

"Think you would recognize him if you saw him again?"

"Maybe, I didn't look at him very long—he frightened me."

"Okay," he said, "will you give a description of the man to Agent Keller while I talk to your mom for a minute?"

"Okay." Abbey turned toward Keller.

Roberts rose and motioned with his head for Susan to follow him into the kitchen. He strolled in, giving it a quick look as Susan followed. The lingering smell of bacon still floated in the air. He paused and studied her a moment. There wasn't a polite way to ask the question, so he just put it plain and simple. "Ms. Porter, does Abbey have any mental problems?"

"No!" she frowned. "What kind of question is that?"

No one needed to tell Roberts he was on shaky ground here. Suggesting to a mother, who might have mental issues, that her young daughter may also have them wasn't exactly his comfort zone.

He slowly stepped back, putting as much distance between him and Susan as the space allowed. He kept his voice low. "Well, it's not every day we get this kind of a report from a child, and when we get stuff like this from an adult, there's usually some underlying mental or psychological thing at work."

Susan's jaw tightened. "I hope you're not suggesting Abbey's crazy." She crossed her arms and moved her feet shoulder-width apart. Her eyes now took on a stern glare.

Roberts leaned back against the counter. *Better try walking this back a little.* "That's not what I said—I'm just concerned that there's something that you're not telling us about Abbey."

Susan posted her fist on her hips and leaned forward. The same way Roberts' mom used to when he was in trouble. "Agent Roberts, I've told you what I know. Abbey has special abilities, but that doesn't mean she's crazy."

"I'm sorry if I offended you, but I have to ask—you understand." *That didn't go over too well.*

Susan said, "No offense taken, but you should believe her. I wouldn't bother you with this if I didn't take it seriously. She doesn't exaggerate."

Roberts wasn't sure where else to go on this one. Anything he said to the child might cause the mother to take offense. The last thing he wanted was a complaint about how he'd accused her daughter of being a nut case. The best course of action was probably discrediting the child's abilities so he could write up the report as unfounded. Going any further trying to unravel something like this was useless. Dick hated long reports that went nowhere and didn't draw sharp conclusions.

"Okay," Roberts said. "I'm glad we cleared the air on that. Thank you."

Susan's expression indicated she still thought he didn't believe her.

He and Susan ambled back into the living room just as Abbey said, "You should have it checked out."

"Have what checked out?" Roberts asked, before taking his seat.

Abbey pointed at Keller, wiggling her finger. "His neck, just below the collar line, there's some kind of infection or something."

Roberts stared at Keller and then back at Abbey. "How do you know?"

Abbey pursed her lips. "Because his aura is different there, a small spot of funny looking green, with red dots in it."

"It's nothing." Keller blushed, pulling his collar a little higher. He looked down at his notebook and refused to make eye contact.

Roberts smiled. "Okay, let's get back to these beads and the man who dropped them." He used his handkerchief to put them back into the envelope. "You said you received a reading or vision of some kind after picking them up, right?"

Abbey nodded. "Yes."

Roberts twisted his dad's ring. "Can you do that with any object?"

Abbey flashed a curious half frown. "That depends on how long the person possessed it, if they wore or handled it a lot, and their feelings toward it."

Roberts again showed his best disarming smiled. "So, you couldn't tell very much about me by handling my toaster?"

Abbey grinned. "No."

"Well then, how about this?" Roberts removed his father's ring and held it out.

Abbey studied it for a moment, examining each side before she spoke. "It's an army ring. Were you in the army?"

"Uh-huh, an officer before joining the Secret Service."

Abbey's big blue eyes caught his. "I'd need to hold it."

She extended her hand, and Roberts dropped the ring into her tiny palm. She closed her fingers around it, and her slim body gave a quick shake as if she'd received a shock. Her eyelids fluttered for a second and then drooped before finally closing. When she opened them, he thought she was looking at him, but she stared over his shoulder into space. Her eyes never blinked. She sat frozen like a sculpture.

Oh crap! Was she having a seizure? Roberts looked at Susan. She seemed unconcerned. When he glanced back at Abbey a few seconds later, her body shook again. She slowly reopened her eyes and handed the ring back to him with a matter-of-fact look.

Roberts slid it on his finger. "Well?"

A smirk crossed her lips. "You tried to trick me."

"Huh?"

"It's not *your* ring."

Roberts sucked in a quick breath, struggling not to show any emotion. He forced another smile. "But I'm wearing it."

"You haven't been for long," Abbey said.

Roberts flinched like someone pinched him. Regaining his composure, he willed himself to relax. "So, tell me something about the previous owner." His attempt to keep the anxiousness out of his voice could have fooled most people, but he had the feeling Abbey saw right through it. His stomach roiled as he waited for her response.

Abbey shifted her gaze to the floor in a timid manner and spoke softly in a respectful tone. "He was a soldier, too, but in a special group of soldiers. They climbed ropes up a high cliff while people shot at them."

Roberts sat back. His skin tingled. He felt the blood drain from his face.

Abbey gave him that deadpan expression as his mind went blank. She locked eyes with him. "Is this your father's ring?"

"Yes."

"He's not alive anymore, is he?"

Roberts felt weak. His muscles had lost the strength to keep him upright. "No, he died last month."

"Your father fought in a war, didn't he?"

"Yes, World War II. With the Second Rangers who assaulted the cliffs of Pointe du Hoc on D-Day."

Abbey's expression darkened and took on a severe look. Her lips flattened. "Do you want to know something else about him?" Her grim face scared Roberts.

"No, that's not necessary. I think I have enough information for now."

Abbey stood and extended her hand. "It was a pleasure meeting you," she said with a satisfied look.

Roberts also stood and a chill rushed up his back as he shook the child's hand. She showed a haunting grin. Roberts shivered and realized he'd taken a step away from her just after he'd done it. It was that grin that unnerved him. It seemed to say *I know all that's been, all that is, and all that will be.* His hands shook uncontrollably. He put them behind his back and clasped one in the other. "Nice to meet you, too, Abbey."

Susan took Abbey back to her bedroom, which gave Roberts a chance to organize his thoughts and get his blood pressure back to normal. How did she do it? What kind of parlor trick was this? *Susan had to be in on it.*

When Susan returned to the living room, Roberts and Keller spent the next half hour interviewing her and completing the protective intelligence questionnaire. Roberts learned a lot more about her and Abbey. The fact Susan had never married Abbey's father was only one of the surprises. He sent Keller to the car—he wanted a word with her, alone.

Walking to the front entryway, he chickened out on asking her how Abbey did the ring trick. It had to be a trick. He'd figure it out, given enough time.

"So, do you believe her?" Susan appeared innocent to the fact Abbey had just freaked him out.

Roberts turned back and met her stare. "I'm not sure what I believe, Ms. Porter." He slipped on his sunglasses before opening the front door. The hot summer sunlight shot into the room, and Roberts' long shadow silhouetted the tile floor. "How do you explain something like this?"

Susan leaned against the door frame and crossed her arms. She had a strange twinkle in her eye like she wanted to confess something, but not enough to say it. "Some people believe these powers are inherited."

"Really?" He stepped outside. *What in the hell was that was supposed to mean?*

"It was nice meeting you and Agent Keller," she said. Her lips parted into a faint smile. "Please tell him they're real. I was born with them." Without another word she closed the door.

Oh, shit. She'd somehow overheard Keller's lewd remark. But how was that possible? Wasn't even in the room.

Susan kept her gaze on the peephole as Roberts marched to the car. Tall and muscular with cute dimples when he smiled. She liked him, and she especially liked the way he interacted with Abbey. His natural good looks, chestnut brown hair, and easy-going manner were all pluses. *Never met a cop like that.* She turned and leaned against the door, her mind drifting back to Abbey's father. Not a mistake, but lots of regrets.

Abbey peeked around the corner of the hall. "Are they gone?"

Susan strolled to her and squatted down. "Yeah." She brushed a loose hair from the child's face.

"Should I have told him about the ring? I think it upset him."

Susan pulled her daughter into an embrace. Abbey still smelled like a baby to her. The warmth of her tiny cheek calmed Susan. "Don't worry about it, sweetie, you just told the truth."

The tenseness in Abbey melted away, and she wrapped her arms around Susan's neck. "He was nice."

"Agent Roberts?"

"Uh-huh."

Susan exhaled and hugged Abbey tighter. "I liked him, too." Susan found this surprising—Abbey liking someone she also liked. Susan hadn't dated much in the last couple of years because of Abbey. Men she found attractive were put off by the child, or Abbey hated them. She never liked any of Susan's gentlemen friends. If they couldn't pass the *Abbey Test,* Susan forgot about them.

"Maybe we'll see him again," Abbey whispered.

Susan stroked Abbey's hair and sighed. "I'd like that."

She'd decided a long time ago if she ever found anyone Abbey approved of, she would make it her mission to get to know him better. At this point in her life, she'd hoped to have a home in Westchester with a big back yard that extended down the hill to a clear water creek, a couple of kids, and a Golden Retriever. Being a single mom in a condo back in Dallas was never her intent, and she'd grown to hate it. She wanted someone she could share her life with. Someone who loved and cared about her and Abbey. Someone who would be there when life's small setbacks weighed heavy on her. Every year that dream slipped a little farther away.

Her mind drifted back to Michael Roberts. Just her luck, the guy they both liked turned out to be someone she'd probably never see again.

FIVE

On the way back to the office, Keller drove while Roberts studied the interview notes. *How would he write this up?* Never had one like that, never wanted another.

Keller broke the silence. "So how come you're out doing PI investigations? I thought the squad leader stayed in the office."

Roberts closed the notebook. "Usually do, but there's no one else, and Dick wanted an experienced agent handling this one."

Keller nodded. "I can see why. That kid was creepy. If this is the kind of cases you guys work in PI, then leave me in white-collar." He glanced at Roberts. "How'd she know so much about your dad?"

Roberts ignored him, but Keller had just asked the most profound question of the day. Did they just witness an actual paranormal event or a carefully crafted trick? No way could she have known about his father. But if she knew about his father from holding his ring, what did that imply about the beads and the president? Headquarters liked clean-cut investigations—no hocus pocus or black magic. Roberts couldn't explain this using the standard format. How could he word it so *he* didn't sound crazy?

Keller slowed for the light and turned on his left turn signal. "Is it true Dick's retiring this year?"

Roberts didn't like to think about that too often. With his best ally leaving, the next twelve months before he could bid for another promotion would be even longer. "Yeah, he hits mandatory in December."

"I hear they're already planning the party. The director's coming down."

Roberts stared out the window but wasn't listening. His mind kept drifting back to the interview and report. His dad had always said, "You must stand for something, or be nothing." Roberts liked that advice.

———

Two hours later, Keller was at lunch and Roberts had completed the report on his interview with Susan Porter and her daughter, Abbey. He walked it to Dick's office and dropped it on his desk. "Here. After you've reviewed this, I'll be in my office if you want to talk about the promotion email."

Dick had his reading glasses perched on his nose and the *Wall Street Journal* spread across his desk. He munched on a sandwich and answered without looking up. "Sure, I'll call you in a minute."

Dick's sandwich reminded Roberts he was starving, but he wanted to talk about promotions more than eat. He headed for the break room. Someone always left treats out. The smell of coffee made his stomach rumble as he turned the corner. The open box of Krispy Kreme donuts on the counter beckoned him. Terri, the twenty-year-old office intern, stood at the counter dipping her tea bag in hot water. As Roberts poured a cup, he reached for the last donut, bumping hands with her.

She quickly withdrew hers. "Sorry, Mr. Roberts."

Terri stood all of four foot eleven and had big, mousey eyes covered by pink-framed glasses. She was studying Criminal Justice at the University of North Texas.

Roberts grinned. "Help yourself." He took a step back.

"You sure?" she asked.

He slapped his stomach. "Think I'll just have coffee." He returned to his office and dug a granola bar from his gym bag. He ate it while checking his emails. His office wasn't as grand as Dick's, but he liked it. He had a door he could close and a nice view of the Mustangs of Las Colinas pony statue across the plaza.

He'd almost finished the coffee when his phone rang.

"Hey, Ace, come on down."

When Roberts walked in, Dick sat reading the report. He glanced up and motioned to shut the door—never a good sign.

Roberts flopped into a chair across from him. "Okay, so what's going on at the promotion board?"

Dick showed his devil smile and held up the report Roberts had just written. "Let's talk promotion in a minute. First, what the hell's this?"

Roberts' cheeks flushed hot. "What do you mean?"

Dick leaned forward and put both palms on his desk. "If I didn't know better, I'd swear you believe that crap the Porter woman tried selling you."

Roberts had expected a little push back, but not this much. He wanted to be honest in the report, but not have Dick think he was an idiot. "There's something to it, Dick, and there's a few things I left out."

"Oh, yeah, like what?" Dick leaned back in his chair and crossed his arms with that *so try and explain this to me* look.

The last thing Roberts wanted to do was try and explain the ring incident to someone like Dick. But he gave it his best shot. About halfway into the story Dick's neutral expression took on an ugly frown. Roberts continued his tale, but the words seemed to grow in his mouth, making it difficult to speak. It was at that point, Roberts understood it didn't even sound convincing to him. He finished the story, but had trouble meeting Dick's stare.

Dick didn't say a word for a few seconds, his mind probably processing how the stunt could have been rigged. Finally, he said, "And you believe she knew this from just holding your dad's ring?"

Roberts wasn't all that sure about anything. He also hated things he couldn't explain. Describing possible paranormal activity wasn't in his nature. That kind of thing could lead to bad misunderstandings in headquarters.

"I just don't know," he said. "The kid saw something in Houston. I'm sure of that, but if it had anything to do with the president, no one can say. But just the fact she and her mother attended the event and called us to report what supposedly happened is suspicious. Don't you think?" He had Dick there—trapped him in a circular argument. The rule in Protective Intelligence investigations—when in doubt, investigate further.

Dick still didn't look convinced. "I can explain the ring thing."

"Huh?"

Dick waved the report at Roberts. "The kid must have seen it was an old ring. Figured you were too young to have owned it new. Lucky guess, that's all."

"But how did she know it belonged to my dad and he climbed ropes while people shot at him?"

"Ace, everyone in the military climbs ropes. My uncle was a combat engineer in WWII. Guy climbed ropes all the time in the European Theater. We even climbed ropes in the Marines. Another lucky guess."

"While being shot at?" Roberts said and immediately wished he hadn't from the expression Dick shot back.

Dick held up the report again. "Look, all I'm saying is that sending this kind of stuff up the flagpole could have big unintended consequences."

Roberts stood his ground. "So, are you suggesting I revise it? To say what? I didn't give any opinions or draw any conclusions. The beads might tell us something if we send them to HQ. At least get an interpretation of the Arabic writing."

Dick's expression hardened and his jaw set a little tighter. He still held the report, and his voice rose. "I can tell you some of those guys in headquarters who don't know you as well as I do may have a few questions. Serious questions. You did nothing to debunk the kid's story."

Frustration swelled in Roberts. "It's what happened, Dick. I can't sugarcoat it for headquarters' consumption."

Dick nodded, and his combative expression softened. Probably didn't want to argue the point. "Okay, relax—I'm just saying some of the same people reading this tomorrow could show up on the next promotion panel. If you want, I'll sign it and back you up. But it's you, not me, who'll work in this outfit for the next twenty years. Reputation is everything with these guys."

Roberts' mind raced. Anger, fear, and the feeling of being trapped caused his stomach to flip. Dick was right. Roberts' desire to lead was an old one instilled from birth. He'd been a leader in sports, his scout troop, and his stint with the army. Taking a leadership position was second nature. But leading meant more than just being out front. It also meant taking a hard stance when you knew you were right regardless of the consequences.

You must stand for something, or be nothing.

Roberts swallowed his fear and met eyes with him. "Sign it and send it up."

Dick frowned, signed off on the report, and dropped it into his outbox. He raked his fingers through his thinning hair and then kicked back in his chair, feet propped on the desk.

"Okay, now we'll talk promotions." He pulled in a long breath. "You're not getting promoted because the gentleman in the corner office is pissed at me."

Roberts understood the gentlemen in the corner office meant Special Agent in Charge Gonzales. "What?"

Dick interlaced his fingers across his stomach. "He's pissed and too chicken shit to approach me personally, so he's taking it out on my prodigy, you."

Roberts jumped up. "That's ridiculous."

Dick just stared at him. "It all stems from a bad posting assignment I gave him when I was doing the advance for the president on a Moscow trip years ago. He wound up in ass deep snow on a rooftop. Never figured the little bastard might be my SAIC someday. We've had several run-ins over the years. He knows the director and I are tight, so he doesn't dare try anything against me. Since he can't get to me, he enjoys satisfying his moronic anger by lowering your promotion points. I send up a high score every year, and he lowers it. His prerogative—he's the boss."

Roberts dropped back into the chair. *So, it was the good old boy game.* "Dick, that's stupid."

"Yeah, he's the worst supervisor I've ever had. I found out he did it after the fact last year. So, this year I talked to him and basically said lay off you. If he had a beef with me, fine, but it wasn't fair punishing you."

"What did he say?"

Dick grunted. "Said he'd think about it. When I saw the email this morning, I knew he'd double-crossed us. Sorry I drug you down with me, Ace." Dick's sorrowful eyes said more than his apology.

Roberts mind searched for understanding. The SAIC liked the old Washington game of playing favorites and holding grudges. Roberts had devoted his life to the Secret Service—now this. A frigging pawn in a ridiculous inner-office struggle.

Dick's lips were tight lines before saying, "The only way out is waiting for him to retire, or you can transfer. It stinks, but that's the way it is."

Roberts stood and strode toward the door. No use getting mad. The special agent in charge had god-like powers granted by headquarters. All the late nights, all the weekends, and holidays worked. *For what? Nothing!* After all the sacrifices, Roberts had no social life, other than an occasional dinner date. Lexi had been his last serious relationship, because total dedication to the job was sure to pay off sooner or later. How wrong he'd been. Half the agents in his academy class had already gotten their promotions. He was behind the curve. Every day he stayed in Dallas dropped him a little deeper in the hole. Now this.

He opened Dick's door. "Well, if that's how it is, I know what I have to do."

Dick flashed the devil smile again. "Feel like having a beer later? I'm buying."

Roberts really didn't want company, but Dick was trying to make it up to him, so what the hell. "Sure—sounds great."

Roberts eyed the outbox. The report lay on top. Dick caught his gaze. *How would headquarters view it?* Had he just signed his own promotional death warrant?

SIX

Traffic sounds drifted down the dark alley as Terrell Washington kept watch. He and Darmon Charles crouched and peeked around the side of the rancid dumpster a hundred feet behind the black sedan. As members of the Naylor Road Crew, Terrell and Darmon had a vested interest in this alley. They fiercely defended their territory while selling marijuana, heroin, and cocaine. Both had records, both were on parole, and both vowed not to go back to jail.

As of late, Terrell and Darmon had helped supplement their meager cut from the drug trade with a little carjacking. They'd killed one person, wounded another, and severely beaten three others in the last couple of months. They both had hip street names, but most everyone just called Terrell by his last name, Washington, and Darmon by his initials—DC.

Washington picked something from his nose and wiped it on his jeans. He looked over his shoulder at DC. "How long ago did you walk past 'em?"

"About ten or fifteen minutes, I guess, just before I met you."

Washington craned his neck a little further around the dumpster, gazing at the rear of the car. "What'a you think they're doing?"

"Nothing, just sitting there."

"Bullshit! People don't just sit in their rides at night around this neighborhood. I've never seen that car before—you say it's got California plates?"

"Yeah. More than likely, tourist."

Washington gawked at DC. "They ain't no tourist. You think they're cops or something?"

DC smirked. "Naw, not in a car like that. Feds maybe, but not even the feds would sit in this place after dark."

Washington fingered his gun. "Forget who they are, or what they're doing. I want that ride." He stood and pulled the wool cap lower. "Give me a head start. I'll slip down the alley against this wall, and you start walking back toward 'em. When they notice you, they'll remember you went past before and figure you're just coming back. Watch for my move."

———

Troy Bishop shifted to a more comfortable position. He hated night surveillance work—especially in the summer. Sitting in a hot car in a dirty alley with the smell of old wine and new urine wafting through the open windows disgusted him. Working terrorism investigations for the Department of Defense, he seldom got stuck doing this kind of thing. But personnel shake-ups, summer vacations, and people calling in sick sometimes forced him into it. The long, boring hours, bad food, and humid nights all served as distractions. But they didn't keep him from noticing the man in his side mirror strolling down the alley. From the gait and slouch, he looked like the same gangster they'd seen earlier.

"That guy's coming back," Bishop whispered. He touched the butt of the .357 automatic pistol under his right thigh and watched the guy in the alley's shadows. Martin adjusted the rearview mirror and took a peek. Martin was new and wound too tight for serious surveillance work. Guy couldn't sit still. Bishop had instructed him to keep an eye on the passenger side mirror. That alley wall outside the passenger window was their blind spot.

"Guess he already cut his deal," Martin said, keeping his eyes on the rear mirror.

When the gangster was directly across the alley from them, a muffled thump echoed from the passenger side and Martin screamed. Bishop tore his eyes from the walking figure to find a pistol poking through the passenger window—straight at his face.

"Don't move," the man with the pistol said, while holding down Martin's bloody head by his hair.

Bishop dropped his hand on the grip of the .357 in the seat as the barrel of another pistol pressed against his left temple. An ugly realization crept through him. *He didn't have a chance. They had him cold.* He raised his hands when the driver's door swung open, and the guy dragged him out by the lapel. Bishop glanced back at the Sig Sauer pistol lying in the shadows on the seat, unnoticed by the attackers.

Bishop held his hands high and contorted his face into a mask of terror. This was his only chance—*better do it right.* "Please don't hurt us. You can have our money—take the car if you want, but don't hurt me or my boyfriend." His quick, convincing surrender must have put the robber at ease.

The guy grinned as he loosely held the gun at an angle, inches from Bishop's face. But he seemed jumpy. His hand shook, and his finger was tight on the trigger. "Got money, queer boy?"

Bishop wasn't sure what was going on behind him, and that was a problem. Martin moaned and mumbled something while the other carjacker tried keeping him quiet. *Had to see where the other guy was.* Bishop chanced a quick look to the rear and the man in front of him slapped him hard across the cheek. The warm, sweet taste of blood filled Bishop's mouth. The guy pressed the pistol against his head. "Didn't tell you to look around, fag. Give me your wallet and that watch."

Not knowing the exact position of the other guy would make it tricky, but Bishop had no choice. "Anything you say, but please don't hurt us." He dropped his right hand toward his pocket, reaching for the .380 automatic he carried as a backup. Quick as a snake, he pivoted to his right and shoved the guy's hand holding the pistol away from his face and toward the pavement. At the same time, he swung his own weapon up to the hijacker's head and pulled the trigger. A hole appeared above the guy's left eye. Dead before he hit the ground.

Bishop didn't stop to watch him fall. He kept pivoting until his arms extended on the roof of the car, the automatic trained on the second guy's head. The shot had alerted the other attacker, and he looked up just as Bishop finished his trigger squeeze. The first round struck him below the bridge of the nose, and the other two in the forehead. The pistol the guy pointed at Martin's head dropped from his dead hand into the floorboard.

The robber fell backward against the alley wall and slowly slid to the street. Bishop turned to the first one he'd shot. A spreading pool of blood stained the pavement around his head.

"Martin, you okay?" Bishop yelled.

When he received no answer, Bishop peeked in the car. Martin just sat there—staring at his hands, smeared with blood. There was a small gash on his brow where the barrel of the robber's pistol had broken the skin. He looked up at Bishop.

"I'm okay," Martin said, "just a headache."

A dog barking in the distance reminded Bishop it was time to scoot. He backed down the dark, trash-littered alley with his lights off. At the first intersection, he pulled back onto the main street. He certainly had no intention of explaining this to the cops—General Cook could do that.

SEVEN

Rene Bertrand could not sleep. His watch read 3:48 a.m. When he walked into the living area of the villa, two of the men sat at the table playing cards. A smoke cloud from their cigarettes hung like a veil across the room. It had been this way every evening—dinner, cards, and smoking throughout the night.

"What's wrong?" the shorter one asked.

"Thought I'd get a breath of fresh air. Is that okay?"

The man considered it, then motioned with his head. "Sure, just stay on the porch." He picked up the radio. "He's coming out—watch him."

Somewhere in the darkness, the outside guard kept an eye on Bertrand. Any escape attempt would probably mean death. Bertrand had doubts whether he would live and collect the rest of the money.

He lit a cigarette as he strolled the balcony. Another sultry night, but a breeze off the ocean made it bearable. He inhaled the salty air and leaned on the railing, rubbing the back of his neck, again recalling the events and bad decisions that put him in this situation.

It all started several months ago when he accepted a dinner invitation. Abu Fahad, an acquaintance, had invited him to dine at Restaurant Guy Savoy—Fahad's treat. Bertrand had little interest in joining the fellow for dinner, but who could refuse such a gracious invitation to one of the best restaurants in Paris?

The meal went well—small talk at the beginning and plenty of drinks through the many courses. Afterward, he and Fahad walked outside and sat on the veranda, where they found a quiet table. The sweet, delicate scent of flowers from a nearby bed relaxed Bertrand. Fahad produced two fine Cuban cigars. The evening passed, and they smoked and sipped Courvoisier XO cognac. Bertrand had just started enjoying himself when Fahad ruined it with the question.

"Tell me, Rene," Fahad said, "how goes things at the magazine?"

Bertrand's job as the foreign correspondent for the French national political magazine, *La Voix*, had become boring. Bertrand shrugged. "Things are slow this time of year. The news cycle should pick up again in a couple of months." No one fully appreciated his talents. He was wasting his time at the magazine.

Fahad nodded and drew on his cigar, studying Bertrand. "I have a deal that might interest you." Fahad leaned forward and lowered his voice. "I represented a consortium interested in influencing French politics toward the Middle East. They are looking for a consultant of your caliber who knows the ropes in government circles. Would you have any interest in such a position?"

Bertrand perked up. "Perhaps. What kind of money are we talking?"

Bertrand earned a decent salary at the magazine, but never enough for his extravagant lifestyle.

Fahad smiled. "Ah, yes, the compensation." He waved the cigar and said, "We could pay 125,000 euros for the initial consultation and an additional 125,000 if the negotiations went favorably."

At first, Bertrand assumed he'd misunderstood the amount, but the man repeated it. Bertrand stared at his host, speechless. With that kind of money, he could begin treating himself to everything he'd lived without for too long: new clothes, new car, and his favorite wines by the case.

"Of course, you may have time to consider the offer," Fahad said, "but we would need an answer within the week."

Bertrand took a deep breath and tried not to show his surprise. He nodded. *Look relaxed—give nothing away.* "So, what are the terms of payment?" To be honest, he did not really care. With that much money at stake, he was not going to say no to any offer.

Fahad moved a little closer. "You would have to sign a five-year, non-disclosure contract. For this, you would receive an annual salary of 250,000 euros. As I said, the initial 125,000 can be deposited within a couple of days. All your living and travel expenses would, of course, be paid, and you'd have an expense account for entertaining."

Did he just say expense account?

Bertrand had long suspected his days at the magazine were numbered. His bad-boy reputation and age conspired against him. His only friend, the editor-in-chief, had confided his retirement plans by the end of the year. Bertrand figured his friendship with Gerard Rye was the only reason the magazine still retained him.

"What would be my duties?"

"Not much different from your current ones," Fahad said. "You know your way around the Middle East and understand the Arab mentality. Your contacts in French government circles, coupled with the fact you also speak fluent English and Arabic, makes you an ideal choice to be our advocate."

"Your lobbyist," Bertrand corrected, before drawing on the smooth cigar.

Fahad smirked. "A rose by another name, eh?"

Bertrand had other reasons for wanting to get out. It went without saying the magazine's management never really accepted him as French because his mother was Algerian, and her parents were killed by French troops during the war of independence.

"Will you consider our offer?" Fahad asked.

This was the sweet dream Bertrand believed he could never achieve. Almost too sweet. "What's the catch?"

"No catch," Fahad assured him. "Our group does want to remain anonymous due to their intent to influence the French political way of thinking. It would not do if it were discovered we were involved in such activities. Complete discretion—you understand. Do you have any questions?"

Bertrand had considered his life after leaving the magazine. He had concluded he had few good options. The magazine would be the pinnacle of his professional career. Everything else would be downhill from there. Less money, less prestige, and more work. This offer was a godsend. "When do I start?"

Fahad grinned. "That's the spirit." He pulled his iPhone out and scrolled to the calendar. "What's your schedule like for the next few months?"

Bertrand did not need to check his schedule. He only had one trip planned, no major interviews, and no hard deadlines to meet. "Nothing important. My only strong commitment is covering the US Presidential Nominating Convention next month. That's a no brainer."

Fahad nodded and typed something into his calendar. "Yes, I do recall you mentioning that during Andre's party a few weeks back. Anyway, we will not need you till after mid-September," Fahad said. "Our plans are still being finalized. I expect we will kick it off in the fall for sure." He rolled the ash off the tip of his cigar and winked. "Certain arrangements must be made with other parties before we can begin. This takes time. Go ahead and attend the convention. It'll give you additional political clout in the eyes of the big bosses. Plan on a stop in Algeria on the way to the United States. I'll set up a meeting with the board and introduce you."

Bertrand did not know or understand why he, of all people, was offered such a fantastic opportunity. Perhaps he *was* much more in demand than he'd realized. It was true, the old adage about "It's not what you know, it's who you know." But he did know one thing for sure. If he agreed, 125,000 euros would soon appear in his account, and another 125,000 by the end of the year.

"We have a deal." He extended his hand to Fahad.

Fahad nodded and shook on it. "Excellent."

And that's how it all started.

The first deposit showed up in Bertrand's new Swiss account right on time. A few weeks later, with all travel preparations completed, he told Rye he would leave a few days early for a short visit with friends in Algeria before making his way to the United States. He was a little anxious about this first meeting. He bought a new suit, got a haircut, and had his teeth professionally whitened. Looked ten years younger.

When he arrived at the airport in Algiers, the limo met him. The drive to the isolated compound was short. It rested on the coastal road about thirty-five kilometers east of the city. Place had a high stone wall surrounding it. Upon arrival, he was directed to an upstairs room of the villa.

Not a very fancy place. Rundown building, outdated furniture, and window coverings almost falling off. His dinner host, Fahad, and two rough-looking men met him.

"Rene, welcome," Fahad said, warmly shaking his hand. "I hope you had a pleasant journey."

The room had an unpleasant musty odor. Bertrand eyed the two thugs leaning against the far wall. "Yes, thank you."

One of the men walked to the door.

Bertrand followed his movement. He looked back to Fahad, who showed a half-grin. "Is our meeting still on?" Bertrand asked.

The thug behind him closed the door. The click of the lock set off alarm bells in Bertrand's mind.

Fahad laid a hand on his shoulder. "I'm afraid there has been a change of schedule. May I see your passport, please?" He held out his hand.

Bertrand stared at him, then looked to the thug by the door. *A bit irregular,* but he surrendered the passport without question.

Fahad thumbed through the document. "Everything looks in order."

Fahad's friendly expression and tone were gone, replaced with a more formal, business-like voice. He held up the passport and nodded to the second guy still leaning against the wall. He strolled over, took it, and walked out the door. The other thuggish looking fellow again locked it behind him.

Uneasiness swept over Bertrand. He opened his mouth to speak, but Fahad held up a hand for silence.

"Please, have a seat."

They both sat at the austere table, stained and sticky with old food.

"I'm happy you accepted our offer, but there are new arrangements we must discuss."

Bertrand listened intently—hanging on every word. He frowned slightly at the term, "new arrangements."

Fahad took a small cigar from his pocket but did not offer Bertrand one. "I must tell you that the overall plans have changed, somewhat."

Okay, that's the second time he's said that. What does it mean?

When Bertrand frowned again, Fahad assured him. "Nothing to worry about—you'll receive the money we promised, but you'll be our guest for the next couple of weeks." Fahad smiled and relaxed back in the chair, lighting his cigar. He swept his gaze over Bertrand, waiting for a reaction.

A cold fear coursed through Bertrand. "But, I must... I'm expected by my magazine to—"

Fahad waved away his objection. "Do not worry about that." Fahad touched his arm. "It has all been arranged."

"But I thought—"

Fahad ignored him, rose, and strolled to the door.

Bertrand went numb and shook. Who were these people—was this some kind of joke?

Fahad stopped at the door and smiled. "If you cooperate, we will live up to the monetary terms promised. If you choose non-coopera-tion...." He stared at the thug who produced a pistol.

Meeting their demands, Bertrand surrendered his cell phone, laptop, and the rest of his identification. The guard took the phone and his laptop and placed them in a separate room. When the cell rang, Bertrand was not allowed to answer. If the caller left a voice message, they permitted him to return the call. He was warned that during the conversation if he attempted to sound an alarm, request help, or try to talk in any type of code, they would kill him. He must pretend every-thing was normal. The tension, insomnia, and constant worry made him physically ill. The old headaches and stomach cramps had started again. It was a nightmare he could not awake from.

Bertrand finished his cigarette and flicked the butt into the court-yard below as another cool breeze blew in off the Mediterranean. The lights of a passing cargo ship cruised along the dark coast. Bertrand shuddered and his spirits sank even lower. Had he fallen in with crimi-nals or terrorists?

While driving the 200 miles north on Interstate 45 from Houston to Dallas, Sayed went over the plan again. He enjoyed driving—always had. Gave him time to think things through. This boring stretch of road held little interest. The hot Texas sun bore down on the landscape, withering what few plants still survived. Sayed recalled earlier visits to the US, the last one many years ago. He first came as a student, then as an officer with Syrian Intelligence assigned to the embassy in Washington.

The trip to Houston had gone terribly wrong. He'd wanted to see for himself how the president's Secret Service detail worked, but somewhere at the event, he'd lost his most cherished possession, his *misbaha*. He shook his head and exhaled. Only a few days had passed. Sayed said a silent prayer to Allah that when the beads were discovered, they'd been tossed into the trash, or at worst, lost and found.

The freeway sign announced *DALLAS 50 MILES*. Out of the corner of his eye he caught a flicker of something in the rearview mirror, the outline of a police car following him in the left lane—not closing, but hanging back, just matching his speed. Sayed's stomach tightened. He glanced at the speedometer; he was not speeding. The rental had proper registration. Sayed eased into the right lane and let off the gas, keeping one eye on the road and the other on the police vehicle in the mirror.

The police car followed him into the right lane and turned on the red lights. Sayed's grip tightened on the steering wheel while he silently rehearsed his cover story. All of his documents were in order—nothing to worry about. Sayed eased off the freeway onto the shoulder. The police car, a black and white Texas State Police patrol unit, came to a stop behind Sayed's. He fumbled for his driver's license, never taking his eyes off the cop in the rearview mirror.

The trooper sat in his vehicle a moment and spoke into the microphone. Probably calling in the license plate number. Or was he informing his headquarters he'd found the car they'd been looking for? No, that was impossible. No one knew he was in America but a trusted few. Sayed glanced at the small green backpack lying on the passenger's seat. He pulled it into the floorboard and laid a sports coat on top, keeping the bag out of sight.

The trooper got out and put on his cowboy hat. He strolled to Sayed's car with a slow gait, his clipboard in his left hand and his right resting on his pistol holster.

Sayed rolled down the window and, in his best English, with a slight French accent said, "Good morning, officer."

The trooper nodded, his eyes scanning the interior of the car. "Good morning, sir. May I see your license and proof of insurance?"

"Certainly," Sayed smiled and surrendered Bertrand's documents.

The trooper did not return the smile as he reviewed the papers.

Sayed remained calm. *Settle down; everything's fine. Just a routine traffic stop.*

"I did not think I was speeding, officer. Only going seventy."

The trooper did not answer. He appeared confused by the foreign driver's license.

Moments passed before the trooper said, "You're a French citizen, Mr. Bertrand?"

"Yes."

"May I see a passport, sir?"

Sayed handed him Bertrand's French Passport.

The trooper studied the passport photo a second, then stared at Sayed. After flipping a few more pages, the cop spoke. "The reason I stopped you this morning was because you failed to display a turn signal when changing lanes."

Sayed released a slow breath. *What a pig!* "I am sorry," Sayed again smiled and shrugged. "I saw you behind me and I only wanted to give you room to pass. That is why I changed lanes."

The trooper tucked all the paperwork inside Sayed's passport and handed it back to him. "No problem. But in the future, if you drive in the right lane, you won't have this problem. In Texas, the left lane is for passing." He released a quick grin, turned, and walked back to his patrol car. Sayed watched him from the rearview mirror. He slid behind the wheel, spoke into the mic, and motioned Sayed to pull back onto the freeway.

Sayed wiped his brow and eased back on the road. He had to settle down. The plan was still on track. He glanced at the French driver's license. Sayed's likeness to Bertrand had not been challenged by US Customs when he entered the country, and now it had just passed another test. The final test was to come. He still had to fool the US Secret Service.

EIGHT

Roberts leaned back in his office chair and read the latest convention intelligence estimate. It pretty much looked like the same one he'd read yesterday and the week before. Nothing on the threat matrix raised any particular concern. Things had been rolling at a steady pace for months, and this looked to be one of the most boring conventions in recent memory. Whenever you had a president seeking a second term, it was like this. About 66 percent of the time, a sitting president was reelected. No drama in the convention was what the Secret Service lived for.

Roberts dropped the document on the pile, stood, and did a lower back stretch against his desk. He longed to be in the field doing anything other than paperwork. But that was the squad leader's job— assist the ATSAIC in running the squad, being Dick's right-hand guy. The rest of the Dallas Secret Service agents ran at full speed. Agents worked twelve- and fourteen-hour days at the different sites getting ready for the president's visit at the convention. Office was like a ghost town.

Roberts stared out his window at the traffic on Las Colinas Boulevard. The early lunch crowd was already on the move.

Donna stuck her head around the corner. A whiff of her thick perfume drifted in as she said, "Hey, Michael. Want to grab lunch with us? We're doing tacos."

Roberts' mouth watered at the thought. He usually accompanied the administrative office specialists for tacos every couple of weeks. They liked him and especially liked that he picked up the tab.

He shook his head. "Not today, I'm the only one left in the squad—better stick around. I'll grab a sandwich downstairs."

A quick frown flashed across her lips. "Okay."

He thumbed through the security survey on the American Airlines Center. They would host the event this year—ground zero for all activity. Presidential staffers, volunteers, media, and security types all did walkthroughs at the convention venues, putting the finishing touches on their plans. No one would believe the tons of paper generated and millions of dollars spent to protect the president at a convention, or, for that matter, at any venue outside DC.

Roberts tried concentrating on the file, but his mind drifted to Abbey and the interview. Two days since Dick sent his report to headquarters, and he'd heard nothing else about it. Now that Roberts had had a chance to cool down, he came to accept Dick's explanation about the ring incident. Roberts had fallen for one of the oldest interview traps known. Abbey took a lucky guess about the ring and Roberts was so quick to confirm it he'd let her off the hook before probing deeper. *Stupid rookie mistake.* He knew better, but when Abbey mentioned Roberts' dad, Roberts spoke too soon. His sorrow was still raw over losing the man, and now it was impacting his work.

Roberts remained curious about the aura reading and if Abbey really had a vision after touching the prayer beads. Was there a way to explain those? He recalled something from his protective intelligence class. He googled the word *Synesthesia.* Yup, just as he'd remembered: *A recognized neuropsychological phenomenon that allows people to see colors from words and numbers. Some even claimed to be able to hear the color. Affects approximately two percent of the population, high degree in females. Often runs in families.* Was that what Susan meant when she said inherited? *May explain the New-Age claim of seeing auras.*

Yeah, that had to be it. Abbey was a synesthete. When she saw the guy's black color close to the president, she naturally assumed the man must hate POTUS and wanted to kill him. Roberts sat back in his chair and regretted some of the wording in his report sent to headquarters. Dick had been right, as usual. Wished he could pull the report back.

The SAIC was out of district, and the ASAIC ran the office in his absence. The call from the assistant special agent in charge took Roberts by surprise.

"Michael, I need you to step into my office."

"Yes, sir. On my way." Roberts dropped the phone back into its cradle. Weird. If the ASAIC had something to say to him, he usually went through Dick. Roberts marched down the corridor, through the Counterfeit Squad area.

"Heads up, Michael," a voice called from the cubicle jungle.

Roberts looked up in time to see a Nerf football sailing toward him. He snagged it and tossed it back to a waiting pair of hands in the jungle. He continued down the hall and took a left into the ASAIC's office.

Ed Paxton sat at his desk reviewing a single piece of paper. A grimace was glued to his lips, and he rubbed the underside of his chin with a finger. Ed always loosened his tie and rolled his sleeves up a turn or two first thing in the morning. Even at eleven o'clock, it looked like he'd been working all day. Roberts liked him. Long-distance and marathon runner. Scholarship in track at Purdue. First Black kid to graduate college from his Mississippi high school class—nice guy.

"Have a seat, Michael."

Roberts eyed the ASAIC's expression again. It had changed to something between pain and curiosity. Ed had his blinds open and the late morning sun streaked into the office right in Roberts' face. Felt like an old-fashioned interrogation room.

Ed laid the paper on the desk and slid it to him. "Do you know what this is about?"

Roberts picked up the sheet and read it. Travel orders for him to Washington that afternoon for a classified meeting the next morning with the president's national security advisor. *What?*

Roberts met eyes with the ASAIC. "I have no idea. What's the deal?"

Ed rested his elbows on the desk and interlaced his fingers, his eyes pinching tighter. "That's what I'd like to know." He held Roberts' gaze but said nothing else.

"Honestly, I haven't a clue."

Ed blew out a breath and lowered his gaze. "Michael, if you've crossed some line, tell me now. Do you know how this looks?"

Roberts was about to answer, but Ed kept talking. "I've been in the Secret Service over twenty years. Four offices, three headquarters assignments, and not once have I ever heard of a field agent, or any other agent for that matter, being called to the national security advisor's office." With each word, Ed's expression became darker and his voice rose. He leaned closer to Roberts. "I'm just not buying you have no idea."

Okay, so the ASAIC was pissed. But was he pissed at Roberts, or pissed he didn't know what was going on?

"I don't know," Roberts said. But in his gut, he knew—the interview with Abbey, the prayer beads. What else could it be? *Shit!*

Ed's lips pressed tight. "I called the SAIC when that came in." Ed pointed at the piece of paper Roberts held. "He told me to get to the bottom of it. Now, do you wish me to tell him that you seriously don't know?"

Robert's swallowed hard and shifted in the chair. No use confessing to anything until he knew what it was about. Besides, he'd done nothing wrong. He couldn't imagine Susan complaining about him. And if she had, that still had nothing to do with the national security advisor. No, something else was afoot—something more significant.

He stared at Paxton. "If I knew, I'd tell you."

———

After a curt dismissal, Roberts headed to Dick's office. He wasn't in, so Roberts returned to his desk and made his flight and hotel reservations. On the way out, he bumped into Dick in the hall.

"Hey, I've been looking for you," Roberts whispered. "Something's going on."

Dick glanced up and down the hall, then motioned him into his office.

"I'm headed to DC for a meeting with the national security advisor. Do you know what it's about?"

Dick took a seat and nodded. "Yeah, just got a call. It's that damn report and beads we sent up."

"What?"

Dick shook his head. "Nobody's talking much about it. I got a heads up from a friend in the director's office."

Dick knew things long before everybody else at the Dallas field office. His *friend* in the Secret Service Director's office kept him well informed. Rumor had it, the friend was a lady—*figures.*

"Anyway, after my friend gave me a heads up, ADPO called. He's refusing to even discuss it over a non-secure line. He did confirm it had to do with the Porter thing, but that's all he'd say."

Roberts' interest piqued. When the assistant director of protective operations got involved, it usually meant trouble for someone.

"Am I in some kind of jam?" Robert asked. He didn't believe he was, but when the ASAIC finished with him, he was ready to confess to anything, including being the second shooter on the grassy knoll. Dick's revelation about the meeting having to do with the Porter interview only heightened Roberts' anxiety. *What the hell have I gotten myself into?*

"I don't think so, but whatever it is sure stirred up a lot of excitement." Dick propped his feet on the desk and leaned back, crossing his arms. "Your guess is as good as mine, Ace. I did find out the director will attend the meeting tomorrow." Dick adjusted his cufflinks and smoothed the front of his shirt.

"That doesn't sound good," Roberts said.

Dick waved away the thought. "I wouldn't get too excited. If they wanted to pick a bone with you, it wouldn't be with the national security advisor there."

Roberts checked his watch. "I have just enough time to pack before I fly out. See you in a day or two, I hope."

"If I hear any rumors, I'll shoot you a call, Ace. Good luck. Oh, before you go, sign this." Dick sat up and scooted closer to the desk, retrieving a get-well card from a pile of papers.

"What's this?"

"Keller's in the hospital."

"Keller? What happened?"

"Apparently he had one hell of a close call. Saw his dermatologist the other day and they found a melanoma on his neck—did emergency surgery the same day. Said if he'd waited much longer, might not have caught it in time. He's out of the woods now. Good thing he got it checked out."

Roberts' mind flashed to Abbey on the sofa with Keller. She must have caught a glimpse of his neck when his collar shifted.

As Roberts signed the card, his thoughts again drifted back to Susan and her daughter. This case got more complicated and less explainable at every turn.

———

The American Airlines flight took forever. They departed late from Dallas; the result of a door that wouldn't shut until a mechanic had a go at it. Flying after 9/11 had become Roberts' worst nightmare, and not because of the extra security. As a federal officer he was never scanned or suffered the indignity of removing garments and shoes. His chief complaints—planes which left late, arrived late, had no food, and packed the passengers in like sardines. But the flight did give him time to think. People say your mind can paint a much scarier picture than reality. They were right. This whole business with Abbey had unsettled him. People like her didn't exist outside of Stephen King novels.

As Roberts exited the plane at Reagan National Airport, he checked his phone for messages. There were none. He had hoped Dick was pulling in favors to find out what this trip was all about. The blank message screen reminded him of how alone he was.

He checked into the Washington Marriott-Georgetown. He always stayed there. Perfect location for getting in a run, plenty of restaurants, and good nightlife.

That evening he had a beer in the hotel bar, then strolled around the corner to a noodle house for a bowl of Pad Thai. Walking back to his hotel, the steamy late July weather and crowded streets of Georgetown felt familiar and comforting. He'd already decided he would request a transfer out of Dallas after the convention. He didn't care where he went, as long as he could get promoted. At least he could start rebuilding his career after basically wasting the last two years. A transfer back to headquarters might even be nice. He still had pals in the intelligence division who'd welcome him back.

Roberts was so close to where he grew up; he would like to have had an extra day or two to check on his mom. Since his dad's death, her age and health had conspired against her.

Roberts owed so much to his parents. He got his intelligence from his mother—she taught school—but he inherited his dad's drive. One of Roberts' favorite memories as a kid was his dad reading with him every night. The old man had a routine. He'd eat supper and work in his woodworking shop in the garage for an hour or two. Then they'd lie on the couch in the living room at bedtime, and Roberts, with his dad's help, would read the classics.

The memories rushed back, memories of the warmth of the old guy lying beside him, the combined smells of fresh cedar shavings and Aqua Velva. Roberts always assumed his dad wanted him to be a good reader. It wasn't until Roberts became an adult that it dawned on him the real reason for the readings. His dad used them as teaching tools. When they'd read a passage, sometimes his dad would ask Roberts to explain what the author was trying to say.

The time they read *To Kill a Mockingbird*, his dad made Roberts explain each chapter. After patiently listening to the explanation of his ten-year-old son, his dad clarified what Harper Lee really meant. A recurring theme began to develop in whatever book they read. His dad drilled into him that, at some point in his life, he needed to make a difference. Do one good patriotic thing for his country. While the US might have problems, it was still the best country in the world. Honor it. Acquire a respected leadership position somewhere he could influence policy for the better. Roberts believed he was doing that by joining the military, but soon realized the entrenched ideas of the army would take decades to change. That's why he looked to federal law enforcement, especially the Secret Service.

Now, he'd even failed at that. Couldn't even get promoted.

Just before bedtime, he had a crazy thought about calling Lexi. He sat on his bed staring at the extra-long pillows—her favorite kind. His regrets about her still weighed heavy on his psyche. He'd probably made the biggest mistake of his life letting her go. Dad always liked her and looked forward to having her as a daughter-in-law. Roberts had never told her of his father's passing. That could be his excuse for the visit. He could be at her place in less than an hour. What would she think about a surprise visit?

No, his relationship with Lexi had ended long ago.

NINE

The next morning Roberts sat in the outer office of the national security advisor's conference room and waited. He'd been told to arrive at nine o'clock. The motto of the Secret Service was: *If you arrive five minutes early, you're usually on time. If you arrive on time, you're usually five minutes late.* Roberts took no chances. He arrived at eight-thirty. Apparently, the meeting had already started.

Roberts' first year in the Secret Service, he'd worked with a crusty old agent on the verge of retirement in the Richmond Office. Bob Fisk told the young Roberts something that now, after all these years, popped back into his mind. According to Fisk, if you're ever called in for something big, just admit to nothing, deny everything, and make counter-accusations. But there was no reason to be nervous. He'd done everything by the book. But he *was* nervous.

"Would you like a cup of tea or coffee?" the receptionist asked. She was cute, with short black hair and brown eyes.

"No, thank you." Roberts exhaled and turned back to the magazine.

The silence of the room was maddening. So much hustle and bustle in the outside hall and streets around the building and so quiet in here —eerie. It wasn't an impressive place. Forest green carpet, leather sofa, three chairs, and a couple of old black and white photos of Washington, DC, probably from the 1940s. The place had a funny odor, like new carpet.

Roberts glanced at the door leading into the conference room and checked his watch for the third time.

Come on! Let's get this over with.

————

Inside the conference room, the President's National Security Advisor, J. Thomas Fuller, sat at the head of the table. He took a sip of stale Starbucks coffee and regretted not getting a fresh one before starting the meeting. "General Cook, would you please begin the briefing."

"Thank you." Cook glanced at Lt. Colonel Bishop to his right and across the conference table at Director Hugh Carroll from the Secret Service. "We have an asset inside al-Qaeda, not on the fringe, but inside al-Qaeda central. He's a former member of bin Laden's staff and met with him weekly before his death—a courier. Code name Emerald."

Secret Service Director Carroll sat back in his chair. "How long's this been going on?"

"Since mid-2002," Cook answered.

Carroll's forehead wrinkled. "If we knew bin Laden's whereabouts for that long, why didn't we kill him years earlier?"

Cook allowed a quick smile to drift across his lips. "He was worth more alive and in place, than dead." Cook laced his fingers together and rested them on the table. "All the big plans passed through bin Laden. He blessed them before they went operational. By keeping him alive and knowing what he was seeing from al-Qaeda cells around the world, we stayed one step ahead of them. When it got to the point he was no longer of any consequence, we took him out." Cook shrugged. "Presidential decision—made for good press optics."

Carroll nodded. "Why am I just now finding out about this?"

"You didn't have a need to know," Fuller answered.

"What's changed?"

Fuller cleared his throat. "Yes, well, that's the rub. There's an al-

Qaeda agent in the US with the intent of killing the president. I just received this information three days ago from the al-Qaeda asset General Cook spoke of. Concurrent with that, we reviewed a report from Secret Service about an interview one of your agents did concerning the possible assassin. I believe Agent Roberts is outside, correct?"

"He was instructed to attend the briefing this morning," Carroll said.

"Fine, we'll get to him shortly." Fuller thumbed through his notebook. "Are there any other questions before we bring him in?"

Carroll shook his head.

Fuller leaned forward and, in a quiet voice, said, "Agent Roberts isn't cleared for this al-Qaeda access information. We shouldn't discuss anything about the asset in front of him." Fuller turned to the fourth man at the table. "Colonel Bishop, please feel free to question agent Roberts as much as you deem necessary. I don't want him leaving here until we've picked his brain clean." Fuller pressed a button on the phone. "Marybeth, send in Roberts, please."

———

When Roberts entered the conference room, he felt the temperature difference. It was at least five degrees cooler than the waiting area. Most SCIFs are cool, but Roberts suspected his nerves also played a part. The windowless room was large. The conference table had ample space for twenty people, with additional chairs along each wall. A portrait of George Washington, in military uniform, hung opposite a big-screen TV. Roberts slid into the red leather chair; his mouth suddenly dry.

There were four men in the room. Roberts had met Secret Service Director Hugh Carroll, recognized J. Thomas Fuller from the news, but didn't know the other two. One was about his age with an athletic build and short dark hair. Guy had a confident, relaxed expression. He also had *the look*. During Roberts' time in the army, he'd met a lot of soldiers who'd seen extreme combat—warriors. Men who'd killed other men. Men who'd faced death many times and survived. They all had the same look. The eyes gave them away—*hunter eyes*. Alert to everything, never relaxed.

The other man sitting beside Hunter Eyes was older. Short, gray-haired and stocky. He also had a military bearing.

At the opposite end of the table, Fuller looked like a king sitting on his throne. With his black, well-kept hair and navy suit, he had an air that only came from an upper-class upbringing, Ivy League education, and a country club lifestyle. His gaze darted from his notebook and landed on Roberts. Then he paused a beat as he reviewed a piece of paper on the desk. Roberts had always wondered about the feeling from the old cliché: *Tension so thick you could cut it with a knife.* He didn't have to wonder anymore.

Without introducing the others, Fuller said, "Agent Roberts, you conducted a fascinating interview a few days ago with a Ms. Porter. Is that correct?"

Fuller's smile could best be described as suspicious. Roberts hated when people flashed that kind of smile. Always meant they already knew the answer to the question being asked. Dick had been right. The Porter report had raised its ugly head.

"Yes, sir."

"Could you relate, in detail, that interview for us?" Fuller sat back in his chair and laid one hand on top of the other, his index finger rapidly tapping the back of his hand.

Roberts had no idea what they were looking for, but all their stares stayed fixed on him. He told the story of his and Keller's interview. The only thing he left out was the ring incident with Abbey. And, of course, Keller's fascination with Ms. Porter's boobs.

"Sounds like quite a tale," Fuller said. "Do you believe what they told you?"

Roberts couldn't tell from Fuller's tone and expression if he was making fun of him or asking a serious question. *Should have taken Dick's advice and toned down the report.*

"Well, sir, the thing about the man in the crowd who wanted to kill the president, I couldn't say for sure. I think they believe it."

Fuller screwed his lips to one side. Sort of an *oh, really* look. After a few moments of thought, he leaned toward Roberts. "We possess credible intelligence there's a foreign assassin operating within the United States. It's possible that may have been the man the child saw in Houston. We also believe he intends to kill the president. Does that appear consistent with what the Porter girl told you?"

Roberts gripped the arms of the chair. *So that's what all this cloak and dagger was about.* He let out a breath. "She didn't say anything about him being foreign, only that she thought he wanted to kill the president." Roberts' temporary relief that *he* wasn't in trouble was now replaced with this new disturbing revelation.

"Yes, of course," Fuller said. "Well, take a look at this and tell me if you recognize anyone." He pressed a button on the remote. A videotape from one of the national news services played without sound on the fifty-two-inch TV mounted on the wall. The president came into view, walking past a rope line of people waving and smiling. A poster displayed across the rope barrier read: *WELCOME TO HOUSTON, MR. PRESIDENT.* When the camera angle widened, Abbey and Susan Porter came into view on the far left just before the video stopped.

Fuller turned to Roberts. "See anyone you know?"

Roberts pointed at the TV. "The child wearing the white and orange dress is Abbey Porter, and the blond woman in blue standing beside her is her mother, Susan."

When the video started again, the camera panned a little more to the left, revealing a tall man with a bushy, black beard and long, black hair. He was dressed in a light gray suit, striped tie, and a fedora-style straw hat shading his face. Aviator sunglasses hid his eyes. That's when the video stopped again.

Hunter Eyes leaned forward in his chair and with his index finger slowly rubbed his lower lip while studying the tall guy on screen.

Fuller stopped the video again and motioned. "We believe that's our man. In disguise, of course. I think for the sake of full identification, the Porter girl should see this, just to confirm it."

"The person in the video matches the description Abbey Porter gave us. I put it in my report," Roberts said.

Fuller smirked. "Yes, I know, I've read it. Now, we believe we know who this fellow is." Fuller pressed another button on the remote.

The TV screen went to a dark blue for a moment. Soon the head and shoulders of a man in his early thirties flashed on screen. He had a professional demeanor in his tan, military uniform, laced with ribbons and medals. A thin mustache lined his upper lip.

Hunter Eyes whispered something to the older guy sitting beside him. Then he motioned at the TV. He seemed to memorize every detail of the photo.

"Gentlemen, this is Colonel Hashem Abdul-Sattar aL-Sayed, formally of the Syrian Intelligence Service. This photograph is over twenty-five years old. He attended college in the United States, University of Michigan." Fuller stopped briefly, turned the page and kept reading. "Served with Syrian external security division and worked in a number of foreign countries, including the US, as an undeclared agent."

Fuller looked up. "Speaks fluent English and French with no accent. Very Caucasian in appearance. Could pass for any American or European."

Hunter Eyes blew out a breath and again whispered something to the older man beside him. The fellow tugged at his collar and shook his head. These two were still a mystery to Roberts. What did they have to do with this?

Roberts' mind raced. Everyone seemed to already know so much about this. He needed to catch up. "How did we identify him as the man in the photograph?"

Everybody shifted their stares to Fuller, and an unnatural quiet settled in the room. Fuller showed another smirk before answering. "We received this information from a foreign intelligence asset. He's confirmed Sayed's intent to kill POTUS."

Roberts wasn't sure why, but that explanation fell flat. *Something didn't add up.* From the expressions on the other's faces, there must be another piece to the puzzle.

Fuller continued. "Your job, gentleman—ensure the protection of POTUS. I say *your* job, because I want General Cook and his people involved in this, also." Fuller's stare landed on the Secret Service Director. "Director Carroll," Fuller asked, "would you object if a member of General Cook's staff joined in this investigation, just as a liaison between the Secret Service and the rest of the intelligence community?"

Hugh Carroll shifted in the chair and cleared his throat as he stared at Cook sitting across the table. "Well, we certainly wouldn't object as long no one interfered."

The guy named Cook offered a suggestion. "How about Lieutenant Colonel Bishop here"—he nodded in the direction of Hunter Eyes —"since he's fully briefed on the operation, Mr. Director?"

Carroll shifted in his chair again and hesitated before saying, "He'll be fine."

Roberts gazed at the two strangers again. *General Cook and Lieutenant Colonel Bishop.* Why were these two guys here? The only military involvement in presidential protection was with communications, transportation, and explosive ordinance detection. How could they help the Secret Service?

"Excellent," Fuller said. He leaned forward and gazed at everyone with that Ivy League, condescending smile. "Is there anything else?"

"Agent Roberts," Colonel Bishop said, "did the people at the Houston event have to get any clearances or show any type of identification before being admitted to the rope line to greet the president? And do we have a record of this?"

Before Roberts could answer, Director Carroll spoke up, "No, it was an open event. They were only required to pass through the mags and submit to a search."

Fuller glanced around the table once more. "Okay, if that's all then—"

Roberts wasn't confident in what he was about to say, but something told him to disregard the little voice of doubt and say it.

"Susan and Abbey Porter might be able to help us."

Fuller cocked his head. "I'm not sure I understand."

Roberts related the story about Abbey and his Dad's ring and also what Abbey had said about Keller's neck. When he finished no one spoke. They all gawked at him as if he'd just said he believed in fairies.

Fuller cut a glance to Carroll before saying, "I see, yes, I see." Fuller interlaced his fingers and a thin smile formed. "Is it your belief that the psychic powers the child claims are real?"

Roberts was on ground so shaky it could give way any second, so he responded cautiously. "I don't know, sir. The girl doesn't know me or my family. She had no foreknowledge of Agent Keller's medical emergency. I can't explain it."

Fuller rocked back in the chair and stared at the table. Director Carroll's ears had turned red and he didn't meet eyes with Roberts. Fuller broke the spell when he asked the Secret Service Director, "What do you think? Should we involve anyone else?"

Carroll shifted his stare to Roberts. "If you believe they might be of some use, go ahead, but you'll have to take responsibility for them."

Take responsibility for them. Roberts knew what that meant.

———

Hugh Carroll was a thoughtful man. You didn't become a secret service director without being thoughtful and careful. He walked around his desk and greeted the visitor to his office that afternoon with a handshake.

"Dr. Thane, you've met Glen Dickerson, director of protective operations, haven't you?"

Dickerson stood and shook the doctor's hand.

"No, I've not had the pleasure," Thane replied.

"Please take a seat," Carroll said. "We want to borrow that medical brain of yours for a few minutes."

Dr. Lawrence Thane, a specialist in psychology and psychiatry, lectured at George Mason University, had a private practice, and retained a Top-Secret security clearance for consultations with the Secret Service. The Service maintained a multitude of subject matter experts for times like these.

Glen Dickerson, in his new role as assistant director – protective operations, or ADPO, oversaw all things protection related. Visiting heads of state, the current first family, vice president and the protective intelligence function of Secret Service all fell under his jurisdiction. He was also a thoughtful man and heir apparent when the director retired.

"Dr. Thane, have you reviewed the reports we sent over?" Carroll asked as he took his seat.

Thane crossed his legs and rested his hands in his lap. "Yes, most interesting."

"What's your conclusion?" Carroll asked.

Thane removed notes from his coat pocket and glanced at them. "By conclusion, I assume you mean is what's indicated in the report possible?"

Carroll nodded. "Yes."

Thane thumbed through the notes again. "This agent of yours, Roberts, I believe is his name."

"Yes, Michael Roberts."

"Is he a good agent—you know, dependable?"

"One of our best."

Thane lowered his head and thought for a moment. "In that case I'd say it's possible. If the agent accurately reported what he observed, no other conclusion could be reached."

Dickerson leaned in Thane's direction. "Are there documented cases of this aura reading which the child claims to possess?"

Thane showed a quick smile. "The science is sketchy. Several efforts to study this sort of thing have been attempted, but with inconclusive results. The young girl mentioned in the report may possess some kind of powers we couldn't measure even if we tried." Thane held up a finger. "But you must be careful with children. The imagination of adolescents, especially young girls, can be a bit tricky. The Salem Witch Trials taught us that.

In the early part of the twentieth century, some serious studies were conducted into the phenomena of second-sight, but I'd personally be careful about reaching any decision about a particular subject without examining her first. Of course, there is the phenomenon of synesthesia. That might explain it." Thane shrugged and his lips thinned. "To be frank, she'd need a full clinical workup before any definitive evaluation could be made."

Carroll rose from his chair and faced the window, gazing out on the skyline of Washington. There wasn't time for such a clinical evaluation, even if the child's mother would agree to it. He tucked his hands in his trouser pockets and turned back around. "We have to know whether to spend any additional time and effort toward this end. What's your call, Doc? Yes or no?"

Thane, like most people in his profession, hated being boxed into a corner with only a yes or no answer. He glanced at the floor, rubbing the bottom of his chin with his thumb. "If the information the girl's provided so far has proven accurate, it would be a mistake to discount it in the future."

Carroll didn't answer. He turned back to the window before dragging a hand down his face. Then he exhaled. *Shit, I'm going to have to go through with this.*

TEN

Rene Bertrand sat at the villa's dining table and played chess with one of his guards, breathing through his mouth because of the odor. The cretin seldom bathed or shaved, and his breath reeked of cigarettes and garlic. He was not the best player in the world, but he was the only one who would sit down occasionally for a game. The other guards appeared too dimwitted. They played cards or backgammon while chain-smoking and sipping hot tea.

Bertrand had become somewhat comfortable in his captivity. Never a brave man, he figured the risk of attempting an escape was greater than the risk of just letting it play out. No one had threatened him since that first day and, while bored, he was somewhat content. Whatever their plans were, whatever their reasons for abducting and holding him, it could not be for anything he'd done. He was a friend of the Arabs; his mother was Algerian. Whatever their rationale, they must eventually release him unharmed. Probably just a straight hostage thing. The Arabs had been holding each other hostage for years. The magazine was used to paying for such inconveniences. But how much would they pay for his release? Besides, if they intended to kill him, he'd already be dead. Right?

Bertrand eyed the man across from him and smirked. This idiot did not have a clue. His opponent rested his chin in his palm and scanned the board up and down. *IQ of a snail!*

Bertrand cleared his throat. "Why am I here?" he whispered.

The man continued studying the board, rubbing his forehead. His gaze shifted from one chess piece to the other. From the corner table, another guard scolded his partner about an illegal play he made during the card game.

From the kitchen echoed the sound of the cleaver on the chopping block. Going by the smell, they were having roasted lamb again. One of the guards, although gruff, could cook. Bertrand's appetite had returned. He strolled to the bar and poured a glass of water, again breathing in the savory smells wafting from the kitchen. The guards stopped playing and gave him a cold stare. Very odd kidnappers. They questioned him repeatedly about his job, co-workers, and people he knew in the news industry. They even took notes. Sometimes, late at night, he overheard them on the phone repeating what he'd told them. *Who were they talking to?*

He returned to the chessboard, and then leaned close to his opponent. "Do you know why I'm here?" If Bertrand could just figure out who they were and why he was taken, he was sure he could assist in his release.

The guard looked up briefly, shrugged, and studied the board again.

Every couple of days they made Bertrand call his boss, Gerard Rye, and check-in. They allowed him use of his computer for sending and receiving emails, but all correspondence remained carefully monitored. Bertrand glanced at the TV. CNN International News played constantly. They demanded he listen and answer random questions they posed throughout the day about world events—as if they wanted him current in case someone should ask.

He gazed at the guard, whose eyes were narrow slits. He'd been staring at the damn board for five minutes. If he did not move soon, Bertrand could have him declared legally dead.

"You must know why I am here? Why not someone else? Why me?"

Without looking up the guard mumbled, "I do not know. Just following orders. Stop asking so many questions and play."

Bertrand chuckled. "I am the one waiting for you—you play!"

The other guards laughed at Bertrand's rebuke.

The guard slowly raised his head and stared at Bertrand through sullen eyes. He reached over the board, sliding his rook one space to the left. He snorted. "Your turn."

Bertrand could not believe it. That was the stupidest move on the board. The moron could have played any other piece, but chose the rook. Leaving his queen exposed meant Bertrand could have her on the next move. He took the rook with his knight. He'd nail the queen next.

Just as he finished his move and looked up, the blow came. Blood dribbled into his beard and mouth as he fell to the floor, holding his broken nose, the warm blood staining his shirt and pants.

The guard stood, raked the chess board onto the floor, and then ambled across the room, laughing. One of the other guards at the table grinned, formed his fingers into a gun, and pointed it at Bertrand. The guard's smile faded as he pulled the imaginary gun's trigger.

Tears filled Bertrand's eyes. He hung his head and cried. A man who would play a half dozen games of chess with you and then deliver such an attack would just as surely take your life. His path was now clear. He must find a way out but had no idea how. The only question—how much time did he have?

ELEVEN

After leaving the national security advisor's meeting, Roberts spent the rest of the day in briefings at Secret Service headquarters and got read into several additional SCI programs. He hated SCI programs. He was a cop at heart. Most of the Sensitive Compartmented Information was spy stuff. He met with the assistant director of protective operations, and ADPO informed him he would be the case agent heading up the investigation during POTUS's visit to Dallas. He would report directly to the headquarters Protective Intelligence supervisor already there.

The case had been bumped up to a Class III status.

A Class III protective intelligence investigation was a rare thing. Most threats against POTUS were of the generic type and handled by a single interview and a report to headquarters explaining how someone had been misquoted or misinterpreted. In ten years, Roberts had arrested only two people as a result of a Class III investigation. The fastest way to find yourself in federal custody was to threaten the president. But to Roberts' knowledge, no agent had ever handled one of this magnitude.

ADPO impressed on him the necessity of staying clear of the military guy—Bishop—whom he believed was nothing but a spy embedded in the investigation by Fuller to keep a check on things. But not even ADPO mentioned the prayer beads, the foreign asset, or Sayed's nefarious connections. Each time Roberts broached the subject, it was waved away, and an excuse made as to why it wasn't important. By the end of the day, he'd figured it out. They'd pushed him out of the loop.

When Roberts got back to the Marriott, he changed into his running gear and went for a jog. DC's evening rush hour had begun, and he ducked and dodged traffic until he hit the shaded running path of Rock Creek Park. That's where he picked up speed. He settled into a good eight-minute pace and relaxed, but the five-mile run was more challenging than he'd remembered.

Less than an hour later, as he entered the hotel side door, he caught a glimpse of a dark sedan with tinted windows and the motor running near the cab stand. Roberts couldn't see the occupant, but there were many dark sedans with tinted windows in DC. He'd even been in a few.

Roberts spent a long time in the shower. Just before he finished, he turned the water to cold. Best way to stop sweating in hot weather. As he dried off, cable news reported on the goings-on of the presidential campaign. According to the White House reporter, the president had just returned to Washington for a few days before traveling to accept his party's nomination in Dallas.

Roberts had a lot to do when he got back home. Showing the video to Susan and Abbey was one of the first things he planned. He looked forward to seeing Susan again. Couldn't quite put his finger on why, though. There was something about her that intrigued him. Roberts hadn't been intrigued by a woman in a long time. It felt good.

Complicating his to-do list was the unwanted partner Fuller had foisted on him, Colonel Bishop. The idea of someone from the intelligence community peeking over his shoulder bothered Roberts. He'd have to keep an eye on this guy. Still hadn't worked out why the military was involved.

For his last night in DC, Roberts decided on Georgetown for dinner. He dressed in khaki Dockers, with a yellow Polo shirt and deck shoes. When Roberts strolled out the hotel's front door, the oppressive summer heat started him sweating all over again. The dark sedan he'd seen earlier pulled under the covered driveway, but he ignored it until a voice spoke from inside the car.

"If you'd like a lift, hop in. I'm hungry too."

Roberts made his way toward the vehicle, bending down as he walked, and looked in the open passenger window. The inside had a new car smell. Bishop sat behind the wheel.

"Where you headed?" Bishop asked.

What was he doing here? Roberts shrugged and craned his neck down the street. "Georgetown."

Bishop flashed a smile. "What a coincidence, my favorite dining location. I know a great fish place right on the river."

"I had fish last night, thanks anyway," Roberts lied.

"Well, they also serve good steaks. We need to talk."

Roberts wanted to shake this guy. "I'll see you soon enough in Dallas. I can wait till then." He turned to leave as a chuckle drifted from the car.

"Fine with me, but aren't you a bit curious about the foreign asset? Didn't it seem strange no one mentioned the prayer beads in the meeting today? They're important, you know."

Roberts stopped as Bishop's words echoed in his ears. He looked back.

Bishop grinned. "The prayer beads confirmed Sayed's identity. Don't you want to know about them and the foreign asset? If you do, get in. Dinner and drinks are on me." Bishop reached across the seat and swung open the passenger door.

Roberts approached the car again and peeked inside. This guy knew all the buttons to push. The coolness of the air conditioner bathed Roberts' face as he slid into the seat. He made a point not to meet eyes with Bishop. ADPO's warning about this guy notwithstanding, he'd get what information Bishop cared to share. Besides, no one else was talking to him.

"The steaks better be good and the beer cold." Roberts grumbled.

The restaurant Bishop chose was Farmers, Fishers, Bakers—some of the best food in Georgetown. The evening crowd hadn't arrived yet, so Bishop asked for a window table. The smell of grilled meat started

Roberts' stomach rumbling. Bishop ordered a Killian's Irish Red and Roberts followed suit. Couples strolling outside with the river in the background, and the heavily wooded area beyond made for a relaxing setting. But Roberts wasn't there to enjoy the view.

After the waitress departed, he leaned forward. "Okay, so what's all this you're talking about back at the hotel?"

Bishop grinned while looking over his menu. "Before we get into that, I want you to know I'm giving you this info on my own. It became painfully evident during the briefing you only had the minimum information. If we're working together, I want you in the loop. You're being told half the story. That could be a problem later."

Roberts didn't answer, but his gaze bore into Bishop. Was this guy about to feed him a line of crap, or break the rules and share real classified material?

"Someone must figure you don't have a need to know, but you can't walk into this thing blind. I need a partner who knows what I know—no secrets, okay?"

This was, to Roberts' way of thinking, the most honest thing he'd heard all day. That is, if Bishop wasn't just feeding him a line. He'd withhold judgment and see how it went. "Tell me about the prayer beads."

The waitress arrived with the beers. "Do you want to order now or wait a while?"

Bishop closed the menu and laid it on the table. "Give us a minute, please."

She retreated, and Bishop leaned closer, the noise of the restaurant drowning out his words. "The beads belong to the assassin, Sayed. The inscription on the medallion proves they were a gift from bin Laden."

Roberts' mind kicked into high gear. "How was he connected to bin Laden?"

"Chief aide and oversaw all al-Qaeda intelligence operations."

"So that's what Fuller meant," Roberts mumbled to himself. He met Bishop's eyes again. Why didn't they just share this with him at the briefing—what's the big deal?

Bishop nodded and took a swallow of beer.

Roberts barely sipped his, working through the mental puzzle. He stared at Bishop. The guy had the kind of smirk that screamed, "I know a lot more than you."

"Ready to order now?" The server appeared again.

After the server left, Roberts asked, "So how come you know so much about this? Where exactly do you fit in?"

"I recruited the asset who's providing the information on Sayed," Bishop whispered. "CIA can't determine if he's telling the truth."

"I'm not clear who you are, Bishop, or what you do."

Bishop took another swallow of beer. The light caught his West Point ring as he turned the glass up to drink.

"Academy man, huh?"

"What?"

Roberts nodded at Bishop's hand.

He glanced at the ring. "Yeah, seems like a long time ago."

"I served a stint with the First Infantry," Roberts said. "Left as a captain and joined the Secret Service. Are you military intelligence?"

Bishop nodded. "I'm officially attached to the 902nd Military Intelligence Group, but that's just on paper. I work at an off-site location outside DC."

"So, what do you do?" Roberts rested his arms on the table.

"Work for an outfit in the Defense Department known as the Protective Preemptive Operations Group, or P2OG. We carry out operations aimed at terrorists and states possessing weapons of mass destruction. Cook's my boss and reports directly to the national security advisor. That's why Fuller's involved."

Now things began to make a little more sense for Roberts—if Bishop was telling the truth. He really couldn't tell if this guy was feeding him a bunch of bull or being completely honest. He took another slow drink before asking, "What's your organic unit?"

"First Special Forces Operational Detachment-Delta."

Roberts stiffened. "You're Delta?"

"Was. Temporarily detached to P2OG at General Cook's request."

Roberts couldn't explain why, but he liked Bishop. If he was Delta, that told Roberts a little about how Director Fuller expected the thing might go down. Delta operators were "direct action" guys. No screwing around. Kill or capture. Was that Bishop's reason for being added to the team? He wasn't a law enforcement agent, and so couldn't be held to the same standard as Secret Service. Having a two-bullets-to-the-brain team member would probably liven things up.

As the dinner progressed, Roberts felt more comfortable with him. He appeared honest, relaxed, and presented no guile or hidden agendas. When they finished eating, Roberts decided it was best to clear the air on the most critical issue. "Are you a spy for the national security advisor?"

Bishop fixed eyes on him. "I realize how it must look. Fuller showed little tact in the way he forced me on your director this morning. I report to Cook, and he reports to Fuller, but I'm not a stooge for anyone."

Roberts gave Bishop a hard stare. "Fair enough." He still didn't trust him 100 percent, but would withhold a final judgment until he saw how the guy behaved. If he were a stooge, it would come out soon enough.

Each took their last sips of beer.

"When do you report to Dallas?" Roberts asked.

"Flying down tomorrow—on your flight as a matter of fact."

A sharp tingle raced up Roberts' back. *How does he know what flight I'm on?*

TWELVE

Sayed was tired of waiting. But emerging from his hotel room, even at night, was a risk he did not want to take. He was in place and undetected. That was the first step. This low-class motel in Richardson, Texas, kept him out of Dallas for the time being. He could hide there until he checked into the hotel reserved for Bertrand—a nice upgrade. Sayed thumbed through the hotel confirmation taken from the Frenchman. All foreign journalists had rooms reserved at the Hilton Anatole in Dallas. His check-in was not for a few more days.

Bored, Sayed studied the transcripts from Bertrand's handlers in Algiers. Everything regarding the man's background, Sayed had memorized. But that was not what worried him. It was the thing he did not know that caused the biggest concern. Some trivial aspect of the Frenchman's life that remained hidden. Something that waited to trip up Sayed as he attempted to pull off the perfect masquerade.

The knock on his door startled him. He glanced at his watch—nine o'clock. He paused with his hand on the doorknob looked through the door's peephole at the dark-haired man on the other side.

Sayed hated this. He had wanted no assistance on this assignment, but the committee had overruled him. The thought that the mission could be compromised by bringing in more people filled Sayed with dread. He kept watching and noticed a second man, taller than the first, standing in the shadows.

Sayed knocked on the door twice. The shorter man knocked three times, placing his hand over his heart. The other man stood behind the first, scanning the parking lot. Sayed took a deep breath and opened the door, stepping behind it to keep himself out of view of anyone passing by.

The two men hurried inside, and Sayed closed and locked the door. They looked around the dimly lit room as if someone might jump out and attack. One wore spicy aftershave that stunk. Sayed studied them. The one with the close-cropped hair was stocky and shorter, and appeared strong. The man's features were hard, like chiseled rock. His deep-set dark eyes showed a firm resolve. The heavy five o'clock shadow gave him a slightly sinister look.

"I am Suleiman," he said and handed Sayed a sealed envelope.

Sayed stared at the envelope. *New transcripts from the Frenchman.* He eyed Suleiman and held up the envelope. "Do you know what this contains?"

The man's eyes never blinked. "No, my orders were to deliver it, not read it."

Sayed looked at the other man. He was taller, slimmer, with long curly hair drooping over his baby face. The black-framed glasses did not inspire confidence. "And what is your name?"

The man stammered and in a quiet voice said, "Zuhair, sir."

Sayed turned from the pair and walked to the other side of the room, his gaze on the envelope. He turned around and pointed at Suleiman. "Where do you live?"

"Chicago."

"Your English could use more work, still too much of an accent." He glanced at the other. "And you?"

"San Francisco, sir," Zuhair replied.

"Your English is excellent."

Zuhair nodded and smiled. "Thank you, sir."

Sayed stared at Suleiman. "Where were you born?"

"Egypt."

"How many years in the US?"

"Four."

Sayed shifted his gaze to Zuhair.

"Los Angeles, sir. Born there."

Sayed nodded. "What do you know of me and my mission?" *A test.* No one in country should know anything about it.

"Nothing," Suleiman replied.

Sayed eyed him another moment. "Nothing?"

Suleiman swallowed and shifted his stance. "We were told to travel here and assist you, if needed."

A satisfying, if not eloquent reply. "And make deliveries?" Sayed held up the envelope.

"Yes, and make deliveries."

"Good," Sayed leaned against the wall. "I do not expect to need you, but if I do, you must be ready. I will be relocating in the next few days. Stay by your phones."

Suleiman looked jittery and nodded like he was in a hurry to leave.

"You are armed?" Sayed asked.

Suleiman withdrew an automatic from his back waistband.

Sayed turned to Zuhair, who unzipped a fanny pack, also revealing an automatic.

"Do you require a weapon?" Suleiman asked.

"No, a weapon would do me no good. If I am forced to use it, my mission would be compromised." Sayed studied the pair. "Do you know why I am here?" It was the same question, asked more directly, but Sayed carefully listened for their responses again.

Suleiman shook his head.

Zuhair said, "No, sir."

Sayed walked to the door. "Very well. Keep a low profile. Any information you have related to me—phone number, address, whatever—memorize and destroy. Wipe it from your phones and computers. Write nothing down."

They both nodded.

Sayed smiled. "I am told you are two of our most trusted people in this country. I will expect you to earn that high praise if the time comes. Our assignment will glorify Allah."

After they left, Sayed tapped the envelope against the palm of his hand and mentally worked through the plan for the hundredth time.

Soon, events might control him. Staying flexible and thinking on his feet was an advantage he knew well. He did have one other advantage, perhaps the only one that counted. The Americans had no idea he was coming. He would be on them like a lion on a lamb before they even realized he was among the flock.

THIRTEEN

R oberts hadn't slept well the last night in DC—too much on his mind. The soft vibrations of the flight from Washington to Dallas started him nodding off. When they hit a rough air pocket, he jumped awake and checked his watch—out for ten minutes. *Better throw some cold water on my face.*

He remained troubled. Why hadn't Secret Service read him into all the information on Sayed? In his line of work, agencies kept secrets from their people for two reasons. They didn't have a need to know, or they didn't trust them with the information. To Roberts' way of thinking, since he was the case agent, he needed to know.

He made his way toward the rear toilet. When he passed Bishop's seat, his new partner glanced up from his book—*Tennessee Williams' Best Short Stories.*

For some reason, Roberts expected him to be reading a Tom Clancy thriller. Tennessee Williams? *Go figure.*

Emerging from the restroom a minute later, Roberts found Bishop waiting outside in the narrow corridor. Bishop held two cups of coffee. He handed Roberts one.

"Thought I'd let you know I'm not going to your office. I'll be at the

local Joint Terrorism Task Force. CIA offered to share their space,"
Bishop whispered.

Roberts had his mouth open to ask why, when Bishop answered it.

"You and I know the way I got pushed on the investigation hasn't
won me any friends at your shop. I'll get in touch when I'm settled."

Roberts was relieved but also a bit disappointed. The Secret Service,
like all federal law enforcement, jealously guarded their status and
jurisdiction. Having Bishop dropped into their lap would frankly piss
off everyone in the office. Bishop was right. His absence did take care
of one problem Roberts had been pondering—how to explain Bishop
to Dick and the SAIC.

Roberts worked his way back to his seat. What had headquarters
told the Dallas office about his DC trip? How much did they know
about all the moving parts of the investigation? About Abbey? About
prayer beads or foreign assets? Roberts strapped in just as the pilot
activated the seat belt light and announced they were on final
approach for DFW International.

An hour later, after dumping his bags in the duty agent room,
Roberts made his way to Dick's office. Behind a closed door, Roberts
told him everything. Dick said nothing, his gaze fixed out the window
as he fiddled with his new gold tie clasp.

After Roberts ran out of information and breath, Dick asked, "Is
that it?"

Roberts sat back and exhaled. "That's it."

"Well, Ace, I tell you, you've been the talk of the office since you
left. The rumor mill started when you got on the plane, and it hasn't let
up since. All the supervisors finally got a briefing this morning, and we
saw the newscast video. Now everyone's on the same page, but I can
tell you the SAIC doesn't like it. You having clearances and authority
he can't control bugs the hell out of him." Dick lifted his brow. "Looks
like you're in charge of the investigation from this end. So, what's your
plan?"

Roberts stood. "First I need to show the video to Abbey Porter."

Dick also stood. His lips formed a pout. "This Sayed guy has balls;
I'll give him that. The son-of-a-bitch walked right into the lion's den,

smack into the middle of a presidential visit in Houston. That takes confidence. A lot of confidence, Ace."

"What do you figure he was thinking?"

"The bastard was checking our security, that's what."

"You think he's in Dallas already?"

Dick bit his lip and nodded. "Yeah, or somewhere near here. He's already in position." He strolled to a wall map of the DFW Metroplex and studied it. "You were right, Ace."

"About what?"

"About everything." Dick let out a long breath, his expression contrite. "The report, the kid, the prayer beads. If you'd listened to me, we would have been caught flat-footed. Sorry I doubted you."

Dick had never apologized for a thing. It took Roberts aback for a second. "Don't sweat it."

For some reason, Roberts felt embarrassed by Dick's apology, so he changed the subject. "I need to catch up on a couple of things and meet with the headquarters supervisor."

"Watch out for Tortorziie. Guy's a snake," Dick said.

Roberts headed for the door, then turned back and met Dick's eye. The reality finally sank in. This wasn't some drill or exercise. There was an assassin in Dallas, and the president was his target.

Dick seldom let a serious expression slip, hiding behind devil smiles, smirks, and frowns. Now, his ashen complexion sent chills through Roberts. "Ace, we're going to have a front-row seat to a presidential assassination attempt."

———

Secret Service Headquarters Supervisor Joe Tortorziie arrived in Dallas and immediately claimed an office vacated by a Dallas supervisor who brought home a stomach parasite from an East African protective assignment.

When Roberts approached the half-opened office door around the corner from financial crimes, a soft whistle drifted into the corridor. Roberts peeked inside and Tortorziie sat behind the desk reading a case report, whistling like a bird. The word SECRET was stamped in red across the top and bottom of the report's cover.

Since Tortorziie was the headquarters man from intelligence division, Roberts had to report to him. He'd worked with Tortorziie during his stint in headquarters a few years ago. They never had any run-ins, but the guy wasn't the easiest to be around. He had *little man syndrome*. Being small of stature, he made up for it by bullying agents who were subordinate to him. He liked spending time rehashing old information that wasn't relevant.

During a meeting Roberts and Dick had a few days ago with Tortorziie, Dick had asked several pointed questions—questions that needed answers. Tortorziie's only response was a crisp "I'll have to get back to you on that." He never did. The way Dick had it figured, either the guy didn't know his job or was just useless.

Roberts gave a quick knock on the door and stuck his head in.

"You wanted to see me, Joe?"

"Yes, come in." Tortorziie closed the folder and dropped it on the desk, littered with similar reports. He was indeed a small fellow. His dark eyes and black hair combed straight back gave him the look of a conman. The reading glasses crooked on the bridge of his nose reminded Roberts of a middle-aged accountant. *Conman accountant, never a good combination.*

Roberts took a seat, and Tortorziie began his lecture. "You're aware of my duties and responsibilities for the convention, no doubt." He exhaled and eyed Roberts. "It now seems I've been assigned a new one —that being this terrorist threat. You've received a full headquarters briefing, I suppose?"

"I got several briefings," Roberts said.

"Good, then you know what I know. Let's run this thing by the book. Any information you get—I get. No going off the reservation. Understand?"

"Right, Joe."

Tortorziie made a habit of holding his pen between his thumb and forefinger when talking. He used it as a pointer, waving it back and forth, or tapping on his desk when emphasizing something. Roberts noticed it during his and Dick's earlier meeting. Then, it was only a minor distraction. Now, Roberts found it annoying.

Tortorziie shuffled through a stack of papers to find the one he wanted. "I've issued a BOLO for Sayed. I didn't indicate the reason—only that he's wanted for questioning, and anyone having information should contact us immediately. I've not worked with the Dallas Police Criminal Intelligence Unit. Are they competent?"

"Very competent, Joe. Say, what do you know about the prayer beads?"

Tortorziie shot him a glance. "What, the ones you recovered from the Porter woman?"

"Yeah."

"I know what you wrote in your report. Is there something else?"

"No, nothing else."

Roberts shifted in the chair. *Either Tortorziie didn't know the significance of the beads, or he wasn't telling the truth.* Had anyone briefed *him*? He *was* the headquarters intelligence agent.

Tortorziie leaned back, interlacing his fingers behind his head. "I understand you intend to show a video of the newscast to the Porter girl."

"Yes."

"Good, let me know if she can make a confirmed identification. Do you understand?"

"Yes, Joe."

"From reports," Tortorziie said, "it appears Sayed was in disguise while he was being videoed. We don't have a perfect handle on what he may actually look like nowadays. We know he's tall, and in his fifties, if we choose to believe CIA reports. Understand?"

"Right."

"Now, I just received information this morning from headquarters that the agency believes Sayed begged to go on this mission. They aren't sure why, but they have their asset working on it. The asset's trying to find out more about Sayed's plans." Tortorziie chuckled. "That puts CIA in a trick box. If the asset appears too snoopy, the bad guys get suspicious and kill him. If that occurs, CIA's golden goose is cooked. If he's not snoopy enough, and Sayed attacks POTUS, then the agency's still screwed for not doing enough to prevent it. It's a lose-lose deal for 'em, unless all the parts collapse together just right. Understand?"

If Tortorziie said "understand" one more time, Roberts would shoot him. He wasn't sure he should ask, but he wanted to know. "Joe, any ideas who this asset is?"

Tortorziie shook his head. "None. They're keeping that quiet. It doesn't matter, does it? The fact is, he's providing information about an attempt on POTUS, and that's all that counts."

"Right, Joe." *This guy didn't have the whole picture.*

Tortorziie tapped his pen on the desk. "Once the convention's over, then case agent designation moves back to the Intelligence Division–Washington. We'll work it from HQ until we or the FBI catches the guy. Your case agent designation will conclude with the departure of POTUS on the last day of the convention. Understand?"

Roberts dug his nails into the chair arms and took a long breath. Joe was one of those guys who liked hearing himself talk. Might have been a great college professor. *Wonder if he rehearses this stuff in front of a mirror at night?* No one needed to tell Roberts that this was his big break. Being the case agent during the convention was his fast track to a promotion.

"I understand, Joe. What's the estimate on whether he may make an attempt during the convention?"

Tortorziie again pointed that damn pen. "Everyone seems to believe that's his plan, but no one's saying it officially, yet. The fact he was in Houston, and just observing, has folks on edge back in headquarters. He's slow and deliberate. That's got everyone worried."

"Any intel on how he might try to carry it out?"

Tortorziie shrugged.

"You think firearm or explosives?" Roberts asked.

Tortorziie shrugged again. "That's what's keeping the director and ADPO up nights. By the way, the director will arrive on Air Force One with POTUS, so keep that in mind. Understand?"

"Okay, anything else?"

"Yeah." Tortorziie again rocked back, pointing his magic pen like a gun. A crooked smile traced his lips just before he said, "You know that being the case agent on something like this cuts both ways."

"Huh?"

"If everything goes fine, especially if we catch the guy in Dallas, that takes you off the hook. If, however, he gets to POTUS during the convention, then your career in the Secret Service is over. Never another promotion, ever."

Roberts had a hundred things he could have said but held his tongue. They stared at each other several seconds before Tortorziie ended the conversation with one word.

"Understand?"

A minute later, Roberts stormed back down the hall to his office. His worst fears were confirmed—Tortorziie was a micro-managing jerk. His assessment about the final outcome of the investigation did, however, ring true. Shit always finds the lowest point, and he sat at the bottom of the septic tank.

Roberts needed to get out of the office. The trip to DC and meeting with Tortorziie made him restless. Passing Dick's office, Roberts glanced in. Dick sat at his desk with his chair facing the picture window. Roberts had caught him in this thoughtful pose several times over the last few weeks—not doing anything. He appeared somehow distracted and not like the old Dick. A sad or perhaps disappointed expression lined his profile.

Roberts strolled back to his office and called Susan. He looked forward to seeing her again, but not Abbey. Keller's assessment of her as creepy wasn't precisely correct, but she made Roberts nervous. He had gotten used to having the edge when interviewing someone. He didn't have that with someone who could practically read his thoughts.

Sticking his head in Dick's office on the way out, Roberts held up his iPad and said, "I'm going to show the video to the Porters."

Dick, having finished his Zen moment, glanced up. "Okay, see ya tomorrow." He wore a long face, and his usually chipper tone was missing. Something troubled him, something bigger than just the Sayed investigation.

FOURTEEN

R oberts drove the short distance to Susan's in his Secret Service Chevy Impala. He liked the fact it had a bench front seat and no middle console. For some reason, Roberts lost items in and between consoles. His car was the only vehicle in the Dallas fleet with a bench seat. Roberts couldn't decide if it made him special or just odd.

When Susan opened the door, she appeared different, but in a good way. She wore a baggy pair of white cargo shorts and a yellow cotton blouse, the top button open. A light pink lacy bra peeked out from under the blouse.

Her eyes sparkled. "Good afternoon. Come in."

She seemed especially happy to see him and he was glad. The coolness of the room was a welcoming relief. Had to be over a hundred outside. Roberts still had no idea why people were expected to wear coats and ties in weather like this.

Susan led him to the sofa. "Have a seat. How about some iced tea? I just made it."

"That's great, thanks."

She went into the kitchen and the sound of glasses clanking and ice clinking drifted into the living room. She reappeared with two iced teas. "I'm afraid it's unsweetened. Is that okay?"

It really wasn't. Being raised in Virginia, his mom, aunts, and grandmothers made sure Roberts became chemically dependent on sugar at an early age. If it wasn't sweet, then it wasn't real iced tea. "Oh, yes, unsweetened is just fine, thank you."

She handed him a glass and sat down on the sofa, keeping a vacant cushion between them. "You have something to show Abbey and me?"

"Yes, a news video of the event you attended in Houston." He took a big swallow of the tea, hiding his grimace as the bitterness hit his taste buds.

Susan sipped hers and leaned back into the cushion. She ran her hand through her hair and to Roberts's surprise, he felt the sudden pull of attraction to her.

"Were we on television?" she asked. Her voice had an excited, girlish quality.

"The news services take a lot of footage. Some gets shown, but most is cut in editing."

"Oh, I see." A slight frown moved across her lips. "Shall I get Abbey then?"

"Yes, she needs to see it."

"Okay." Susan walked toward the hall leading to Abbey's room. Something about the way she moved caught his eye—the sway of her hips. Yes, she did look different today—desirable.

A few minutes later Susan and Abbey strolled back into the room and he stood. The child studied him, but said nothing. A feeling of uneasiness crept into his gut.

Susan stroked Abbey's hair; a habit Roberts had noted before. Some kind of signal? Or just the comforting touch of mother to daughter?

"You remember Mr.—I mean Agent Roberts."

Abbey sat on the sofa, and Roberts sat beside her. She surveyed him as if she were taking an inventory, making sure he was still the same person. She released a quick grin. "Hello. Where's Agent Keller?"

Roberts' hair prickled. *Christ! Right out of the gate. Asked about Keller.*

Abbey's big blue eyes revealed something, but he couldn't figure it out.

He cleared his throat and edged away from her. "He's on sick leave. Just got out of the hospital."

Susan jerked her head back. "Is he all right? What happened?"

Roberts turned to Abbey. "You probably saved his life. That funny coloring on his neck was something serious. Life-threatening, really, but he's okay now, thanks to you."

Abbey's mysterious smile contained no humor. It was a sad smile. "I'm glad," she whispered.

Roberts momentarily lost his train of thought, and his mouth dried up. After taking another sip of tea, he said, "I have a video I'd like you to watch. It shows you and your mom when you were in Houston during the president's visit."

"All right," Abbey said with little enthusiasm.

He turned on his iPad and loaded the file. Waiting for it to open, Abbey stared at him. Roberts wanted to say something to break the silence. Abbey didn't utter a word, just kept that deadpan expression, her gaze boring a hole into his soul. Why didn't she say something? Why just stare at him?

"So, what have you been doing this summer?" he asked.

"Reading and practicing the piano," Abbey said.

"You play the piano?"

"She's terrific. Coming along well, right, Abbey?"

Roberts handed Susan the iPad as the video started. She studied it, waiting for her and Abbey to show up. Abbey sat ramrod straight, expressionless. The president walked across the airport tarmac while the camera panned to the left.

Susan pointed. "Look, Abbey, there we are." The video held the president in mid-frame with Susan, Abbey, and the other guests in the background. When the camera moved a little farther to the left, the image of the tall man with the bushy beard beside Abbey came into view. Abbey kept her gaze on the video—her expression blank.

Roberts reached over and pressed the pause button with the picture of Abbey and the tall man in center-frame. "Is that the man who dropped the beads?"

When she didn't reply, Susan turned and asked, "Well, is it him?"

Abbey sat motionless, and tears formed in her eyes. One ran down her pink cheek.

Susan touched her leg. "What's wrong?"

Still gazing at the screen, Abbey's small lips quivered, and her shoulders heaved. "Yes, that's him," she said, before falling into Susan's lap, crying.

Susan held her close and stroked her hair, kissing her head. "That's okay, Baby, it's okay."

Roberts was shocked—the child had feelings after all. He'd thought her an emotionless zombie, but there she was, crying like a regular six-year-old.

Susan ventured a glance at him while handing back the iPad. "Can we turn that off, please?"

"Sure." He pressed the stop button.

Susan straightened Abbey up and put her hands on the child's shoulders. She gently wiped the tears away. "What's wrong?"

Abbey rubbed her cheeks with the back of her hands and sniffled. She stared at Roberts through red eyes. In a voice no louder than a whisper, she said, "I've thought a lot about it." She wiped away another tear. "I'm sure now. He's going to kill the president."

Minutes later, Roberts sat by himself on the sofa, waiting for Susan to return. She'd taken Abbey back to her room and spent a few minutes settling her down. Sitting alone, Roberts considered what she'd just said. *He's going to kill the president.* She'd been right about Keller's neck, his father's ring, and the man in the crowd being dangerous. Were her words prophecy? If he tried putting *this* into a report, it would make him look foolish. *Let it go.*

Susan came back into the living room and sat down. She had that nervous twitch people get after a major shock. "I gave her something to read—it relaxes her."

"I'm sorry she got upset. Are you okay?"

Susan waved away the idea. "She's fine, and no, I'm not okay."

"I apologize, but we needed—"

She glanced his way. "Oh, no, I'm not angry with you. You've got a job to do—I'm just upset she cried." Susan swallowed hard and licked her lips. "You see, since she was an infant, she's only cried three times.

Twice after she got hurt, and the third time today. This business has affected her much more than I'd realized." Susan stood and rubbed her hands down her legs. Her gaze darted around the room. She grabbed his half-empty glass. "More tea?"

"No, thank you, I'm fine." Roberts settled deeper into the cushions. "Have a seat. I'd like to know a little more about you and Abbey, if you don't mind."

Susan couldn't hide being upset very well. The uncertain droop of her mouth and anxiousness in her eyes spoke volumes. "Certainly, what would you like to know?"

Roberts smiled his best smile to put her at ease. It must have worked, because she sat down and relaxed, her left arm along the top cushion, inches from his shoulder. The way she sat caused her blouse to open, revealing much more of the bra and a sweep of creamy white skin.

Roberts shifted his gaze back to her eyes. "Tell me about her father," he said.

Susan made a face. "Stan and I worked together for a couple of years on Wall Street. We also lived together for a while and I got pregnant." She stared in the distance. "I viewed it as exciting and assumed he wanted to get married. He didn't," she said, with an emphatic stare.

"I worked through the pregnancy and lived with him, but the relationship only became more strained after I refused an abortion. He wanted out and so did I. So, after Abbey's birth, my dad asked me if I wanted to work for him back in Dallas." Susan smiled and nodded. "A ploy by the old schemer to get his grandchild closer to him and Mom."

Susan turned away, brushing hair from her eyes. There was an awkward silence. She sniffed and put a hand to her mouth. "Stan saw Abbey only once, I'm told—in the maternity ward." She turned back to Roberts and took in a long breath. Her eyes had misted. "So that's how I became a single mom." She stared at her lap and rubbed her hand across her shorts. "Abbey and I moved here, and I keep the books for my dad's business. I go in every other day for a couple of hours but do most of the work remotely from home."

"I see." Roberts' stare drifted to the blouse again.

"I'm very protective of Abbey," she said, "I want her to succeed in life. I'll do whatever it takes to ensure that. That's what a good parent does. Do you have children?"

Roberts shook his head and shifted on the sofa. "No, I'm not married." He paused a second before saying, "Susan, I need to know something about Abbey—about her powers, that is."

Roberts still had doubts about the kid, but he'd done more research and found a University of Toronto case study involving emotion-evoked synesthesia. According to the study, there was a form of synesthesia in which a seven-year-old subject saw colored *auras* around the head or body of persons that were linked to his emotions. If Abbey really could see auras, then he'd better not discount something he could use.

Susan leaned slightly in his direction. "What?"

"Before I ask, I want to tell you something you can't repeat. Promise?"

"Sure."

Roberts needed to tread carefully here. Passing on this kind of information without authorization could be a career-ending move. Once they pulled your Top-Secret clearance, you'd be finished as an agent. But he needed to convince her of the importance of his request. He'd been taking so many career chances the last few days—what was one more? "We think she's right about that man in the video. We believe he's here to harm the president."

Susan's jaw dropped and she leaned even closer. "Who is he?"

"We've identified him, but that's classified. I don't even have all the information, yet."

"I see."

"You know, there might be a way Abbey could help us."

"I don't understand."

"She saw his black aura, and had the vision about him wanting to kill the president," Roberts said. "After what she said today, I need to know—do you see any other way she could help us locate this guy? We think he's in the Dallas area and may try something during the convention."

Susan shook her head. Her confused expression gave him pause.

Roberts eyed her a moment before saying. "We need to explore all options. Abbey could make the difference in whether we lose another president in Dallas."

"I don't get it. How could Abbey possibly help? Are you talking about some kind of remote viewing, or something? Abbey can't do that."

"No, not remote viewing. Abbey's the only one who's seen the guy up close. He was wearing a disguise in the video I showed you, but he can't disguise his aura. Abbey can see things the rest of us can't."

Susan didn't answer, just gazed at him.

Roberts cleared his throat. "If I could swing a couple of passes for you and Abbey, would you attend the convention with me?"

Susan's lips parted into a grin. "Seriously?"

"Yes, seriously."

She thought a few seconds. "Would we be in any danger?"

Roberts had expected this—only natural. He couldn't make any guarantees because he had no idea about Sayed's plan. Best to keep it general for now. "No more than any other delegate or guest. I could even arrange a photo session with you two and the president, if you'd like." He hoped this final enticement would close the deal. If he was to put his plan into action, Abbey must be involved. Convincing Susan was the first step.

Susan's grin faded and she slowly shook her head. "I don't know… something doesn't feel right here. Having Abbey traumatized by seeing this guy again isn't something I'm in favor of. I don't think I want—"

Before Susan could finish her thought, a small voice sounded from the hall. "Mom."

Roberts looked around and Susan stared over his shoulder as Abbey walked toward them. She wore a blank expression, that weird deadpan look. The one that creeped Keller out.

"I want to help," Abbey said.

Susan squatted, and Abbey walked into her waiting arms.

"Baby, I never meant for you to hear any of that."

Roberts wished he could quietly slip out and leave them to this private mother-daughter moment, but he couldn't. He was the reason for it.

Abbey eyed Roberts. "Is what you said true, about me being the only one who can see the man? That I might be able to help catch him?"

"Yes, Abbey," he said.

Susan pulled in a long breath and her eyes squinted. Roberts couldn't tell if she was angry, upset, or just thinking something through.

"Then I want to help," Abbey said again in a quiet tone. She touched Susan's cheek. "Don't worry. I'll be able to spot him before he can hurt anyone, including us."

Susan looked Roberts' way and nodded. He released a silent sigh of relief.

"Are you sure, Baby?"

"Sure," Abbey repeated. Without another word, or making eye contact with Roberts again, she turned and walked back toward the hall.

Susan reclaimed her seat on the couch. "Agent Roberts, looks like for better or worse, we're in."

"Good, I'll make the arrangements. And please, call me Michael."

"I'd like to know a few more details."

"Sure. What would you like to know?"

Susan bit her lower lip a second before asking, "Let's talk about it during dinner."

"Dinner?"

"Yeah, dinner. You eat dinner, don't you?"

"Yeah." Roberts hadn't expected this, never done this before, but knew several other agents who had. More than one had drawn an official reprimand. You never fraternized with witnesses in a case—especially a Class III investigation.

He couldn't figure out what she was going to say next by her expression, and that worried him. It was one of those looks you see in a mall as someone strolls along window shopping. If he wanted her cooperation, if he wanted Abbey's help, he had a decision to make. Stepping a little farther out on an already thin limb wasn't his nature.

"Do you have someplace in mind?" he asked.

She cocked her head to the side. "Is that a yes, then?"

"That's a yes."

She lowered her outstretched hand along the top of the sofa and accidentally brushed his shoulder. "Great, how about tomorrow night? Abbey can stay with her grandparents."

"Seven o'clock?"

"Fine." Her shoulders relaxed and she leaned back a little more into the couch.

"We'll talk more about everything over dinner," he said. "I'll get you two in the office tomorrow afternoon for photos and have your convention credentials in a day or so."

"I've never been to a convention. Are they as crazy as it looks on TV?"

"Crazier. This is my third."

This time she intentionally touched his shoulder, but the flirtatious expression was gone. She wrinkled her forehead. "If I feel something's wrong, I want the option to back out at any time. I won't put Abbey in danger, even for the president."

FIFTEEN

Roberts arrived at the office early the next morning, the visit with Susan yesterday still fresh in his mind. A stroke of genius, inviting her and Abbey to the convention. By keeping Abbey close to POTUS, she could act as an early warning system to Sayed's presence—giving the Secret Service time to respond. The term canary in a coal mine seemed a crass way of describing it, but probably an accurate one.

He headed to Tortorziie's office. Reporting everything to a headquarters man wasn't something Roberts was used to. With Dick, he didn't have to check in or ask permission; all he had to do was show results.

When he stepped through the door, Tortorziie stopped typing and turned. He showed the kind of look door-to-door solicitors probably get from most people.

Roberts leaned against the frame. "The Porter girl confirmed the video. She identified the guy as the one who dropped the beads."

"Good, I'll make the notifications," Tortorziie said and went back to his typing, ignoring Roberts.

This morning, Tortorziie wore some kind of funky aftershave, which stunk up the small office. Had a spoiled cabbage odor.

"I can see you're busy, so I'll let you get back to work." Roberts backed out of the office. "Oh, I almost forgot, Ms. Porter and her daughter are coming by this afternoon to get credentialed for the convention. If you want to meet them, they'll show up between two and three."

Tortorziie snapped his head around. "What?"

"I said they'll show up—"

"I heard that part. What did you say about getting credentialed?"

"I've invited them to the convention, and I'm getting them guest badges."

Tortorziie frowned. "On whose authority?"

"On mine."

Tortorziie reached for his pen. "Michael, what makes you think you have that authority?"

Roberts hadn't expected push-back on this. "The director told me to use them if I believed they might be of assistance."

Tortorziie sneered. "Of course, he did, but you don't have the authority to do anything unless it's approved by a headquarters' supervisor."

Roberts met his stare. "Do you have the authority?"

Tortorziie exhaled a tired breath. "If I choose to exercise it." The pen started a slow tap on the desk.

"Then do it. I need them."

"For what possible reason would I want them at the convention, and with guest passes to boot?"

Roberts didn't understand why the guy questioned his decision. Could it be because he hadn't cleared it with him first? Was this just a little power game? *Little man syndrome.* Whatever the reason, Roberts decided not to play. He could read people and make decisions—he made one now.

"Joe, I need the girl at the convention with me because she's the only person who can recognize Sayed. The mother goes with the kid, okay?"

"You know, Michael"—Tortorziie sneered again, leaning back in his chair, the pen now used as a pointer—"people talk about you in headquarters, and they aren't saying very nice things."

Blood rushed to Roberts' face. "Are you going to authorize the passes?" His harsh tone made it clear he wasn't willing to negotiate.

Tortorziie shrugged. "No, it's not necessary."

Roberts' voice rose. "The Porters will arrive this afternoon, and I'm having them credentialed. If you try and stop it, I'll call ADPO."

A bright red glow rushed up Tortorziie's neck and lit up his face. He sprang from his seat and said, "Now see here." He poked the pen inches from Roberts face.

Before Tortorziie could blink, Roberts snatched the thing and flung it into the trash basket in the corner. "If you ever point that damn thing at me again, you'll be digging it out of your ass," he whispered in a menacing tone.

He slammed the door on his way out.

Roberts stormed down the hall. His mind sorted through his options. He closed the door to his office and flopped into the chair, waiting for the call he knew would come. Letting the guy get to him like that wasn't his nature. Tortorziie, although an asshole, maintained a good reputation in the Intelligence Division. Roberts, on the other hand, couldn't even get promoted. What was he thinking?

Well, what's done is done. He wasn't going to let Tortorziie or anyone else run the investigation and then drop him in the grease if it all went to hell. Whichever way it played out, he'd take the credit or blame, but only if he called the shots.

The rest of the morning passed slowly, waiting for the phone to ring. Roberts stared at it, willing someone to call. Every minute it didn't ring only increased his anxiety. He occupied himself with administrative paperwork until Dick stuck his head in.

"Want to a grab a sandwich?"

"Sure."

"Let's go." Dick slipped on his jacket. "I'll drive—meet you at the front in two minutes."

On his way out, Roberts passed the SAIC and ASAIC talking in the hall. When he neared, their conversation stopped. They eyed him, and he expected daggers to appear any second.

"Good morning," he said.

They both glared at him—neither replied. Figures. The SAIC was a petty, jealous, small-minded man who hated not being in total control of everything that went on in his field office. The ASAICs had to follow along or risk the SAIC's wrath come performance review season.

When Roberts exited the building, the temperature was already in the nineties. Another hot July day. Easing into Dick's waiting car, Roberts fished for the tangled seatbelt as Dick pulled onto the street. Dick flipped the AC on high and weaved through the light traffic. Roberts was conflicted. Should he tell Dick about the argument? If anyone would understand, it would be him.

"So, how's it going, Ace?"

Roberts stared out the window. "Not so good. Me and Tortorziie had a little tiff earlier."

"Yeah, I got a call about that."

Roberts tensed. "From the SAIC or ASAIC?"

Dick glanced at him. "Neither, Hugh called me."

Roberts' mind froze, trying to figure out who Hugh was. No one named Hugh in Dallas. "Hugh?"

Dick kept his eyes on the road. "Yeah, Hugh Carroll. You know, the director of the Secret Service."

"Oh, that Hugh." Roberts' appetite left him.

"Seems he wants to know if you're crazy or just stupid?"

Great. Now I've pissed off the director. Roberts shifted to a more comfortable position. "Do I get a choice?"

Dick shrugged but didn't look his way. "Beats me, but that little worm Tortorziie called ADPO. He's pretty upset, said you were out of control down here, and wanted you replaced as case agent." Dick glanced in his direction.

"And?" Roberts asked.

"ADPO called the director and told him he intended to send someone from Intelligence Division down to replace you. Said he might also recommend a reprimand, under the circumstances."

"So that's it then." Game, set, match—he'd lost.

Dick made a right turn. "Mind if I finish my little story?"

"Sorry."

"The director called me and asked what I thought. I told him you weren't crazy or stupid, and my money stayed on you."

"Thanks. What did he say?"

"Said he'd call me back."

Roberts stared straight ahead, afraid to meet Dick's eyes, waiting for him to say something else. Anything so there wasn't silence. "Guess I screwed up pretty good, huh?"

"Michael, everyone including the director, knows Tortorziie is a lightweight prick. But you still can't threaten the man."

Here it comes. "So, did you hear back from the director?"

Dick pulled up to the sandwich shop and shifted into park. "Yeah, about fifteen minutes ago. I'm afraid I have some good news, and bad news, Ace."

Roberts pulled in a deep breath. "I could use a little good news about now."

"All right, here it is. You're still case agent, but you're not reporting to Tortorziie anymore."

Roberts perked up. "Huh? So, what's the bad news?"

"I'm the new case supervisor. You report all information directly to me from now on."

Roberts let out a breath, and a morning of tension drained from him. "I don't get it. How's that bad news for me?"

Dick opened the driver's door, glancing back over his shoulder before getting out. "Cause if you ever try and shove a pen up my ass, I'll shoot you before you get my pants down."

Yup, there was the devil smile again.

———

Three hours later, when Susan and Abbey arrived at the office, Roberts walked them to the processing room for fingerprints and photographs. Susan appeared especially happy to see him—Abbey acted disinterested. While Abbey was having her photo taken, Roberts stood close to Susan and chatted. He happened to glance into the hall, and Bridget stood staring at him. Her usual smile wasn't present. After a moment, she walked away without a word.

Dick made his way to the processing area just before they left. Susan had bent over, retying one of Abbey's shoes, before Dick strolled in. He stopped at the door, and his eyes widened as he zoomed in on her. Roberts had seen that look before and almost laughed out loud. Susan glanced up at the newcomer.

"Dick, I'd like to introduce Susan and Abbey Porter. This is my supervisor, Dick Crosby," Roberts said.

"Hello." Susan rose and shook Dick's hand.

Dick stood extra straight and puffed out his chest. His eyes had an excited look, and he showed his broadest smile. "I'm delighted to meet you both." He shot a quick glance down at Abbey, but couldn't seem to take his eyes off Susan. It was his usual reaction to any attractive woman who stepped into the office.

No one spoke for what seemed too long before Dick shuffled his feet and said, "Well, I'll let you get finished. Don't want to hold you up."

Roberts escorted Susan and Abbey to the lobby. While they waited for the elevator, Susan's hand brushed his. She had a mischievous grin. She and Abbey stepped into the elevator. Just before the doors closed, she said, "See you at seven."

Roberts experienced a feeling he hadn't had in a long time. He actually looked forward to an evening meal.

Dick was leaning against his office door as Roberts walked back down the hall. "I can see why you would want her at the convention," Dick said.

Roberts shook his head. "It's not what you think."

Dick released a smirk. "What am I thinking, Ace?"

The ringing phone greeted Roberts when he got back to his office.

"How's it going?" Bishop asked.

Wondering when he'd show up. "Great, what's up? Find a place to stay, yet?"

"I'm just down the street in the Omni Mandalay."

Roberts shifted the receiver to his other ear. *Impossible!* The Secret Service had tried to reserve a couple of rooms for some DHS bigwigs there five months ago—no dice. "How did you get in there? That place has been booked forever."

There was a pause before Bishop answered. "General Cook used a favor. Anything happening?"

"No, other than I almost got canned as case agent, and the Porter girl identified our suspect from the video."

"Sounds like you've been busy."

"Yeah, well..."

"I'm in room 2411 here, and my extension at the task force is 5775. You have my cell number," Bishop said. "By the way, did you guys get the word? Looking like there's an Al-Qaeda cell here in Dallas operating in support of you know who's mission."

"Where did you get that?"

"NSA intercept," Bishop said. "You'll probably hear something later. I've got to go. Take care."

Roberts reared back in his chair. The day's events had only confirmed what he already knew. Being on the horns of a dilemma wasn't just uncomfortable, it was dangerous. He had information, thanks to Bishop, that no one else in Secret Service appeared to have about the prayer beads, foreign asset, and latest intel. He also had an ace in the hole, thanks to Abbey, who might be able to identify Sayed from his aura before he could carry out his plan.

Roberts had always been a company man. Sports had taught him loyalty to the team. He'd done everything asked of him, and more. But the Secret Service, like other federal law enforcement, was mired in tradition, procedures, and protocols that allowed for little deviation. If Roberts were to use his Bishop and Abbey advantages, he'd be on his own—going off the reservation. If the thing blew up in his face, he could lose his job. Certainly, no more promotions. The director hadn't tried to block him using Abbey, but his support was tempered: *You'll have to take responsibility for them.* The director also authorized him to work with with Bishop, but everyone knew he'd been forced into that call.

The safe bet, the company-man bet, was to more or less ignore Bishop and Abbey. No hocus pocus or working with someone outside the Service. No one could fault him for following the established rules. But they would.

Never another promotion, ever.

Roberts drew in a long slow breath. His reputation was already shot. His chances for promotion drifted a little farther away every day.

Even if there was only a one in a million shot of saving the president, could he ignore it?

You must stand for something, or be nothing.

As the day drew to a close and the hum of office activity decreased, Roberts wrestled with the problem. Just before leaving to pick up Susan, he decided. Abbey and Bishop were his team.

Now—how to make it work?

SIXTEEN

Driving to Susan's that evening, Lexi popped back into Roberts' mind. She had changed him—changed the way he viewed relationships. He didn't go on many dates; two or three with the same woman was the average. After that, he became bored or scared. He'd find dozens of reasons for not asking them out again. He enjoyed the physical company of beautiful women, but not the baggage that went along with a long-term involvement. Knowing his time in Dallas was short meant he shouldn't start a relationship which would entail forcing a woman to have to move when the next transfer rolled around. He'd had bad luck with that.

Roberts still recalled that miserable day in early January over two years ago. He'd shaken the rain off his umbrella as he entered the noisy Bayside Restaurant in Chevy Chase. He and Lexi always ate there to celebrate special occasions. She waited at a table for two in the corner. The smell of shrimp cooking in garlic wafted past as he meandered through the crowd. He bent down and gave her a hello kiss. Something was up. The glint in her eyes always told him. She had that satisfied smirk and could hardly sit still. He took his seat and unfolded his napkin as she spoke.

"I have the most exciting news," she said.

"Really? So do I."

She placed her palms on the table. "Okay, but I'll go first. Dr. Jameson talked to me this afternoon." A wide smile parted her lips before she took a deep breath. "They've asked me to stay on after my residency as part of the research staff. Me, Lexi Cummings, genetic researcher at Johns Hopkins. Can you believe it?"

The elation and excitement in her voice only lowered Roberts' spirits. His well-rehearsed story fell apart. There was no delicate way to break the news. "Yeah," he said, "that's great... really great."

The waiter stopped and told them about the day's specials and left a couple of menus. Lexi had already ordered a martini for herself and a gin and tonic for him. He took a long drink, finishing half of it.

She glanced at the wine list. "We should celebrate. Let's share a bottle of something expensive. Oh, I forgot about your news. Tell me."

Roberts didn't look at her. He scanned the menu and mumbled, "I've been transferred." When she didn't answer, he glanced her way. The smile was still in place. He'd told her months ago his time in the Intelligence Division would be coming to an end soon and he'd have to find a new home in a field office.

She propped her elbows on the table and leaned closer. The look of expectation caused him to hesitate. "So, which one did you get, Washington or Baltimore?" She pleaded. "Oh, please say Baltimore, sweetie, please."

He shook his head. "Dallas."

Her smile melted. "Texas?"

"Yeah, Texas."

"But you didn't request Dallas. You asked for—"

"Dallas, Lexi. The others on my wish list were already filled—no openings."

She scowled and her gaze drifted to the table for a few moments. When she looked up, she whispered, "But what does this mean for us?"

Roberts had been rehearsing this next part for most of the afternoon. He gave her his best sales pitch. "It'll just be for two or three years. Besides, there are lots of goods jobs in Dallas for a doctor like you. They have a wonderful medical center and loads of opportunities for talented people."

Her jaw set, and she gave him a cold stare. "Do you think I want to work in Dallas, or, for that matter, any place in Texas, when I've been offered a position at Johns Hopkins? For God's sake, Michael, don't you understand?"

Roberts understood. They agreed not to discuss it anymore that evening.

The engagement continued for several months after he'd arrived at his new post. They tried the long-distance relationship thing, with one or the other traveling to Baltimore or Dallas every other week, but excuses for not making the trip got easier on both their parts. Phone calls also became scarcer. Soon they agreed to postpone the wedding. As the months passed and the emails got fewer and fewer, they came to the same conclusion.

Receiving her engagement ring in the mail that day ended it. Roberts seldom drank more than one or two drinks, but that night he got drunk enough to have a long talk with himself. He decided to go after a career—to hell with relationships. He never spoke to Lexi again.

Roberts arrived at Susan's a little before seven. She answered the door and invited him in. She wore a purple, sleeveless blouse that accentuated her figure and a tight-fitting white skirt.

Something about her always excited him. Not just her looks, but the way she tilted her head when she smiled, the way she listened to him as if his every word mattered. He hadn't felt like this about a woman since Lexi. And he wasn't sure he wanted to.

She gave him a beer and a smile before she disappeared into the back to finish getting ready.

Each visit to the house seemed a little different. The earlier scent of cinnamon was now replaced by a whiff of petunias. Ten minutes later, she hurried back into the living room, putting on her last earring. He finished the beer and stood.

"Sorry, I'm terrible with time. Shall we go?" she said.

They made their way out of Irving and into Dallas. She tilted the passenger seat back and got comfortable.

"Do you always go out to dinner with the people you interview?"

Roberts kept his eyes on the road and his expression neutral. Figured that would come up sooner than later. "Not till now."

She blushed. "Really?"

"Really. Why did you ask me?"

She thought about it a few seconds. "I guess curiosity more than anything."

"Curiosity?"

She slid her sunglasses on and shrugged. "I've never dated a cop."

"Why would you think cops are different than anyone else?"

"I don't know. I just never thought of myself dating one, that's all. So, what do your other *friends* think about you being a cop?"

He glanced her way. Figured that would come up as well. "I don't know. We never talked about it."

"Oh." She fiddled with her purse snap a moment. "I've been thinking about the convention."

"Yes."

She leaned closer. "What do you want us to do? I mean, Abbey and me."

Roberts wanted to word this just right. No need causing any anxiety. "I'll arrange everything at the convention. You'll be fine. I'll pick you up every morning and deliver you home every night."

She raised her voice slightly. "No, I mean what do you want us to do? Do we follow you around or..." She kept her stare on him, demanding an answer.

"Yes, you'll stay close to me. If the man we're looking for shows up, he probably won't resemble the guy in the video. We believe it's a disguise. He can hide his outward appearance, but not his aura. Abbey will tell me, and then we'll take it from there."

Susan's lips pressed together. Her eyes drifted down as a thought must have entered her head. "Are you sure all this is safe?"

"Don't worry. I won't let anything happen to you or Abbey." An empty feeling raced through his stomach. *He couldn't make that kind of promise.* Without knowing Sayed's plan, no one could say how much danger they might be in. "You guys will travel to all the locations with the president, from the arrival at Love Field, until the departure. I'll always be with you." He glanced her way in time to see her bite her lip. "You'll see. It'll be okay."

"You recall what I said, if I feel bad about something."

Roberts nodded. "Yeah, you can back out anytime."

Susan relaxed into the soft leather seat and grinned. "So, where are we going?"

"It's a surprise. You'll love it."

Roberts' surprise was the Dallas Fish Market Restaurant on Main Street. The valet parked his car while he escorted Susan inside. Walking into the cool room was a welcome relief from the steam bath of the street. She scanned the decor and ran both hands down her skirt.

"There was a big write-up on the executive chef here last month. One of the top ten in Dallas," he whispered as they approached the greeter.

The smell of something being cooked in butter floated through the air. "Never tried this restaurant," Susan said.

They were seated at a table for two near a window. They ordered drinks and Susan gazed at the traffic and evening commuters. She repositioned her water glass and rubbed the back of her hand before saying, "Seafood is my favorite."

"Mine too," he replied.

They scanned the menu and she asked, "Any suggestions?"

"Everything's good. Go crazy."

She cracked another grin.

The waiter took their drink orders and soon returned with Roberts' Stella Artois and her white wine. He ordered the blackened grouper and she, the seared jumbo Maine scallops.

Roberts wasn't sure where to start with the small talk. He was badly out of practice on the dating scene. What few dates he'd been on the last year had ended on a sour note.

He cleared his throat. "So, you attended SMU?"

"Yes."

"Expensive."

"I was on scholarship. Studied business and finance. Received an MBA."

"Scholarship? Are you a brainiac?" he chuckled.

Her chin dipped and her cheeks turned red. "Kind of. Valedictorian of my high school class. Graduated magna cum laude from SMU."

He sipped his beer. "I can see where Abbey gets her looks and intelligence." In a quiet voice he asked, "Is there anyone special in your life now?"

She'd opened her mouth to answer when she must have realized the nature of the question. She shyly grinned. "Agent Roberts, is this part of the official investigation... or a private one of yours?"

"It's for me. Are you offended?"

Another grin. "Not offended, just surprised." She shook her head. "No, there's no one special." The redness drifted to her ears. "What about you? You know my life's history, and I know nothing about you. Are you from Texas?"

He shook his head. "Nope, Virginia. Went to school there. Spent a few years in the army, and then went right into Secret Service. Not much to tell." Roberts hated talking about himself.

She smirked and leaned her forearms on the table. "Oh, I bet you have a lot more to tell." She glanced at his left hand. "Why the Secret Service? I thought everyone wanted to join the FBI?"

Roberts shrugged. "Different strokes..."

She ran a finger around the top of her glass, and her gaze briefly drifted back to his left hand again. "Never married?"

"Nope." *Okay, here comes the marriage questions.*

This seemed to intrigue her. She slowly nodded. "Why?"

"Never found the right person." *That was a lie.* Hope she couldn't see it in his face.

She took a slow sip of wine and eyed him. "How old are you?"

"Thirty-six." He sat back in the chair and waited for the next inquiry.

She stared at something on the table and didn't speak.

"Why?" he asked.

She shook her head. "Oh, nothing."

He let his silent stare do its work.

After a few seconds she said, "It's just that most people your age are already married."

"You're my age and you're not married," he said.

Her head snapped up. "I am not."

"Not what?" He smiled. "My age, or married?"

A smirk moved across her lips. She wiggled her finger at him. "You're quick."

"Yeah, well, mama said I was special."

She laughed. Not a giggle, a full-throated belly laugh. He liked making her laugh like that. She wiggled a finger at him again. "I'll have to keep an eye on you."

"Promise?"

She sipped her wine and studied him. Roberts understood what she wanted to know. Lots of guys his age had relationship issues. Thankfully, she dropped the subject, but it would most likely pop up again.

By the time the food arrived they'd discussed the hot topics. Her growing up in a big city like Dallas, as opposed to his childhood in the Virginia countryside. They both loved snow skiing. He thought the Beatles best defined the rock-and-roll of the 60s, and she insisted it was the Stones. He enjoyed her company; she helped him relax. That's another thing he hadn't experienced in a long time. For the last hour, he'd not once thought about the convention, Sayed, or his career.

They didn't rush the meal. After dessert they had coffee and a couple more drinks. It was almost ten o'clock before they left, and the drive back to Susan's put him in a great mood. He knew her now, and the previous tension between two strangers was gone. But Roberts had concerns. Since he couldn't get promoted in Dallas, he would seek a transfer as soon as the convention concluded. Leaving another piece of his heart like he did with Lexi didn't appeal to him. The fewer commitments, the better for a guy who was only passing through.

He walked her to her door. He wasn't ready for the evening to end. She slid the key in the lock and looked his way. It was one of those looks you see from somebody who wants to ask a question, but isn't exactly sure if they want to know the answer.

"If you can come in for a while, I have a bottle of Chianti Classico that begs for two people to share it."

Roberts had been hoping she would ask. "Okay, you've convinced me."

She got the glasses while he opened the wine.

"That's about the only thing we didn't discuss tonight—wine preferences," she said.

He twisted the corkscrew. "Red—always red."

She set the glasses on the counter as he popped the cork.

Roberts had never been shy with women. He felt most had the same urges as men. When he found a woman he liked, he wasn't afraid to make the first move.

Her eyes met his just before he pulled her to him and kissed her—a slow, gentle kiss that explored her soft mouth. She wrapped her arms around his neck and pushed closer. Her hungry response surprised and excited him.

The phone in his jacket pocket vibrated, and he broke the kiss with a sigh. That was the problem being the PI Squad leader. The damn thing rang day and night.

He unwound himself from her embrace. "This is Roberts."

"Agent Michael Roberts?" an unfamiliar voice asked.

"Yes, who's this?"

"Ben Clawson, Intelligence Division. I have some information to pass to you if you can get to a SCIF and secure phone."

"I assume it's related to my case and the POTUS's visit."

"Most definitely."

Roberts calculated how he could pull this off. Didn't want to leave Susan, but needed to take the call. "I'll call you in about twenty minutes, if that's okay?"

"Fine," Clawson said. "I tried contacting ATSAIC Dick Crosby, but got no answer. You were next on the call list."

"Call you right back." Roberts hung up and dropped the phone into his pocket. He softly rubbed Susan's bare arms. The most enjoyable evening he'd spent in the last year and now this...

She frowned. "Who was that?"

He took a step back. "My ATSAIC isn't available, so I have to call headquarters from the secure phone in the field office. I won't be long."

"What's an ATSAIC?"

Roberts said, "Assistant to the special agent in charge. We have almost as many acronyms as the military."

Susan's eyebrows rose and she rotated the wine cork in her fingers. She leaned back against the kitchen counter. "I hope I don't end up drinking this whole bottle myself." Just the tip of her tongue licked her upper lip.

There was absolutely nothing she could have done that would have excited him more. He released a slow breath. "I'll make the call and be right back. I promise." He gave her a peck on the lips.

Driving through the night with the windows down was one of Roberts' secret joys. The feel of the wind on his cheek and the night smells of the city always made him feel more alive. He passed a park, and the whiff of fresh-cut grass took him back to the family horse ranch in the Shenandoah Valley during hay-cutting season. Growing up, he never wanted to leave, but after college he didn't want to go back. A slow, easy life wasn't what he needed. Proving himself good enough and better than the rest had become his goal. His dad understood this logic—wish he'd had just one more day with the old man.

Roberts parked in the lower level of the office garage. He called the Intelligence Division on the encrypted phone and they connected him with Clawson.

"Okay, here it is," Clawson said. "CIA reports their asset now says Sayed definitely plans the attempt on POTUS at the convention. There's talk of some kind of explosive device, but we still haven't confirmed that yet."

A nauseating sensation rushed through Roberts. "What else?"

"That's it."

Roberts was disappointed. Everyone already assumed the convention would be the target. The only new information was the explosive device. "You mean that's the whole thing?"

"Yup, don't you just love those CIA guys?" Clawson laughed.

"Right," Roberts replied. Dick had been right. *We're going to have a front-row seat to a presidential assassination attempt.* "ATSAIC Crosby needs this information. Any luck calling him?" Roberts asked.

"Nope, just tried again before you called."

Roberts couldn't imagine where Dick might be. The guy always answered his phone. His favorite line was, if I don't answer by the third ring, I'm either dead or in the shower. *Hope he's in the shower.* "I'll contact him and make sure he gets briefed," Roberts said.

"Great, one less thing for me to do."

Roberts considered the new information while walking back to the parking garage. If the convention was the target, there was a lot more to consider. He first needed to pass this info to Dick.

His mind on the bad news from Clawson, Roberts had already gone up the stairs to the upper garage before he caught his mistake—he'd parked on the ground floor. By then it was easier just to go to the upper garage elevator and take it down. His mind went back to Susan, that cute tongue licking her lips. She and the bottle of Chianti Classico waited just a few minutes away.

Roberts punched the elevator button and waited. He also hit the send button on his phone to call Dick. A second later, there was the sound of a cell phone ringing in the almost empty garage. He glanced around, but only a few cars were scattered here and there, and none Secret Service. A moment later, another ring from a phone echoed through the garage as his phone also called Dick's cell number. Roberts left the elevator landing and walked toward the closest car, a late model, dark blue BMW 5 series. The windows were down, so he peeked inside. Dick lay unconscious in the front seat.

SEVENTEEN

"**D**ick!" Roberts grabbed the door handle and gave it a jerk. Locked. He reached inside the open window to release the lock as the possibilities raced through his mind. Heart attack? Stroke? This wasn't his Secret Service car. Roberts' stomach twisted as he pulled the door open and leaned over to check Dick's pulse. The cause soon became evident—Mr. Booze.

The interior smelled like a cheap cocktail lounge. *Oh, shit.*

Roberts scanned the garage to see if anyone was watching. Thank God it was so late. A few hours earlier and the place would have been filled with cars and people. All clear, so with great difficulty, he pulled Dick out of the driver's seat and helped him to the passenger side. Trying to fold a drunk back into the small car wasn't easy. Dick slumped, only about half awake, and not in a good mood after being disturbed. He mumbled half-sentences and garbled them to the point he may as well have been speaking a foreign language.

After numerous tries, Roberts finally shoved him in the seat and buckled the belt. Thank God the keys were still in the ignition.

Once Roberts reached Dick's house and helped him inside, his boss finally opened his eyes.

"Where the hell am I?" Dick said, speaking his first intelligible sentence of the night.

Roberts had an arm around his waist and half-carried him toward the sofa. Guy weighed a ton. "You're home."

Dick squinted and must have recognized the place. A silly chuckle before he said, "Guess I'm a little overserved, huh?"

"You could say that. Here, sit down." Roberts eased him on the couch. "I'll make us some coffee, okay?" He didn't wait for a reply before heading to the kitchen.

Dick mumbled something, then waved an arm in a mock salute and slurred, "Good idea, Ace."

Roberts scanned the kitchen counter and searched a couple of cabinets before finding what he needed. When the coffee began perking, he stuck his head around the corner. From the living room, Dick's garbled voice boomed. "Think I'll splash a little cold water on my face. Be right back."

Roberts caught sight of him stumbling down the dark corridor. Soon the sound of running water drifted into the living room. The little water on the face had turned into a full-fledged shower—complete with singing. *Oh, brother!* Roberts wasn't sure, but it sounded like Dick had combined "The Wreck of the Edmund Fitzgerald" and "The Night They Drove Old Dixie Down" into one bizarre melody.

After pouring himself a large cup, Roberts sat down in the living room. The dark, heavy oak furniture, rich wood floors, expensive wall and window coverings spoke of a life few agents would ever know. If a man's home was his castle, then Dick was, indeed, a king. The room reminded Roberts of the vice president's study, only nicer.

The extra money Dick made from his stocks and gambling funded a lavish lifestyle. He lived big, with three divorces to prove it. Photos of his exes lined the fireplace mantle. He claimed his marriages resulted from being an incurable romantic, and he always kept an eye out for a future ex-Mrs. Dick Crosby. If he couldn't give half his net worth away every five or ten years to some deserving woman, then he didn't figure life was worth living.

Dick traipsed back into the room dressed in a black terrycloth robe and barefoot. His shoulders were hunched, and he had that old man shuffle thing going, the kind of walk that makes you think you should get ready to catch them. A wet bath towel was draped around his shoulders and drops of water streamed on the floor in his wake. Although still a little wobbly as he finished toweling his thinning hair, he was noticeably more sober.

Roberts got him a steaming mug of coffee, and Dick flopped into a chair beside the couch. The puffy dark circles under his eyes aged him a decade, but he'd taken the time to slap on an expensive aftershave. Some things never change.

Roberts didn't know what to say. A tinge of embarrassment hit him, seeing his friend and supervisor in this sorry condition. Best to let Dick bring it up first. Just make a little small talk. Roberts sniffed the air and looked Dick's way. "That smells good. What do you have on?"

The old devil smile crossed Dick's lips as he settled back into the chair and took a sip of coffee. "I have a hard-on, but I didn't know you could smell it."

Roberts just shook his head and grinned.

Dick sipped more coffee. "Boy, that's good."

"How you doing?"

Dick shifted in the chair and crossed his legs, pulling the robe over his knee. "I'm better now, thanks."

"You were lucky I found you and not the police."

Dick's nodded. "Yeah. I owe you one." Sitting back in the chair, Dick took another sip and ran a hand down his weary face.

"What's wrong, Dick? This isn't your style."

Dick looked away and tapped his hand on his leg for a few seconds. He took another swallow of coffee and sighed.

"Guess I'm just a little scared."

"Scared? Of what?"

"Of this," Dick replied. He looked around the room and spread his arms out, as if taking in the whole scene.

"I don't understand."

Dick gathered his thoughts for a moment. "I've been an agent a long time. In less than four months, that's all going to change. I have no family, no hobbies, and without the job, no reason to wake up most mornings. I can't just sit here every day with nothing to do. I need a reason to get up." Dick lowered his gaze.

"You can do anything you want," Roberts said, "you've got money. You could travel, or find another job, or take up a hobby."

Dick swatted away the idea. "I know all that, but it's not enough. This case of yours got me thinking about how much I'll miss the work. Where else can a man find this kind of rush? On a golf course? On an Alaskan cruise? I think not."

Roberts wasn't surprised by these revelations. Dick's reputation of being somewhat of a maverick in the Secret Service didn't make sense to Roberts; he always suspected Dick considered it a privilege to be a special agent. Supervising the Protective Intelligence squad held a lot more drama than most jobs. Coming down from a high like that wouldn't be easy.

"I'm sorry. I didn't know," Roberts whispered.

Dick uncrossed his legs. He shot a furtive glance Roberts' way and shrugged. "I know it's a stupid way of looking at it, so save your breath."

"Anything I can do?"

Dick snapped, "Yeah, don't feel sorry for me. I don't need that kind of help. Sorry I screwed up your evening."

"That's okay, I wasn't doing—oh shit, I almost forgot. I need to make a call." Roberts reached for his phone. "Be right back." He trotted into the front entry area.

"Think I'll have another cup of joe," Dick muttered.

Roberts dialed Susan's number and waited. He checked his watch —12:26 AM. On the fourth ring, a groggy voice answered.

"Hello."

"Susan, it's me. I'm sorry, but something came up."

"What time is it?"

"Almost twelve-thirty—I'm sorry. Can I take a rain check on that bottle of wine?"

The voice woke up a little. "Sure. How about dinner at my place tomorrow. We'll drink it then."

"You're on. About seven?"

"Yeah, seven's great, good night, Michael," her sleepy voice whispered, and the line went dead.

Roberts was impressed by Susan's response. Most women would be pissed to the tenth degree about being stood up. Didn't matter whether it involved national security or helping out a friend in a jam. Lexi would have gone crazy, but not Susan.

Roberts made his way back into the living room and found Dick sitting in the chair fiddling with a string on his robe.

Dick asked, "Why in hell were you at the office this time of night?"

"Got a call from Intelligence," Roberts said, "it's confirmed—the convention's the target. They're speculating Sayed might use some kind of explosive." Roberts watched Dick for a reaction.

"That's going to complicate things. Was that all?"

"Yeah, that's it," Roberts whispered, letting disappointment lace his words. "Now for my question." He gave Dick the look he reserved for suspects. "Why in the hell were you parked in the garage shitfaced?"

Dick stared at his lap and took another sip of coffee. "Beats me. I'm at a bar one minute and being woken up by you the next. Don't remember driving or parking in the garage. Never happened before." Dick's voice took on a defeated tone. "Guess I'm slipping."

This wasn't a satisfactory answer by Roberts' way of thinking. This kind of behavior got agents suspended. Sometimes they got fired, and in the event of an accident with injuries, indicted. But what could he say? Dick already knew all of this. He warned the troops against it in every squad meeting.

"Well, no harm done this time," Roberts said.

Dick shook his head, his face stoic. "Ace, don't be like me."

"Huh?"

Dick looked at him. "I said don't be like me. I've spent my whole working life in this outfit, giving everything I had to the job every day." A grin cracked the corners of Dick's mouth. "And now I'm retiring with nothing, except a few million bucks."

Roberts chuckled. "Lots of agents wished they had that problem."

Dick sipped his coffee and spoke in a low, serious voice. "You know what I mean. No wife. No kids. No grandkids." He gazed at Roberts.

"I'm about to be alone... really alone for the first time. That's what scares me."

Roberts wanted to say something reassuring. Something clever to dispute Dick's assertion, but nothing came to mind. The only thing he could think to do was clear his throat and look away.

Dick stood. "I'm going to get a little sleep. Guess your car's still at the office. There's a bedroom in the back for you."

"That's all right, the couch is fine."

"We can take our time getting in tomorrow. Nothing scheduled. Good night, or good morning, or whatever in the hell it is," Dick mumbled while shuffling down the dark hall.

He moved like a broken-down old guy on his last leg.

––––––––

The next day, Roberts spent his office time catching up on paperwork. When he got the call and invitation from Bishop late in the afternoon, it was a welcome relief. At five o'clock, Roberts and Dick strolled through the well-appointed lobby of the Omni Mandalay Hotel a couple of blocks down from the Secret Service office on Las Colinas Boulevard. Soft music drifted through the air and the sound of a fountain and waterfall echoed as they turned left toward the bank of elevators. A great lawn in the back and wisteria-covered arbor stretched out to a lake. This was Roberts plan, but he was now second guessing his decision to invite Dick.

Dick gazed toward the wall of windows. "Nothing wrong with Bishop's taste in hotels." He grunted and pushed the up button.

Roberts had probably made a big mistake. After Bishop called him to come by for a drink, Roberts had asked Dick to join them. Roberts felt if Dick and Bishop met, it might instill more trust. If Dick and Bishop didn't hit it off and Dick told Roberts not to work with Bishop in the investigation, his plans would fall apart. Roberts needed Bishop more than Bishop needed the Secret Service. How could he mitigate this? Two Type A personalities with guns and alcohol. Yeah, big mistake.

They took the elevator to the twentieth-fourth floor and Roberts knocked on the door. Dick stiffened his stance and raised his chin as the door opened.

Bishop answered the knock holding a drink. "Hello, Michael," he extended his hand.

"Troy Bishop, I'd like you to meet Dick Crosby, my supervisor," Roberts said.

"Mr. Crosby." Bishop nodded.

When Bishop and Dick shook hands, they also locked eyes.

"Call me Dick. Everybody else does."

"Fine," Bishop said, "just call me Bishop, have a seat. I hope gin and tonic's okay."

"That's great," Dick replied. He strolled over to the window as Bishop mixed the drinks. Dick pulled back the curtains on the corner suite, and the lake and downtown Dallas came into view. He let his stare take in the full room before saying, "Nice place."

Dick was never one to mince words, and he didn't do it now. He meandered back to where Bishop stood. "How did you swing this place during a convention?"

Bishop turned to Roberts and winked while pouring the drinks. "Just lucky it suddenly came available. Do you want a twist of lime or straight up?"

Once settled with his drink, Dick asked, "How's it going at the Joint Terrorism Task Force?"

"Good," Bishop took a sip and sat back in the soft leather chair.

"Any leads on Sayed?"

"Not yet. FBI has everyone canvassing their sources to determine if he's in town."

Roberts asked, "Did you get the word, the convention is the target?"

Bishop sat his glass on the small table. "Yes, I received a call day before yesterday. Are you guys looking for him?"

"We put out a BOLO a couple of days ago," Roberts replied.

"We've also sent copies of his photos to all hotels in the area. We listed our interest as wanted for questioning only," Dick chimed in.

Bishop kept his eyes on Dick. "Word I got today was that,

according to the asset, Sayed doesn't have an egress plan. That doesn't sound good."

Dick did a double-take. "What?" He turned to Roberts. "Did I miss something?"

Roberts shrugged. "First I've heard about it." If Sayed had no egress plan, then he didn't plan to escape. This was something Secret Service should have known. Perhaps they did, but Tortorziie hadn't shared it yet.

Dick cleared his throat. "Appears your intelligence is better than ours, Mr. Bishop; we'll have to follow up on that, thanks." Dick kept shifting in his chair. Couldn't seem to find a comfortable position.

Bishop showed the same relaxed manner he did that day in the National Security Advisor's office. Cool and calm—like he was waiting for a table in a nice restaurant.

Dick stretched his legs and took his first sip. "So, tell me, Mr. Bishop, how exactly will you be assisting us in this investigation? I'm not certain I understand." Dick's lips didn't show the "devil smile." It was more of a silly smirk. Dick hated other agencies sticking their noses into Secret Service protection business. Roberts understood. The few times this had happened, the outside agency managed to screw something up and they bowed out, leaving Secret Service holding the bag.

A tinge of anxiety rushed up Roberts' back. Dick understood fully —*what was he up to?*

Bishop studied Dick a few seconds before answering. In a quiet voice he said, "I'll lend whatever assistance possible and act as the liaison between Secret Service and the Terrorism Task Force."

Dick again sipped the drink a little too quickly, nodding, appearing to carefully consider what Bishop just said. Dick raised his head and stared at the ceiling. "Liaison," he repeated. He stretched the word from three syllables to at least six. "Michael, don't we have a Secret Service agent permanently assigned at the task force as liaison?"

Of course, Dick knew this because the agent reported directly to him, so Roberts didn't bother answering. He still didn't like the way this was heading. Dick had the look. He was getting ready to make his move; deliver the kind of zinger he was famous for. Roberts slid his chair back a few inches and kept both feet flat on the floor.

"Yes," Dick whispered, tapping his chin with his index finger, "I do recall us having an agent in the JTTF." He dropped his gaze down to Bishop. "So, if we already have a liaison, what are you there for, exactly?" Dick's eyes pinched, and he leaned in closer to Bishop.

Bishop never showed any facial change at this direct challenge. But the beating pulse on his temple indicated he now understood Dick's game. Bishop rose and in a nonchalant manner asked, "Can I freshen up your drinks?"

"No, thanks, we're fine," Dick snapped.

Bishop took his time mixing another for himself and strolled back to his chair. This now became a duel. Roberts waited. Getting between these two could be dangerous. Better just let the big dogs fight it out.

Bishop reclaimed his seat and casually crossed his legs before saying, "I report to General Cook. Who he reports to is his business. If you're concerned I'm a spy for the national security advisor, then don't work with me. My understanding is that your director himself agreed to this cooperation. If you, at the field office level, decide to disregard your own director, that's fine."

Roberts grinned, round one to Bishop. Throwing in the "disregarding the director" thing was brilliant. Dick, like everyone else, was being pushed into a direction he didn't appreciate. They may have to do it, but they didn't have to like it.

Dick's head jerked and he blinked a couple of times. He shook off Bishop's quick come-back and prepared for round two. "I'm aware of the director's wishes to work with you and the Terrorism Task Force on this business," Dick said in his most sarcastic voice, "I'm just wondering what your real mission is. From what Michael tells me, your background isn't criminal investigations, but military and intelligence."

Bishop looked down at his dress pants a moment and smoothed a crease. When he looked up, the cool hunter's eyes bore in on Dick. "My background is special ops, with an emphasis on weapons of mass destruction."

"So, what are you really here for?" Dick's expression became a blank slate and his lips flattened.

Bishop met Dick's stare for a few seconds before answering. The pulse on his temple faded. In a low, even voice he said, "I'm to assist either you or the task force in finding Sayed." He waited a beat before saying, "If we locate him, and bringing him into custody is not possible or practicable, then I'm not to allow his escape."

Roberts sucked in a quick breath. Many people believed Secret Service killed most assassins who attacked the president. Nothing was further from the truth. Only happened once in history. But what Bishop was implying...

Dick didn't say anything right away. But his sarcastic expression faded. He also probably understood. Never one for not having a complete understanding of the facts, Dick asked, "What does that mean, exactly?"

Bishop's face was a death stare. "You know what it means. I'm your failsafe—I'll kill him."

EIGHTEEN

Sayed drove around for almost half an hour before he finally found it: one of the few remaining public pay phones in the DFW Metroplex. Secluded at the far end of a rundown mom and pop grocery in south Richardson, it was the ideal location. He dialed the number, and the phone rang twice before the voice answered, repeating the number he had just dialed.

Sayed scanned the parking lot and whispered, "Do I still have a green light?"

A long pause from the other end of the line was not what he had expected. There could be only two answers. Green meant go, red meant the operation was compromised—get out now. An escape plan had already been established. In three days, he could be in Pakistan.

"Green," the voice answered.

Sayed quickly broke the connection. The Americans were so good at electronic interception and eavesdropping that every second he stayed on an unsecured line meant risking his location becoming known. He departed the area and drove around for over an hour, making a series of turns and watching who might be following. Sometimes he would quickly accelerate, then come to an abrupt stop as he ducked into an alley, checking for tails. He continued the surveillance detection route back to his hotel.

His thoughts drifted to the sheikh. The man had been like a father to him, a role model for all to follow. Sayed still carried the guilt of not being with him when the SEALs came. But the assassination of a US president would avenge the sheikh's death and help renew the brothers' confidence worldwide. Allah had bestowed this opportunity on them with the appearance of the Frenchman. Now it was up to Sayed.

————

The setting sun still sent heat waves shimmering off the sidewalk as Roberts pulled into Susan's condo complex. The temperature on his car's thermometer read 102.

She met him at the door with a kiss on the lips. That cute impish smirk she did so well flashed before she said, "That's where we left off last night—dinner's ready. Hungry?"

"You bet," he said. He'd been looking forward to this all day. She looked great, as usual, and tonight she wore a pair of designer jeans and a sheer pink cotton blouse. He looked around. "Where's Abbey?"

Susan took his hand and led him to the kitchen. "Grandparents, she's spending another night."

How convenient.

As he helped her put the finishing touches on dinner, he couldn't help the steady stream of questions scrolling through his mind. Where would things have gone if they hadn't been interrupted? How close of a relationship did he want at this point in his career? Was he wrong to string her along if he had no follow-up plans?

He helped with her chair, caught a whiff of her perfume, and forgot all his questions. Each minute he spent with her, he wanted another.

Susan poured the Chianti Classico. "Good thing you came back before I drank it myself."

Roberts took his seat. "Sorry about last night. Not exactly a nine to five job."

She finished pouring the wine. "You're forgiven if you'll forgive me for serving a red with chicken. Let's eat."

Roberts was a quiet person—never really enjoyed conversation that much. But with Susan, it came easy, and she could talk intelligently on any subject. Tonight, she speculated about what kind of season the Cowboys might have this year. A woman after his own heart. He took a bite of salad and said, "You mentioned something during our first meeting that I'm still trying to figure out."

"What?"

"When I asked about Abbey's ability, you said something about it being inherited and told me to tell Keller that they were real, you were born with them. Did you overhear what he said about your—"

She laughed. Matter-of-factly, she said, "No, but I knew."

Roberts had hoped for more of an explanation, but she didn't elaborate. He kept eating, rolling her answer around in his head. "Wow, this is all great."

Susan flashed a satisfied smile. When he couldn't take it any longer, he asked again.

"What did you mean by inherited powers? Inherited from whom?"

Susan placed her fork on the plate and put both elbows on the table before taking a sip of wine. "Ever since I was a little girl, I've just known things. Not all the time you understand, but sometimes." She shrugged. "There's no predicting it." A blush ran up her neck. "Blame it on Mom's side of the family. They started it."

Roberts didn't answer. He allowed his stare and silence to do the work.

She dabbed her lips and looked down like she might be deciding whether she wanted to continue. "My maternal grandmother had many of the same abilities as Abbey." Susan allowed a grin. "My grandfather always let grandma have the final say on any business dealings. Used to say she could tell a shyster by his looks. What little I inherited from the old girl isn't worth discussing." She smiled. "But Abbey appears to have received her full gift."

"So, it's just the females who inherit it?"

"I don't know." Susan forked a piece of white meat. "Guess so."

He studied her a moment. "You know if this were the seventeenth century, you'd all be put on trial as witches."

"Probably." Her eyes twinkled. "I've almost outgrown mine. I can seldom tell what someone's thinking anymore. Sitting so close to Agent Keller that day, it just popped into my head: *store-bought.*" She grinned. "Besides, a woman doesn't need special powers to tell what people like Keller are thinking most of the time."

A quiver raced through Roberts' stomach. *Could this be real?*

Susan showed a grave expression. "I'll tell you something else, if you want to know."

Roberts was hooked. He leaned closer. "Yeah, I do."

She pointed her fork at him. "Do you believe in ghosts or spirits?"

Roberts thought for a moment. He wasn't sure where he stood on the spiritual world. *What was she leading up to?* "I try and keep an open mind."

"After my grandparents died, my mother was at their old house, gathering up some family things, and she saw my grandmother."

Roberts leaned closer. "She saw her spirit?"

Susan glanced down and shook her head. "That's not how she described it." An embarrassed expression followed. "Mom wasn't much of a churchgoer. She said what she saw was more of a shadow of grandma. Her words were *psychic shadow.*"

Roberts didn't know what to say. "You believe her?"

Susan shrugged. "I've read up on it. Apparently, people with strong extrasensory abilities give off a great amount of psychic energy. This becomes stored in places they spend the most time. Occasionally it manifests itself as an outline or shadow of the person. It's not the spirit, but the stored psychic energy causing the image. You don't have to be dead to cast a psychic shadow."

Roberts had enough experience in psychological matters to understand. During times of extreme emotion, or in the middle of a full psychic episode, people sometimes believed they heard voices, saw things, or receive information from God, spirits, or even the planet Mars. Wasn't at all uncommon. Lots of events in life could trigger it—bereavement was one. Anyone losing a mother could be forgiven for believing they saw something.

"Perhaps she did. Or at least thought she did," he said.

If Susan had told him this on the day they first met, he would have discounted it as the musings of a deranged woman. But since meeting

Abbey and having had a full demonstration of her abilities, Roberts couldn't ignore anything anymore. He filed the information in a back folder of his mind.

They dropped the subject and talked about favorite movies, including *Saving Private Ryan* for him and *Under the Tuscan Sun* for her. Susan seemed relieved he didn't press her for more information on her family. She'd probably told him the story to get it off her chest, but didn't want to discuss it any further. It was getting to the point he could interpret her expressions and body language so well he could almost read *her* mind.

After dinner, he helped her clear the table. The bottle of Chianti was gone, so she reached into a high cabinet for another. She tipped back on her heels, losing her balance. He caught her in his arms. They were in the exact spot in the kitchen he'd kissed her the night before. As he brought her back to a standing position, she kissed him softly on the lips. He responded with a more aggressive kiss. Susan got more aggressive still, pushing closer, pinning him against the counter.

She broke the embrace, and her eyes searched his for a second. She nibbled at his lip. Without speaking, she took his hand and led him out of the kitchen. The long shadows of evening stretched across the floor on the way to the dimly lit bedroom. Candles flickered on each nightstand. A delicate smell of lavender floated in the air. They stood beside the bed. Never taking her eyes off his, she slowly pulled out his shirttail and ran her hands up inside, caressing his back with soft fingers. She nibbled his lips again and stepped back, unbuttoning her cotton blouse.

Things were happening a little faster than he'd expected. He wasn't complaining, but he hadn't anticipated being at this point so early.

Roberts slipped the blouse off Susan's shoulders, allowing it to drop to the floor. He kissed her softly on the neck. She smelled and felt wonderful. She leaned into him, rolling her tongue softly over his lower lip as he took her into a tight embrace. His fingers caressed the back of her bra looking for the clasp. *Nothing.* Okay, probably a front snapper. He eased back from her and let his fingers drift to the area between the cups. He fumbled and felt for several seconds trying to locate the snap or hook. Susan released a little giggle.

He'd embarrassed himself. "Sorry, guess I'm a little out of practice."

She giggled again and nibbled his ear. "It's a slipover," she whispered.

"Huh?"

"The bra, a slipover." She took his hands and directed them into the bra cups, raising them a few inches. Roberts couldn't have been more turned on. She'd totally surprised him. He wanted her. The thought he would explode any second was the last one he had before his phone rang. It didn't register at first, but by the second ring he realized who it was.

"You've got to be shitting me," he said. He checked the caller —Dick.

She grabbed his arm. "Don't answer it."

That was the best suggestion anyone had made all evening. He almost went with it before something stupid kicked in and he answered the call. "This is Roberts."

"Hey, Ace—need you to meet me in the office right now," Dick said.

"What's happened?"

"We've got ourselves a lead on Sayed."

Susan caressed his chest and nudged closer, making it difficult to concentrate.

"A lead? Okay, I'll be right there." Roberts ended the call.

She had a look. Surprise, frustration, and aggravation all rolled into one.

"What?" she asked.

"I have to go—we've got a lead on the suspect." He tucked his shirttail back in.

She brushed the hair from her face and lowered the bra. "You have to go right now? What suspect?"

Roberts finished straightening his shirt. "The guy who wants to kill the president."

"He's in town?"

"Possibly. We're going to find out."

Susan dropped on the bed and lounged on a stack of pillows. "Are you coming back?"

Everything in Roberts' being told him not to leave. What difference could an hour make? It could make a difference with Dick—maybe the president's life. He exhaled a long breath and bent down. He let his hand drift beneath one of the bra cups and gave her an extra-long and wet kiss. She shivered at his touch. "Sure am. Be back before you know it."

She sighed. "Think that's the same line you used last night."

NINETEEN

As Roberts walked down the hall toward Dick's office, Susan stayed on his mind. Was somebody trying to tell him something? Being interrupted twice in two nights was probably a sign from above—a sign he needed to tamp down his relationship with her unless he wanted to have regrets in a few months when he left.

As he marched across the threshold, the smell of fresh brewing coffee greeted him. He poured himself a cup from the small pot on Dick's credenza before sitting down. Dick wasn't in his suit. He wore jeans and an open collar blue Oxford. His feet, clad in brown leather deck shoes, rested on the edge of the desk. Yeah, he could be mistaken for Nicholson easily.

"Hope I didn't interrupt your evening," Dick said. He sniffed the air as a grin spread across his lips. "New perfume?"

Roberts shot him a glance. He was not amused. *Twice—twice in two days*. "Your timing could have been better. What do you have?"

Dick took a swallow of coffee. "Years ago, when I supervised counterfeit investigations, I came across a guy called Rick. He got jammed up on a little counterfeit charge by the locals. I interviewed him and believed he was innocent. I proved it, and got the charges dismissed."

"Yeah, okay. And?"

"I developed him as an informant, and he's fed me pretty good info ever since."

Roberts was still confused. What did counterfeit and a guy named Rick have to do with Sayed and the president? "So, where does an honest man get all his information on criminal activity?"

Dick scoffed. "Hell, Rick's not an honest man. He's one of the biggest crooks in Dallas. He just wasn't guilty of that particular counterfeit charge."

Roberts shook his head. His mind drifting to Susan waiting... that bra. "I'm not sure I—"

"Anyway," Dick interrupted, "Rick hasn't killed anybody—to my knowledge. Mostly small stuff, you know, a little numbers racket, some black-market cigarettes, and various other criminal enterprises. He runs a club in Deep Ellum, Rick's Café Casablanca, off Canton Street. It's a bar with a jazz and blues theme."

"Rick's Café Casablanca? Like the club in the movie?" *Christ.*

Dick grinned. "Yeah, he's from Morocco. Of course, Rick isn't his real name—I can't pronounce his real name—but he fancies himself a Bogart-like character. Has his hand in, or knows something, about every organized crime thing in the Metroplex. He called about an hour ago, said he saw the BOLO and might know where Sayed is."

Roberts couldn't believe it. "How did he see the BOLO? It's only sent to cops."

Dick pointed at Roberts. "First thing you need to know about Rick is don't underestimate him. Second, don't disrespect him. He's touchy about respect."

"How in the world could he know anything about this guy if he's a wanted terrorist and just rolled into town?" This whole situation began to take on an element of the absurd.

Dick shook his head. "No idea. That's what you'll find out. Here's the address of the club. He's waiting there for you." Dick handed him the slip of paper.

"Think I should take one of the squad guys as back up?"

"Naw, they've busted their butts all week. I'll have them on standby, if necessary." Dick thought for a second. The devil smile appeared as he took another sip. "Take Bishop. Let's see how he does in the field."

———————

Fifteen minutes later, Roberts and Bishop drove toward downtown. Roberts briefed him on what Dick said. Bishop, to his credit, didn't appear any more impressed about the incident than Roberts.

Roberts drove into the heart of Deep Ellum, heading toward Rick's Café Casablanca. He and Bishop had their windows down, and the sounds of a big city not quite ready to go to sleep floated in with the warm air. A few people milled around, but the hot evening drove most into one of the bars or restaurants.

Deep Ellum is the old warehouse district of East Dallas and was the prime location for jazz and blues in the twenties. The district reached its high point as the primo entertainment hot spot with bars, night-clubs, and restaurants in the 1990s, but that had all changed by the time Roberts had moved to the city. Now, tattoo parlors, head shops, restaurants and various retail stores dotted the place. There were still many music venues, but only one authentic jazz and blues club left—Rick's Café Casablanca.

Scanning the area, Roberts didn't see any parking spaces. Cars were packed into every lot and along both sides of the street. They'd probably end up several blocks away. Just up ahead on the left, a car backed out of a club parking lot across the street from Rick's. Roberts sped up and whipped into the place before another car could pick it off.

Bishop grinned. "Heard you Secret Service guys received special driver's training. Never understood why until now."

Roberts only grunted, but noted this was the first time since meeting Bishop the guy had shown the slightest bit of humor or mirth. *Might be hope for him yet.*

As they opened their doors, Bishop gazed out the front windshield. "Interesting sign."

The green, blue and yellow neon striking rattlesnake with the club's name, "The Snake Pit," hung just above their vehicle.

Roberts flopped his US Secret Service placard on the dash before hitting the lock button on his key fob. "Hope my car's still here when we get back."

When they approached Rick's, the young doorman eyed them. Dressed in all black, he probably weighed close to 250 and stood about six foot five. He leaned back against the building, slowly rubbing his long goatee. "There's a five-dollar cover, gents."

Roberts flashed his credentials. "Rick's expecting us."

The guy examined the identification and stepped inside the door. "Hey Tina! Come here," he shouted above the music.

Roberts never went to clubs. Live music venues weren't his thing. *Did Susan like places like this? Would she wait up for him again? Was this a BS lead?*

The hot, humid night had already started Roberts sweating. He pulled the front of his shirt away from his chest and stomach as the sound of a bass sax drifted out the door. A young woman with red lipstick, short black hair, and a powder blue summer dress stepped out. She wore a lot of eye makeup. Gave her a raccoon look.

"These guys say Rick's expecting them. They're feds," the doorman said.

She shot them a hard stare. "Rick *is* expecting you. Follow me." She whirled around and pushed the door open.

The club was in full swing as they made their way through the crowd. The jazz band on stage was dressed in clothes from the forties. Gave the old classic tune a more authentic feel. The white walls reflected what little light drifted from the band area. In the dark room, it took a few seconds for Roberts' eyes to adjust. He focused on the blue summer dress ahead, staying close behind while Tina wove her way through the spaces between tables. Bishop brought up the rear. The amplifiers blared about twice as loud as Roberts liked.

They followed her through a winding trail of conversations and laughter. No one paid them any mind as she strolled up to a bar on the far wall, which took up the whole side of the room. As they approached, bartenders and waitresses scurried to fill drink orders. The girl in the summer dress whispered something to one of the bartenders and turned to them. Her raccoon eyes blinked a couple of times and she said, "Wait here," before heading back to the main entrance.

Roberts and Bishop exchanged dark looks as the bar employees went about their business, never giving them a second glance. A few seconds passed before the bartender lifted the phone to his ear and punched a button. He glanced at them and spoke in muffled tones, the music drowning out the conversation. Moments later, a young man opened a door near the end of the bar, revealing a well-lit back hall area. He was also dressed in black, and about the same size as the doorman. His shaved head glistened, as if oiled, but the shoulder holster with a black semi-automatic held Roberts' attention. The guy motioned for them with his fingers.

"This way, gentlemen."

They squeezed around the edge of the bar and stepped through the door. The guy closed and double-locked it behind them.

"May I see your identification, please?"

Roberts and Bishop displayed their credentials and the guy studied them. From Bishop's expression, Roberts could read his mind. He thought the same thing. Did this guy even know the difference between genuine or false creds?

The man returned their identification. "Follow me."

Walking through the maze of passages and doors, cameras bristled from every wall and security beams chirped as they passed. This type of security was usually reserved for major crime bosses. Roberts had to wonder if Rick had graduated to something bigger than black market cigarettes. They turned a corner and another large guy sporting a shoulder holster stood in front of an oversized door. Their escort stopped and nodded to the sentry. The guy knocked on the door and an assertive voice from within said, "Come!"

As they entered, the man behind the large desk rose and smiled. When the door closed, he spoke. "Good evening, I'm Rick." He extended his hand as he came around the desk to greet them.

If Dick hadn't warned Roberts about respect, he might have laughed out loud. Rick was a runt. He stood about four foot eleven, and, soaking wet, didn't weigh 120 pounds. Elvis-style black hair covered his small, misshapen head and accentuated the dark circles under his deep-set eyes. The white suit and blood-red tie looked like they were part of a silly costume. Roberts shook the tiny, outstretched hand. It was soft, but had a firm grip.

"Nice to meet you. I'm Michael Roberts, and this is Troy Bishop."

Rick only grinned and nodded at Bishop, not offering his hand. "Please, gentleman, take a seat."

Rick sat in his elevated executive chair. Roberts and Bishop lowered themselves into the short, leather chairs directly in front of the desk. Rick sat a head taller and lounged back, crossing his legs. The side door opened, and a young man wearing dark trousers and an open-collar white dress shirt entered, carrying a tray with a ceramic pot and three glasses. He also wore a semi-automatic. Setting the tray on the desk, he poured the boiling water into the glasses, which overflowed with fresh mint leaves, then withdrew to the corner of the room. During the entire episode, the kid never made eye contact with them or Rick.

Rick fussed over the teas while Roberts studied the place. Not large, but well-appointed. The ornate Persian rug covered a rich, cherry wood floor, which complemented the mahogany bookcase behind the desk. The walls were adorned with paintings and photos of different Middle Eastern vistas. The many family photos on the bookcase gave it a slightly homey feel. But it wasn't homey. With no windows and the door and interior frames reinforced with half-inch steel plates, the room was a fortress. A lazy ceiling fan circulated little air. The place had a stale odor of cumin and garlic. Roberts was ready to leave before Rick finished preparing the tea.

Rick put several spoons of sugar in his tea, smiling at Roberts. "Sugar?"

"No thanks," Roberts and Bishop said in unison. In the Middle Eastern tradition, Roberts understood certain things must be done by the host to welcome a guest before discussing any business. Roberts understood this, but just wanted to get it over with. He seriously doubted Rick knew the whereabouts of Sayed.

Rick passed them their teas and sat back in his chair with a satisfied expression. He gently blew on his glass, holding it with a thumb at the top and index and middle fingers at the bottom.

Roberts got down to business. "Dick said you might know where we could find the person described in the BOLO. Is that correct?"

Rick nodded to the server in the corner. The young man approached, keeping his head down. "Allow me to introduce my nephew, Abdelilah Rahmouni, my youngest sister's son."

The young man bowed his head even lower.

"He attended mosque Friday and observed a suspicious stranger," Rick said. "The stranger fit the description of the fellow you're looking for. The man never attended that mosque in the past and did not converse or offer friendly fellowship with any of its members."

Roberts tilted his head. *Is that it?* Was this guy kidding? Since the guy was Dick's pal, and sensitive about respect, Roberts tried keeping a straight face. He cleared his throat. "Is that so unusual?"

Rick's eyebrows flew up. "Most certainly," he leaned forward and glanced back and forth between Roberts and Bishop. He squinted and zeroed in on Roberts as his voice rose. "We Arabs are a naturally friendly people, not the barbarians the news makes us out to be, especially to guests and strangers. The man's behavior was most suspicious."

"So, what's your conclusion?" Roberts asked the nephew.

Rick snapped, "He found it unnerving—quite unnatural."

"I see." Roberts rubbed his eyes. Deciding to play along a with this a little longer, he asked, "If he's a stranger, how do you know where he lives?"

"I instructed Abdelilah to follow him, of course," Rick answered, in a matter-of-fact way.

"You followed him?" Roberts asked. *This just didn't add up.*

"Certainly." Rick grimaced. "A man in my position cannot allow a stranger who acts suspiciously to just invade the mosque without checking up on him. We must be careful these days." He pointed at Roberts. "All sorts of undesirables trying to infiltrate the country to do God knows what!"

"Yes, I see." Roberts glanced at Bishop. He relaxed in the chair like he didn't have a care in the world, calmly sipping his tea, and enjoying the show. He somehow kept a straight face, but his eyes showed a tinge of the kind of mirth he exhibited in the parking lot earlier. Guy knew BS when he heard it.

Roberts figured Rick must being playing some angle, but he hadn't shown his hand yet. "You say the man resembled the picture we sent out in the BOLO?" Roberts asked.

"Yes, sir," Abdelilah answered before Rick could speak.

Rick frowned. Abdelilah lowered his head again and took a step back.

Roberts pulled out his pen and notebook. "Where does he live?"

Rick produced a small yellow piece of paper and studied it briefly before handing it to Roberts. "Here is the address. He resides in a small hotel in South Richardson—again, very suspicious. Most Arabs visiting the Metroplex stay with friends or family. That is our way. While it is possible he is here on business, or a new arrival, it is improbable." Rick sat back and steepled his fingers. He had that kind of look that indicated he was confident he'd solved all Roberts' problems.

Roberts was less convinced. *Rick was full of shit*. Probably just trying to garner additional favor with Dick in case he ever needed a federal agent's help again. This whole thing felt contrived, just to make Rick look like he was still a loyal informer. The tea had slightly cooled, enough for Roberts to take his first sip. *Nasty*. Needed sugar.

"Thank you, Rick." Roberts sat the glass on the desk. "Anything else?"

Rick stood. "Please tell Dick to call or come by sometimes. I see him so infrequently he is becoming a stranger."

"I will." Roberts rose and shook hands with the small man.

"Abdelilah will show you out."

Reaching the fresh air outside, Roberts gazed at Bishop. "You were a lot of help back there."

Bishop laughed. "What could I say? You were doing too good of a job to interrupt."

As they rounded the corner of the club and crossed the street, a man wearing biker colors leaned against the trunk of their car. When they approached, he stood to his full height; the guy was taller than the club's doorman. Roberts studied the monster biker with the potbelly, long brown hair, and dirty beard. *What does this moron want?*

"This your car?" the guy drawled in a Texan accent, spitting on the ground.

Roberts stopped short of the moron. "Yes."

The biker's right hand remained hidden inside his pocket. "This here parking lot's for Snake Pit customers only."

Roberts eyed him. "We're just leaving."

"I don't reckon you are. There's a fine for parking in this here lot if you ain't a customer."

Roberts cocked his head toward Bishop, who had the same relaxed expression he always wore. Roberts figured he'd just badge the dude and be on their way, but the biker had other ideas. The man withdrew the hand from his pocket and flicked open a switchblade.

Neither Roberts nor Bishop moved.

The biker began cleaning his fingernails with the point of the blade, looking up at them with a goofy grin. "Yeah, the way I've got it figured, you owe about fifty dollars—each—for illegal parking."

Roberts eased his hand closer to where his pistol rested under the jacket. He swiveled his head to make sure they were alone. "We didn't see a *NO PARKING* sign. Do you work here?"

The guy pointed the knife at him. "Don't you worry about where I work, smartass. Your only worry is if you can come up with a hundred bucks between you."

"You know, if I didn't know better, I'd think this was some kind of armed robbery," Bishop said. He'd assumed a shoulder-width stance on the balls of his feet. That pulse in his temple had switched on again.

The biker spit in his direction, showed a chilling stare, and pointed the switchblade at him. "Well, you can just think what you like, but you're either walking or giving me the money."

Roberts elected not to identify himself—a better idea came to mind. He took another look around to make sure no one was watching.

"Okay, have it your way." Roberts pulled his service weapon. He pointed the Sig Sauer .357 magnum at the fool's collassal head. Who knows how many times the giant had successfully pulled this robbery scam and gotten away with it? It was clear from his expression this was the first time a victim had brought a gun to his knife fight.

Roberts nonchalantly began cleaning *his* fingernails with the pistol's front sight, keeping the barrel trained on the man. "Now, what I think I would rather do is just get in my car and drive away before anyone gets hurt. What do you think about that idea?"

A chuckle sounded from Bishop.

The moron's jaw went slack, and he moved to the left, never taking his eyes off Roberts.

Roberts kept the pistol trained on him. "You should probably put that knife back in your pocket. I might start thinking you're trying to rob us and do something crazy."

Without a word, the biker closed the knife and slid it back into his jeans. Bishop grinned and moved between the biker and the vehicle toward the passenger door. At that moment the man exploded with rage. Something inside the drug-soaked pea brain must have snapped. He charged Bishop, huge hands grabbing his lapels. For a big man, he moved fast.

The force of the attack drove Bishop back hard against the car. Roberts raced around to lend a hand. He shouldn't have bothered.

Just before Roberts was about to grab Bishop's attacker, Bishop folded his arms tightly across his chest, locking the biker's hands in place with his own. Bishop quickly dropped straight down on his knees. The idiot's muscles, tendons, ligaments, and bones weren't constructed to move in the direction Bishop forced them while trapped.

The loud crack of both wrists snapping sounded like a muffled gunshot. The dude howled in pain. Bishop shoved him backward, and he rolled on the ground into the fetal position, moaning and crying.

Bishop jumped up and dusted off his pants, casually looking at Roberts. "Do we call the police, or leave?"

Roberts scanned the area again—no one had noticed the encounter and no vehicles slowed or stopped. "Let's get out of here." As Roberts backed out of the parking space he said, "That was a pretty slick move."

Roberts had seen moves like that in action flicks, but always assumed they couldn't be performed unless choreographed with a director. Bishop didn't need a choreographer, and he *was* the director.

The pulse in Bishop's temple twitched a couple more times before turning off. His blood pressure probably never rose above average. "I don't like people grabbing me," he said.

"So noted," Roberts mumbled.

TWENTY

It was another steamy summer night with no breeze or anything else that resembled comfort, the kind Dallas is famous for this time of year. Roberts glanced at Bishop. "Well, this is the place."

He and Bishop sat inside the car in the parking lot of the address Rick provided, a small motel located off Central Expressway in Richardson, ten miles north of Dallas. It was an older property with the rooms on a single floor forming an L shape around the parking lot with half the lights burned out. A stray cat slinked in front of their car and sniffed at some trash.

Bishop settled a little deeper in the seat and stared at the row of doors in front of them. "What's the chance Sayed's staying here?"

"About as good as reaching into a bag of bills and pulling out the only hundred glued to the bottom."

"That good, huh?"

Robert's couldn't fully appreciate Bishop's sense of humor. "You're in a cheery mood for the middle of the night."

Bishop shifted in his seat and leaned his head against the rest. "It's just my nature. So, what's the plan?"

"Let's see what the night clerk can tell us."

With Roberts in the lead, they hiked to the office. He rattled the office door handle a few times before the night manager put down his book and walked to them. The manager gazed through the glass while Roberts displayed his badge.

The guy unlocked the door. "You need a room?" he asked.

Roberts shook his head. "No, just some information."

The manager looked in his mid-forties, dark tan, with long graying hair. Stale cigarette smoke clung to him. He limped back to the counter and waited for them.

Roberts peeked at the guy's name tag. "Jeff, I'm with the Secret Service, and I need your help regarding a guest in room 17."

The manager eyed Roberts and Bishop. "Can I see that identification again?" The man retrieved his glasses from behind the desk, studied Roberts' credentials, and handed them back before setting his glasses on the counter. "Sure thing, what do you want to know? He's not in any trouble, is he?"

Bishop browsed several business cards scattered across the cluttered front desk. The manager kept his eye on him. "That's what we're here to find out," Bishop said.

The man typed something into his desk computer and turned the screen so Roberts could see. "Well, here's his information."

Roberts copied the name, Ibrahim Al Karak, and the man's address into his notebook. It was clear from the name the guy was Middle Eastern. All the blanks on the form were filled in and none of the information raised any suspicion. "Have you seen him since he arrived?"

The clerk scratched the stubble on his chin. "Once or twice."

Roberts produced the photos he viewed that day in the national security advisor's office, one of Sayed in uniform, and the other of a heavily disguised Sayed standing beside Abbey in Houston. "Does he look like either of these guys?"

The manager bent over and closely examined each. He slid his glasses back on and looked again. "No, not all that much... well, maybe a little like this one." He pointed to the photo of Sayed in uniform. "Only, the guy in room 17 isn't so thin and is older."

Bishop strolled around the tiny lobby, studying notices and certificates on the wall. He didn't bother looking at the manager before asking, "Have you seen him driving a car?"

The man turned Bishop's way. "I think so, but I'm not positive."

Roberts scanned the registration information again. "There's no car listed. Would you know which one it might be?"

The guy made a point of staring at the ceiling before saying, "Nope, can't say for sure, sorry. I didn't check him in—day shift."

"Is anyone else in the room, or is he alone?" Bishop asked.

"He's alone... far as I know," the manager said, his voice losing some of its confidence.

"All right, thanks, that's all we need for now." Roberts grabbed the photos, and he and Bishop headed for the door.

The manager followed them. "What do you want me to do?"

Bishop turned to face him. "Forget we were here."

Back in their car, Roberts examined the notes. "Well, that was a pretty useless conversation. Guy doesn't know anything for sure except his own name. I'm going to call Dick."

Dick answered on the first ring, and Roberts told him about the occupant in room 17 and the license plate numbers of all the vehicles in the parking lot near that room.

"I'll get right on it and let you know," Dick said. "It may take a while, so go get a cup of coffee. I'll call when I get something."

They found an IHOP, and Bishop bought them two large coffees to go. They returned to the motel and parked in a dark area near the office. None of the vehicles had moved. No light showed around the curtains of room 17, which lay about thirty yards directly in front of their car. Guy was probably either asleep or out on the town.

Bishop kept checking the passenger side mirror. He had his pistol lying in his lap as he sipped the coffee. Roberts started to ask him about it but decided he must have his reasons. Roberts hated waiting. In a world of computers, jet aircraft, and where billions of dollars were transferred in less than a second, this part of investigations was mentally and physically exhausting. He fidgeted in the seat, praying Dick would call soon.

Bishop's hunter eyes never left the door of room 17, except to occasionally give a glance out the car's side mirror. He seemed somehow at peace, a man used to waiting for hours or perhaps days on end—waiting for the perfect moment.

An hour later, Roberts swallowed the last few drops of the lukewarm coffee. "I've drank so much of this tonight I won't sleep for the next two days."

Before Bishop could reply, Roberts's phone rang.

"Ace, got something to go on now," Dick said. "Think I'll come out and join you."

"We're parked in the shadows of the office on the west side."

"See you in a few minutes."

"Dick's coming out to meet us," Roberts said.

Bishop didn't answer.

Roberts briefed him on synesthesia and his plan to use Abbey as an early warning system during the president's visit. "What do you think?" Roberts asked.

Bishop shot another glance out the rear passenger-side mirror before saying, "Could work. Don't know much about extrasensory things. That's your department."

Roberts had hoped Bishop would endorse his idea. Roberts needed all the encouragement he could muster. After the president arrived, things would get ramped up. This was the quiet time—the time to tweak the plan before it went operational.

"Found out something new," Bishop said. "It's old information, but worth considering."

"What?"

"CIA thinks Sayed's ill."

"Ill?"

"Yeah, physically sick. They've been pumping the asset pretty hard for anything he has on Sayed. Asset just remembered something that happened a couple of months ago. Sayed disappeared; no one talked about where he was or what he was up to. Asset overheard some guys talking recently about Sayed's time in the hospital. Said he'd gained a lot of weight. Didn't even look like himself anymore."

"So, a sick person goes into the hospital and gains weight?" Roberts asked.

Bishop hunched his shoulders. "Who knows? The asset thinks Sayed might have a tumor. Certain tumors cause fluid to build up. Puffs people out."

"What do you think?"

Bishop smirked. "This asset isn't their brightest or best. CIA medical experts have a different take. They suspect it's an endocrine problem. Something went haywire with the thyroid or pituitary. That could also cause rapid weight gain."

"If Sayed believes he's terminal, that might be why he volunteered for this assignment."

"Maybe," Bishop said.

They sat in silence for the next ten minutes until Bishop spoke again. "One thing is certain. If Sayed is terminal, he has nothing to lose. Makes him even more unpredictable and dangerous."

Dick pulled alongside and turned out his lights. A moment later, he slid into their backseat. "So, what did Rick say about this guy?"

Roberts related the story of Rick's suspicion that the person resembled Sayed.

"That's weak as pond water," Dick said.

"Yes, very weak. What did you find out?" Roberts asked.

"I ran the name you gave me against the license plates in the parking lot. One of them came back to Ibrahim Al Karak. Then I ran a full criminal check—nothing."

"How sure are we that the guy in the room is Al Karak?" Bishop asked. "Sayed could assume the identity of anyone as a cover."

"We won't know till we talk to him." Dick leaned back in the seat. "Ohio DMV emailed me a photo." Dick handed the picture to Roberts and said, "Doesn't look much like Sayed from the photos we have."

Roberts studied the driver's license picture of Al Karak before passing it to Bishop. "What are the odds he altered his appearance?" Roberts asked.

"Pretty good, I'd say," Bishop muttered while studying the photo. "Anything from ICE?"

"Nope, according to records, he's a US citizen—born here," Dick said.

"If he's assumed the identity of a US citizen, you can bet he's put together a foolproof back story should anyone care to check, probably one that shows him being born in the US," Bishop said.

Roberts turned around to the back seat. "How do you want to handle it?"

Dick did a long exhale and ran his hand slowly down his face. "Well, since our old pal Rick put us on to him, we have to interview the guy. Can't ignore a lead no matter how screwy it sounds." Dick leaned forward and rested his arms on the back of the seat between Roberts and Bishop. He lowered his voice as if someone might be listening. "This whole business is firmly built on quicksand. I advise we don't kill the guy, but we shouldn't take any unnecessary chances." Dick gnawed his lower lip a few seconds before staring at Bishop. "Do you have a ballistic vest?"

Bishop shook his head. "No, didn't bring one."

"Okay then, Ace, you go in first, and I'll follow. Bishop, you cover us outside and come in last. Is there a back door or back window?" Dick asked.

"No, what you see is what we have. One way in, one way out."

Dick opened the rear passenger door. "Okay, Ace, let's get the room key. Bishop, maintain the eyeball."

At Dick's request, the night clerk took them to a vacant room configured the same as the target room so they could study its layout before making entry. When they got back to the cars, Dick popped his trunk and dug around for his bulletproof vest.

Roberts dropped his vest over his head and whispered to Bishop, "He loves this stuff. Doesn't get to do it much anymore with his supervisor job."

Dick struggled with his ballistic vest, pulling it over his head and securing it around his girth. He jerked the elastic straps and slapped them on the Velcro. He checked his pistol, extra magazines, and flashlight.

Bishop crossed his arms, leaned back against the car, and eyed Roberts and Dick "gearing-up" for combat. Bishop didn't check a thing —mark of a man who was always ready for a shit storm.

Dick turned to Roberts. "I'll open the door with the key. You go in fast and hard when I turn on the light. Watch his hands until we clear the area. If the whole thing goes tits up, at least we'll have him in a crossfire." Dick looked at Bishop. "You come in and clear the closet and bathroom after we've secured him. Any questions?"

They all stared at each other. Roberts shook his head and Bishop flashed a confident grin.

Dick unsnapped his holster. "Let's go."

———

The irony was inescapable to Roberts. He and Dick would make the entry while someone who'd trained for years in Delta on this kind of stuff, and had done it dozens of times, came in last. That's the way the system sometimes works. Take the best-qualified person and put them in the rear.

Dick took his place at the door and put his ear against it. The area behind the window curtains remained dark as Dick slowly inserted the key into the lock.

Sweat formed on Roberts' upper lip, and the stench of his own body odor wafted past his nose. He raked the back of his hand across his mouth. He'd done this lots of times and always experienced the same reaction. Probably not a bad thing. Kept him focused.

But something about this one just felt wrong.

He glanced back at Bishop. The guy had the same relaxed expression he did at the Snake Pit. Dick slowly turned the key and knob until the door cracked opened. He looked over his shoulder at them and nodded. Dick gave the door a hard shove and the interior chain caught with a loud clang.

"Damn." Dick stepped back and kicked the door open.

Roberts scrambled into the dark room with his flashlight.

Dick flicked on the light switch as a male voice screamed something in Arabic. The well-lighted room now revealed a man in his late forties or early fifties with a hairy barreled chest sitting up in bed.

"Don't kill me... please don't kill me," the man pleaded.

Dick trained his gun on the fellow and screamed, "Police! Don't move."

Bishop scurried past and checked the bathroom and closet. "Clear," he yelled, walking back into the bedroom.

Neither Dick nor Roberts ordered the man to raise his hands; it wasn't necessary. He held both high while they kept him covered. There was a slight resemblance to Sayed—very slight.

"Stand up and keep those hands where we can see them," Dick said.

The man looked like he might keel over from a heart attack any moment. His face had turned an unhealthy scarlet color, and his breath came in quick, shallow pants. "What have I done... what have I done?" he kept asking. He slid from the bed and stood by the wall. "What have I done... what have I done?"

Roberts checked the bed and nightstand for weapons. "Nothing," he said and holstered his pistol.

Dick also holstered his weapon and sat the man down. They spent the next forty-five minutes calming the guy, conducting the interview, and searching the room. The man acknowledged being Ibrahim Al Karak and had plenty of identification to prove it. He seemed bewildered at the questions. If his story checked out, Al Karak was the best model citizen Roberts had ever met. Software engineer with a degree from MIT, owned his own small company, wife, two kids, one dog, and the songs on his phone were pure sixties and seventies gold.

Dick instructed Bishop to watch him while he and Roberts went into conference outside.

Once they got out of earshot Dick asked, "What do you think?"

To Roberts, the deal had stunk the second Rick told him about it. It hadn't gotten any better with age. He shook his head. "I think Rick screwed us on this one. When was the last time you went to his place?"

"Couple of years."

"I don't know what he was like then, but the guy I met has a security team right out of the Godfather. Whatever he's into now, I'm guessing you wouldn't be comfortable keeping him as an informant anymore. Think he wants to appear helpful in case he ever needs a federal favor."

Dick shuffled his feet and grinned. "Yeah, probably, but I'm still taking this guy to the office and getting prints, just to be sure."

"Good idea. We'll transport him and meet you there," Roberts said. "Hey, what's our plan if this guy comes up clean?"

Dick grimaced. "You know, Ace, sometimes you just ask too many questions."

———

After searching the guy's car, they drove to the office. When they turned the corner into the prisoner processing room at the field office, Roberts grimaced at the handwritten sign taped to the electronic fingerprint machine. *BROKEN – SERVICE ALREADY REQUESTED.* The device could take prints, send them to the FBI, and receive a response in a few minutes. Doing it the old way took days.

"Hell," Dick said. He stared at Roberts. "What do you think, Dallas Police Department?"

"I have a better idea," Roberts said. Move him to the polygraph room. I'll see you in a few minutes."

Roberts felt like a rat for even having the thought. Calling them in the middle of the night was wrong, but he couldn't do this without Susan and Abbey.

Susan picked up on the third ring. "Hello," she whispered.

"I need a favor."

"What, right now? Thought you were going to be right back."

"I'm sorry."

"Okay, what do you need?"

"I want you to come to our office and bring Abbey. Can you be ready in ten minutes?"

"She's not here, remember? My parents babysat her last night."

"Crap!"

There were a few seconds of dead air before Susan said, "I'll call my mom. Give me ten minutes and we'll pick her up on the way back to your office."

Roberts hated the thought of waking half the family, but this needed to get settled. Taking the prisoner to DPD for processing was embarrassing for a federal agency and still didn't guarantee anything if the guy's prints weren't in the database.

Ten minutes later, Roberts picked up Susan and they swung by and collected Abbey on the way back to the office. Susan didn't talk much. Roberts couldn't tell if she was pissed or just half asleep. She shot glances at Roberts during the drive.

The only thing he'd told them was there was a man they needed Abbey to look at. Poor Abbey had drifted back asleep during the drive and Susan woke her just before they entered the Secret Service parking garage.

Abbey yawned and rubbed her eyes as they walked down the hall of the deserted field office. Roberts apologized again just before they entered the door adjacent to the polygraph room.

Bishop stood in one corner and Dick in the other. Both had a cup of coffee. Roberts stared at Al Karak through the one-way mirror into the polygraph room next door. He was seated and also had a cup of coffee, and a worried expression.

Roberts introduced Susan to Bishop, then squatted down eye level with Abbey.

In a soft, even voice he said, "I want you to look at someone and tell me if it's the same person you saw in Houston, all right?"

Abbey frowned and swallowed. Rubbing her arms, she glanced over at Susan before saying, "Okay."

Roberts took her hand and led her to the one-way mirror. She was too short, so he slid a chair over and lifted her onto it. The tension in her small arms and shoulders surprised him. *She was way out of her comfort zone.* But who wouldn't be at this time of the morning? She was in an unfamiliar place, with strangers, and asked to identify someone who'd terrified her. Roberts had another guilt attack for coming up with this crazy idea. But he needed to know. Know if the man was Sayed—know if Abbey was as good as he believed.

Roberts leaned forward and spoke in a quiet voice over her shoulder. "Now just relax and study him a minute before you say anything. Don't be afraid. He can't see or hear us. He'll never know this even happened."

Abbey stared at the man on the other side of the glass. Roberts stood behind her and held a hand on each shoulder to steady her on the chair—she was shaking. Susan joined Dick in the corner. Her lips flattened and her forehead wrinkled as she watched Roberts and Abbey at the glass.

Roberts again spoke softly. "He's about the same height as the man in Houston, Abbey, but he may appear different now."

Roberts wanted her to verify the guy was Sayed, but also didn't. Because if she confirmed it was Sayed, and it was later determined he wasn't, then Roberts' plan for using Abbey at the convention would be flushed down the toilet. Everyone would find out he had no backup plan. Everything in the Secret Service had a backup plan—every motorcade route, every ingress and egress, every flight plan called for one. If it was discovered he had nothing... Well, that's not the type of guy Secret Service would want to promote to a supervisory position.

Abbey analyzed the guy a few seconds longer before releasing a shallow breath. "That's not him."

Roberts moved closer and tightened his hands on her shoulders. "Are you sure?"

"Positive," she said. The decisiveness in her voice was convincing.

Dick stepped forward and cleared his throat. "Could you be mistaken, Abbey?"

She looked up at him and grinned. "No, his aura's blue."

———

Fifteen minutes later, Roberts had dropped Bishop at his hotel. He offered to take Susan and Abbey for an early breakfast, but Susan declined. She was unusually quiet. Was she mad or tired?

Either way, Roberts was impressed by how Susan and Abbey had handled themselves. He had asked things of them he would be hesitant to ask of his closest friends or relatives, and they had risen to the challenge. Was there nothing Susan wouldn't do for him? Roberts had a pang of conscience. Was he asking too much? Was there too much danger to involve them? Was his relationship with Susan clouding his judgment as an agent?

Dick had started apologizing to Al Karak for the mix-up as soon as

Abbey gave her assessment. While Susan and Abbey made a quick stop in the ladies' room, Roberts strolled back to the interrogation area. When he rounded the corner, Dick asked Al Karak, if he was an MIT graduate and owned his own IT company, why was he staying in such a ratty motel?

Al Karak's cheeks flushed and his chin dipped before saying in a quiet voice, "We almost went under in 2020. Had to let most of my people go and cut expenses by forty-two percent just to stay afloat. I handle most direct sales now as well as manage the company. No extra money for nice motels."

Roberts cleared his throat, and Al Karak looked his way. Roberts asked him if he, by chance, knew Rick.

Al Karak nodded. "I gave him an estimate the other day on upgrading his company's IT system. When he demanded I cut the estimate in half, I laughed in his face."

Dick blanched. "Okay, let's get you back to your motel."

That was the problem with protective intelligence leads regarding the president. Everyone and everything, no matter how screwy the information, had to be investigated. And when the lead proved to be as stupid as suspected, someone had to apologize—a lot. Guys like Rick sometimes used the system and wasted agents' time. And that was one thing they couldn't afford to waste.

Roberts managed to pull one thing of value out of the whole experience—he felt more confident about Abbey's abilities. He might just have made a good decision when he decided to involve her. But it was still early days. They had several more ahead of them.

Everyone was exhausted and exasperated, all their efforts to locate Sayed a bust. Time was up. The convention opened later that Sunday morning. The president would arrive Wednesday afternoon, and they were no closer to finding the terrorist than they had been a week ago.

They'd have to shift from investigative to protective mode. It would be up to the FBI and other law enforcement and intelligence outfits to locate Sayed. The Secret Service now had to expend all their resources protecting the president at the convention.

If there was one thing Roberts hated above all else, it was playing defense.

Roberts dropped Susan and Abbey back home. Everyone said their goodbyes and he studied them as they followed the sidewalk to her door. Roberts understood something now that had been bugging him. With Bishop, Susan, and Abbey, he was sure he'd chosen the right team.

TWENTY-ONE

W hat do you make of it?" J. Thomas Fuller asked General Cook.

Fuller relaxed in his office chair and relished the aroma of the impressive French blend while Harry Cook read the CIA report. He didn't answer immediately, but grunted. Fuller admired Cook's attention to detail—that, and the fact the guy seemed to work every waking hour. Holidays, birthdays, weekends, Cook never appeared to sleep, or for that matter, go home. For his part, Fuller despised working on Sundays. Twelve- and fourteen-hour days during the week were more than enough for him. He longed for the day he could return to his professorship in International Studies at Princeton.

If he wasn't such close friends with the president from their college and fraternity days, he would have refused the job. But how do you turn down an offer from your lifelong friend, and the president? This world of spy satellites, covert agents, and secret operations left Fuller with a cold unsettled feeling most of the time. While hailed as the best national security advisor in decades, he was a teacher at heart, and now just wanted to go back home. Fuller took another slow sip of coffee and waited on Cook's response.

Cook laid the report aside and removed his reading glasses. "This changes everything."

"That's what the directors of CIA, Secret Service, and FBI said after they read it."

"If we believe this report," Cook tapped the paper with his finger, "then we must reconfigure our whole defense of POTUS."

"General, the report from Emerald mentions an explosive device with five times the power of a conventional bomb, which can't be detected by ordinary means. Is this possible?"

Cook considered the question a few seconds before answering. "A lot depends on what the term 'conventional' means. I wish we could debrief this asset. I'm not an expert on these things, but many explosives can be successfully masked. It also depends on the type. Nitrate based are the easiest to detect, but not all explosives are nitrate. Peroxide based are harder to uncover, but more easily made. But they're very unstable—heat, shock, or friction could cause an unexpected denotation." Cook exhaled and laced his fingers in his lap. "My best guess is some kind of RDX variant that we're not aware of. They're always tinkering with that stuff to make it more powerful."

Fuller finished his coffee and set the cup on the saucer. "The Secret Service director is requesting as many Explosive Ordnance Disposal personnel as possible in Dallas before the president's arrival. We're even ripping them from critical overseas assignments."

Cook folded his glasses and slipped them back into his pocket. "Makes sense. Not much else he can do. If there's an explosive device in play, they'll find it."

Fuller changed the subject. "Have we heard anything from your man in Dallas... what's his name?"

"No, Bishop is working with the local Terrorism Task Force and Secret Service, but nothing yet."

"I don't like the feel of this one, Harry—I don't like it at all," Fuller whispered. He had an uncomfortable bout of queasiness flutter through his stomach. He frowned as he studied the portrait of Kennedy on the opposite wall.

———

In Algiers, the real Rene Bertrand hardly slept at night. He did most of his sleeping during the day so he could spend his nights watching. The small transom above his door was his spy hole, where he stood on the stool observing the comings and goings of his captors. Three always on duty during the night, and sometimes five in the main living area during the day and evening hours. This never changed.

His escape would not be easy. The only chance would be late at night when there were fewer guards and his absence would not be noticed until morning. Bertrand noted the habits of the night shift. Always the same three. Always two inside and one outside, changing posts every couple of hours. No one ever checked up on Bertrand at night, so this worked in his favor. The guards played cards or backgammon and occasionally switched the TV channel. In any case, by two o'clock each morning, they were all asleep. If Bertrand decided to go with his plan, that was his time—two o'clock.

Bertrand did not know why he had been snatched. What could be their motivation for holding someone unless for ransom? But he was not being held for ransom. The outside world believed he was free, and in Dallas covering the Presidential Convention.

Bertrand had never done a courageous thing in his life. Attempting an escape would take courage, courage he might not have. But something told him if he did not try, he might never get out alive. Every night he spent time convincing himself escape was the right move, building his confidence that it was the only safe bet. The thing he must do to survive. He was almost there.

TWENTY-TWO

While the parking attendant drove his rental car into the garage and the bellman led the way with his luggage, Sayed strolled through the front door of the Anatole Hotel in Dallas. His false identity as the French journalist, Rene Bertrand, was his only defense against detection. Cool air greeted him when he entered the main lobby and strolled toward the check-in counter.

Sayed scanned the area, quickly memorizing everything and everyone, putting each face in his mental vault. Because of the early hour, there were several choices of front desk personnel. He scrutinized the group, selecting the youngest, a woman with a wide smile. She appeared the most susceptible for what he planned.

"Good morning sir, checking in?" she asked.

"Yes, I have reservations," he replied, using his French accent.

"Name, please?"

"Rene Bertrand."

He noted the name tag she wore: *JULIE*.

This was one of the most vital aspects of the mission. The last thing Sayed wanted was a room in an area where the rest of the foreign press circulated. He did not know if any journalist knew Bertrand, but the risk scared him. Being identified as a fraud was the greatest danger. He felt confident he could fool a stranger into thinking he was the Frenchman, but someone who already knew the man...

The press corps and foreign journalists would be assigned a block of rooms in one part of the hotel. He needed to avoid being dropped into that cesspool at all cost. Julie was his ticket.

She typed the information into the computer. "Oh, you're part of the foreign journalist group, aren't you?" She looked up and showed that wide, full smile.

Sayed smiled back. "Yes, I am."

"Do you live in Paris, Mr. Bertrand?"

"Yes, have you traveled there?"

"Oh yes, my husband and I spent our honeymoon in Paris three years ago—I just love it."

Sayed had her. He had made the connection. He reached into his wallet and withdrew a Bertrand business card.

"Please, Julie, the next time you visit, give me a call. I have many contacts in the entertainment business. I can get you discount tickets on almost any show or concert in the city. Perhaps if the timing is right, free passes as well." Sayed allowed another friendly smile. Those last words triggered the desired effect.

"Are you kidding?" she asked in her sweet, Texas drawl. "That's fantastic! Thank you so much."

"It is my pleasure for someone so beautiful," he bowed his head.

She blushed. "Mr. Bertrand, how will you settle your account with us?"

"American Express." he presented Bertrand's business credit card. "I wonder if I might ask a small favor, please."

She flashed another smile. "Certainly, what can I do for you?"

This was first-week basic intelligence officer training. *Manipulate others to serve you.* "Well, I am afraid I am not as much of a partier as the rest of the foreign journalists, if you know what I mean." Sayed frowned. "I cannot sleep when there is too much going on in the halls and adjacent rooms. Could I possibly get a room separate from the others, in a quieter area, so that I might rest better?"

She showed a serious expression and nodded. "I know just what you mean." She shrugged. "But the hotel's all booked up because of the convention. Your room's part of the block reservations for journalists. I can't change that."

Sayed grimaced. "I had hoped you could find something, anything, so I might get a better night's sleep during my stay at your lovely hotel. I certainly would not object to paying an additional room fee, if required."

She shot a glance toward a tall man at the far end of the counter and then back to Sayed. "Hold on. I'll see what I can do. No promises though."

Feeling exposed, Sayed glanced around at the crowd of people milling in the vast lobby. He had stayed cooped up in that infernal room in Richardson so long that just waiting at the counter felt like he was standing naked in public—naked with a secret so big everyone must be able to see it on his face. He shook off the negative thoughts.

Julie whispered to the tall man, and they both turned and stared at Sayed. She showed the Bertrand business card and whispered again. The man typed something into the computer as Julie lightly touched his shoulder. After conferring for a moment, she returned.

"We can upgrade you to the Tower for the same price," she said, "but don't tell anyone. Okay?"

"The Tower?"

"Yes, it's part of the hotel, but separate from the main area. It's very nice, a better room than you have reserved. We just had a cancellation."

Sayed released a grin. "That is perfect, thank you."

After completing his check-in, she winked. "It helps when the front desk manager is your husband—see you in Paris."

A minute later, Sayed followed the bellman through the spacious Atrium lobby to the elevators. He was satisfied with himself—*He still had it.* All it took to secure a room away from the other journalists was a Bertrand business card and a promise he would never keep.

Sayed gazed at the ceiling of the Atrium lobby. Hundreds of panes of glass allowed the bright sunlight to fill the area. Trees, shops, and dozens of plants lined the walkway. The red brick interior with green ivy cascading from each of the seven balconies reminded him of the

Syrian Intelligence Ministry. As he strolled deeper into the hotel, the décor lost its contemporary feel, and statues, sculptures and artwork all took on an Asian flavor as they neared the Tower elevators. Sayed glanced at his folio; the room number indicated the 25th floor. That should keep him out of sight.

After tipping the bellman, Sayed went into the bathroom and washed his hands. He reached for a towel and caught sight of his reflection in the mirror. Leaning closer to the glass, he touched his cheek. The plastic surgery correcting the eyes and nose was completed weeks earlier, and no signs of swelling or bruising remained. A little coloring had transformed his hair to a lighter shade of brown. The thirty pounds he had gained filled out the facial features and gave him the larger belly. Sayed reached into his jacket pocket and held the Frenchman's passport up to the glass. He gazed at the photo of Bertrand. Now, his face stared back.

———

Roberts always loved Sunday afternoons—his favorite time of the week. He enjoyed the lazy time to catch up on things. But waking up on Sunday afternoon stunk. The ringing of the phone by his ear sounded like a fire alarm, pulling him from a pleasant dream involving faint smells of candles, lavender, and Susan. He cracked open his eyes. Too much light streamed through the half-closed blinds. The clock read a quarter past noon.

Four hours sleep—not good.

Roberts answered the phone and cleared his throat. "Hello," he mumbled, in a quiet, raspy voice.

"Are you going to sleep all damn day? You can sleep when you're dead."

Dick's sick humor wasn't what Roberts wanted just now. Guy had had less sleep than him. He'd never known anyone who could do without sleep like Dick. Probably the secret to his success.

"Ace, you there?" Dick asked in a concerned voice.

Roberts cleared his throat again. "I'm here, Dick. What's up?"

"Need you and Mr. Bishop in the office, pronto."

What now? "Okay, I'll call him."

An hour later in Dick's office, Roberts finished reading the top-secret report before passing it to Bishop, saying, "An undetectable bomb? That makes no sense. We can easily detect bombs."

Dick studied Bishop while he read the report. "Mr. Bishop, this asset you recruited, the one passing this stuff to CIA, isn't pissing down our back and telling us it's raining, I hope."

Bishop grinned, never taking his eyes off the report. "I don't believe so."

Dick rocked back in his chair. "Going on this new information, we should reassess our threat profile. I don't understand how he figures he'll plant a bomb and detonate it with our security package in place. Hell, we have agents, police, EOD, counter-snipers, counter-assault, counter-surveillance—you name it. He can't place a bomb anywhere close to POTUS."

Bishop stared at the floor a moment, like he might be mentally working something out.

"Any ideas?" Roberts asked Bishop.

"We shouldn't discount anything with this guy."

Dick ran his hands over his hair. "Ace, what's your plan as far as the girl?"

"I'm taking Susan and Abbey to the arrival at Love Field, and we're staying near POTUS during all his public appearances."

"You think this idea of yours has a chance?" Dick asked.

Dick had that look again, the one Roberts hated, the one that said *this is dumb—it'll never work.* Roberts didn't need that just now. His doubts already outweighed his confidence. He trusted Abbey, but betting the president's life on her... Dick had backed him on the suggestion it might work, and now even *he* doubted the plan.

Roberts wasn't much of a gambler. Like most Secret Service Agents, he didn't like leaving anything to chance. But this bet was his career, his reputation, and possibly the president's life. An afterthought slipped into his mind. And perhaps Susan's and Abbey's as well.

TWENTY-THREE

S ayed completed his prayers, showered, and went to the hotel dining room for a late lunch. He sat in the back of the restaurant, hidden from most guests, taking note of all who entered to see if they showed him any recognition. He planned to finish lunch, register for the convention, and slip back into his room unnoticed.

Walking out of the restaurant, he consulted his hotel map and found the Edelweiss room. He casually strolled past, peeking inside. Several registration tables were staffed by volunteers, and only a few people waited in line. Sayed swiveled his head up and down the hall and, seeing no one else walking his way, hurried inside the room.

The middle-aged woman, with short red hair and large, green-rimmed glasses, greeted him. "Are you registering, sir?"

"Yes, I'm Rene Bertrand from *La Voix*."

She squinted. "From where?"

"*La Voix* is the magazine I work for in Paris." He handed Bertrand's *La Voix* identity card to the red-headed beast.

"Oh, yes, I'll get your packet." She spent a moment thumbing through a large box of nine-by-twelve envelopes before turning back. "Here you go. Just complete the paperwork inside and present it to that man over there." She nodded to her right.

Sayed glanced in that direction. At the next table sat a Secret Service Agent, his identity confirmed by the red lapel pin and radio earpiece. Keeping his eyes on the agent, Sayed took the envelope to a worktable in the corner and dumped out the registration forms. The Secret Service man carefully reviewed each set of credentials presented by the other registering journalists. He then stamped the papers and directed the reporter to the next table to be photographed.

Sayed finished the paperwork and approached the desk, holding out the completed forms to the agent. In a calm, relaxed voice, he asked, "Are you the person who gets this?"

The agent was about thirty with short black hair. His skin tone indicated Hispanic origin. The guy's eyes scanned him, never blinking. A nervous tingle crept up Sayed's back. *Something felt wrong.*

The agent held out his hand. "Your passport, please."

Sayed handed him Bertrand's passport.

The agent inspected the document. Without looking up, he asked, "Do you have an identity card from your employer, Mr. Bertrand?" The agent opened a folder on the table and ran his finger down a list of names.

"Of course." Sayed again extracted Bertrand's office identification card from his wallet and handed it over.

The agent looked at the two photos of Bertrand, one on the passport, and the other on the identity card. He put them side by side and stared into Sayed's eyes.

"Have you lost a little weight recently?"

Sayed understood why he'd asked the question. Sayed had put on as much weight as he could before the mission but still was not quite as heavy as the Frenchman, Bertrand. He laughed and said, "Yes, thank God. I even trimmed my goatee for this trip," pointing at the office identification card showing slightly fuller facial hair.

The agent did not laugh. "One moment." He opened a second folder and examined the two photos taped inside. Although he tried to shield the pictures, Sayed caught a quick glimpse. He went numb.

It was not possible. He immediately recognized his earlier photo from his Syrian intelligence days, and of course the second one taken at the Houston airport less than a week ago.

Betrayed—the only possible explanation. Sayed took in a slow, measured breath and maintained an even expression, but his stomach had turned to shit. He calmly gazed outside at the hall. Could he make it to the door and into the lobby before being shot? Or was this the trap? Had they been waiting for him to show up all along before moving in?

Surely the agent would recognize him—it was right there in front of him.

The agent's facial expression never changed. He studied Bertrand's ID and passport photos, comparing them to the two pictures of Sayed taped inside the folder. Sayed took another breath and also scrutinized the images. He began to relax; the photos the agent reviewed did not resemble him anymore. He now appeared as a middle-aged man, stockier, with medium-length light brown hair, short well-trimmed goatee, and mustache with different eyes and nose. He also possessed all the documentation for his false identity—Rene Bertrand.

Maintain a confident façade. This is the point the agent might test you. Sayed forced himself into a friendly smile.

The agent looked at him again and squinted with a severe and accusatory glare. He held the gaze a moment too long. Sayed's legs grew weak waiting for him to say something—anything. Sayed forced a wider smile and leaned toward the agent.

"Is there a problem, sir?"

After another moment, the agent closed the second folder. "No, no problem, Mr. Bertrand." He stamped the papers, initialed them, and motioned Sayed toward the photographer for his convention ID photo. The picture took only a few seconds, but turning it into a proper convention identity document took another ten minutes. Sayed waited his turn with the other journalists. He didn't offer his name, and no one asked. The others made small talk about the flight over, the sweltering weather, and how the credentialing process got slower with each convention. Sayed kept one eye on the agent at the table and the other on the door, scanning everyone who entered. How much information had the traitor told them? Who could it be? *Could this still be a trap?*

When they called Bertrand's name, Sayed was so deep in thought he missed it.

The man raised his voice. "Is Mr. Rene Bertrand still here?"

Sayed woke up and realized he had just drawn unwanted attention to himself. He stepped up, apologized, and accepted his new convention credentials.

His ticket to the president.

The laminated card had his photo, the news agency he worked for, and the words *FOREIGN JOURNALIST* printed in bold red letters at the top. A royal blue lanyard was attached. He fitted it over his head and adjusted it around his neck. The ID came down to mid-chest and would allow him full access to all convention activities. Sayed sorted through the various schedules and pamphlets as he walked back into the hall. Everything looked in order. Had to be careful. If this were a trap, he would be under surveillance now. He would spend the rest of the time in his room, out of sight.

Sayed took in a slow breath and allowed himself a moment of triumph. He had done it—halfway there. Now just wait for the president's arrival and close the deal. Someone touched his shoulder, and he jerked around.

"Rene, how in the world are you?"

Sayed braced himself and his breath caught. He had prepared for this, but the suddenness still took him aback. The fellow was a heavy set, middle-aged man, at least six inches shorter than he. A thin tuft of graying brown hair outlined the bald head, and the small glasses perched on his nose gave the man a comical appearance. A glance at the convention credentials around his neck identified him as Reggie Peters—*London Evening Standard.* Sayed's wide smile greeted the stranger.

"It is you," the man blurted out, "wasn't sure at first."

"How are you, Reggie?" Sayed pumped the stranger's outstretched hand.

"Top of the world, and you?" Peters' brow knitted, and he gawked at Sayed. "You sound different. Caught a cold in this infernal weather?"

Sayed took the hint. His voice did sound different than Bertrand's. He had practiced from the tape recordings but still spoke with a more nasally diction than the Frenchman.

Sayed coughed and wiped a handkerchief under his nose. "Afraid so. Cannot seem to shake it."

Studying Sayed, Reggie said, "You've lost a bit of weight. Good for you."

Sayed grinned and slapped his midsection. "Well, I've been watching my diet. How are things at *The Standard*?" He had to break off this conversation, but doing it too soon might draw attention.

Peters leaned in closer. "Have a new editor—doesn't know a damn thing about reporting. One of the new super-bright millennials. Biggest prick I've worked for in years."

Sayed looked around the hall for eavesdroppers before answering, "Yes, well they come and go, but we always remain, eh, Reggie?"

"Well said, Rene." Reggie placed his hand on Sayed's shoulder and drew closer. He lowered his voice and in a conspiratorial tone whispered, "Have you set us up yet?"

Sayed squinted at the stranger. *What was he talking about?* "Set up?"

"Come, come, you're always the first for checking out the local birds." A mischievous grin cracked the corner of Peters' lips. "Any good leads? I've saved up. Think I'll try a couple of expensive ones this trip."

It became clear what the Englishman meant. Sayed stammered for a reply, but his mind had stopped working—a total blank.

Peters said, "We tore them up in 2016—Philadelphia had some nice ones." He grinned and lowered his voice another notch. "I still recall that last night. Yours was a number—the blond with the ponytail and big tits."

"Yes, of course, Reggie." Sayed's stomach soured with disgust for the man. Sayed needed to get away. This idiot could undo his plans if not handled properly.

Sayed again wiped his nose with the handkerchief. "I am feeling a bit tired right now." He touched his forehead with his index finger. "Those antihistamines I am taking keep me in a fog. If I hear back from my contact, how about something later this evening?"

Peters beamed. "Of course. Shall we meet for dinner?"

At this point Sayed would have agreed to anything that could get him away from this fool. "Yes, of course. About seven?"

"Fine, seven it is. I'm in 344. Call me there or on my cell."

"By the way, Reggie, my cell phone isn't working for some reason —must get it checked out."

"Understood, see you at seven." Peters waved over his shoulder as he strolled toward the main lobby.

Sayed rushed upstairs and sent an urgent email to Algiers: "*Who is Reggie Peters?*"

———

Rene Bertrand was asleep when the captors stormed in.

"Get up," the guard said from the open door.

Bertrand rolled over and faced him, still groggy.

"I said get up," the man yelled, advancing and grabbed Bertrand by the scruff of the neck. "You must answer an email."

This was new. And what was the big hurry? He had answered emails on several occasions and also returned calls from his cell. Always under the supervision of the guards. Always with a gun against his head. The CNN International broadcast gave him the essential world news every day, so he sounded convincing enough in his phone conversations. For all intents and purposes, he was a free man in Dallas covering a national political event. His captors even forced him to send daily convention updates, using what he had learned from the CNN broadcasts, to his magazine.

Leading him into the living area, the guard roughly pushed him into a chair where his laptop computer was powered up and waiting. Bertrand scanned the sender's name but it was not familiar, nor was the email address. Who the hell was asking him about old Reggie Peters?

The cold barrel of the pistol nudged his cheek. "Answer it, you dog," the guard said.

Bertrand's hands shook. He rubbed his fingers to settle down and hit the reply tab: "Peters is an old friend and associate of mine from England. He works at the *London Evening Standard*."

Bertrand waited while the mysterious party on the other end

digested the message. When no reply came, he looked at the guard. "Well?"

Before the man could answer, another question popped up: *"What do you do when you are together?"*

For the first time in captivity, Bertrand found something to make him smile. He typed: "Chase whores and drink."

The reply came immediately: *"Tell me something about him that everyone knows, and something that only you know."*

Bertrand's mind sorted through the expected response. He took a slow, easy breath and typed: "He is the oldest and best reporter on staff at *The Standard*. He just started taking Viagra last month."

"What is his cell phone number?"

Bertrand typed the number and waited. For what, he did not know.

"That is all for now," came the terse reply.

Bertrand wiped a bead of sweat from his upper lip. Why all this about Reggie? As soon as he thought about the question, the switch flicked on in his mind. The hair lifted on the back of Bertrand's neck. An ice-cold chill rushed down his back. Was someone impersonating him in Dallas? *No, that was not possible.* How could Reggie mistake this stranger for him? Unless the stranger resembled him. Someone who appeared so much like him that he could fool an old friend?

TWENTY-FOUR

Sayed paced his room. He had fooled Peters, but he could not do it for long. The Englishman must be dealt with, now.

He retrieved his rental and drove to a payphone. He had two calls to make. The first was to his controller. When the monotone voice answered by repeating the number he just called, Sayed spoke slowly and clearly.

"The mission is compromised. They have photos of me and obviously know why I am here. There is a leak in the organization."

"Get out now," the controller said, "we will make preparations to pick you up at relocation site number one. Do you require assistance getting there?"

Sayed did not hesitate with his answer. "I am not leaving. Still operational at this point."

The controller's voice dropped to a whisper. "Are you certain?"

"I am confident I can continue. This call is a warning to *you*. Someone with knowledge of the operation has betrayed us. Find him!"

Sayed disconnected and muddled through the problem. Whoever the traitor was, he most probably resided outside the United States. The two sleeper agents knew so little about him and his mission; he did not suspect them. Their instructions were limited: report to Dallas

and take orders. No, this rot went to the very core of the organization
—deep inside al-Qaeda.

He called Suleiman and requested a meeting. Sayed understood
meeting the sleeper agents too often was risky. If he or they had fallen
under surveillance, it might jeopardize the mission, but he could not
afford to wait.

In every assignment, something unplanned always happened. It
was how one handled unexpected emergencies that separated the
experienced foreign intelligence officers from the inexperienced ones.
Keeping a cool head and working through the problem with deliberate
focus had always paid off for Sayed. It would pay off now.

On a hot, steamy Sunday afternoon, no one noticed the two cars
parked behind the warehouse. Sayed presented his dilemma and
proposed his idea. Suleiman quickly agreed, but Zuhair hesitated.

"Do you see a better solution?" Sayed asked Zuhair.

He bowed his head and quietly said, "No, sir."

"Good," Sayed said, "it is settled."

Before departing, Sayed told the sleepers that a traitor lurked
within the organization. No one could be trusted. No outside contact
with anyone was allowed until after the assignment had concluded.
From here on out, they would only deal with him and ignore any
instructions from their other contacts, especially if they contradicted
Sayed. He would give the orders now.

Sayed drove back to the hotel and contemplated his next step. If
done wrong, the whole thing could still fall apart. He checked his
watch—five o'clock—and called Peters' cell.

"Peters, here."

"Reggie, something has come up. Give me a rain check on dinner
tonight."

"Damn, having a drink in the Gossip Bar right now. Can you
join me?"

Peter's voice sounded slurred and thick.

"Afraid not, but the other thing came through. Have two set up for
ten o'clock."

"Marvelous. Knew you wouldn't let us down." Peters chuckled.

"We will meet them and bring them back to the hotel. They're frightened of walking into the lobby unescorted. The vice cops, you know."

"Yes, I understand. Where will we meet?"

"I will pick you up you at the Tower entrance just before ten. I am driving a rental—gray, Toyota. I will park on the curb near the valet area."

"Wonderful, see you then," Peters said.

"Reggie, do not forget your little blue pill. You will need it later."

"Ha, ha—I never leave home without them."

———

J. Thomas Fuller relaxed at home with a biography on the current Dalai Lama. Fuller had a love-hate relationship with Sunday evenings. Loved the fact the phone seldom rang, hated that tomorrow was Monday. Reading for pleasure was what he missed most about leaving academia. All his hours as national security advisor were spent reading reports, meetings, and phone calls. There was never time just to unwind and enjoy the pleasures of literature. The ringing of the encrypted phone in his study drew him out of his world of bliss and slammed him back into reality.

"This is Fuller."

"Mr. Fuller, this is Gary Zeno at the NSA action desk."

Fuller set his book aside. "Yes."

"As per your directive last week, I'm calling to inform you that we intercepted a transmission thirty-seven minutes ago from a caller in Dallas, Texas, to a high-value target in Afghanistan."

Fuller sat up in his chair. "Go on."

"I've just forwarded you the text of the intercept."

Fuller logged on to his Top Secret email. "Continue."

"Sir, we ran the caller through voice recognition and have a 94 percent confidence it's the subject of your directive—Sayed."

Fuller read the email as Zeno continued talking.

"The call originated from a payphone off Stemmons Freeway. That's west of downtown, sir."

"Very well. Continue monitoring that target. I want to know about every contact they have in Dallas." Fuller's voice rose. "And in the future, I don't want it to take thirty-seven minutes before I'm notified."

"Yes, sir," Zeno said before disconnecting.

Shit! Fuller no longer felt like reading—couldn't concentrate. Had something happened in Dallas? Could Sayed have been tipped off? Any sane man in his position would abort the mission. But not Sayed —a fanatic. Oh, to have this fool's confidence. But why so much confidence?

Fuller retrieved the book he'd been reading. He opened it to the bookmark and settled back into the story. Fuller still couldn't concentrate. He again set the book aside and stared to the far side of the room in thought. They'd missed something in their Presidential security protocols—something big.

———

Roberts and Bishop sat in Chili's, each on their third beer. The waitress had finally given up on the pair ordering food. It was a slow night and since she wasn't busy, she leaned against the bar with her arms crossed, glaring at them, probably wondering if they were drinking their dinners tonight.

Roberts didn't know why, but he had started doubting his plan. It all sounded so good a few days ago, but as they neared the president's arrival, the enormity of the thing settled onto Roberts' shoulders. No other agent had ever dealt with a threat this serious before. Roberts' confidence needed a boost. Maybe Bishop could offer something encouraging.

"Need to ask you a question," Roberts said.

Bishop sat back in the booth. "Ask."

Roberts downed the last swallow and raised his hand, signaling the waitress. "How is it you ended up in Dallas?"

"Wondered when you'd get around to that," Bishop said, before also finishing his beer. He pushed the empty aside and whispered, "The way this threat developed, Fuller didn't know which agency might end up taking the lead. He instructed General Cook to have several people from P2OG available to embed. When your report about Abbey and the prayer beads rolled in, that looked like the best shot for intercepting Sayed."

The waitress dropped off two fresh beers and Roberts tested his. "But why you, here?"

Bishop gave a half-shrug. "I'm Cook's go-to-guy. Wherever he feels there's the highest likelihood for action, that's where I go. I'm getting hungry. You ready to order yet?"

Roberts had no appetite. He had too much riding on this. What he'd told Susan... he'd as much as guaranteed her and Abbey's safety. He couldn't guarantee anyone's—not even the president's.

"Hey," Roberts said.

Bishop had begun scanning the menu. He lowered it and eyed him.

"Is there anything new from the CIA asset?"

Bishop shook his head. "No, but he's working on finding out where Sayed is staying in Dallas. Says he might have something in the next day or two."

The CIA asset had always troubled Roberts. He didn't trust most informers or assets—especially those working for money. Often, if they didn't have any fresh intel, they'd just make up something to justify being paid.

"You recruited this guy. You trust his intel?"

Bishop shrugged. "The guy's a total rogue. Looks like an opium runner." Bishop placed his index finger in the center of his forehead, "with a big ugly mole right here. But the intel he provides is solid. Never caught him in a lie."

Roberts changed the subject. "You said you got all shot up in Afghanistan. Mind telling me about it?"

"Not much to tell. My team and I were already in Pakistan, training their Special Services Group on 9/11. After the attacks in the US, we were directed to hook up with the Northern Alliance and deployed to Tora Bora."

Bishop's hunter eyes stared at some point in the distance, recalling the event.

"Our mission was to direct laser target designators at caves for the bombs and missiles. When it became clear bin Laden was no longer there, we went after al-Qaeda stragglers."

Bishop took a long, slow swallow of beer and exhaled. "We were clearing a house early one morning. Intel said there was an al-Qaeda big-wig inside. Tossed a grenade through the window and breached the door." Bishop squinted and frowned. "There was so much smoke and dust it was hard to see."

Bishop didn't say anything for a while. He just stared at his beer glass. Finally, he took another long swallow. "Terrorist inside popped a grenade on us as we searched the place. I spent a while in hospitals and physical therapy."

Roberts' earlier assessment about Bishop was confirmed. A soldier who'd killed many times and almost been killed. Problem was, he wasn't a Secret Service agent. Roberts lowered his gaze to the table. He couldn't do things the way Bishop did. War zones and public places in the US required different methods. Roberts had been wrong. Talking to Bishop didn't encourage him. Quite the contrary. It left him feeling more alone and isolated than ever.

TWENTY-FIVE

Sayed pulled the vehicle against the curb and waited—five minutes till ten, but Peters had not arrived. Where could the fool be? In his rearview mirror, Sayed spotted the young valet walking toward the car. *No, go back. I do not need your help.* Sayed rolled the window down, hung his head out and, in his best French accent, said, "Just waiting for a friend."

The young man waved, wheeled around, and walked back to the valet booth. At that moment, Peters exited the hotel, took a right, and marched toward the car. He stopped and bent down, peeking through the passenger window before smiling.

Sayed motioned him inside.

"Thought it was you." Peters laughed and slid in the seat.

The fool wore some god-awful cologne that was probably supposed to smell like musk, but instead had a manure odor. Sayed pulled the car into the traffic going south on Market Center Boulevard as Peters buckled his seat belt. He wiped sweat from his face with a handkerchief. "How far is it?"

"Down the road, not far."

In less than a mile, they turned right behind the warehouse where Sayed had met Suleiman and Zuhair earlier. In the shadows of the back alley, another vehicle sat, its parking lights on. Sayed parked and turned off his lights. "We are here."

"What's all this damn cloak and dagger, Rene?" Peters asked.

"The girls are very suspicious. They can make a bundle this week, but not if they are in jail. This is how they want it, Reggie."

Peters leaned toward the windshield. He squinted and searched the darkness, checking out the vehicle. A frown crossed his lips. "I understand, but this is a shabby place for conducting business, don't you think?"

"Give me your money. I'll talk to them and make the deal," Sayed said.

Peters dug out his wallet and handed Sayed two hundred dollars. "Be right back."

Sayed walked to the driver's side of the other car and pulled out his wallet. He pretended to hand Zuhair money, sticking his hand inside the car's window. "Is everything ready?"

"Ready," Zuhair said.

A moment later, Sayed slid back into the driver's seat and handed Peters back his two hundred dollars. "I paid the man for mine, but he will not let me pay for yours. He wants to confirm you are not a cop." Sayed led out an exasperated breath. "Just pay him so we can get out of here. You will not be disappointed once you see the two girls in the back seat—they are top of the line. Let's get this party started."

"Well, I never. Oh, all right." Peters got out and strolled into the darkness toward the car. About halfway there, he stopped and looked back at Sayed.

Sayed leaned forward in the seat. *Come on... come on. Just a little closer.*

The warm breeze shifted, and Sayed caught the whiff of something foul from the nearby dumpster. Finally, Peters moved a little closer, edging his fingers along the car's hood while he sauntered toward the driver's window. He bent down and looked inside.

How long before he'd realize there were no girls in there?

A dark figure slipped around the side of the dumpster behind Peters. Suleiman clasped Peters' mouth with his left hand and the knife found its mark. The swift movement impressed Sayed. Only a muffled cry escaped Peters' throat before he fell. Suleiman kept the blade in him and dropped on top of Peters as he slumped to the concrete. Suleiman pulled the knife from the dead man and rolled him over, wiping the blade on Peters' trouser leg.

Sayed got out of the car and motioned at Zuhair. "Take his wallet, cell phone, and watch. This must appear to be a common robbery and murder. Also get his hotel room key."

From around the corner of the warehouse, a man's slurred singing floated through the darkness. Sayed jerked his head in that direction. "Hurry, someone is coming."

Zuhair rolled Peters over and hurriedly ran his hand through his pockets. He stuffed the contents into a bag and handed it to Sayed.

Sayed stepped back and glared at it. "Fool! I do not want that," he waved it away. "Get rid of it."

TWENTY-SIX

Detective Thurman Howard pulled his unmarked car behind a remote news van already on scene. The van's extended live broadcast antenna stood like a monument to the tragedy the place had seen only a few hours earlier. Howard laid the half-chewed cigar in the ashtray and checked his reflection in the rearview mirror. The seventies flat top had finally given way to longer, salt and pepper hair combed straight back. Reaching across the middle console, he grabbed his notebook off the passenger seat. *How many of these have I worn out?*

Thurman Howard had worked thirty-eight years for the Dallas Police Department. For thirty-one of those, he wore a detective's badge, and the last twenty-seven he worked homicide. Few people ever achieve status as legends in their own time, and fewer still deserve it, but Thurman had. For the last twenty-five years, he'd instructed homicide classes in the Dallas Police Academy, and because of this, every new officer knew him before graduation. And every new officer learned only to call him Howard. Calling him by his first name meant an ass eating.

Howard solved almost all his cases. His case-cleared stats afforded him leverage few other detectives enjoyed. Never got the run-of-the-mill murders. They saved the complicated ones for him.

The steamy weather greeted him when Howard stepped from the car. Already hot at eight-fifteen in the morning. Probably another scorching afternoon. His summer attire was a blue plaid, short-sleeve shirt, with a button-down collar. The coffee stain on the leg of his light gray dress slacks had mostly dried.

He made no effort to hide his pistol. It hung, as always, on his right hip with the detective shield clipped beside it. Howard wasn't a big man, but he stretched his five-foot-nine-inch frame ramrod straight before adjusting his belt below the growing beer gut.

All the activity centered around the alley up ahead. Yellow crime scene tape stretched from the corner of one building to the other, outlining the evidence search area. Several police vehicles and crime scene units were parked near the alley. The group of press and onlookers stood outside the tape perimeter with a uniform officer manning the entrance.

"Morning, Officer," Howard said, squeezing through the narrow space of curious bodies.

"Morning Howard. How's it going?"

Howard glanced around the alley. "Never better. You the first on scene?"

"No, Corporal Shaw got the call." The officer pointed to another uniform deeper in the crime scene area.

"Thanks." Howard slipped on his sunglasses and strolled toward the forensic team. The sweat caused his shirt to stick to his back, and he pulled it away with his left hand.

Kneeling beside the body, the forensic team supervisor spotted Howard. In a loud voice he spoke up. "Everybody, keep your hands on your wallet. Howard's here." The sneer indicated he wanted the banter to begin.

Howard strolled up and posted his fist on his hips. "Hope you didn't kill this guy with your stupid sense of humor, Kelly."

"Nope, knife in the back."

Howard moved closer to the corpse. He pointed at the ground ahead of him. "This area clean?"

Kelly shot him a glance. "Yup."

Howard squatted beside the covered body. He pulled the sheet down below the face. "Dumped or killed here?"

"Killed here. No scuff marks or abrasions. Found this." Kelley handed Howard a clear plastic bag with *EVIDENCE* stamped in red. Inside rested a laminated ID with a royal blue lanyard attached.

Howard studied the ID. "Reggie Peters, *London Evening Standard*. This limey came a long way before getting himself killed, didn't he?"

"Yeah." Kelly stood. "We're finished here. Got photos, searched for evidence and searched the body."

"Find any other identification?" Howard asked.

Kelly peeled off a pair of blue Latex gloves. "Nope, that's all. Wallet's missing. From the outline on his wrist, looks like he had on a watch. That's missing too."

Howard opened his mouth, but Kelly beat him to the question. "And before you ask, no phone either."

Howard scratched his chin and held up the plastic bag with lanyard. "Just this?"

Kelly unzipped the Tyvek coveralls and waved the sides to let air in. "Yeah, go figure. Never guess where we found it."

"Where?"

Kelly pointed at the body. "Guy had it around his neck, tucked *under* his shirt out of sight. You need anything else, or can I have them load him?"

Howard pulled out his handkerchief and mopped his face. "Go ahead." He strolled toward Corporal Shaw, who was talking to a uniformed sergeant, Stony Davis. Stony was an old pal. Used to rodeo in his younger days—bull rider. They'd worked the streets together years earlier and still got together with the wives every few months.

As Howard approached, Stony spit a sunflower seed hull on the ground, grinned, and extended his hand. "Morning, Howard. So, you got this one, huh?"

"Yeah, guess so." Howard eyed the sergeant as they shook hands. "You've stopped dipping snuff and got hooked on sunflower seeds?"

Stony's neck took on a red glow. "Yeah, well, you know. Deborah's been on my ass again..."

Howard patted the sergeant's back. "Don't worry about it." He leaned closer and whispered into his ear. "Wimp."

Stony's cheeks and ears also glowed red, but he didn't offer a comeback. "This is Corporal Shaw." Stony motioned to the other uniform officer. "First on the scene."

Howard nodded a hello. "Who called it in?"

Shaw stepped forward. "We met a garbage truck driver about an hour ago. Said when he rolled down the alley for the dumpster"—the officer pointed over Howard's right shoulder at a man standing beside a garbage truck—"he found the guy."

Howard looked around. "He see anyone else?"

"Nope."

Howard tucked the notebook under an arm and dropped his hands in his pockets. "Any witnesses?"

"No, but we found a wino passed out around the corner of the warehouse," Shaw said. "Didn't have enough money to buy a cup of coffee, and no weapon. Said he didn't see or hear nothing."

Howard gazed at the gray warehouse glistening in the bright sunlight. "What about this place. Who owns it?"

"Warehouse manager came by just after the forensic team arrived. We let him view the body," Shaw said.

"Doesn't know the guy. Never seen him around here before," Stony chimed in.

Another drop of sweat formed on Howard's nose, and he wiped it off with the tip of a finger. "Guy have a car?"

"Nothing found in the area. Maybe the killer took it," Stony said.

Howard nodded his approval—they'd covered all the steps necessary for a preliminary homicide investigation. He sighed. "All right, put it in your report—I'll pick up a copy later."

Stony turned to Howard. "This guy a foreign reporter, you think?"

Howard peered at the sun. "I reckon so. Probably for the convention."

"What brought him here last night, you figure?"

Howard chuckled. "Drugs, whores, little boys. Who knows? You all done, Stony? I think the forensic team's pulling out."

"Yeah, we're finished," the sergeant answered and spat out another hull.

Walking back toward his car, Howard pondered Stony's question. What was the guy doing there? Figuring that out would be the hard part. All dead bodies tell a story. The killer always leaves something and takes something from the crime scene. Forensics might help. Whoever the victim met there last night killed him. But that's the way it was in Dallas on hot summer nights. People meet up. One kills another. And the survivor goes on his merry way.

First thing on the itinerary—figure out where this limey had been staying in Dallas.

———

Howard spent the remainder of the morning on new case paperwork back at the PD. Each murder demanded its share before the real investigation started. He worked through lunch, munching on a ham and cheese sandwich and chips between typing and reading the original offense report. He seldom went out to eat with the guys. His wife made him a lunch that he carried in a paper bag to work. He most enjoyed the home-grown dill pickles she canned every season. Always put a few cloves of garlic and a handful of cayenne peppers in each jar. Gave 'em a snappy flavor.

His sergeant stopped by and told him he'd received a call from the lieutenant, who received a call from the captain, who received a call from the deputy chief. The gist was, the mayor's office took a particular interest in the case because of the political and public relations implications. Bad enough a foreign journalist got killed his first night in town. The city solicited the convention, and except for the Super Bowl and Olympics, this was the biggest catch a city could expect as far as tax revenue.

A quick resolution was needed. It took Howard two phone calls before finding Peters' hotel—the Anatole. He'd swing by there before heading home today.

Mid-afternoon, Howard's phone rang. The medical examiner's secretary told him the doctor would like a word. Could he come by?

Howard grinned and finished off his can of Coke. He collected one of his best short cigars from the locked desk drawer where he hid his humidor. He always enjoyed visiting with his old pal, Dr. Fleming.

Twenty minutes later, the ME's secretary motioned him down the hall. Howard suspected he wasn't fooling her. She, as well as everyone else in the ME's office, knew what he and Dr. Fleming were up to—a complete and undeniable violation of all city and county rules. There were *NO SMOKING* signs everywhere, but Howard and Dr. Fleming ignored them. They'd been smoking in Fleming's office long before the signs went up.

Howard strolled into the open door of Fleming's office with the same smirk he always gave his friend. Fleming rose and welcomed him with a handshake. Fleming was older, a little grayer, taller and slimmer. He stooped when he walked.

"Sit down. We need to talk." Fleming hung the *IN CONFERENCE* sign around the doorknob before closing and locking the door. He turned the large air purifier on its highest setting.

Howard unwrapped his cigar before he sat down. Fleming scooped up his pipe and they both lit their tobacco of choice without another word.

The worst kept secret in the county. The fact Dr. Fleming and Detective Howard "talked" a couple of times a week, with the air purifier on high, was the office joke.

Howard liked Fleming's office—it had flair. On one wall hung a life-size color dissection chart of the human body, and the opposite wall held Fleming's numerous awards, commendations and citations. Behind his desk stood a dark wood bookcase sagging from the medical book collection. A single photo of his wife rested on his desk.

Howard held up the cigar, exhaled a long stream of white smoke, and sat back in the chair. "Glad you called; I'm having one of those days—needed this."

A frown formed on Fleming's lips. "This time, I really do need to talk to you, Thurman."

Dr. Fleming remained one of the few who insisted on calling Howard by his first name. He didn't care—he liked Fleming. Howard slumped lower into the soft leather like he didn't have a care in the world. Wished he had his own office with an air purifier. "So, what's wrong?"

Fleming tested the draw of his pipe and exhaled a puff of smoke. "It's that English guy they brought in this morning—that's what's wrong."

"You've already started? With your backlog, I figured you wouldn't get around to him until later this week."

"Started? I'm finished."

Fleming seemed more animated than usual and a bit flustered. He got this way when politicians got involved in his cases.

"I got a call before the body arrived," Fleming said, "instructing me to do the autopsy immediately and personally." He eased back in his chair and nursed his pipe. "Consider this my informal report."

"Okay, what's so serious? Just another dead foreigner, right?"

After taking another slow draw, Fleming said, "Don't know, but I have some rather interesting information I can share with you about his death."

Howard straightened up and leaned forward. "Such as?"

"Such as, he was killed by a professional."

"A professional what?"

"Killer, Thurman—a professional killer! What the hell do you think?"

"How could you know that?" Howard grunted and pulled another round of smoke from the cigar.

Fleming grinned and in his condescending voice asked, "How long have we known each other?"

Howard considered the question for a moment. "Long time."

"You asked me once if I'd ever served in the military, and I said I had."

"Yeah."

"Well, you never followed up on it. If you did, you would have learned I served with the 75th Rangers in Vietnam."

"Ha! You? A Ranger?"

Fleming's eyes squinted. "We all had other lives, Thurman. I left the army and used the GI bill to go to school. Got my medical degree and never looked back."

"Okay… okay, I'm sorry. Go on with your story."

Fleming took another draw from the pipe. "Anyway, in training, they taught us killing techniques with a commando-style dagger." He rested both elbows on the desk, holding the pipe between his fingers.

Howard eyed him. "And?"

"That's how this Englishman met his death—with a commando-style, narrow-blade, killing dagger."

Howard blew another slow stream of smoke toward the ceiling. "Hell, you can probably order those things from the internet, can't you?"

"Sure, but they don't come with instructions," Fleming said as he reached for the envelope on the desk.

Emptying the contents, several eight-by-ten color photographs of the body slid out, taken during the autopsy. On one magnified shot, a blue latex-gloved hand spread open the wound.

Fleming pointed at a photo. "Look here. See the ragged skin around the wound entrance? The killer knew his business."

Howard stuck the cigar in the corner of his mouth, leaned forward, and traced his finger across the photo.

Fleming continued. "When you stick a six- or eight-inch dagger like that into human flesh, it creates suction. You must twist it several times before removing it to release the pressure. If you don't, it's hell getting out—not like in the movies. That's what this killer did." Fleming tapped the photo and showed a satisfied expression. "See the jagged edges of the skin? If it weren't twisted, it would be smoother."

Howard gave him his full attention. "So, you think the murderer got some kind of military training?"

"Not just military. Special Forces-type training. You don't get that good by reading about it in a book—you have to do it."

Howard brushed some loose ash from his shirt. "Anything else?"

Fleming tapped the photo. "Yeah, the killer didn't go just anywhere in the back. He hit the kidneys."

Howard's eyebrows knitted together. "So?"

"The quickest way to take the fight out of someone is the kidneys or throat. Also, here." Fleming spread the photographs across the desk and pointed at a photo of Peter's face. "See that slight bruising on the right cheek?"

Howard moved forward a little and studied the photo. "Uh-huh."

"That, my friend, is where the assailant used his left hand to clamp the mouth shut. See, the three bruises line up exactly to someone's three middle fingers." Fleming held up his hand and wiggled his long slender fingers.

Both men were leaning over the photograph, heads almost touching. The combined smoke haze from the pipe and cigar settled around them like fog.

Howard was intrigued. "How can you tell the blade's length?"

"I measured the puncture wound. Also, this." Fleming rummaged through the photos again until he found the right one. "See the blood on the pants? That's where the murderer wiped the blade on the victim's trousers after he killed him. I compared the puncture wound length to the blood smear, giving me an estimated overall length of approximately seven inches, give or take an inch."

Howard puffed the cigar and pinched his throat. "So, this wasn't your typical third-ward stabbing? No chance this could have been done by some druggie or john?"

"Not likely." Fleming drew the smoke deep and released it before settling back into his chair.

Something was very wrong here. Not at all another hot summer night killing in Dallas. "This guy's in town for probably less than a day before he gets whacked." Howard met eyes with Fleming. "How did he manage to piss off someone enough in that amount of time for them to hire a professional killer—unless they did it themselves?"

"That's your department, Thurman," Fleming emptied his pipe into the ashtray by tapping it several times.

Howard nodded and took one final deep pull from the cigar. "The guy must have known someone in Dallas." Then another thought appeared. "Or someone from Europe who's here now knew the victim," he mumbled. When Fleming rose, Howard snuffed out his cigar, and the smoke dissipated, pulled by the currents in the air purifier.

Offering his hand for the customary goodbye shake, Fleming's eyes took on a concerned look. "Be careful of this one, Thurman. He's dangerous."

———

Dick hated talking to Special Agent in Charge Gonzales. After that run-in in Moscow, their relationship had taken a nosedive and augered deep into the ground by the time the guy was promoted as his SAIC.

Dick walked into Gonzales's office to find him lounging back in his executive, black leather chair. Half-closed blinds shielded the two walls of windows from the blazing sun. The office overlooked the canal of Las Colinas, the best view in the building—rank had its privileges.

As soon as the SAIC saw Dick, a curious smirk appeared.

Dick paused. *This ain't good—the guy's up to something.*

"Sit down, Dick."

Taking his seat, Dick stayed on his guard. He seldom met with Gonzales alone, preferring witnesses in case it broke bad. None of the office supervisors trusted or liked the man, but they had more to lose than Dick, so they always backed the jerk.

The SAIC fiddled with some papers on his desk. Couldn't keep that silly grin off his lips. "How's the business with the Porter girl going?"

Dick tensed. This was some kind of a setup. "Everything's fine. Roberts is taking care of it. No problems that I can see."

Gonzales played with a gold-plated letter opener. He tossed it on the desk and interlaced his fingers, settling his stare on Dick.

"Headquarters may be reconsidering the Porter girl matter. Got a call a moment ago from ADPO."

Dick didn't say a word. He already knew the answer.

"Wanted my opinion on whether I believed it was all a waste of time. I told him it was most certainly a waste of time. A waste of time and resources that we could put to much better use."

The smug "so what do you think of that" expression made Dick want to slap him.

The SAIC smiled and relaxed in his chair.

"Nothing to say? No quick come back?"

Dick rose. "Is there anything else?"

Gonzales sneered. "How ironic, ending your career on such a low note. If not for your friendship with the director, I'd have transferred your ass years ago. Now all I have to do is wait. How long is it before you get the gold watch? Three and a half months and you're gone. You and that nut case, Roberts, better hope nothing happens during the convention. If it does, that'll wash both of you out of here and save me the trouble."

Dick stopped at the door before leaving. He turned back and faced the man. With his most serious expression and in a solemn tone, he said, "I hope you know what an inspiration you are to the office, sir."

The SAIC's wide smile disappeared and a perplexed look replaced it as Dick slipped into the hall. He wasn't worried about that guy's opinion. Two things worried Dick. Could they keep the president safe? And what would become of Roberts if their plan didn't work? If anything happened to the president, Roberts was set up to take the fall. Retiring at the end of the year left Dick unable to help him. Gonzales would make Roberts' life a living hell until he tired of it, then send him to a dead-end assignment in the middle of nowhere where he would be forgotten.

TWENTY-SEVEN

Every time an op was rushed like this one, something always went to hell, was the thought on Lieutenant Richard Henderson's mind as he and the other SEALs assembled their gear in the hanger at the covert base on the Afghan Pakistani border. Voices from a nearby radio squawked out current weather, wind, and visibility conditions for the rolling mountain terrain.

Chief Petty Officer Salazar lifted the medical kit and slung it over his shoulder as the others dispersed. He approached Henderson, and keeping his voice low said, "Sir, that's not much to go on."

Henderson grimaced. "Yeah, it's weak, but without eyes on the ground, that's the best we've got."

Henderson had been involved in a dozen of these types of missions. The SEALs had been instructed to intercept and capture a high-value target traveling by car north of Islamabad. No other information on the subject—just a vehicle description, complete with license plate number. Another unknown male accompanied the target. Neither had been seen with weapons. A spy satellite had located it, and a drone had been deployed to maintain contact until a team could be dispatched.

Henderson had a bad feeling about this one. Thing was thrown together too fast. Little information on the target.

Henderson hoisted his pack and weapon and led the team outside the hanger toward the Blackhawk, already wound up and ready to go. He gazed at the threatening sky. It had darkened again. The short afternoon rainstorm a couple of hours ago was just a preview of what was to come. The rain on the tarmac smelled fresh and small puddles glistened like circles of sparklers as the team ran to the chopper. If this thing went down as planned, they'd be back in less than a couple of hours. If it didn't...

With everyone strapped in, they slid off the pad and spun northwest toward the interdiction location. Henderson fitted the headset and mic over his head before leaning toward the team and motioned them to listen up. He yelled over the engine.

"Guys, since this thing is so squirrely, don't take any chances. We'll do a capture or kill, whichever way they'll let it go down —understand?"

Everyone showed a thumbs up and finished their final equipment checks. Henderson moved closer to a window and looked out. The rolling mountain terrain, its ridges covered by truck-size boulders and scant pine forest, rushed by. He rested his head against the airframe and closed his eyes. He allowed his mind free range and calculated all the options. After ten minutes, he keyed the headset mic. "Pilot, do you have an updated location from the drone?"

A static-laden voice replied, "Yes, sir, the vehicle just turned off the main road and is heading due east in the direction of Pindi Point."

Henderson searched his map for the location. Perfect—woody, hilly terrain and only a two-lane road with no towns or villages nearby. If they could just get there fast enough to deploy ahead of the vehicle.

The voice of the co-pilot broke his concentration. "Five minutes to LZ, sir."

Henderson pressed the transmit button. "Copy, five minutes to LZ."

He held up five fingers at the team and yelled, "Saddle up."

Everyone acknowledged with a nod.

Henderson checked his watch. Plenty of light to do the extraction and return to base before dark—as long as the rain held.

Minutes later, they were on the ground. The pilot reported no road traffic in the immediate area except the target vehicle, five miles to the west. As the helicopter departed and the dust settled, Henderson and the team scurried for cover.

After the whine of the chopper faded, total silence surrounded the team. The high pine forest's smell reminded Henderson of his parents' home nestled in the mountains near Flagstaff.

He pointed at three SEALs. "Ron and Dave, deploy the spikes just over the crest of the hill. Bill, spot them from the center of the road. I don't want those guys in the car seeing the strip until the last second."

Three SEALs broke cover and headed up the road carrying an over-size rucksack with the spike strip. Henderson pointed to his right and eyed the other team members. "We'll hit them up there. Just before the crest. Set up your fields of fire."

The other SEALs raced up the hill and deployed in the woods. Henderson searched the road with his binoculars. A small, black car kicked up a dust trail about a mile out, closing fast. Henderson ran through the woods toward his men. "They're coming."

He dropped to the ground and fought to bring his breathing back to normal as the car got closer. *Almost there... just a few more yards.* Henderson trained his rifle on the advancing car moments before it hit the spikes at the crest of the hill. Both front tires blew, and the vehicle swerved hard to the right as the rear tires also deflated. The driver couldn't control it, and it crashed headlong into the shallow ditch. Nothing happened for a couple of seconds. No one moved. A cloud of dust shrouded the occupants of the car.

Henderson and three other SEALs dashed forward, weapons at the ready, while the others kept them covered. There was nowhere for the car occupants to go—their only option, surrender.

Speaking in the local dialect, Henderson screamed, "Exit the vehicle with your hands up!"

The dust had settled, and he squinted at the dark, tinted car windows trying to see anything. *What was going on inside?* Movement caught his eye through the passenger window. If they were preparing to detonate a car bomb, there wouldn't be enough left of the team to send home in a shoebox. Henderson screamed the order again and tightened his finger on the trigger.

A SEAL jerked the driver's door open, and a shot rang out. He fell backward as other pistol fire boomed from inside the vehicle. Everyone opened up at once. The deafening roar of automatic gunfire drowned out any sound from inside. At one point, Henderson thought the passenger had lifted his hands as bullets tore through the vehicle.

The team fired over eighty rounds before Henderson called a halt and eased forward. With all the windows shot out, it was clear the two occupants were dead. Henderson opened the passenger door and the body of a small, swarthy man rolled out. His mouth gaped open, showing a gold tooth. He also had an ugly black mole in the center of his forehead.

TWENTY-EIGHT

Waiting. That's what Sayed was left with. Waiting and wondering how the rest of the assignment would play out. The unexpected encounter with the Englishman had been handled, but nothing happens in a vacuum. He remembered a scientific axiom his father told him once: *For every action, there is an equal and opposite reaction.* What reaction could he expect from this? In a city the size of Dallas, a single murder shouldn't engender any undue suspicion. Should it?

Sayed's journey to this place had been a long, winding road, a road where chance encounters, coincidences, and tragedies had all played a significant part.

Sayed was born to privilege. His father was the port manager in Latakie, Syria, where Sayed spent his early life. His mother was a devout Sunni. She and young Sayed studied the Quran every day, and he learned the lessons of The Prophet at her knee. Sayed's father was absent for the most part. Early mornings at the port and late nights with his friends and business associates. He made a good living for his family but seldom gave them what they desired most—his time.

In 1974, when Sayed was fourteen, his mother took him to a wedding. One of his mother's friend's sons was to be married. The

Sayed family was all invited, but as usual, Sayed's father was too busy. Of course, Sayed hated the idea of missing a football game with his friends to attend a wedding, but his love for his mother was so great he'd never disappoint her by refusing.

After the ceremony, Sayed had been introduced to the tall, skinny, seventeen-year-old groom—*Osama bin Laden*.

Sayed attended college in the US and received an appointment with the Syrian General Intelligence Directorate through his father's connections. Because of his knowledge of America and fluency in English and French, he was assigned to the External Security Division. His work there impressed many people in high places. It was only a matter of time before he would be in charge of a major department.

In 1985 he met and married Rasha. Only she understood and loved Sayed the way his mother did. She understood the dangers and secrecy of his work and faithfully played the part of devoted Muslim wife and mother to their twin daughters. But she was more than just a faithful wife and mother; she was his light. Her love and encouragement sustained Sayed in a way that he craved. Rasha was so much a part of Sayed that he felt alone and insecure when he traveled without her. He was only half a person without her—something most Muslim men would never want to admit.

In 1988, Sayed was covertly deployed to Afghanistan to monitor the Soviet-Afghan war. The leader of Syria, Hafez al-Assad, had personally selected him for this assignment. His mission: determine the fighting effectives of this new Mujahideen group, al-Qaeda, and its charismatic leader, Osama bin Laden. With the passing of years, Sayed had long since put the wedding and name bin Laden out of his mind. But when he saw the intel photo of the man, it all came back. The eyes, the crooked smile, the soft voice Sayed remembered from the seventeen-year-old groom.

Sayed spent two months with bin Laden's group. He took part in ambushes against Russian military convoys, ducked and hid with the other fighters when Soviet aircraft circled overhead, and spent the evenings listening to bin Laden's message and teachings. From his strict religious upbringing, Sayed found himself agreeing with bin Laden's ideas. The United States foreign policy *was* oppressing

Muslims in the Middle East. The Jews *did* control the media around the world. And expelling the Soviets from the Prophet's Land was doing Allah's work. Sayed came to understand that revenge killings of civilians were justified under Sharia Law and Jihad. He was inspired and invigorated at the thought of Muslims being able to determine their own destiny without the interference and meddling of a foreign power.

For the first time since being married, Sayed didn't feel incomplete without Rasha. He longed to remain with the sheikh, fight the Russians, and defeat the infidels. He shared the sheikh's teachings with Rasha, and she became equally enthused.

The next two years, Sayed followed the goings-on of al-Qaeda and Osama bin Laden from his post in the Syrian Intelligence Service. And more importantly, he kept a back-channel communication with bin Laden. Although the distance kept them apart, they established a degree of mutual trust and respect.

In August of 1990, when the US launched Operation Desert Shield, the United States sent thousands of infidels to occupy Muslim lands— Holy Lands where shrines of Islam had stood for centuries. Mecca, Medina, and dozens more were in danger of being defiled by heathens with unclean hands. Bin Laden denounced the use of foreign troops in Saudi Arabia, and Sayed, as his disciple, encouraged Syria to follow bin Laden's lead.

This is where Sayed's trouble with Syrian President al-Assad started. Sayed's secret back channel to bin Laden was discovered and he fell under suspicion of passing Syrian government secrets to the al-Qaeda leader. After a lengthy internal investigation, Sayed was cleared of the most damning charges. But his explanation of the secret communications with bin Laden fell on deaf ears. He was demoted. The only thing left was to resign. His career was in tatters. Rasha came to his rescue. In 1992, she agreed to go with him to join bin Laden in Sudan. By then, she was as devoted a disciple of the sheikh as Sayed. They packed up their family and moved to Khartoum later that year. Bin Laden welcomed Sayed back and instructed Nasser al-Bahri, bin Laden's personal bodyguard, to assign the newcomer to the protection detail.

In 1996, two significant events happened. Sayed and his family left Sudan with the sheikh and moved to Jalalabad, Afghanistan. And the sheikh issued a *fatwa*, declaring war against the United States.

By 1998, Sayed's days as a bodyguard were over. He and a special team, trained by him, infiltrated and successfully executed two bombings of US Embassies in East Africa. At last—they'd struck at the great snake that had been choking the life out of the Middle East. The sheikh praised him for the daring and complicated raids. Sayed had at last been restored to a position of trust by the man he most revered. His promotion to al-Qaeda intelligence chief soon followed.

March 6, 1999, wasn't any different than most days in Jalalabad. The weather was overcast, and temperatures were average for that time of year, with highs around 20 degrees Centigrade. Storm clouds boiled up to the south, threatening rain later.

Sayed and his family had at last established a routine. The initial move years ago from liberal Syria to the more conservative Sudan had been a struggle for the family, especially the girls. The next move to the more conservative Afghanistan even challenged Rasha. Moving every few years to more fundamental Muslim countries took getting used to. In that prepubescent time of their lives, the girls felt the need to complain and argue about everything far more than Sayed liked.

The family lived in a modest two-bedroom apartment. The sheikh had a villa on the outskirts of town and several smaller dwellings within twenty miles. He seldom slept in one place too many nights. Since Sayed was senior staff, he enjoyed the perks of the position. Once a month, the sheikh hosted a small gathering—what he called his "family reception." The sheikh was a family man and understood that his staff, who had family with them, needed a break every so often. He encouraged the bonding of al-Qaeda families.

Rasha and the girls were excited. Rasha had become friends with a couple of bin Laden's younger wives, and the children played well together. An evening away from home was much needed and appreciated. After the girls finished school, Sayed loaded the family into the Range Rover the sheikh allowed him to use.

As they approached the walled villa, Rasha examined the guards at the gate entrance. "Are there more now? When you worked here, it did not seem like there were so many."

"The threats have increased. Jihad against the Americans comes with a price," Sayed said.

She did not answer, instead breaking up an ongoing fight in the backseat between Yara and Rima. "If you do not behave at the sheikh's, you will answer to your father."

She nudged Sayed in the ribs and shot a playful glance.

Sayed grinned. He had never laid a hand on the children. Their mother was the disciplinarian of the family.

The sheikh, always a gracious host, personally welcomed each family with his wives at his side. "Blessings be upon you and your family," he said when greeting them.

Sayed gave him the customary hug and whispered, "I have finished." He patted a pocket on his robe. "Have them here."

That turned out to be the biggest mistake of Sayed's life. How many times had he thought about it? How many times did he wish he could take back those words?

TWENTY-NINE

Today, the old business of party-nominating conventions had become just a formality. Gone were the days of floor fights for the nominee for president. The official first day of the convention was yesterday—Sunday. Months ago, the rules committee, the nominating committee, the platform committee, and half a dozen other groups met and insured a well-choreographed show. The real deal started today—Monday.

All this Roberts explained to Susan and Abbey while he drove down Stemmons Freeway toward the American Airlines Center that afternoon. They'd enjoyed a late lunch and now weaved their way through the always heavy Dallas midday rush. A wreck had slowed traffic almost to a stop just before his exit.

"Will we see the president today?" Abbey asked.

She sat between Roberts and Susan in the front seat of Roberts' Secret Service car.

"Not today, honey. He's not here yet," Susan said and stroked the child's hair.

Roberts changed lanes. "He'll arrive later this week."

Abbey pointed at the device under the console of the dash. "Is that a police radio?"

Roberts reached for the mic. "Yup, want to see how it works?" He didn't give her a chance to answer before speaking into the mic. "Dallas—Roberts."

The voice on the other end sounded crisp and official. "Roberts—Dallas, go ahead."

"Radio check—how do you copy, over?"

The voice answered, "I copy you five by five—how me, over?"

"Copy you the same—out."

Abbey did not comment, but stared up at him with one of her elusive smiles. He liked her smiles. She'd changed from the shy, quiet, and strange little girl he'd met a few days earlier, becoming more personable and outgoing. Probably just starting to warm up to him.

He flipped on his blinker and wormed between two cars to exit the freeway, taking a back route to the building's rear loading dock. The American Airlines Center anchored the seventy-two-acre Victory Park development, just north of the Dallas Central Business District and historic West End. The AAC's exterior was constructed of brick, limestone, and granite, with sweeping signature arches hanging over each of the four entrances.

Stopping at the first checkpoint, Roberts placed the Secret Service placard on the car's dash. A bored-looking uniform Dallas police officer nodded and held out his hand. Roberts surrendered his credentials.

"Good afternoon, Officer," Roberts said.

The officer bent down and peeked inside the car. "Afternoon." He returned Roberts' identification and waved them through. They parked in an area designated *POLICE VEHICLES ONLY*, and he escorted Susan and Abbey to the rear loading dock.

"So, what are we going to do here if the president hasn't arrived yet?" Susan asked.

Roberts kept walking, not meeting eyes with her. "Oh, you know. Just familiarization with the place. Thought you'd want to see it before things got too crazy." He had another, more important reason, but he didn't want to share it with her. This one was just between him and Abbey.

Several delivery trucks waited; the area was busy with people pushing carts of boxes or guys with clipboards checking off deliveries. A second uniform stood at the dock's far end, leaning up against a wall, chatting with a cute redhead. Roberts led Susan and Abbey up a flight of stairs and entered the side door. When they stepped in, a Secret Service agent sat at a desk to their right. He glanced up, examining Roberts' lapel pin and convention credentials around his neck. Roberts didn't know the guy. He was one of the dozens of agents sent to Dallas on temporary assignment to supplement the field office agents during the convention.

Roberts dug into his pocket. "Almost forgot to give you guys these." He extracted two GUEST identification IDs. "Put these on."

Susan and Abbey strung the chains holding their laminated photos around their necks.

Roberts asked the agent, "Anything happening?"

"Nope, all quiet. Lots of last-minute deliveries, but they're cleared before getting here."

"Things will pick up this evening. Were you given the pictures of the guy we're looking for?" Roberts asked.

The agent opened a folder, and the two photos of Sayed were stapled inside. "Got 'em."

Roberts motioned for Susan and Abbey to follow him. He took the lead through the maze of back corridors and passageways. A woman's voice boomed from overhead through speakers in the main arena area, its echo through the back halls becoming clearer with each step. A sudden burst of applause startled Abbey and she jumped. Roberts opened a set of double doors and the spectacle of the enormous hall revealed itself.

Hundreds of people filled the area, walking around, talking, laughing and wearing all the regalia that make political conventions famous. No one listened to the woman on the podium, but with each pause they all clapped and cheered.

Susan said, "So this is it, huh, the show?"

"Yup," Roberts said, noting the look of delight on Abbey's face. He hadn't told Susan, but he'd brought them here today partly to see if she could handle hours of noise and mingling with strangers. Seeing her excited—rather than intimidated—was a huge relief.

"Come on, we'll take a peek at the security room."

Making their way down the drab, back hall, they went up a short flight of stairs and around a corner. On the door hung a sign, *US SECRET SERVICE – AUTHORIZED PERSONNEL ONLY.*

Roberts opened the door and revealed a wall of closed-circuit television monitors, another wall of city, state, and national maps. He was surprised to find Bishop there, seated at a console, finishing a slice of pizza with two Secret Service agents from the field office.

"What are you doing here?"

Bishop wiped sauce from his chin. "Figured the guys might like some pizza and Coke for lunch."

One of the agents toasted Bishop with a cup. "We got a new best friend."

Roberts gave Susan and Abbey a tour of the place, explaining how everything worked. He needed Abbey here for an experiment. She appeared enthralled, and her big eyes widened at the sights and sounds of the security room. After a quick look around, he motioned for her to join him in front of the wall of monitors. Susan chatted with Bishop and wasn't paying attention.

"Abbey." Roberts squatted eye-level and whispered, "I need a favor."

Her eyes sparkled. "Okay."

"Can you see the colors of the people in this room?"

"You mean their auras, Michael?"

She'd never called him by his first name, and although he liked it, she said it in a way that made him feel uncomfortable.

"Yes, that's right, their auras. Can you see them?"

"Sure."

He turned toward the group of agents. "So, what colors do you see?"

She paused a moment, studying the three men. "They're all white and light blue."

Roberts pointed across the room. "Even Mr. Bishop, over there?"

"Yes," she said. "Why?"

"Just curious." He directed her attention to the dozen TV monitors.

"Check out the TVs and tell me if you can see the colors of the people in the arena."

She shook her head. "No."

"No, you won't do it, or no you can't see the colors?"

Abbey grinned. "No, I can't see their colors."

"Are you sure?"

"Yes, I've tried before with our TV. It only works on real people, not their images."

"All right then." He stood. "We'll do it the old-fashioned way."

Bishop motioned while walking to the door. "A word, please."

Roberts followed him into the hall.

Once outside, Bishop said, "DHS is setting up special cameras that have a feed to their best facial recognition software. Everyone entering the hall gets a still shot sent up for evaluation."

"Yeah, they're doing the same thing at the president's hotel. But if Sayed had major facial reconstructive surgery, would the software still pick it up?"

Bishop shrugged. "Depends on how major."

Roberts looked down the corridor. "Figures. Anything else?"

"Yeah, did you guys get the word about the intercept?"

"What word?"

"Sayed was electronically intercepted the other day calling from Dallas," Bishop whispered. "He knows we're on to him. His controller offered to have him abort and bug out, but he refused. Says he's still operational. Looks like he intends to finish the job."

"Where in the hell did you get that information?"

Bishop made a face. "General Cook called me. Your people haven't disseminated it down to you?"

Roberts shook his head. "It's probably in the intel loop, but I haven't been told yet."

"Your guys should pass that kind of stuff on faster," Bishop said. "Did you hear about the journalist killed last night in Dallas?"

"Yeah, heard it on the news this morning. Bad luck on his part, getting killed his first night in town."

Bishop leaned back against the concrete wall and crossed his arms. "Maybe not bad luck."

"What do you mean?"

"Not sure, but I heard from the Terrorism Task Force the detective working the case is thinking about a different angle."

"Such as?"

"A professional hit."

Roberts rested his hand on the wall Bishop leaned against. "Who'd want to kill a reporter?"

Bishop grinned. "Who wouldn't?"

Roberts chuckled. "Think we should talk to the detective?"

"Can't hurt," Bishop said.

THIRTY

They again dragged Bertrand from his bed and seated him in front of his computer. He felt awful today. Another round of stomach cramps and a splitting headache. Another email question awaited him from the mysterious person in Dallas. A quick grin traced Bertrand's lips when he read it.

"Who else do you know who will attend the convention?"

Bertrand secretly enjoyed this. The guy using his identity sounded nervous, and he liked the idea of manipulating the son of a bitch. He typed back: "I know about a dozen journalists who will be there."

"How well do they know you?"

"We correspond regularly and do dinner a few times a year when on assignments," he typed.

"Do any know you as well as Peters?"

"Yes, several."

"Nothing else for now."

Bertrand sat back. That should give the asshole something to worry about—even if it was a lie. Bertrand felt a little better. He might be a prisoner, but he did not have to submit.

———

Sayed had hardly slept, and what sleep he got was not good. The Peters thing upset him. Killing the swine didn't concern him, but the fact that he'd been recognized had. How many more like Peters were waiting in ambush? He could not afford to let someone get that close again.

He had prayed most of the morning in hopes of Allah giving him guidance and felt no better after the effort. He did not understand this. It was the once-in-a-lifetime chance for Islam to show the world they were not afraid of the West. That they could and would strike anyone who dares invade the sacred lands of their fathers. He, Sayed, had this great blessing bestowed on him to be the bearer of the sword that would strike down the infidels and send fear into the hearts of all who would transgress against Allah and the Holy Lands.

But Allah kept putting obstacles in his path. Why? To test his resolve? Was this the final test to determine if he was worthy of this critical task? He would prove himself worthy.

His years of training would guide him. He knew what the police and Secret Service were thinking. They were looking for him, and he was right under their noses. That's precisely where he intended to stay. He was in place. Now all he had to do was wait.

He made a decision: he would feign illness and remain in his room most of the time until he killed the president. He must do nothing to raise any suspicion, nor have any suspicion directed against him. All he needed was time. And time was on his side.

———

There was never any love lost between Thurman Howard and any federal law enforcement agent. He'd known several good Dallas cops who'd gone fed, and figured they were okay, but he wouldn't give a nickel for the rest. The FBI couldn't investigate much of anything without local help. ATF and DEA were just as bad, or in some ways worse.

Years ago, when he'd worked a federal narcotics case with DEA, a young, hotshot agent followed him, trying to find out who his informant was. The kid wanted the informant as his own and could offer the guy more money than Dallas PD. Howard allowed the agent to tail him into a blind alley, took him by surprise, and then chewed his ass out before sending him on his way.

As far as the Secret Service, they were just a bunch of pretty-boy, Ivy League, three-piece police with expensive shoes and stylish haircuts. Not real investigators, but attractive security guards. His only experience with them in a local counterfeit investigation still left a bad taste in his mouth. Their smug, *I know it all* condescending attitude made him swear he'd never have any further dealings with 'em.

It wasn't with any degree of friendliness that he met Roberts and Bishop that Monday afternoon at the Dallas Police Department. In the conference room with Sergeant Brown, Howard figured he had home-field advantage. After the introductions, Roberts got right to business.

"Detective Howard, thanks for visiting with us. We understand you're the investigating detective for the Peters homicide."

Howard rocked back a little in his chair and glanced at his sergeant. "That's right."

"Could you tell us what progress you've made thus far?"

"Why is the Secret Service interested in a Dallas homicide case?" Howard asked.

"We're working an investigation involving an individual who is a credible presidential threat, and we're concerned our two investigations may have a common nexus."

Howard wouldn't lie but saw no reason to share any more information than necessary. He told them about the findings from the ME and the dagger theory.

Bishop eyed Howard. "You think that's what happened?"

Howard lowered his gaze. "Don't know anything about daggers, but otherwise, the whole thing smells like a basic robbery and killing."

Roberts asked, "Do you find it unusual the guy got killed his first night in town?"

Howard shifted in his seat. "Not particularly. Coincidence probably."

"Any additional info which might help us in our investigation?" Roberts asked.

Howard shook his head. "Nothing, at this time." He didn't like the way the one called Bishop kept staring at him. Something about the eyes said, "I don't buy your story."

Roberts handed Howard his business card as he stood. "Well, we won't keep you away from your work any longer. Please, if you discover anything regarding a possible suspect, we'd appreciate a call."

Studying the card, Howard stood and shook hands with the two men. "I'll call you."

After they left, Howard tore the card in half and dropped it into the trash on his way out.

———

Roberts marched out the police department's front door into a blinding summer sun, Bishop close behind. Roberts wasn't satisfied with the interview. Something about Detective Howard's expressions, tone, and general demeanor convinced Roberts that Howard felt some threat regarding their visit. From the time they entered, a fog of animosity had filled the room.

Bishop slipped on a pair of sunglasses before asking, "Is it just me, or did Detective Howard seem a bit edgy?"

Roberts also fitted his shades on his face while fighting the glare off the sidewalk. "No, he seemed *a lot* edgy. Must have issues."

"So, you think there's any connection between Sayed and the English guy getting killed?"

"I was hoping to get a better read on that after talking to Detective Howard. I got nothing."

Roberts dropped Bishop off at the American Airlines Center before heading back to the Secret Service office. As Roberts walked into Dick's office, his boss was on the phone. He hung up after a quick goodbye, a frown outlining his mouth. Roberts hated Dick frowning. It usually meant he'd done something wrong, or forgotten something.

Roberts took a chair. "What?"

Dick sat back. "Tortorziie just called. It seems the NSA—"

"—intercepted Sayed calling from Dallas?"

"How the hell did you know?"

"Bishop filled me in earlier. He always gets the latest intel before us."

"That bastard Tortorziie is holding out on us," Dick snapped. "Probably assumes we don't need it. I'll have to have a word about that." Dick changed the subject. "You think this limey journalist business has anything to do with Sayed?"

"Don't know, but Bishop and I just left the Dallas Police Department. We interviewed the investigating Homicide detective in the Brit's murder."

"And?"

"He's less than excited about working with us." Roberts related the details of the murder.

Dick's shifted position and asked, "Why would a professional kill a foreign guy that had been in Dallas only a few hours?"

"That's what I've been asking myself," Roberts said. "Doesn't make any sense, unless it's just a case of being in the wrong place at the wrong time."

Dick tightened the knot on his tie. "I hope you don't start believing in coincidences."

"I could use the squad tomorrow if they're available."

"What's your plan?"

"I've been thinking." Roberts leaned his forearms on Dick's desk. "We might get a lead on the murder by showing the dead guy's photo around and interviewing anyone who may have come into contact with him. That probably means the entire foreign journalist's corps. They're the most likely to know something about who he was hanging with prior to his murder. Something someone saw might lead us to Sayed, if he's involved."

Dick thought about it a moment before saying, "Good idea. I'll have them start tomorrow morning. Anything else?"

"No." Roberts settled back and crossing his legs. "Anything going on here?"

"Nope." Dick sighed and stared at him for a moment, then exhaled and ran both hands back through his hair.

That's what he did when something bothered him.

He eyed Roberts. "Let's just work this foreign reporter lead. It's a long shot, but the only thing we've got right now." Dick's voice dropped a little and took on a strange quality. "Sayed didn't run when he had the chance, which means he still believes he can pull it off." Dick stood, shoved both hands in his pockets, and eyed the Dallas city map on the wall. "Which means he's found a way past our security. If that's the case, let's make sure we've covered all the bases. We need to recheck everything and everybody, starting with the journalist."

Dick flopped back down in his chair. "Only a select number of people are given that kind of close access to the president. And from what I'm hearing, that's exactly what Sayed needs—close access."

THIRTY-ONE

S ayed finished his café lunch at the Anatole. With all the foreign journalists at the American Airlines Center attending the convention, he wasn't afraid of being recognized by anyone at the hotel. Besides, he wanted to establish himself as actually staying in the room. Once he became difficult to locate, the *did he even reside in the hotel* question was bound to come up. He headed to the front desk, keeping a wary eye on people around him, with the idea of exchanging some larger bills.

At first, the man standing at the counter ten feet away wearing the short-sleeve shirt and dress slacks did not jump out as noteworthy. But then Sayed overheard his request to see the manager. The guy was older with a potbelly and salt and pepper hair, combed straight back. He turned slightly as he thumbed through a copy of *D Magazine* he had pulled off the counter. A badge and gun hung on his belt.

A fellow in a business suit approached. "I'm Jerry Kiel. How can I help you?"

The waiting customer spoke, "Mr. Kiel, I'm Detective Howard, Dallas Police Homicide. Could I have a word, please?"

When the man said police, Sayed turned his face in the opposite direction. The hotel manager ushered the guy behind the counter and into an office. Sayed collected his money and hurried to his room. If the police were here regarding a homicide, there could be only one reason— Peters. Sayed grimaced. How did they connect him to the hotel so soon? This meant that in the future, leaving his room would be too dangerous. Damn his luck, why did Allah keep putting these challenges in his path?

———

Howard waited until the hotel manager closed his office door before speaking. "Mr. Kiel, I'm investigating the homicide of one of your guests—Reginald Peters. He worked for a newspaper in London, and I need a list of all the foreign journalists registered here. Need to ask them a few questions about their connection with the murdered man."

Kiel's mouth dropped open and he took a step back. "My God. Was that the murder I read about the other day?"

Howard nodded. "Yes, sir. He was a guest here."

"I see, well, I can have the front desk manager provide that," Kiel said. "I trust you won't disturb our guests' stay or intrude on their privacy. I'd rather this not become common knowledge."

"No, sir, that's not my intention." Howard flashed his most disarming smile. "Just a couple of questions. That's all, I promise."

"Very well, I'll get the room list."

"I'll also need to interview a few of your staff and peek inside the dead man's room."

"Certainly, I'll get a key for you."

Ten minutes later, Howard walked through the door of Peters' room. Housekeeping had already cleaned it—bed made, and fresh towels neatly arranged on the racks. Howard examined all the deceased's clothes and luggage. He found what he wanted on the bathroom counter.

He almost missed it. It lay under a tube of toothpaste, a small white slip of paper from a hotel notepad.

Tower entrance—ten o'clock.

The ME's report estimated Peters' time of death occurred between 10:00 PM and 12:00 AM.

Clues don't get any better than this.

He folded the paper and slipped it into his pocket.

Howard strolled to the Tower entrance and glanced out the front doors. Heat waves shimmered off the parking lot. Temperature was over a hundred again. Two young valets stood under the green awning. Howard readied himself for the blast of hot air and pushed the doors open, approaching the two men.

"Afternoon, gents. Can you help me out?"

The men looked in their early twenties and both were very tall and skinny, wearing dark dress slacks and white, short-sleeve shirts. Sweat poured from them, despite the large box fan moving super-heated air their way. *What a crummy job.*

"Yes sir," the closest said.

Howard displayed his badge and evoked the name of the general manager. "Wonder if either of you recalls seeing this man last night?" He showed them a copy of the identification photo recovered from Peters' body.

They examined it as Howard wiped the first drops of sweat from his neck. "Another hot one, huh?"

"Sure is," one answered, taking a long swallow of water as he studied the photo. After a moment he looked up at the other valet. "Hey, ain't this the guy we saw last night? The one who you said looked like your uncle?"

"Yeah, the guy who met the car, I remember," the second one agreed.

Howard's pulse quickened. "You saw this guy last night?"

"Yes, sir, he came down just before we got off."

"Got picked up by another man," the second one said.

Howard had the scent. "Did the other guy have a car?"

"Yeah, a light-colored four-door. Isn't that right?" he turned to the first valet.

"Best I can recall. Got the impression he was also a guest here. Looked like he'd pulled around from the garage."

Howard scratched his chin and wiped a bead of sweat forming on his nose. "Make, model, license plate number?"

The one beside Howard said, "I don't know, do you?" looking at his partner.

The other shrugged. "Don't recall."

"The guy driving, what did he look like?" Howard had his pen out ready to write.

"I didn't see him that well—Trey went up to the car."

Howard gazed at the other valet. "What about it, Trey? Get a look at the driver?"

"No, not a good one. He sat in the car and just stuck his head out and waved me off. Said he was waiting for someone."

"Think you'd recognize him, again?"

"Not sure. It was pretty dark."

Howard stared at the young fellow. "Okay, I'll settle for just a description."

Five minutes later, Howard sat in the Tower lobby cooling off and started making phone calls from the list the manager provided. He saw no use in getting into rush hour traffic, so he called all forty-four names. Most were not in, so he left messages. But he was able to contact over a dozen and conduct face-to-face interviews in their rooms.

The first part of the interview was most important. Howard wanted to find someone who could identify the driver of the car that picked up Peters. From the valet's description, he was a white guy, in his fifties with a short, well-trimmed beard who spoke with a foreign accent. No amount of questioning could help the valet recall what kind of accent. He just knew it sounded foreign. Howard had checked, but there was no video of the car from the outside cameras, so no license plate number to check. A few journalists recalled several people fitting the general description but could provide no names.

The second part of each interview went the same. "Have you seen this man?" Howard asked as he displayed the photo of Peters. "Have you seen him in the company of anyone else? Do you know anything about his murder?"

A few remembered seeing him earlier in the bar and restaurant, but he dined alone. No one recalled him meeting anyone.

Howard checked his watch, 6:05 PM. Another long day. He called it quits, phoning his wife to tell her he was on the way home. With the discovery of the note in the bathroom and getting the suspect's description, he had taken a big bite out of this case.

Howard thought briefly about sharing the new information with the Secret Service, but after a few seconds, discounted the idea. There was a lot more of them than him. They could figure it out on their own. Besides, he intended to solve the case and drop it in their laps with a big, fat bow on top. That would show them who the top homicide detective in this town was.

———

Sayed sat in his dark room and listened to Howard's phone message over and over. Did he suspect him, or was he just leaving the same message for all the journalists? It troubled Sayed the rest of the night.

THIRTY-TWO

Following Roberts' instructions, the next morning as each member of the foreign press corps exited the bus at the American Airlines Center, a member of the Secret Service Protective Intelligence Squad met them. They were asked the same questions Howard asked the day before. Several told the agents the police had questioned them the previous evening. All appeared concerned about the murder of one of their colleagues.

Roberts called Howard an hour later. He didn't sound interested in talking. Roberts pointed out that they were doing the same job and suggested they join forces. Howard showed only modest interest in partnering up.

When Roberts marched into Dick's office that Tuesday morning, Dick was reading a report marked *TOP SECRET*. He laid it aside.

"Ace, according to this," Dick nodded at the report, "the super-secret CIA asset described Sayed's bomb as some sort of new, hyped-up explosive. Sounds like a crock to me." Dick reared back and laced his hands behind his head. "Almost every explosive Ordinance Disposal type in the armed forces is showing up here today. With the room shortage, they're be billeted in National Guard and Army

Reserve facilities around town. Guess the Joint Reserve Base will get the bulk of 'em."

"You think sending extra explosive experts will do any good?" Roberts asked.

Dick kicked back a little farther and rested his feet on the desk. "Hell no, but it makes somebody feel better. Brains, not brawn, are the answer." Dick pointed an assertive finger toward Roberts. "How are the interviews going?"

"We've almost finished. Still have a few left."

"Any luck?"

"Not much. Detective Howard's also conducting interviews of the same people."

"He come up with anything?"

"Says not. I just spoke to him, but…" Roberts lowered his head and searched for the exact words.

"What's wrong, Ace?"

Roberts stared at Dick. "Detective Howard isn't playing nice."

Dick sat up. "What?"

Roberts shrugged. "I can't figure it out. He seems standoffish and doesn't want to cooperate with us. Think he understands the seriousness of this?"

"I could make a call to the PD—see if I could shake things loose."

"Don't do that, Dick. All I got is a gut feeling. No use screwing up our good relations with the whole department over one detective."

Dick eyed him. "We're talking about the protection of the president. Don't let a cop compromise our mission—screw him."

"Don't worry, I won't. Think I'll swing by the Anatole and do a little snooping."

"Good idea." Dick exhaled and ran a hand down his face. "Don't forget the agent briefing at two o'clock."

At precisely ten o'clock, Roberts walked through the front door of the Anatole and almost bumped into Thurman Howard. He was busy writing something in his notebook when Roberts approached. "Morning, Detective Howard."

At the mention of his name, Howard spun around, his eyes meeting Roberts'.

"Hi."

"Thought I'd come over and see if you needed a hand with anything."

Howard stared at him a few seconds before he spoke. "Still have a few interviews left."

"Yeah, me too." The awkwardness of the meeting hung thick in the air. "You do realize the president arrives tomorrow? We need to knock this out."

Howard only nodded before turning and walking away.

Roberts reviewed his list while walking through the lobby. *What was Howard's problem?*

Roberts headed to the front desk. The Protective Intelligence Squad had interviewed all the journalists except four. He checked with the receptionist and discovered the reporter from India had had a family emergency and returned home. That left just three that needed interviewing: the Brazilian, Francisco Lago; the Frenchmen, Rene Bertrand; and the Saudi, Hamaza Asfour.

Roberts took the elevator up and knocked on the Brazilian's door. When he got no answer, he called the room's phone number, but only got a voice recording. Roberts left a voice message to contact the Secret Service Field Office. Roberts also called the Saudi's room, again no answer. He left another message. Then he called the Frenchman's room, no response. Roberts left a third message. *Better go ahead and knock on the other two doors while I'm here.* But before he could, a call beeped in—*Dick.*

"Ace, get back to the office. We've got a change of plans."

———

Sayed had just gotten out of the shower when his phone rang. He wrapped the towel around him and approached the phone and listened to Roberts' message. Five minutes later, someone knocked on his room door. Sayed stared out the peephole. The policeman he'd seen the day before waited outside in the hall. The detective had left a message the previous evening, but not attempted a personal interview until now. This meddlesome cop could undo all his plans. Sayed had seen the news broadcast the night before about the English reporter killed in Dallas. This policeman would keep trying until he interviewed Sayed. That wasn't a chance he could afford to take.

THIRTY-THREE

Dick relaxed back in his office chair. "The president's coming in early."

"How much early?" Roberts asked.

"Two hours. This'll screw up the schedule. Good thing we found out before the briefing. You need to make all the notifications regarding the early arrival. By the way, do any good at the Anatole?"

"One checked out and returned home—some emergency, but the other three journalists weren't in."

"Okay. Also, coordinate with the squad about contacting you if they conduct any suspect interviews during the visit? I want you in the loop on everything happening at any POTUS venue."

"I'll take care of it. Anything else?"

Dick's expression darkened, and he studied Roberts for a moment. "Ace, anything you need, just ask. Both our asses are on the line this time. Since we got the director's backing, that means *his* ass is on the line. We'll work our angle and let the rest of the guys do their thing. But don't take any chances or assume anything. There's a whole team waiting to chop us off at the knees if we screw this up. Class III threats like this don't happen very often."

A nervous growl erupted from Roberts' stomach. "I know."

"We'll be under the microscope every minute."

"I know."

An hour later, Roberts had made the notifications, briefed the PI Squad, and gulped down a sandwich. He strolled into the agent briefing just before it got started. The conference room hummed with activity. The tables had been removed, and extra chairs brought in, but the place still overflowed. The smell of coffee hung heavy in the air as agents lined up to get a cup. With all the seats taken, dozens of agents stood in every corner leaning on walls and windowsills waiting for the meeting to start.

Roberts greeted some old friends and avoided the likes of the SAIC and Tortorziie. Events like this always turned out to be huge home-comings, with agents from all over the country getting reacquainted. Just before the meeting began, Bridget strolled up and stood beside Roberts. They exchanged quick smiles. It took the Presidential Protective Division lead advance agent a while to call order so he could speak.

"Would everyone please take their seats?" the lead advance asked for the second time.

Roberts listened while the agent went over every day, every time, and every venue POTUS would attend while in Dallas. Roberts, Susan, and Abbey would be at each one. Finally, after a half hour, they got to the intelligence situation report.

Tortorziie was introduced and began the briefing. He discussed the planned demonstrations and went over the designated demonstration areas at each site. He briefed on the number of protective intelligence teams working each venue and what radio channel they would moni-tor. Then he addressed the most critical subject.

"Ladies and gentlemen, what I'm about to tell you is classified Top Secret. The media hasn't picked up on it yet and that's the way we want it. We believe there is a non-confined Class III in district, prob-ably in the city. This individual traveled here for the express purpose of assassinating the president—possibly with an explosive device."

A wave of whispers passed through the crowd. Agent's furrowed brows and focused eyes stayed on Tortorziie, waiting for him to explain.

Tortorziie again spoke, "We have two photos of the suspect. One is many years old, and the other shows him in disguise. His name is Hashem Abdul-Sattar aL-Sayed, and his descriptive data is included on the briefing sheets being passed out. Agents at magnetometer checkpoints—you'll have an EOD team and bomb dog at all your locations. As far as the rest of you, there are three to four times more EOD teams working this visit, so call if you need one. If the Class III is encountered, he'll most likely have the device with him.

"Every PI team will have an embedded EOD element and dog. If you see something suspicious, call a team. Do not, I repeat, do not leave your post in an attempt to deal with a suspect. It's possible he has confederates working with him and may try a distraction to slip in. And last, but certainly not least, just before this meeting I was handed a non-confirmed intelligence report that the subject might attempt to deliver the explosive package using some sort of drone aircraft. Again, this is not substantiated. I'll attempt to run down the source and get back to you with any other developments."

Roberts had wondered if Tortorziie would include Abbey in the official intelligence briefing. He didn't, but his hateful stare shifted to Roberts.

Two new agents from the Dallas office glanced at each other. Each had a *this shit is real* expression.

Tortorziie looked over at the lead advance agent and said, "That's all I have, Tony," and sat down.

The room fell silent. No agent in the history of the Secret Service had ever heard what this group just did. Someone would try and kill the president right under their noses. That meant that one or more agents would probably die attempting to shield him. Everyone looked at the agents around them. No one had to tell Roberts what they were thinking.

Roberts meandered back to his office and called Bishop. "Hey, you busy?"

"Nope, what'cha need?"

"Swing by the Anatole and try and locate the last three journalists. I went there earlier, but they weren't in. The French guy's in the Tower and the other two are staying in the main hotel. We need to know if they have any information about who the murdered guy was last seen with and a description of the person if possible."

"Is it really that important this late in the game?"

"Could be. I just want them resolved before POTUS arrives. I need to stick around here and get the squad ready for the arrival. I'm emailing you their names and room numbers."

"No problem, I'll take care of it," Bishop said.

It bothered Roberts that he'd just lied to Bishop. He had nothing else to do with the squad, but he needed to think. He didn't want the distraction of running all over Dallas looking for witnesses who probably couldn't tell him a damn thing.

Roberts closed the door to his office. Needed total quiet—a silent place to concentrate and review all the briefing material from the meeting. He'd search for the point or location in POTUS's schedule that Sayed might exploit. At what place was POTUS most vulnerable? There wasn't any—the thing was airtight. All the security arrangements had been checked and double-checked. All the attendees at the convention had been vetted and vouched for. How could Sayed expect to succeed?

There's something they'd missed—something big.

Roberts played this mental exercise for almost two hours before his phone rang.

"I have good news and bad news," Bishop said.

"Okay."

"I found the guy from Brazil and interviewed him. He didn't know anything. Never even saw the English guy."

"Is that the bad news?" Roberts asked.

"No, the bad news is I couldn't locate the other two. The one from France and the Saudi. Checked at the front desk, and they told me the French guy, Bertrand, called down requesting privacy. Said he got food poisoning. Asked to discontinue maid service until further notice so he could rest. Knocked on his door—no answer. Left him a message to call you at the office."

"Maybe the food poisoning is why he wasn't answering the door or phone when I tried," Roberts said.

"Could be."

More likely he was sleeping off a late-night drunk. Roberts had seen many reporters get into the party-hard mood on the company expense account at political events. "What about the Saudi?"

"Left him a message also," Bishop said. "Guess you're with POTUS the rest of the week."

"Yup, me, Susan and Abbey."

"I'll be circulating around the venues. Hey, Michael."

"Yeah."

"You're plan's solid. It'll work. I'll see you later," Bishop said before hanging up.

Roberts sat back and grinned. There was nothing anyone could have said which would have given him more confidence.

Roberts called Susan and confirmed the plans for picking her and Abbey up the next day. She hinted he was welcome to stop by for a while if he had time, but he lied and told her he had to work late.

After everyone in the office departed for the day, he sat alone with his thoughts. He stared out the window as the sun dipped below the horizon. He wasn't hungry, he wasn't tired, and he wasn't anxious. He was curious. Sayed knew something they didn't. If Roberts could just have a little more time, he might figure it out.

THIRTY-FOUR

As he walked down the hall past the row of doors in the tower at the Anatole Hotel, only one thing troubled Suleiman—his partner, Zuhair.

Zuhair was not a bad operative. He was inexperienced though—nine years Suleiman's junior—and like most Americans, had lots of bad habits. Sharing a room with him this last week had been a nightmare. Often, he refused morning prayers, claiming he did not feel well. Those stupid video games he played half the night kept Suleiman awake. He lectured Zuhair about staying faithful to the Prophet, and Allah, but the guy didn't want to listen. Suleiman counted himself lucky he lived across the country from Zuhair. Working with him daily would be horrible.

They approached the door and Suleiman knocked twice. After a brief wait, he knocked five more times. Suleiman looked behind him at Zuhair, noting how he scanned the empty hall with short, jerky movements. This guy was drawing more attention to them than he was worth.

The door opened and they hurried inside the almost dark room. They had received specific orders: Do not make personal contact or go near the hotel unless summoned. Suleiman could not fathom what the urgency was for a second meeting—and at the controller's hotel to boot.

Sayed had dark rings under his sunken eyes. He flashed them a morose stare.

"Another situation has developed." Sayed related to them that a detective was snooping around, investigating the Englishman's murder. "I believe they also want to interview me."

"How did they connect you to his death?" Zuhair asked.

"Fool! How should I know? Someone may have already told them something that would implicate me. Besides, my cover story will not hold up under hard police interrogation."

"Then you should change hotels," Suleiman offered.

Sayed walked away, looking at the floor, rubbing the back of his neck. "For reasons I cannot discuss, I must remain here, but this policeman cannot be allowed to find me. You need to take care of him. Keep him away from me."

Suleiman stuck his hands in his pockets and shrugged. "Killing him might create more problems than it would solve."

"Then do not kill him. Just put him out of commission."

"He will have a gun. Might be forced to kill him. I do not know if we could stage an accident if he is armed," Suleiman said.

Sayed caught his eye and snapped. "I do not care how it is done—just do it."

———

Howard relaxed in the lobby, plowing through the last few journalists on the list. He only had five left. "I wonder how many the feds have done?" he mumbled before dialing another number.

Howard would never ask a fed for anything, even if it meant taking twice as long to accomplish the same task. His stubborn streak kept him independent of them, and that's the way he liked it.

———

Suleiman and Zuhair circled the lobby and scrutinized Howard on the couch. They strolled into a corner of the Tower Lobby.

"I think that is him on the sofa," Suleiman whispered. The guy fit the description, but Suleiman wanted to make sure. No sense killing the wrong guy.

"He's old for a policeman. Not as big a problem as we thought," Zuhair said, nodding at Howard talking on his cell.

Suleiman eyed the detective. "We will keep watch. See what he is up to. Our best chance is after he leaves here."

"Right." Zuhair took a seat in a nearby chair.

Suleiman joined him. "When he leaves, we will follow and determine where he is going. If he goes back to the police department, we will let him go, but if he goes anywhere else, an opportunity might present itself."

Howard disconnected from the call and finished writing in the notebook. He checked his watch and got up.

"Stay here," Suleiman said, "I will follow him. If he gets away from me, I will call you."

Zuhair nodded.

Howard walked the length of the hotel toward a bank of elevators. In the main lobby, Suleiman strolled past as the detective pressed the up button. He let Howard enter the elevator while he waited in the lobby.

Ten minutes later the elevator returned and Howard marched out. Suleiman trailed at a discreet distance as the detective ambled back toward the Tower. Something about the way the guy walked told Suleiman he was probably on his way out.

Suleiman slid his cell from his pocket and dialed Zuhair's number. "Get in the car and wait for me. Looks like he may leave at any time."

Howard walked out the Tower entrance and got into his car. Zuhair barely had time to pick up Suleiman and fall in behind. Zuhair drove a little too fast through the hotel parking lot, trying to catch Howard before he got out of sight.

"Slow down," Suleiman said, "You will draw attention."

———

The heat had lessened as twilight settled on the city, falling to ninety-eight with a heat index around a hundred and five. Howard took a look at the traffic on Stemmons Freeway, trying to decide if he would dive into that mess or take the back way home. The furtive action of the vehicle in his rearview mirror caught his attention. Howard glanced back a second time while exiting the parking lot onto the side street.

Closing the distance behind him was a late-model, dark Ford. The setting sun blocked Howard's view, turning the two people in the front seat into silhouettes. Probably just his imagination. He changed lanes and slowed, giving the vehicle a chance to pass. It changed lanes, staying a few cars back, out of his direct vision. Howard changed lanes again and accelerated well over the limit. The Ford did the same, hanging back several car lengths.

Well, I'll be damned. Those two Secret Service boys want to play the same game the DEA Agent did years earlier. This should be fun.

Howard made a few right turns then a few left turns just to play with them a little while considering his options. When he realized exactly where he was, the perfect plan became apparent. When he confronted them to eat their asses out, he wanted to be on familiar ground.

He stopped at the red light with the dark Ford still two cars behind. When the light turned green, he gassed it, changed lanes, and ripped down the street. He couldn't keep from laughing as he glanced in the rearview mirror at the Ford darting through traffic trying to keep up.

The alley he'd been searching for appeared just ahead. He took a right into it, parked, and jumped out, leaving his car running. Just before the dark Ford arrived, Howard swung behind a smelly dumpster. He kept his eyes on the street. As the Ford raced past the alley's entrance, the man in the passenger seat pointed at Howard's parked car and turned to the driver. The sound of brakes locking up filled the alley as their vehicle stopped just out of view.

––––––––

Zuhair backed up and swung into the alley before putting the vehicle into park. He twisted his head toward the detective's car by the dumpster as Suleiman pulled his pistol. "What's he doing?" Zuhair asked.

"He is playing with us, trying to lose us." Suleiman snorted. He jumped out of the car, keeping his pistol out of sight near his leg, and walked down the alley.

Zuhair ran behind him. "Do you know where we are?"

"Of course, I know." He hurried his pace while Zuhair followed.

"What if he called for help?"

Suleiman spun around. He was tired of his partner's stupid questions—time to act! "Then we will kill them, too. Now, let's go!"

———

Howard heard someone yelling from the entrance to the alley but couldn't understand any of the words. Sounded Arabic. As the pair crept toward his car, Howard peeked around the dumpster and understood his error in leading them there.

They weren't the Secret Service agents.

He thought it would be funny to surprise them here, in the alley where Peters had been killed. Who were these guys, and why were they after him?

Dusk closed in as the pair neared his car—guns drawn. Howard released a slow breath and pressed closer to the dumpster. He wiped the sweat from his eyes and unsnapped his holster. Too late to call for help now. It didn't make a hell of a lot of difference who they were—they aimed to kill him. Howard didn't panic. He was a Texas lawman. And in the best tradition of Texas lawmen, he drew the .45 and waited.

Keeping out of sight behind the dumpster, he held his breath as they approach his car. He didn't like the odds, but he had surprise on his side. If only he had that extra magazine of .45 rounds he kept in the glove box. He'd just have to make all his shots count. He braced himself against the dumpster and leveled the pistol toward them.

———

Rene Bertrand checked his watch. It was early Wednesday morning; by Friday the convention would conclude, and he might be of no further use to his captors.

His nightly spying had paid off bigger dividends than he had expected. He understood their ways now. He knew them, their personalities and habits. After a shaky start, he played the part of the subdued and submissive prisoner, never arguing, always doing what they asked. His act finally lulled them into dropping their guard, and their initial military-like bearing now gave way to a relaxed malaise. He had even figured out the lock on his bedroom door. The nail file in his shaving kit worked well. They had not bothered taking it, so he practiced for hours each night, unlocking and then relocking his door while they slept. It took less than twenty seconds.

Only the commander, the short husky one with the full beard, still adhered to the old rules. He came in around mid-morning and stayed for a few hours. The rest of the time, the others did as they pleased. The night shift was the worst, or best, for his purposes. They slept—all of them. One in the other bedroom, one on a sofa in the living area, and the last, outside, probably in a car. The guard currently outside, the young skinny one, always strolled through the door each morning rubbing sleep from his eyes.

Rain had fallen most of the night, and the pitter-patter still on the roof confirmed it wasn't over yet. The soothing sound of rain on the car would have the outside guard in a deep slumber by now. But how would Bertrand know for sure? He cracked his bedroom door open and listened. The sound of soft snoring greeted him when he peered into the living area. Only a table lamp lit the room. He crept barefoot across the floor and peeked out the front window—nothing but darkness.

Bertrand glanced at the sleeping guard on the sofa before flicking off the outside door light. He tiptoed back to his room, closed and locked the door, and got beneath the covers. He waited five minutes— nothing. If the one outside were awake, he would check on the light turning off—would he not? Bertrand waited another five minutes and then got up to peek out his door. The one on the sofa had not moved. Bertrand slipped on his shoes and fixed the pillows the way he had practiced to give the impression he was fast asleep under the blankets.

Bertrand crept to the front door and inched it opened, its faint squeak seeming so loud in the dark, quiet room. The guard on the sofa grunted and rolled over, facing Bertrand, his eyes still closed. The sound and scent of rain floated into the room through the half-opened door as Bertrand froze—did not even breathe.

Should he chance closing the door? Would it wake the guy up?

Bertrand scanned the area. Perhaps he should grab something heavy and crush the guy's skull. The guard mumbled a few soft words in his sleep and rolled back over to face the sofa cushion.

Bertrand took a deep breath, eased the door fully open, and slipped onto the dark porch, softly closing the door behind him. He squatted and let his eyes adjust to the darkness. With his night vision intact, he tiptoed across the covered porch, avoiding a large planter and sack of firewood lying against the wall. He stopped at the top of the stairs leading down to the courtyard. Rain poured off the roof and splattered on the top step, soaking his shoes. Holding out his hand, he collected some. He drank the cool water—it never tasted so sweet.

The Toyota SUV, with the sleeping guard inside, was parked in the corner of the courtyard. Holding the guardrail, Bertrand took the stairs one step at a time. A light on an electric pole illuminated the outside, but Bertrand remained in the shadows as he descended the stairs. The drops of rain reminded him of tiny falling stars as they streaked past the light. His objective, the front gate, was dead ahead.

Bertrand stepped off the last stair and his feet gave way in the slippery mud. The fall scared him, but he released a quiet chuckle. *He had escaped.* Pulling himself off the wet ground, he worked his way to the gate and reached for the latch but stopped with his fingers an inch away. It might be alarmed. He moved back into the shadow of a large hedge and studied the gate through the rain—no wires. Possibly wireless, but why would they bother? Taking a chance, he again ventured forward and lifted the latch. As it released, it made a shallow click. He slipped outside and took one last glance at his former prison before closing the gate.

Bertrand scanned the vacant coastal highway toward Algiers. There was little traffic on the road this late. A drainage ditch ran parallel with the highway, separating it from the sometimes-high tides of the Mediterranean. This could hide him from any search traffic coming from the villa.

Bertrand wiped rain from his face and oriented himself before heading east. A risky plan, but when they found him missing, the search would probably concentrate west toward Algiers. If he traveled east, he reasoned, he could catch a west-bound ride, and possibly avoid the most intense search area while still on foot. The most important thing right now was getting as far away from this place as possible.

Ankle-deep water rushed down the ditch when Bertrand lowered himself into the stream. Floating debris brushed his legs as he carefully moved along the ditch. He would follow it and put as much distance between him and the villa as he could before first light. Because of the rain, dawn would come later, which meant the idiots back at the villa would probably just sleep longer.

Bertrand took one careful step at a time. He could not afford to fall and injure himself tonight. Freedom, how he had taken it for granted all these years. The lyrics to an American song ran through his mind while he struggled through the watery, dark ditch. Something about freedom and having nothing to lose. He did not recall the singer, but repeated the words over and over while making his escape.

———

The two men with guns stopped short of Howard's vehicle in the alley, one on each side. It had gotten just dark enough that they appeared as shadows against the fading western sky. No streetlights shined into the dark alley, so Howard figured they couldn't see inside his car. He was no more than twenty feet from the farthest guy. In training, he'd made shots twice that far with deadly accuracy. He also figured two stationary targets were better than two moving targets, so he made his move.

Howard took aim at the one farthest from him, thanking God for his pistol's night sights. He drew in a deep breath and let half out before starting his trigger pull. He gave no warning before he fired.

The impact of the first big .45 round hitting the man in the lower chest spun him around, and he dropped to his knees. Howard fired again and the guy's head snapped back from the impact. Howard fired several more times, and the second man screamed before he, too, hit the pavement. The guy's arm, with gun still in hand, stretched in Howard's direction.

With both suspects hit, Howard moved from one side of the dumpster to the other, remaining in the shadows to watch the two. Couldn't tell how bad they were hurt. Finally, he pulled out his cell phone and called for an ambulance and police backup. Were they alone? Were there others lurking just down the street, ready to finish the job? He stayed behind cover, scrutinizing the pair for several more minutes. Because of the darkness, he couldn't tell if they were even still alive.

The dumpster radiated heat from the hot afternoon, and sweat bathed Howard's face. He wiped his brow and eyes and rubbed his wet hands on his pants. A minute later the sounds of approaching sirens broke the stillness. *Shit.* He couldn't let another cop or EMT walk up on this mess before he checked out the suspects. With reinforcements around the corner, Howard kept his pistol trained on the one still holding the gun and broke cover.

———

Suleiman's breath came in shallow gasps, the pain in his chest unbearable. Twice he had almost passed out, but he fought the darkness. He would not let it take him until he killed this man who had shot him. Suleiman had no doubt his injury was fatal. How ironic, sniped from the same dumpster he had hidden behind before dispatching the Englishman.

A peaceful bliss descended over him. By slaying this policeman, he would avenge himself and make his final contribution to the mission. The plan, whatever it was, would succeed. Allah be praised!

The distant whine of a siren grew closer as Suleiman waited. Soon an ambulance pulled up to the alley entrance, and the flashing red and blue lights backlit the old policeman approaching him. Suleiman waited for his chance. He moved his head a little to the right and stared down the sights of his pistol at the approaching man. Suleiman's finger tightened on the grip. He let the man get ten feet from him before swinging the pistol up and pulling the trigger.

The fellow grunted and staggered back.

As the darkness closed around Suleiman, his last vision was of the policeman falling toward the pavement.

————

Howard had been shot before—years ago in the leg. It hurt like hell, but he didn't lose his head then, and he didn't lose his head now. This time, felt like someone hit him in the chest with a hundred-mile-an-hour hard ball. Howard stumbled a couple times before losing his footing, beginning a backward tumble. Before he hit the ground, he put his remaining rounds into the guy who'd shot him.

Howard hit the concrete hard, slamming his head. He could hardly breathe and tasted blood. It didn't hurt much, but there was numbness on his left side. His mind clicked into high gear, and he rolled to his left. If he had a nasty chest wound, he didn't need blood pooling around his lung—better to let it bleed out.

THIRTY-FIVE

Wednesday morning began a little cooler than previous days in North Texas. The sky was overcast, and a light breeze made conditions bearable. But by nine o'clock, the breeze had stopped, the skies cleared, and the hot sun again bore down on the city. Roberts stared out Dick's window, waiting for him to finish the phone call. Bored, Roberts got up and strolled around the office, examining the treasures Dick had on display in the shelves and on the walls.

"Thirty-five years," Roberts whispered.

Dick hung up the phone. "You say something?"

"No, nothing." Roberts took a seat.

Dick leaned back and adjusted his cufflinks. "You got everything ready on your end?"

"Yes, we finished the last of the interviews except two, the French guy and the Saudi guy. Honestly, I have doubts either of them will be of much help. We've interviewed forty so far. Those guys are so focused on politics and partying, no one paid much attention to who Reggie Peters met that night."

Dick's eyes pinched. "So, what's going on with the French and Saudi guy?"

"They're not returning our calls or answering their door. We'll keep trying. Word is the Frenchman, Bertrand, got food poisoning. We'll get management involved and get a key if they don't call soon."

Dick's lip curled. "A Saudi, huh?"

The whole squad understood Dick's attitude toward the Saudis. He still held the belief they couldn't be trusted. It all started when he discovered that fifteen of the nineteen 9/11 al-Qaeda hijackers were Saudi Arabia citizens. This paranoia only deepened after the disappearance and mysterious death of the journalist Jamal Khashoggi, last seen entering the Saudi consulate in Istanbul.

"Concentrate on the Saudi first," Dick said. "After you pick him off, go after the frog."

Roberts nodded.

Dick changed the subject. "I've squared it with the detail for you, Miss Porter, and the girl to ride in the spare limo. That way you'll arrive with the motorcade and get ahead of POTUS at every venue."

"That's great. Thanks."

"Be at the airport at least an hour before wheels down and get checked through."

"Right, what about—" Roberts stopped mid-sentence and answered his ringing cell phone.

"Roberts, here."

Bishop's voice sounded strained. "You heard about the policeman shot last night?"

"I heard about a shooting, but they didn't release any names."

"Well, they've released it to the task force. It's Thurman Howard."

"What?" Roberts stood and met Dick's eyes.

Alarmed, Dick stood as well.

"Yeah, and he killed the two guys who shot him."

"What happened?"

"Don't know all the details, but the two guys appeared to be Middle Eastern."

"I don't like the sound of that."

"Me neither."

"Someone's got to talk to him."

"I'll do it. You have a date with the president," Bishop said.

"Thanks, let me know how it goes."

Roberts related what Bishop told him. With each word, Dick's expression darkened. He took a seat and remained silent, just tapping his finger on the desk, staring at Roberts.

"You understand this is no coincidence. There's a connection to the Peters' murder."

"Yeah," Roberts said, "I know. Bishop's on his way to the hospital."

THIRTY-SIX

To say Thurman Howard was the luckiest man in Dallas would have been an understatement. The fact he got shot in the lung with two trained medical personnel less than thirty yards away was only half the story. The closest hospital, one and a half miles north of where he fell, was Parkland. The Dallas County Hospital became famous during the assassination of President John Kennedy. Kennedy, Lee Harvey Oswald, and Jack Ruby all died there. Despite its grisly history, it remained the designated Level 1 trauma center for the visit of POTUS. If you were seriously injured in Dallas, that's where you wanted to go.

Bishop made a call and determined he could see Detective Howard for a few minutes if he came right now. Bishop stopped and steadied himself before walking through the hospital door—not his favorite place. He stepped into the lobby and took the elevator to Howard's floor. Bishop hated hospitals. In his mind, everyone did except the people who worked there. He especially hated military hospitals. He stopped, rechecked the room number on the piece of paper, and took a left down the long corridor.

The antiseptic smells, sounds, and overall feeling of the place caused a rush of memories. Bishop frowned, recalling the last time he was in a military hospital in Afghanistan. His mistake had cost a friend's life and almost gotten him killed, as well. When they hit the door of the al-Qaeda safe house that morning, he didn't have his head on straight. There was too much confusion right after the explosion, and Bishop just wasn't thinking as he searched for survivors.

He'd slowly advanced toward the man lying face down on the floor. Dude didn't move—looked dead. *Should have made sure.* Bishop kept his rifle on the guy as the sergeant moved in closer to roll him over. As Bishop approached a large column supporting an oversized arch, the insurgent rolled on his back. Bishop got a glimpse of the grenade in the man's hand before it blew, throwing Bishop back against a wall. If he hadn't been standing slightly behind the stone column, he'd have died. The last thing he'd remembered before blacking out was Sergeant Edwards calling his name. Edwards, also severely injured, died later that day. Sometimes after an especially stressful assignment Bishop would awake to a pained voice in the dark calling his name, *Bishop... Bishop... help me.*

Since then, Bishop had re-instituted the "double-tap rule." Combat troops in forward areas who regularly came into contact with insurgents knew it well. Enemy combatants who appeared only wounded could still kill you. The best policy in dealing with these fighters—take no chances. Two additional shots into the wounded man assured your safety. HQ never sanctioned it. They hated it—fewer prisoners to interrogate. Not something you mentioned around the Thanksgiving table with family, but a reality none the less.

Bishop strode up to the uniformed policeman standing in the hall and held up his military intelligence credentials. "I'm expected."

The officer examined the creds and nodded toward the door behind him.

Bishop put his hand on the handle and turned to the officer. "Is Sergeant Brown here yet?"

"He just went in, sir."

"Thanks." Bishop slipped into the room. A whiff of antiseptic attacked his nose. He held the door after entering and let it softly close. The lights were turned down, and when his eyes adjusted, the form of Sergeant Brown sitting in the corner came into view. He had been the supervisor who sat in on the meeting at the police department the day Roberts and Bishop met Howard. They shook hands, and Bishop motioned toward Howard in the bed.

"How's he doing?"

Brown glanced toward Howard. "He fades in and out, mostly out. They have him heavily medicated."

Bishop was careful about his next words. "I don't want to disturb him any more than necessary, but I need answers to some questions. His investigation into the murdered English reporter is probably what almost got him killed last night. I need to know why."

Brown glanced at Howard and slowly shook his head as he turned back to Bishop. "Don't know how much he can help in his condition. Besides being shot, he suffered a pretty good concussion when he fell. Doctor says he might have some short-term memory loss."

It was clear the sergeant didn't want Bishop there, but this was bigger than Thurman Howard. "Just one or two questions, please."

Sergeant Brown stared at Howard and his brow creased. He nodded. "One or two, that's all."

Bishop approached Howard. A clear, plastic tube wove up under the sheet into Howard's upper chest area and disappeared somewhere under the bed. Thing had streaks of blood. An IV hung from a rack near the bed connected to Howard's right arm. An oxygen hose fitted in his nostrils and wrapped around his head. The rhythm of the pulse and heart monitor beeped as Howard took regular breaths. The drawn shades and dimmed lights gave the place a surreal quality.

Howard was asleep, his eyelids twitching. Bishop bent low and, taking one last look at the sergeant, whispered into the wounded man's ear.

"Detective Howard, can you hear me?"

Howard grunted, his mouth moving, saying nothing. Bishop touched his arm and spoke louder.

"Howard, it's me, Troy Bishop. Do you remember?"

Howard's eyes fluttered open.

"I talked to you with Special Agent Roberts. We met a couple days ago. Remember? At the police department?"

"Roberts," Howard mumbled, and blinked his eyes.

"Yes, Roberts and I met you at the police station, remember?"

Howard blinked several more times and whispered, "I remember."

Bishop touched Howard's arm again, giving it a light reassuring squeeze. "Who shot you?"

Howard licked his lips and swallowed hard before he spoke. "Didn't know 'em."

"Why do you think they attacked you?" Brown asked.

Howard turned his gaze from Bishop to his sergeant. He closed his eyes a moment. Suddenly they flew open, as if he'd just figured out the answer. The sudden movement startled Bishop, and Sergeant Brown jerked his head back.

A thin smirk appeared on Howard's lips when he turned back to Bishop. "Too close," he said in a raspy voice.

"You're crowding him. Step back a little," Brown ordered with a wave of his hand.

Howard frowned, turning his head to meet the sergeant's gaze. "No, I got too close."

"Too close to what, Howard?" the sergeant asked.

A grin spread across Howard's lips as his eyes slowly drifted shut. "The truth," he slurred and again faded into another deep sleep.

It wasn't often that Bishop allowed himself to get surprised or excited. It was even less often he felt anxious about events, but what Howard said shook him. There had always been a missing piece to this puzzle. A piece that only Sayed knew, that Sayed controlled. Was that the truth Howard meant?

THIRTY-SEVEN

Bishop stepped back. Keeping his eyes on Howard, he moved to the other side of the bed beside Brown. "Any idea what he meant?"

Brown shrugged and shook his head. "Truth about what?"

"That's what we need to find out. The two Middle Eastern guys, do we know anything about them?"

"We got their property and car, but nothing jumps out as significant —except..." Brown stared at the floor.

Bishop moved closer. "Yes?"

"Except, I recall Howard saying something about a theory Dr. Fleming had concerning a dagger being used to kill the English guy."

"Go on."

"They found a long knife in the car, under the passenger seat."

"Was it a dagger? Where is it?" Bishop asked.

"I haven't seen it. It's in the police lab, I think, being dusted for prints."

"I'd like to see it."

"Sure, we'll take my car." Brown paused a second and laid a hand on Howard's arm before walking from the room.

Brown called on the way to the station and learned the knife and other items had been processed for prints and were back in the property room. Bishop read a copy of the Dallas police report on Howard's shooting while the evidence officer pulled the sealed plastic bags off the shelf. Bishop carefully examined each bag. Then he copied information from the assailant's driver's license and the vehicle identification number into his notebook. An analyst at the Terrorism Task Force could determine the history of these two within minutes.

"Have they taken prints of the dead guys?"

"No, not sure we need to," Brown replied. "We can get everything we need from their identification."

"If it's all the same, I'd like prints."

Brown gave a curious half smile. "Sure, we can do that."

Rummaging through the rest of the evidence, Bishop found it. A seven-inch long dagger. He inspected it while still in its plastic bag. "Is this it?"

Brown examined the knife. "Has to be. Heard we recovered some blood evidence off the hilt—it's being typed against the English guy's. Should know something later today or tomorrow. You ever seen anything like that?"

Bishop studied it a moment. It had a long, narrow, black handle and blade with a sharp point. Easy to puncture clothing and get right into flesh without much effort. "Oh, yeah. This is a replica of what the World War II British Commandos used. Very effective for close-in fighting." Seeing nothing more that interested him, Bishop asked, "Can we go to the morgue?"

Doctor Fleming wasn't in when they arrived, but an assistant escorted them to the autopsy room. If Bishop hated the smell of hospitals, he despised the smell of morgues. Something he couldn't quite describe—sort of a metallic, raw chicken, formaldehyde odor. The combat field morgues erected in the rear areas were their own horror show. No amount of combat could harden you to that. Bishop figured this trip might be a wasted effort, but if nothing else he could at last see the face of the enemy. That's the problem fighting insurgents. With their hit and run tactics you seldom got a good look at them, except when they were dead. Every time Bishop got a chance to see one, he took it—boosted his morale.

The attendant wheeled the two gurneys from the cold storage locker. Bishop, Sergeant Brown, and a Dallas police forensic officer waited while the pale green sheets were removed. Except for some scratches on the chin and right cheek, the one identified as Suleiman appeared uninjured. After the rest of the sheet slid off his naked body, the damage became apparent. Thurman Howard's Colt .45 had done its job well. Suleiman had the initial chest wound and several additional ones in the lower abdomen and pelvic area.

The guy called Zuhair was almost unrecognizable. Looked like his face had exploded. Brown grimaced at the sight. Only the picture from his driver's license could serve as positive photo identification.

Bishop let out a low whistle. "Howard nailed this one good."

The forensic officer spent the next half hour taking prints from the dead men. Bishop collected them, and the sergeant drove him back to his car.

———

At the Secret Service office, Roberts rose from his desk as Bridget O'Neal hiked past his door.

"Hey, Bridget," he called.

No doubt about it, she was the most beautiful female agent he'd ever seen. Irish blood ran deep in the five-foot-eight redhead. With her looks and figure, a professional modeling career wasn't out of the question, but she had a cop's personality. New to Protective Intelligence, she'd transferred from the Counterfeit Squad only a few months ago. Picked up the program fast and developed into a first-rate investigator.

Bridget leaned into his office. "Hi, Michael, what's up?"

"Can you help me out?"

"Sure."

She still had an interest. Roberts could see it from her expression. He and several squad members met for dinner a few months ago. She was also there. She'd gone home and changed first. Showed up in a tight black sweater and jeans, looking better than any woman in the place had a right to. In the crowded hall near the restrooms, bumping into each other could have led to a kiss. They both felt the same attraction but knew workplace romances were never good—especially in this job.

"I need a favor," he said. As her group leader, he could have made this an assignment, but only asked it as a favor. He handed her the piece of paper. "We didn't finish the interviews of the journalists. There's still a couple left. Can you try and knock them out?"

She glanced at the paper and folded it. "No problem. I'll do it right now."

"Interview the Saudi first. Dick has a special interest," Roberts said. "Knock out the French reporter after that. We've tried to catch them for the last few days, but haven't had any luck. Heard the French guy got food poisoning and may have sought medical treatment. In the hospital, for all I know. Try and find out what the deal is, get hotel management to at least do a welfare check on them."

She winked. "Consider it done."

Conducting the final two interviews was the last thing on Roberts' to-do list before the president arrived. It was now a moot point since it appeared Howard had killed the guys responsible for the English reporter's death. With the murder of Reggie Peters solved and the suspects deceased, Roberts could at last concentrate only on Sayed. Roberts put the matter of the last two reporters out of his mind. The president and vice president would arrive in a few hours. Things were about to get crazy.

———

Bridget O'Neal didn't get far before the overhead page summoned her. She reported to Joe Tortorziie's office as instructed.

Tortorziie laid the papers aside when she entered. "Agent O'Neal?"

"Yes, sir."

"I've got an assignment for you."

"An assignment?"

Tortorziie glanced down at his copy of the Protective Survey and Instructions to Agents document. "Yes, I understand you're the reserve PI agent for the visit."

"Yes, sir."

"I want you to do a few favors for me in your spare time—for the director, to be exact."

"What kind of favors?" This wasn't Bridget's first presidential visit. She'd been the reserve PI agent before. On that previous visit, the event brought out all the nuts, so she was the busiest one in the office. They called, made threats, and had to be interviewed. She'd worked half a day on a direct threat and ended up arresting the suspect. The man was still going through his 180-day psych evaluation in Missouri.

"Nothing much," Tortorziie said. He handed her a note pad from his desk. "Find a place that sells this wine and make sure a chilled bottle is in the director's hotel room before he arrives. Also, buy a couple of his favorite cigars and leave them with the wine. I think he smokes the Padron7000."

She stiffened. "Does the director expect this on every trip? This isn't my job."

Tortorziie's eyes narrowed. He stood and pointed his pen at her. "Agent, the director expects only good work from his people, as do I. This is something special we're doing for him, understand?"

"Sir, I have enough to do already. Agent Roberts just gave me an assignment at the Anatole—"

At the name of Roberts, Tortorziie's nostrils flared and he shook the pen in her direction. He shouted, "I'm the person responsible for the intelligence advance for this visit! Roberts doesn't have any authority."

Bridget accepted the list. *No point angering the little man.*

"Place this card beside the wine and cigars. Here's a fifty," Tortorziie said.

She left the office and stormed down the hall rolling her eyes and muttering under her breath, "Kiss ass."

THIRTY-EIGHT

R oberts drove too fast to Susan's. He should have left the office earlier, because she'd invited him for a light lunch before they went to the airport. On the way, he turned the plan over and over in his mind. Using Abbey most effectively remained the challenge. That and keeping Susan calm. If anything spooked her, the plan would unravel and leave him with nothing. To be honest, Roberts still had a few doubts about Susan. Her strange beliefs about her mother seeing her own mother's psychic shadow preyed on Roberts' mind more than it probably should. Wasn't normal.

Susan surprised him when she answered the door. Knowing her flair for the sexy and provocative, he'd suggested she wear a slightly more conservative outfit for the president's visit. The black business-cut skirt and cream-colored high-neck blouse looked great. With an outfit like that, she could pass for a presidential staffer—never a bad thing. He expected a lot of attention would be directed toward her and Abbey during the visit. The fact they'd displaced two other presidential staffers from the spare limo would engender questions and, no doubt, comments.

"You look fantastic," he said.

She blushed and fiddled with the string of pearls. "Glad you approve. Ready for lunch?"

"We don't have much time. Is Abbey ready? I wanted to talk to her before we leave."

"She's ready. We ate earlier. I put her down for a short nap."

Susan already had lunch set out on the table. "Help yourself."

They took their seats and Roberts gobbled his sandwich, a bad habit he'd gotten into from his years on protection. Working a protective detail only allowed someone five or ten minutes to eat a meal most days on duty. Since arriving in Dallas, he'd slowed down and now ate like a sane person, but the excitement of the visit made him default back to his old protection habits.

Susan gaped at him eating, drinking lemonade, and talking at the same time. Her amazed stare finally drew his attention. He put the uneaten portion of the food back on his plate and grinned. "Sorry."

Susan laughed and waved her hand. "It's fine." She took on a more serious expression. "Say, I watched a Netflix movie last night about the FBI's unit that tracks serial killers. In the movie it said the Bureau had conducted research, and that's how they profiled them."

Roberts nodded. "Yeah?"

"Well," Susan's eyes squinted, "why doesn't the Secret Service do something like that to profile presidential assassins?"

Roberts took another small nibble of his sandwich before saying, "We did."

"Huh?"

"Twenty years ago, we published the Exceptional Case Study. Examined eighty-three people who killed or attempted to kill public figures in the United States from the previous sixty years."

"Really?"

"Yeah." He smiled. "Know what they found?"

"What?"

"There is no stereotypical assassin. Too many variables."

"Oh." She frowned and looked down.

Roberts felt bad for crushing her great idea, so he cleared his throat and squeezed her hand. "It was a good thought though."

The shadow of a smile blossomed back on her lips.

"Time to get ready," he said. He grabbed the small black nylon bag he'd brought in and removed his suit jacket. He dug in the bag for the encrypted radio and attached wires for his earpiece and sleeve mic. After securing the radio to his belt, he readjusted the .357 semi-automatic on his right side. Then he checked the handcuffs that rested in the small of his back and glanced at the two extra magazines to the left of the belt buckle. "Ready," he said.

Susan sat back, crossed her arms, and grinned. "Better hope you don't fall in water over your head. With all that extra weight, you'll drown for sure." She stood and slung both arms around his neck. She smelled good—her perfumes always drove him crazy. Her warm body and soft beating heart pressed against his chest. They kissed. Probably the longest and wildest kiss they'd ever shared.

Susan whispered, "You finish up, and I'll get Abbey." She headed toward the back hall.

Roberts downed the last few bites of food and rechecked his equipment before slipping on his jacket. He wanted to cool things with Susan, but he couldn't help himself. Something kept pulling him back into her arms at every opportunity.

Susan led Abbey back into the living room. She was wide awake and giddy.

He squatted down. "Ready to go?"

"Will we see the president today?" she asked.

"You bet, just like in Houston."

The second he made the remark, he knew he'd screwed up. Abbey's expression soured.

"Well, not just like Houston," he said. "I'll be with you and your mom." He touched her arm. "You know I'm counting on you, right?"

She dropped her gaze to the floor and mumbled, "I guess."

"Abbey, if you see the man from Houston, don't be afraid. I won't let anything bad happen." Roberts raked a loose hair from her face.

She looked at him with a frightened expression, like the one she'd shown before. Her voice shook and she only spoke above a whisper. "What will you do if you see him, Michael?"

He glanced at Susan before turning back to Abbey. "Well, I'll just have to arrest him, that's all."

Abbey's eyes took on an unsettling stare—her voice low and threatening. "I don't think you'll be able to arrest him."

Roberts' heart skipped, but he maintained his composure. "Sure, I will. Just wait and see."

She put her small hand on his left cheek. Her palm felt cold and dead. "If you try, he'll kill you."

A sudden chill rushed over Roberts. He hadn't expected this. The last few days she'd acted like a regular kid. Her big eyes stayed fixed on him, never blinking—those old wisdom eyes he'd seen the first day he'd met her.

Abbey's voice rose with excitement. "If you see him, shoot him before he kills you."

Susan gasped and said, "Abbey! I can't believe what I'm hearing from you."

Abbey looked at her mother, her face ashen and her lips trembling. "I don't want him to get hurt."

"Come on. We'll be late." Susan grabbed Abbey's hand and shuffled toward the door.

The same sense of foreboding Roberts experienced on meeting Abbey invaded him again. A wave of anxious dread rushed through him. It was sickening and nauseous.

The drive to Love Field took less than twenty minutes. Abbey sat between Roberts and Susan while he again explained exactly what he wanted them to do.

Susan asked, "Will we get our picture taken with the president today?"

Roberts squirmed. "Dick's squared it with the staff, but not until later in the visit. He'll tell me, and I'll let you know."

Putting off having the photo with the president was Dick's idea. The way he calculated it, if they waited till the last day, Susan might think twice about backing out halfway through—a cold, deliberate attempt to manipulate her. Dick didn't do things like that often, but when the president's life hung in the balance, he could be a conniving son of a bitch. Roberts had mixed emotions about this. While he understood Dick's concerns, he knew Susan's heart. She wouldn't allow a petty thing like a photo with the president to put her child in danger.

Traffic started backing up when they neared the airport. Roberts took a right into one of the private air terminals. They stopped at the police checkpoint near the entrance. Roberts displayed his credentials and the officer waved them in.

Roberts said, "The vice president has already arrived."

"They don't travel together?" Susan asked.

"Nope," Roberts said. "When the president and vice president travel to the same location, most of the time they do so in separate planes. Protocol and security concerns dictate the vice president arrives first, if possible, and he greets the president upon his arrival."

Roberts called Dick on his cell and told him they'd just passed through the checkpoint. Dick directed them to the rear of the private terminal. The presidential motorcade had begun forming up. Heat rose in shimmering waves off the tarmac while they waited for Dick in the car. The temperature on the car's thermometer hung at a hundred and four.

Someone knocked on Roberts' window. He snapped his head around to find Bishop staring at him. The guy had a way of turning up at places and times Roberts didn't expect. Come to think of it, he also had ways of disappearing with no trace. Roberts rolled down the window a few inches. "Hop in the back and cool off."

"No thanks. Can we talk?" Bishop smiled and nodded a hello to Susan and Abbey.

Roberts followed him to the shade of a nearby building. A whiff of burnt aviation fuel drifted through the air.

"How did things go with Howard?" Roberts asked.

Bishop spent the next five minutes filling him in on what Howard told him and what he'd found out from the police department and morgue. "The dagger they found under the seat of the dead men's car is just like the one Howard described that probably killed the English journalist."

Roberts' mind raced. "So that confirms it. Those two guys killed the Limey, huh?"

Bishop wiped his face with his handkerchief. "Appears that way."

"No idea why?"

"None."

"But Sayed is connected, I'm guessing," Roberts whispered.

Bishop's lips flattened. "Yeah, that's the question. My vote is yes, most definitely."

Two airport employees strode past and stared at them.

Roberts lowered his voice. "Dick thinks the whole thing might be somehow connected with the press. He's requesting Washington reconfirm all the credentials for the foreign journalists."

Bishop stared across the blazing tarmac and squinted at the glare. "Makes sense."

Roberts changed the subject. "You know, you're a first-class investigator. If you ever decide you want out of this spy stuff, you'd make a great cop."

Bishop shook his head. "No thanks. Cops have too many rules."

"Hey, did you hear anything about Sayed using a drone to attack POTUS?"

Bishop grinned. "Yeah, it's a BS story. Don't worry about it."

Roberts mopped a line of sweat from his brow. "Let's get in the car. It's cooler. Dick's meeting us in a few minutes." Roberts turned toward his vehicle.

"If you think this is hot, try Afghanistan this time of year," Bishop said. "Got something to check before the arrival. See you later."

Before Roberts could answer, Bishop had disappeared around the corner. Roberts got back into the car just as the bomb dogs finished sweeping the motorcade vehicles. All cars were being swept for explosives, even the police escort cruisers.

"Can I pet the dog?" Abbey asked.

"They aren't those kinds of dogs," Susan said. She and Abbey had been watching the goings-on with fascination—not uncommon for those who'd never attended a presidential airport arrival. Dozens of police cars, black limos, and SUVs dotted the tarmac. The place overflowed with police, Secret Service, and staff. The well-wishers' area was roped-off and covered by a long rectangular tent—offering a little shade. Tubs of bottled water floating in melting ice had been placed at strategic locations under the tent.

Roberts put his hand on Abbey's shoulder and pointed at the greeters. "That's where you saw the president when you were in Houston. This time you'll ride in his motorcade."

For the first time that afternoon she smiled—it made his day.

THIRTY-NINE

"Morons, imbecilic, mongrel dogs," Sayed muttered. He shook his head and stared at the television in disbelief, watching the noon news from his hotel room. The press now reported the details of the Thurman Howard shooting. How could they have allowed the old policeman to kill them both?

With his only backups dead, Sayed's mind clicked into overdrive. His long-held plans to remain in his room must change. It was only a matter of time before the police might force entry, especially if they somehow connected him with the Englishman and policeman's attacks. This left him only one choice. Every second in the room placed him in greater jeopardy. Before leaving, he grabbed the small green backpack and made sure the DO NOT DISTURB sign was still on the outside of his door.

Departing from a side exit of the Anatole, Sayed caught the bus at the corner.

————

Roberts felt sorry for Dick, walking down the tarmac toward them. The front of his shirt was wet from sweat, and his face glowed a bright red.

He slid into the back seat, blew out a breath, and greeted Susan and Abbey.

"Well," Dick said, "number two's almost finished lunch. Number one's arriving in about twenty minutes. No need boarding the spare limo until there's a wheels down."

Roberts turned around and faced him. "Is the schedule still holding?"

"Yeah, he's going straight to the hotel," Dick said, "he'll have afternoon meetings, work on his acceptance speech, and have dinner in the suite with his staff." Dick paused, staring at Susan. "I must say, Ms. Porter, you've never looked lovelier." He showed the devil smile.

She beamed. "Why thank you. Aren't you a charmer?"

Roberts knew Dick. He'd be all over Susan if he didn't know about the thing she and Roberts had going on.

A small, warm hand touched Roberts'. Abbey stared up at him with that *child trying to be brave* expression. He squeezed her hand and winked. Her forced grin seemed pitiful, and he could only imagine what went on inside that little mind.

Even with all the security, Sayed still believed he could pull it off. Roberts' mind drifted to dark places. The thought that the chief executive's life might rest in the hands of this six-year-old wasn't a comforting one.

Dick sat up from his reclined position and spoke into the mic clipped on his left sleeve. "Security room, this is Crosby. Go ahead with your transmission."

Roberts couldn't hear the response as Dick operated on a different frequency designated for only the vice president.

Dick frowned. "That's clear—is a PI team en route? Okay, keep me informed."

Roberts asked, "What's happening?"

Dick didn't answer at first. His tongue licked his upper lip as he stared at the floorboard. "A post stander saw someone who resembles"—Dick paused, eyeing Susan and Abbey—"our suspect."

"Where?"

"Near post two."

Roberts thumbed through his site post assignment log and found post number two. It was the terminal's front entrance. He and Dick shared a concerned stare.

Susan fidgeted, shooting furtive glances at Dick then Roberts. After several seconds, she asked, "Do you two need to go somewhere?" Her hand had drifted across Abbey's lap and found Roberts'.

"No, that's the PI team's job," Roberts answered. "They'll let us know what's going on as soon as they can sort it out."

Several long minutes passed, and Abbey also laid her hand on Roberts'. It was cold. He was about to say something to comfort her when Dick spoke into his sleeve mic.

"Airport security room, this is Crosby. Go ahead." He listened, his eyes squinting.

Roberts caught a glimpse of Susan's expression. What's she thinking? He needed her calm and relaxed. Their whole strategy centered on Abbey being able to spot Sayed.

Dick spoke into the mic again. "Okay, thanks."

"Well?" Susan asked. The pent-up nervousness in her voice made it sound strange and foreign.

"It's nothing—some airport worker on his day off tried using his credentials to sneak in for a peek at the president. We've tossed him," Dick said.

Susan let out a slow breath and her shoulders relaxed. She attempted a smile but failed. Abbey slid her hand back into her lap.

Roberts needed to do something to break the tension—a distraction of some kind. "Well," he said, "it's about ten minutes before wheels down. Let's take a walk."

"Great idea," Susan said. She opened her door and dragged Abbey out by the arm.

Dick pulled himself from the back and said his goodbyes before heading toward the terminal.

"Let's walk past the greeter area," Roberts said. "I want Abbey to check them out." Roberts slipped on a pair of sunglasses.

The trio crossed the hot tarmac, Abbey's hand in his. They probably resembled the typical family strolling to within a few yards of the crowd of sweating well-wishers. The blazing sun was relentless. Several ladies' foundation had started sweating off and a few eyeliners weren't as crisp as they'd probably been earlier. Those foolish enough to wear a suit, or any kind of jacket, had them folded over their arms or slung by a finger over their backs.

Roberts bent down and whispered, "Abbey, do you see him?"

She shook her head. When he glanced up at Susan, she was twisting her head in all directions, wringing her hands. The next few days would be long and tiring—if she didn't relax and settle down, she'd become a nervous wreck.

The tempo increased the last few minutes before wheels down. Other than the official greeters and guest, only law enforcement personnel involved in the arrival now occupied the secured tarmac area. Drivers cranked their vehicles and started the air conditioners. The security room radio broadcast boomed through Roberts' earpiece.

"Air Force One's on final approach."

Searching the sky, Roberts could just make out the faint outline of the massive plane in the distance. He reexamined the arrival area. Everything looked tight. The Dallas Police escort motorcycles cranked and several took off to set up blocking positions on the road outside the airport.

Roberts touched Abbey's shoulder. "Look. Here he comes." He pointed and directed her attention at the plane growing larger by the second. She shielded her eyes and studied it.

He rested both hands on Abbey's tiny shoulders as Susan squinted and also shielded her eyes.

Like most Secret Service agents, Roberts would never admit this, but it still took his breath away seeing that beautiful plane land. Waiting on the tarmac when this symbol of America touched down inspired reverence in all who witnessed it. The huge, blue and white Boeing 747 had electronic countermeasures for jamming enemy radar and the ability to defend itself from missile attacks.

Several hundred yards across the airport, Air Force One's rear wheels sent up puffs of white smoke when they made contact with the runway and the engines reversed thrust as the plane slowed.

The airport security room broadcast a general announcement over the radio: "All posts, we have a wheels down, 1354 hours."

"What's that car doing?" Susan pointed at the black Suburban falling in behind the plane as it taxied toward the arrival area.

"That's CAT," Roberts answered.

She turned and gave him a blank look.

He cupped his hand to her ear and said, "C-A-T—Counter Assault Team. They protect the offside and rear of the plane while it's taxiing, loading, or unloading the president. If an unauthorized vehicle approaches, they interdict it."

The engine whine of Air Force One became loud enough that Susan had to yell over it. "I assume interdict means shoot."

Roberts only nodded. Out of the corner of his eye, he saw two Dallas Police cruisers depart—the bomb sweep unit and the scout car. They'd look for trouble or suspicious activity along the motorcade route. He searched the distance airspace. All air traffic ceased during the time Air Force One was landing or taking off. A lone helicopter hovered about a mile away—*Huntsman*. The scout chopper would precede the motorcade looking for possible trouble along the route.

As it approached them, Air Force One slowed its taxi to a crawl. One peculiarity of Air Force One pilots—they prided themselves on nailing the arrival, exactly. No matter the arrival time, regardless of headwinds or tailwinds, they adjusted the mission profile to accommodate it.

Arrival time for this flight was two o'clock, 1400 hours. By intentionally slowing their taxi, they'd make sure the wheels were blocked at precisely the right time. Meanwhile, everyone else melted in the sun, awaiting their official arrival. Roberts shifted from one foot to the other, allowing a bead of sweat to trickle down his butt crack on its way to his boxers. A quick smile cracked his lips—*Oh, yeah. This was special.*

A couple of minutes later, Roberts' earpiece crackled as the security room announced: "All posts, we have an arrival—1400 hours."

Uniformed Air Force personnel blocked the wheels, and agents scurried for position. Jet exhaust hung heavy in the air when the armored limo and follow-up from the vice president's motorcade slowly made their way planeside. The vice president emerged from the armored car and stood while the stairs rolled into place for Air Force One.

"Look, Abbey, the vice president," Susan said.

Roberts bent down and pointed him out. "He's been having lunch with some city and county bigwigs waiting for the president to arrive."

An Air Force officer ascended the stairs and locked the massive door in the opened position. The lead advance Secret Service agent jogged up the steps and disappeared inside the aircraft. Soon he and the special agent in charge of the president's detail emerged and surveyed the arrival area. Satisfied, they descended the stairs.

The president's motorcade eased planeside, parallel to the vice president's. The back of Air Force One was a beehive of activity. Staffers, traveling press, and additional agents poured out of the rear stairs and rushed toward their designated vehicles. The president would not exit until all the motorcade cars were loaded and ready to depart.

Dick trotted up behind Roberts. "Okay, you guys get in. I'm riding in the PI car." He flashed a devil smile. "Enjoy your trip."

That last comment confused Roberts. *What was that supposed to mean?* Roberts, Susan, and Abbey took their places in the plush interior of the black, armored spare limo. They sat on one side of a set of facing seats—both dark blue velour, with the presidential seal on each. This car, and the official presidential limo, were identical. Dick had told Roberts that one senior staffer and a Secret Service agent would join them.

The Director of the Secret Service, Hugh Carroll, made his way down Air Force One's steps and stood beside Roberts' vehicle.

Roberts tensed. *Crap, not the director.* If that wasn't bad enough, the president's chief of staff stepped around to the opposite door. Anytime you rode with guys like this, there was an opportunity for a grand screw up. One misplaced word spoken without thinking was all it took to sink a career. Having Susan and Abbey along only complicated the thing.

"Oh shit," Roberts whispered, "thanks a lot, Dick."

Susan turned. "Did you say something?"

The band struck up "Hail to the Chief," the red carpet rolled out, and the two uniformed Air Force personnel, flanking the stairs, rendered a salute. The president walked out of the plane to the top of the stairs with the first lady—all smiles and waves—and escorted her down the steps to greet the vice president. The visitors cheered, the Secret Service scurried to waiting armored vehicles, and Roberts tensed at the thought of the trip with the director and chief of staff. The president visited with the vice president and the official greeting party a moment. Lots of handshaking and smiles all around before strolling toward the armored limo, again waving at the crowd of well-wishers.

After the president entered his black Cadillac, Director Carroll and the chief of staff got into the spare with Roberts, Susan, and Abbey. Police sirens screamed as the motorcade rolled forward.

Roberts took the initiative. "Mr. Director, allow me to introduce Ms. Susan Porter and her daughter, Abbey. Ladies, this is Secret Service Director Hugh Carroll."

"Ms. Porter, I'm happy to meet you," Carroll said. "And you too, Abbey."

They both smiled. "My pleasure, Mr. Carroll," Susan answered.

Carroll nodded toward the man on his left. "This is the President's Chief of Staff Ronald Moore."

The small man in the navy-blue suit said nothing, but looked up from texting. He stared at Roberts and Susan—his mind probably working overtime. Looked like no one briefed him on who they were or why they traveled in such a coveted place.

Carroll must have noticed the chief of staff's expression, because he touched Moore on the sleeve in a very relaxed manner. "Ms. Porter and Abbey are assisting us on a little protective intelligence matter with this visit."

"Is that so?" The expression of doubt never left Moore's face.

"Yes, I understand they're a great help." Carroll crossed his legs and gave Susan a quick nod.

She blushed and stroked Abbey's hair. "Thank you for saying so, sir."

Carroll made small talk during the short trip to the Renaissance Hotel. Moore eyed Susan and Abbey while talking on his cell phone about the president's afternoon schedule.

Watching Susan and Abbey, Roberts was reminded that, for those who had never ridden in a presidential motorcade, the experience rated as something special. Their expressions and wide-eyed looks were typical. Usually, there was a lead police cruiser, one or more spare limos, primary limo, follow-up, PI car, CAT SUV, communications van, staff vehicles, ambulance, and two police cars guarding the rear. The full motorcade might be fifteen to thirty cars. The size and configuration always depended on the purpose of the visit and threat level. This was a large motorcade.

Abbey had her face against the window as police motorcycles with red and blue flashing lights and sirens blaring zipped past. She whispered, "Wow."

Susan gazed out the opposite window with the same awed expression.

The Secret Service referred to the presidential limo as "The Beast." The late-model Cadillac only had two original factory parts—the hood and trunk. The rest of the car had classified modifications to include carrying an electronic cooler in the trunk filled with the president's blood.

Abbey caught Robert's gaze and grinned. She and Susan both appeared more relaxed, which was good. Starting a visit relaxed was the key, because it only got crazier from here.

When the motorcade exited the freeway, the hotel came into view. The ellipse-shaped, thirty-story pink granite Renaissance had stood as a fixture in Dallas since the 1980s. Compared with the mammoth Anatole across the freeway, it was a small hotel but still an elegant place for POTUS to spend the next few days.

They made their way behind the building, and cars dropped out as they neared the back loading dock. Only the five-vehicle "secure package" made the final turn. The secure package consisted of the most important vehicles, including the spare limo.

A previously erected, massive white tent came into view. The days of open arrivals and departures had ended with the attempted assassination of President Ronald Reagan in 1981. When the limo and follow-up drove inside the tent, its flaps dropped, hiding the vehicles behind a thick canvas skin and allowing the president to exit the limo unseen.

The spare limo stopped just outside the tent, and Roberts ushered Susan and Abbey up the side ramp and into a door.

They rushed in and trotted down the rear hall. POTUS and his entourage were fast on their heels. Several uniform police officers and agents lined the back hall, ensuring no one but the president and his party entered. All hotel employees had received prior notification the place was off-limits during arrivals and departures.

Abbey followed her instructions and gave everyone a hard gaze. They walked a few feet past the rear service elevator and stopped. An agent held the elevator door for the president while Director Carroll, the chief of staff, and the rest of the official party entered and started their ascent to the twenty-eighth floor.

"Well, that takes care of the arrival," Roberts said, and leaned against the wall. He dug the protective survey from his pocket and gave it the once over.

"I can't believe I did that," Susan exclaimed. She had an excited, almost giddy expression.

Roberts grinned. "Fun, huh?"

"Yes, I loved it. What about you, Abbey?"

Abbey's wide smile answered Susan's question.

"Come on. Let's check out the place," Roberts said, and led the way through the maze of back halls. Emerging into the white granite lobby, Bishop greeted them.

"You made good time," Roberts said.

Bishop's grave expression concerned him.

"Excuse me a minute," Roberts whispered to Susan.

Walking through the lobby with Bishop, Roberts asked, "What's happened?"

Bishop glanced around before answering. "We've confirmed it. They're al-Qaeda."

"Who?"

"The two guys who attacked Howard."

"You sure?"

"Tossed their apartments in Chicago and San Francisco—found proof," Bishop said. "In the San Francisco apartment, we found a wadded-up map of Dallas from a printer and some notes about flights to DFW. We've grabbed both laptops and are searching for more clues about Sayed. Nothing's come up so far."

Bishop's words back in the restaurant in Washington echoed in Roberts' ears. *I want you in the loop. You're only being told half the story.*

"So, if their al-Qaeda, then…"

"They're connected to Sayed," Bishop finished his sentence.

International threats to the president were usually overblown. Domestic threats were what agents worried about the most. Most international threats usually were found to be inaccurate or made by someone without the means to carry them out. Roberts had always hoped the intelligence was wrong, that somehow someone presumed or assumed too much. With this new revelation, Roberts could reach only one conclusion. Sayed was still in Dallas, and he still believed he could kill the president.

Fear welled up in Roberts, tying his gut in a tight knot. A fear of doubt. People were being attacked and killed. Anyone near the president was in jeopardy. Roberts had never believed Sayed stood a chance of getting close enough to POTUS to endanger him or anyone close to him. But the guy wasn't going to be waved off. *Crap, things like this didn't happen in real life.* In real life, assassins who realized they might have been compromised called off the hit and ran as fast as they could away from the target. Sayed was proving to be the exception.

Roberts left Bishop and paced across the lobby toward Susan and Abbey. They were watching the junior staffers and traveling press lining up at the hotel registration counter, fighting for their place in line. Susan started laughing when he approached.

"You'll never guess what we just saw," she said. She showed a genuine smile again.

"What?" he asked.

"Two reporters almost came to blows over who's checking in next. You should have seen 'em."

"Yeah, a lot of hyped-up personalities in this lobby today," he said. "I need to run upstairs for a few minutes. You two okay here for a while?"

"Sure, anything wrong?" Susan asked.

"No, just touching base with Dick on a few things. You got my cell number if you need me. Find a comfortable place and I'll see you in a few minutes."

"We're fine—Abbey loves people watching, and so do I."

Roberts squatted beside Abbey. "Keep your eyes peeled. Remember, you're my deputy."

Abbey nodded and smiled again—a new record, three times in one day.

"Okay," she said.

Roberts stepped into the elevator designated for the president's floor. The Secret Service agent manning it glanced at Roberts' Secret Service lapel pin and credentials hanging on the chain around his neck before closing the door. When the door opened, another agent checked everyone before they stepped off. The whole floor belonged to the president, his staff, and the Secret Service. A uniformed police officer with a bored expression leaned against a wall as a backup. Roberts hiked down the hall where a group of agents stood outside the security room. A few doors down, more huddled near the president's suite.

Dick walked out of the security room and handed some papers to a guy on the president's detail. Roberts caught his attention, and Dick headed his way. They walked to a quiet corner away from the rest.

"What's going on?" Dick asked.

Roberts told Dick about his conversation with Bishop.

Dick blinked a couple of times. "Damn. Does Tortorziie know?"

"I don't think so."

"Okay, I'll tell him," Dick said.

"I'm considering cutting Susan and Abbey out of the deal," Roberts said. "Things are starting to get too dangerous. There's no way we can guarantee their safety."

Dick pursed his lips. "We've bet everything on Abbey, Ace. If you think cutting them out is best, I won't argue with you, but we've got nothing else."

Roberts had put himself in this crummy situation, and he had only himself to blame for the decision he now had to make.

"You don't have to decide tonight," Dick said. He slapped Roberts on the shoulder and showed the devil smile. "POTUS is in for the rest of the evening. Do something and relax—we got this."

"Relax?" Roberts sighed.

"If I had a good-looking woman waiting for me in the lobby, you can bet I'd figure it out," Dick said. "Hang around a little while longer and then cut out. Dinner, a few drinks, and chasing mama naked around the bed will take care of things—see you tomorrow." Dick turned and headed back to the security room.

Roberts couldn't believe Dick wasn't more concerned. Of course, Dick had been around a long time. Probably seen more than his share of unusual threats. Roberts assumed Dick's confidence stemmed from the overwhelming police presence. No one could get near the president without being checked numerous times. Somehow, this raised Roberts' anxiety instead of lowering it. Sayed had no intention of going head-to-head with the security forces. He intended to use stealth and deception.

Roberts choked down his anxious thoughts and strolled to the elevator. He retraced his steps and found Susan and Abbey lounging in a couple of comfortable chairs in the side lobby. The sweet smell of grilling meat drifted past as he walked up. This should have stimulated his appetite, but Roberts had little desire for food at this point. He sat beside Susan and pulled the protective survey from his coat pocket, studying it a second. "Appears he's in for the evening."

Susan's demeanor wasn't exactly lively, but her eyes still showed excitement. "So, what now?"

"We'll give it a while here and then have dinner if you like. Where shall we eat?"

"I'm still enjoying this party mood," Susan said. "Can we eat here?"

Roberts stuffed the survey back in his pocket. "Sure."

Susan swiveled her head around the crowded lobby. "But can we get reservations this late?"

"That depends," he said.

"On what?"

"On whether you like steak."

"I *love* steak."

"Then we'll eat at the Asador."

She glanced over her shoulder. A few customers milled around the reception desk of the Asador Restaurant. "Won't they be booked up? How will you get us in?"

Roberts winked. "Made reservations three days ago."

She placed her hand on his arm. "Smart guy."

But Roberts didn't feel smart. He had some serious decisions to make regarding Susan and Abbey. Decisions he wouldn't need to make now if he *had* been smarter.

———

Since the president and vice president were buttoned up for the rest of the evening, Bridget and her Dallas Police partner finally got a few minutes of downtime. Her partner was hungry, so she dropped him off at a snack bar in the Anatole Hotel lobby. The tempting smell of grilled cheese sandwiches almost caused her to waver as she walked to the elevator. On the way, she called the Saudi journalist's room number. He answered on the first ring.

Bridget identified herself and told him she was coming to his room for an interview. Ten minutes later, after walking out of Hamze Asford's room, Bridget called Bertrand's room number. When it went to voice mail, she pushed the elevator button for his floor. The hallway was empty as she searched for the room. Disregarding the DO NOT DISTURB sign, she pounded on the door. After no answer, she went back to the lobby. Bridget wanted to knock out this last assignment and have a couple of drinks. Chasing all over town to fill Tortorziie's shopping list for the director had put her in a bad mood early, and she needed some decompression time before the long day tomorrow.

A front desk attendant hurried over. "Yes, are you checking in?" The sides of his head were clipped short. He had long greasy hair on top that half-covered his eyes. He raked a lock back and smiled.

She showed her credentials. "No, just need some information."

The guy's smile faded. "Oh, you're one of them. How may I help you?"

Bridget put both palms on the counter and leaned toward him. "We're concerned about the welfare of Mr. Bertrand. We've tried contacting him for days, leaving messages, but he doesn't answer. Think you could help us out a little?"

The attendant exhaled a tired breath and typed something into the computer. He studied the screen a moment and typed something else before saying, "Appears he's left word with housekeeping. He doesn't wish to be disturbed." He glanced at Bridget a moment before continuing. "Says he's ill and just needs rest. Housekeeping leaves towels in the hall and just knocks on the door. Mr. Bertrand indicated he'd call for a room clean when he feels better." The man glanced up again from the monitor with a contented expression. The kind that said, *That's all I can do.*

Bridget gazed back with her police stare, saying nothing, until she made him look away.

Wimp.

"So, do you think he's still alive up there? Anyone checked on him lately?" Her tone sounded coarse, and that's the way she wanted it.

The attendant cleared his throat. "I can call the front desk manager if you like."

The guy had that prissy, nasally hum that made Bridget crazy.

"Can I leave a message and have Mr. Bertrand call me?" she asked.

The wimp pointed behind her at a nearby table with a red phone. "You may use a house phone for that if you like. The room has voice mail."

Bridget understood she had to back down a little. She couldn't force this guy to do anything. Interviewing a hotel guest who wasn't a suspect in an ongoing investigation could be tricky. She didn't have any legal authority to back her on this, which meant she'd have to attack it a different way.

"Never mind, I'll be back tomorrow." She marched away before the wimp said something else that would cause her to strangle him with his own tie.

———

Roberts, Susan, and Abbey relaxed in the lobby of the Renaissance Hotel and sipped colas he'd procured from the bar. Abbey's shoulders slumped and she yawned every so often. She studied each person who entered, eyeing some more than others. Roberts was happy she took her assignment so seriously. Cutting her and Susan loose wasn't something he took lightly, but with everything going on, it was the only fair thing. He'd never forgive himself if anything happened to them.

When they made their way toward the restaurant, Roberts asked Abbey, "Are you still having fun?"

She didn't answer, staring back with a blank expression.

"I think she's getting a little tired," Susan whispered.

The Asador was packed. The customers were in a good mood, and a few were already lubricated up enough that their voices drowned out the others. With people shoulder to shoulder, the place had a stuffy feel. The waiter took their orders and suggested an excellent wine. Still officially on duty, and in the president's hotel, Roberts declined. He and Susan ordered steaks and Abbey a hamburger.

After the long day, the dinner conversation was noticeably subdued. Roberts picked at his food. Bishop's information about the two terrorists and figuring out if he should cut Susan and Abbey out of the plan had destroyed Roberts' appetite. Susan and Abbey didn't have that problem. They wolfed theirs down and ordered ice cream for dessert.

On the way home, Abbey leaned her head against him and became quieter than usual. He didn't realize she'd fallen asleep until they were almost there. Roberts glanced down at her. He'd put his career and the president's life in her hands. She was so fragile and small.

Susan turned to him and grinned. Her hand slid to the back of his neck. She began massaging it, working out the tension.

When they arrived, Susan gently lifted the sleeping Abbey from the seat. Roberts unlocked the front door and let them in. He took off his jacket, and Susan mouthed, "Be right back," and carried the child down the hall. Roberts dumped the ten pounds of gear he'd put on a few hours earlier and slipped off his shoes before searching the kitchen cabinets. He found a bottle of single malt Scotch—needed a drink before talking to Susan. He almost added a few cubes of ice but didn't. Single malt should stand alone.

He dropped on the couch and savored the whiskey. He only drank hard liquor occasionally, usually after a long day working the president. Susan took her time putting Abbey to bed, so he made another drink and finished it. He leaned back on the sofa, closed his eyes, and the last of the stress drifted away. The sensation of someone sitting on the couch brought him back.

"Hope you're not asleep," Susan ran her fingers along his cheek.

He opened his eyes. She had dimmed the lights.

"No, just relaxing," he whispered. He'd been thinking about Susan —a lot.

"Want another drink?"

"Nope, had my limit."

She'd changed into a negligee—a sheer negligee. A long, beige one that left nothing to the imagination. Roberts let himself take in her beauty. She took his empty glass and set it on the coffee table.

"Is everything okay? I mean, with the president?"

He gently ran his fingers across her bare leg and touched her hand. He squeezed it and, in a voice filled with emotion, said, "I'm cutting you and Abbey out of this deal."

Susan's head jerked back and she frowned. "What?"

"Something's happened… something bad." Roberts looked down. "I can't guarantee your and Abbey's safety any longer." He lowered his voice. "Probably never should have promised it."

Susan sat up straighter and pulled her hand from his. "I don't understand."

"I know, but I can't explain. I appreciate your wanting to help, but…"

Susan stared at him a long time without speaking. Her spine stiffened a little more. "You recall what I said before this started?"

"Huh?"

She cleared her throat. "That if I didn't feel right about something, I could pull out."

"Yeah, well, that's what I'm—"

"That still goes."

Roberts wasn't sure if it was the fatigue or the two Scotches, but he had no idea what she was trying to say.

She took his hand again and scooted closer. "I don't want out. I've thought a lot about what you said. That Abbey could prevent another 1963 in Dallas." She nodded. "You were right."

"Susan, I—"

She put her fingers over his lips. "Don't worry. When I feel threatened, I'll pull the plug."

"Yeah, but the danger's greater now, Susan. People have been killed," he whispered.

"When I feel threatened, I'll pull the plug," she repeated in a more assertive tone. She had that determined expression people get when to argue with them further would only aggravate the situation.

"Besides," she said, glancing down the hall, "Abbey will warn us if there's any danger."

He dropped the subject for now and took her in his arms, pulling her on top of him. She'd applied some kind of powder or something—smelled good. When her lips met his, he ran his hand up her leg and caressed her inner thigh. She shivered, and her tongue rolled inside his mouth. The warmth of her pressing against his chest sent tingles through him. The relaxed sensation from the drinks loosened his tongue. He finally said what had been on his mind.

"I think I love you, Susan."

Roberts wasn't sure why he said it, but he didn't regret it. It just kind of popped out. It could have been the moment, or perhaps it was just something he should have said days ago when he first thought about it. Either way, he was surrendering his heart again. Something told him Susan would take better care of it.

She stared at him with a wide-eyed look. He'd even surprised her. Her expression softened and she showed a small grin before whispering, "Oh, you silly man. I love you, too."

Her voice had a sweet, smoky quality. She kissed him hard and pushed closer. It looked like the end to a perfect evening. Until Abbey screamed.

———

A second later Susan was up, the negligee open, and running toward Abbey's room. Roberts fumbled in the pile of gear he dropped in a chair before finding his pistol. He raced down the dark hall with about a million thoughts running through his mind, none of them good. He arrived seconds after Susan. He surveyed the child's room—nothing. The lamp on the nightstand was on and Susan sat on the edge of Abbey's bed, holding her—stroking her hair.

Susan whispered, "Abbey, that's okay, baby—that's okay, it's only another dream." Susan turned his way, her lips pressed together into a grimace. She loosened Abbey's arms from around her neck and lowered her back onto the pillow. Susan brushed Abbey's cheeks, drying the tears, and kissed her on the forehead. "Wanna sleep with me tonight?"

Abbey nodded and wiped her nose with the back of her hand.

"Okay, be right back." Susan rose and wrapped the negligee across her front. She stepped back into the hall and closed the door, her face no longer radiant with desire—she'd become a mother again.

"Sorry, she's had bad dreams since Houston. I'd hoped she'd gotten over them. Suppose the excitement today triggered something." Susan's chin dipped and she stared at the floor. "After a bad dream, I let her sleep with me the rest of the night."

"I understand. Better you stay with her."

Susan walked him back to the living room. Roberts put on his shoes and gathered his gear.

"What time tomorrow?" She kept her arms crossed, not revealing any more than necessary.

"The president's not leaving until late morning. I'll pick you up at eight, okay?"

Susan walked him to the door and gave him a long goodnight kiss. Taking his free hand, she directed it back under the negligee, between her legs. He wanted her, right then—right now. After a moment, she broke the embrace and opened the door. "We'll see you at eight—good night."

Just as Roberts stepped outside and Susan closed the door, his phone rang.

"Hello, Roberts here."

"Hi Michael," Bridget's silky voice said.

"Hey, what's going on?"

"Just thought I'd let you know I went to the Anatole. Interviewed the Saudi. Guy recognized the English reporter, Peters, from the photo. Said he saw him having a drink at the Gossip Bar in the hotel, flirting with the barmaid the day he got killed. Hasn't seen him with anyone else."

"What about the French guy, Bertrand?"

"No dice. That guy's still not answering his door or phone. Called his room for the last few minutes, but no answer. What should I do?"

Roberts considered it a moment. "Get some rest. Let's try a different tactic tomorrow. Since he's never around during the day or evening, we'll hit him early in the morning. Stop by on your way in tomorrow and see if you can catch him."

"Okay, will do."

"There's something squirrely about him. Either he's not getting the messages, or he's ignoring our calls. Either way, get into that room tomorrow no matter what. We have to wrap this up." Roberts had had lots of experience with journalists—not all good. They seldom got into a hurry cooperating with the authorities, but this French guy took the prize.

Bridget paused before saying, "There is one other possibility. He might be dead like the English guy."

"Yeah, if no one's seen him for a couple of days, that's a possibility. If you find him, check all his credentials again and ask if he knows the English reporter, and if he saw him talking to anyone. We're still batting zero. We need a break," Roberts said.

"I'll take care of it. Stopping off for a nightcap before calling it an evening. Want to join me?"

Roberts had no doubt what a nightcap with Bridget would lead to. He turned and examined Susan's door. "No thanks, I'm beat. Think I'll hit the sack."

———

After Roberts left, Susan stood with her back to the front door for a long time. She still had a comforting feeling from his touch. Without him realizing it, what Roberts had just said to her made her greatest wish come true. She hadn't expected it, and that had made it all the more exciting.

She quietly opened Abbey's door for a quick check. She'd drifted back to sleep. Susan strolled into her bedroom and sat on the side of her bed. She opened the nightstand drawer and rummaged through it until she found the old white envelope of photos. She dumped the contents on her bed and spread them across the covers. Susan picked out the only picture left of Abbey's dad, Stan. The rest, she'd destroyed years earlier.

She studied it a long time, the memories flooding back. It was the one taken the first year they met, that summer weekend at the friend's beach house in the Hamptons. The photo showed Stan relaxing in a chaise lounge, in a pair of swim trunks and sunglasses, gazing at the camera with his wind-blown curly hair a mess. They'd boiled lobster on the back deck that evening, sipped delicious white wines, and laughed. Stan was such a charmer. That's what made him such a good broker—clients loved him. That night they'd taken a long shower and made love. He'd won her heart that weekend. That's all she'd ever wanted. Someone to win her heart.

More memories rushed back quicker than she'd expected, bringing tears. Tears of regret, tears of sorrow, tears of betrayal. Susan ran her fingers across the photo. Why had she saved it all these years? She'd not seen or spoken to the man since shortly after Abbey's birth. But something kept her from destroying the last picture—the last link with the past. She stared at it several more seconds and her eyes misted again. Susan took a long breath, gathered the other old photos, and stuffed them back into the envelope before laying it back in the drawer. She shot a final glance at Stan's photo, tore it into several pieces, and flushed them down the toilet. She wiped away the last tear she'd ever shed for him.

FORTY

Thurman Howard's dreams weren't exactly nightmares, but they weren't the imaginings of a settled mind. As the pain medication wore off, his brain cleared a little. *The dark alley, gunshots, and the sweet blood flooding his throat.*

He woke a little more and opened his eyes. The lights were low, so he figured he was alone. A throbbing pain pulsated through his lung, and his mouth tasted of medicine. Was his shooting connected to the dead English guy? Had to be. The Anatole Hotel, the guy with the beard who spoke with an accent. He'd picked up the murdered man. Howard needed to tell all this to his sergeant. They had to know what he knew. They had to catch the guy.

He rolled over a little and pain shot through his left side. He grunted and mumbled, "That hurt—it hurts."

Howard hadn't noticed the homicide detective reading his book in the corner until he stood and strolled beside the bed. Howard turned his way as the man's shadow fell across the covers.

"Howard, do you hurt?" the detective asked.

"Uh-huh."

He must have drifted back off for a few seconds because voices whispering woke him up again. The detective by his bed was talking to someone in the room, "Can you just give him something for the pain —to help him rest?"

Howard cracked open both eyes. A tall, middle-aged nurse with curly brown hair stood at the foot of his bed, reviewing his chart.

She looked at the detective. "Dr. Carlo said only as much as needed to keep him comfortable."

The detective spoke again, "Just a little. For tonight."

She eyed the chart once more before saying, "Oh, all right, but just a little—to help him rest."

Her hands reached for Howard's IV tube. He didn't want to sleep— couldn't afford to sleep! He had information, vital information to the investigation he needed to share with someone, anyone. He needed to tell his sergeant what he'd just remembered. But his lips could no longer form the words. In desperation he blurted out, "Sergeant Brown."

The detective bent over and looked at him with a grin. "Howard, I'm not Sergeant Brown—I'm David... you know, David Travis, remember me?"

Yeah, Howard knew Travis—this idiot couldn't tie his shoes without instructions. Howard attempted to speak but could only open his mouth. A familiar, relaxing sensation cascaded through him. His eyelids closed and his memory clouded. He forced his eyes back open and reached out toward Travis. He gazed at his hand, which had somehow separated from his body. He shook his head—he needed to stay awake. Everything was connected. They needed to know the truth he knew. He fought to keep his eyes open, but couldn't. They closed again and he drifted back into a dark, quiet space.

FORTY-ONE

The following morning, Sayed requested the cab drop him off across the street from the Anatole, and he made his way through the parking lot toward the Tower entrance. In the darkness of the early morning, few people stirred. He enjoyed the solitude and quietness. Reminded him of early mornings with the sheikh at his compound.

Sayed had been playing a dangerous game of cat and mouse with the authorities. A very dangerous game. He hurried to the elevators. Moments later, he stood on his floor. A room service waiter with a large tray knocked on a door at the end of the hall as Sayed slipped into his room.

The waiter gave Sayed an idea. He had taken a risk returning to the hotel, but it was necessary. At this point, as far as the authorities knew, he was only a reporter who was proving difficult to reach. If he suddenly disappeared without a trace, what would the Secret Service do? Would they cancel his press credentials? That would wreck his plans. Would a lookout be issued for the French journalist, Bertrand? As long as they believed he still resided in the room, they must assume he just didn't want to be bothered with calling them back or being interviewed.

Sayed carefully examined the room, making sure no one had searched it in his absence. He took a relaxing shower, then ordered room service. After finishing breakfast, he listened to the police and Secret Service messages on his room phone's voice mail. Sayed pulled back the covers on the bed and mussed up the sheets and a couple of pillows. He rang housekeeping and informed them he felt much better and requested a full room clean today before five o'clock. He left a twenty-dollar bill folded in a note which read, *Sorry for any inconvenience.* Before he left, he urinated in the toilet but did not flush it. On his way out, he took the *DO NOT DISTURB* sign and put it back on the inside door handle.

Sayed had no idea what the Americans knew of his plans, or if they knew anything at all—it did not matter. Whatever they thought would prove wrong, in any case. He called for another cab just as dawn broke.

———

At eight o'clock, General Harry Cook took off his reading glasses and massaged his eyes with thumb and index finger. He rolled his neck and grimaced. He'd been in his Pentagon office since six that morning and still ran a low-grade fever. He needed one good day's rest to shake this aggravating summer cold. After the convention concluded, he vowed to take a couple of days off. Three solid weeks of work were enough.

Cook took another sip of coffee to soothe the rawness in his throat and searched in the desk drawer for another throat lozenge. Before he found it, his encrypted phone rang. He glanced at the incoming number—national security advisor.

"Good morning, Mr. Fuller. What do I owe the pleasure?"

"Good morning, General. We have a problem."

Cook couldn't help but grin. Fuller never called unless there was a problem, especially on the secure line.

"What's happened, sir?"

"We've just become the victims of a phenomenal screw-up. I'm forwarding you an after-action report from a SEAL team. They attempted a stop-and-capture of a high-value target in Pakistan, near a place called Pinti Point. Driver came out shooting, wounded one of their team members. They riddled the car, killing the driver and passenger."

Cook tried to figure where Fuller was going with this. He usually got right to the point, but this was different. He pushed the receiver closer to his ear.

"Anyway," Fuller continued, "after running the driver's identification through CIA, we got a hit—definitely a bad apple. One we've been looking for a long time."

Cook had a sinking feeling. "And the passenger?"

Fuller paused a beat too long before answering. "They got a hit on him too. Never realized he was in the car until too late. He's the Agency asset—operational code name, Emerald. The one CIA has been getting all their information about Sayed from."

Cook took in a slow breath and exhaled. "Son of a bitch, so now we're flying blind."

———

Thursday morning, Roberts sipped his third cup of coffee in his apartment as he dressed. Today would be the longest and most tiring of the visit. The forecast called for temperatures in the triple digits with high humidity. Well, hopefully, wherever he got transferred, it might be cooler than Dallas.

If he could just get Susan and Abbey through today, the president would receive the formal nomination tonight. POTUS only had one quick event tomorrow before heading back to DC. By noon he'd have wheels up and be back en route to Washington.

If Sayed was going to make a move, today was probably the day. With the president visiting several venues, Sayed had ample chances to intercept him either in transit or at the venue itself. Since no one had figured out his method of delivering the bomb, everything was still on the table.

———

Bridget O'Neil was on a mission. The clerk at the front desk of the Anatole had royally pissed her off last night. She parked in the hotel's lot and stormed toward the entrance with the rising sun.

"Okay, let's see if you can avoid me this early, Mr. Bertrand," she mumbled as she dialed his room on her cell phone. It went to voice mail again. She left another message and her number as she made her way to the front desk manager. A stately gray-haired gentleman soon emerged from the back office and inquired how he might help.

Bridget showed her credentials. "I need to check out a room."

His eyebrows pinched. "A room?"

"Yes, we're concerned about one of your guests and want to ensure he's okay."

"I see." The manager turned to the keyboard. "Name?"

"Bertrand, Rene Bertrand," she said.

After a moment, he asked, "Have you attempted to contact the room?"

She stared at him with her best stink eye.

A blush ran up his neck and he muttered, "Of course, you must have." He studied the monitor. "It appears he's fine."

"Why would you say that? Have you talked to him?"

"No." His tone had a condescending ring. "But he contacted our hotel staff an hour ago."

"What?"

"Yes, ordered breakfast early this morning and signed the bill. I have a copy from room service if you wish to see it."

She shook her head. This put a different wrinkle on the thing. At least he was still alive. "Never mind. That's okay."

The manager stared at the screen again. "He requested housekeeping clean his room today."

Bridget's mind searched for an answer. If the guy had been in his room all this time, why wasn't he answering the door, or returning the urgent messages they'd left? Something smelled wrong. "I want to look inside the room," she said.

The manager gasped. "Go inside a guest's room? I'm afraid I can't authorize that."

Bridget paused. If the guy demanded a search warrant, she couldn't claim an exigent circumstance, couldn't say the guy was a suspect in a case. She'd have to play the game. She leaned toward the counter. "Who can authorize it?"

The older man stepped back putting distance between them. "I'll have to contact security."

"Call them."

Two minutes later a security officer dressed in blue blazer and tan slacks strolled up. Bridget introduced herself, presented her identification, and made the request.

He studied her ID. "Secret Service, sure, no problem. This isn't a criminal thing, I hope."

"Nope, just checking to see if he's okay."

They arrived at the room, and the security man knocked. After no response, he used his master key card and opened the door. He called Bertrand's name several times and announced security before entering. They stepped into the dark room. A single light shined from the bath, and Bridget switched on a bedside lamp. She scanned the area. The blinking phone message light caught her attention. She listened to the message—the one she'd left minutes ago. An empty food tray sat on the edge of the disheveled bed. A note lay on the dresser with a folded twenty-dollar bill.

"He showered this morning," the security officer said from the bath.

Bridget walked to the bathroom door. The officer held up a large, white towel. There were drops of water on the sink and floor. She strolled in and touched the towel—still wet. Something stunk. She glanced down to the toilet. *Nasty bastard... doesn't even flush.* But she was still perplexed. Why wouldn't he answer the door or phone? Only one explanation.

"Asshole." She turned and stomped back to the dresser.

"Who?" The security officer asked, following her.

"Bertrand. The asshole's too busy to return calls from the police."

She scribbled a terse note on the back of one of her business cards and left it stuck in the corner of the dresser mirror. As she finished the note, a nagging feeling hung in her gut. There was still something wrong here. Checking her phone, she had just enough time to meet her partner. She'd contact Roberts later and brief him. He'd figure it out.

FORTY-TWO

Roberts waited on Susan's sofa for her and Abbey to finish getting ready. He looked over today's schedule. Susan hadn't opened the blinds yet, and the place had a gloomy, uneasy feel. Roberts switched on the table lamp as he flipped from one page to the other. He concentrated on the times and places the president would be most exposed. A few minutes later, Susan hurried into the living room, her expression aggravated. Abbey followed meekly behind. Susan had dressed her in a royal blue dress with silver trim, and she looked like a little princess.

"Sorry." She led Abbey toward the door. "We girls took too long this morning, didn't we?"

Roberts didn't waste time trying to figure the hard stare she sent toward Abbey. Who could read signs between females?

He stood. "So, we're ready?"

Susan glanced up from stuffing the last few items in her purse. "Ready."

She looked great, as usual. The black skirt and crimson, high neck blouse screamed power woman.

Abbey was quiet, probably still tired from yesterday. Roberts didn't like it when Abbey was quiet. Never knew what might be going on in that little head.

They arrived at the Renaissance Hotel about 8:20 and parked across the lot from the entrance. As they followed the sidewalk under a blazing morning sun toward the front door, the scream of approaching sirens brought them to a halt. Two Dallas Police cruisers rounded the corner of the service road and raced up the drive toward the hotel. Susan froze, her shoulders tightening. She drew Abbey closer. "Michael?"

He stopped as a fire truck wheeled down the freeway service road in front of the hotel.

Susan scanned the parking lot and hotel entrance. "What's happening?"

He shook his head. "Don't know."

A tiny, cold hand grabbed his.

The fire truck, lights flashing, stopped on the service road blocking one lane of traffic. Roberts eyed the truck. The fireman stayed put. Roberts had learned long ago that when firefighters run hot to a scene and don't get out, it's a bad sign. The uniform police officers ran into the front entrance, and a few seconds later people wearing confused expressions streamed out.

"Let's get out of here," Roberts said.

They walked back to his car and piled in as a large blue and white police truck approached the entrance. Roberts' worst fears were confirmed. The Dallas Police Bomb Unit vehicle skidded to a stop and two bomb techs ran inside.

Susan's head was on a swivel. "What's going on?"

Abbey's trembling hand rested on his leg.

"Hold on and I'll find out," he said.

The crowd milled around the hotel entrance. A police officer pointed at them and waved his hands for them to move further away.

Roberts dialed Dick's cell. Waiting for an answer, he peeked at Abbey. Her scared eyes met his. He winked. "We're okay, don't worry."

Dick answered with a curt hello.

"We're outside the hotel. What's going on?" Roberts listened for a few seconds. "Didn't the site agent brief them?" A grin spread over his lips. "So, is it safe? Okay, we'll meet you in the lobby." Roberts disconnected and glanced at Susan. "False alarm."

Her jaw dropped. "False alarm! That's it? What happened?"

He sat back in the seat and dropped the phone into his pocket. "When we secure a hotel for the president, we brief the phone operators and staff on the procedures to follow in case of a bomb threat. We instruct them if someone calls in a threat, they aren't to raise the alarm, but quietly inform us, and we'll handle everything. We have bomb specialists and explosives detection dogs at the hotel all the time."

She frowned as she gazed at the hotel. "Was there a bomb threat, here?"

"Yeah, about ten minutes ago some nut called one in. The operator on duty informed an assistant front desk manager and he made a bad decision—called 911 instead of calling us." Roberts opened his door and got out.

Susan didn't move.

He stared at her. "What?"

"How do we know it's safe?"

"Because we've checked it out. It's safe."

Susan and Abbey slid out of the car keeping their eyes on the hotel. From their looks, Roberts understood he had some more explaining to do.

"Relax. We get calls like this on every visit."

"But how do you know?" Susan held Abbey by her side, the concerned frown still firmly in place.

Roberts glanced back at the hotel and then at her. "Because we haven't evacuated the president. If there were any doubt, the working shift would have thrown him into the limo and been gone by now. Besides, the caller said it would explode," he checked his watch, "two minutes ago."

Susan's eyes fixed on him and she gnawed her lip. "Michael, how can you live like this? It's just too—"

"Don't worry. This kind of stuff is pretty much SOP for a visit. We just roll with the flow."

In a voice that exuded little confidence she said, "Okay, but let's go easy." She took Abbey's hand and followed Roberts across the parking lot.

As they walked into the lobby, Roberts searched for Dick and found him near the front desk, talking with an older man wearing a hotel nametag. The crowd had filed back in and the emergency vehicles departed. Bomb dogs and their handlers dispersed, and Secret Service agents drifted back into the shadows. Dick finished his conversation with the guy and walked over to Roberts. Dick smiled at Susan and Abbey.

"Good morning, ladies."

"A little excitement this morning, Mr. Crosby?" Susan asked.

"Just a little, appears an inexperienced manager is being sent home to reflect upon his most recent decision," Dick said.

"We still on schedule?" Roberts asked.

"Yup, no changes. Just relax here in the lobby, and I'll let you know if I hear anything." Dick drew his sleeve mic to his mouth. "This is Crosby—go ahead." Listening for a moment through his earpiece, he answered, "I'm en route." He turned to Roberts. "See you later."

Susan released a nervous sigh. From her looks, she was still concerned, but trying to put on a brave face. "Nothing like a little thrill to finish waking us up."

After the initial adrenalin rush, the next hour seemed long and tedious. They sat on a sofa in the lobby, Abbey scanning everyone who walked past. Roberts' mind started wandering just as Abbey quickly stood, staring at someone across the lobby.

Roberts leaned beside her. "What do you see?"

She didn't answer, but strolled to the left, never taking her eyes off her prey.

Susan jumped up and followed Roberts as he trailed Abbey, gripping her purse so tight her knuckles whitened. Roberts reached under his jacket and unsnapped his holster as he scanned the area Abbey had in her sights, but saw no one resembling Sayed.

Abbey whirled around. Her expression had softened. "Not him," she said.

Roberts kept his eyes on the group of people that Abbey had been watching. "You sure?"

She nodded. "Uh-huh."

When he turned back to Susan, she let out a long breath and her shoulders slumped. *Yeah, wound a little too tight for protective intelligence work.*

About 11:30, radio traffic picked up in Roberts' earpiece. The motorcade began forming up behind the hotel, getting ready for the noon departure. The shift leader and special agent in charge of the president's detail were sorting out last-minute logistics. At 11:50, the motorcade agent announced the cars were ready.

A voice behind them said, "Time to go, folks."

Roberts glanced over his shoulder. Dick motioned and pointed toward the rear service door. Susan bounced up and grabbed Abbey's hand. Probably relieved to be doing something. They walked through the hotel's back halls, through the kitchen, and out the back door. Dozens of agents and police waited for the president's departure. Dick led Roberts, Susan and Abbey to the spare limo.

"Make yourselves comfortable; we'll depart in four minutes."

Roberts opened the limo door for Susan and Abbey, and they hurried in. Minutes later, a rush of people burst from the hotel's back service entrance and ran toward the vehicles. Drivers waited with air conditioners on high as the mob scurried around, searching for their assigned cars. One of the last to emerge was a man in a Marine class-A green uniform. He craned his neck, looking down the line of cars and SUVs, then trotted in their direction. He carried a small black piece of luggage.

He stuck his head in the car. "Spare limo?"

"Yup," Roberts answered, "hop in."

The tall man removed his cap and took a seat across from Roberts and the girls, making sure the luggage stayed by his side. "I'm Bob Nolan," he said.

Roberts introduced himself, Susan, and Abbey.

"Always worried about getting in the right car," Nolan explained. "It changes."

Susan eyed the chest full of ribbons on the Marine. He wore the silver oak leaf of a lieutenant colonel and had a lean, handsome, weathered appearance.

A voice came through Roberts' earpiece. "All posts, we have a departure from the hotel, 1159 hours."

The flaps on the tent jerked back, and the limo and follow-up lunged forward, picking up motorcade vehicles as they traveled through the back parking lot. Police sirens wailed as cycles blocked the intersection before the line of cars pulled into an empty street and onto the service road.

Unlike most people, Roberts hated motorcades. Most of the public believed the president was safe in transit. Nothing was further from the truth. It was a dangerous place. The majority of attacks against US presidents took place boarding the limo, while in the limo, or as they departed in the limo.

Susan still hadn't taken her eyes off the Marine, and neither had Abbey. Someone in military uniform always became a curiosity piece in this sea of dark suits and police blues.

Finally, in a matter-of-fact way, Susan leaned forward and asked. "So, what do you do for the president?"

The Marine shot a surprised glance at Roberts. Susan's question, while innocent, was nonetheless indiscreet. The officer stared at her, probably wondering about this lady and child with official guest credentials.

The lieutenant colonel offered a disarming smile. "I advise the president on national security and military matters." Though friendly and polite, his tone made it known—he didn't want to discuss it further.

Roberts would fill Susan in later. The black case he carried went by many names; most called it *The Football*. It contained the launch codes for nuclear weapons.

Dallas Police motorcycle officers stopped vehicles from entering Stemmons Freeway until the procession passed. Roberts watched the drill and wondered how many people had found themselves victims of a presidential motorcade over the years. How many late appointments, explanations to bosses, wives, and husbands? Roberts shook his head. If you must be near the motorcade, it's probably best if you're part of it.

The cars slowed when they entered the back of the American Airlines Center. Vehicles dropped out as they approached the rear underground parking garage. Only the five-car secure package proceeded down the concrete ramp. The overhead door lowered when the last vehicle entered. Agents dismounted the follow-up and ran to the limo when it stopped. The shift leader made a general broadcast, "Command post—we have an arrival."

"Copy your arrival—1211 hours."

———

Roberts, Susan, and Abbey hurried ahead toward the stairs. The hot, stuffy garage belonged to the Secret Service—agents posted everywhere. The CAT SUV brought up the rear. The heavily armed assault team waited—ready to deploy at the first sign of trouble.

Roberts and his posse headed up the stairs to the back hall. Bishop waited on the landing and opened the door for them.

"Buying pizza for the guys again?" Roberts quipped.

———

Thurman Howard's wife sat on the small sofa in the hospital room and read her book. Bright sunshine filled the room as Howard finished his first solid meal since the shooting. He turned up the glass, enjoying every drop of the sweet orange juice. His throat had a dry scratchy feel. Sergeant Brown stood by his bed and took the glass after he finished. Howard glanced at his friend with a weak grin, the most he could muster.

"Guess I screwed up, huh?"

"I don't see how. You killed the two guys who tried to kill you. They had you outmanned, outgunned, but not outfought. You showed 'em, Howard." Brown's voice lowered. "Sorry you had a bad night last night. I mean sleeping, and all."

Howard just stared at him. "Huh?"

Brown grinned. "They said you thought I was in the room with you last night."

Howard struggled to recall. Had he seen Brown last night? His memory was still fuzzy since the shooting. No, he'd asked for Brown last night. He touched his sergeant's arm. "Do me a favor: don't let them give me any more of that stuff for pain, okay? It messes my mind up too much."

"Howard, that's your call now. I heard the doctor tell your nurse this morning. You can control the pain medication yourself from now on."

Howard raked his hand through his disheveled hair. "That's good."

Brown strolled to the end of the bed. "Is there anything else? Need to get to work."

"Yeah."

"What?"

Howard gazed at the far wall and searched his memory. "I can't recall right now." He touched his head with his finger. "Guess some of that stuff's still floating around up here."

"Well, don't worry about anything, old buddy—you'll be out of here and back at work in no time."

Howard had something to tell Brown, and it aggravated him that he couldn't remember.

Brown patted him on the leg and strode toward the door. "You get some rest—I'll see you first thing tomorrow morning."

Howard looked up at the television. A live shot of the presidential motorcade leaving the Renaissance Hotel stirred a tiny memory.

The president—it had to do with the president. And it was important.

FORTY-THREE

Roberts moved his group to one side as a stampede of footsteps came up the stairs behind them at the American Airlines Center. Standing shoulder to shoulder against the opposite wall in the back hall leading to the podium were a dozen men and women waiting to meet the president. The president was dressed in a dark navy suit, light blue shirt, and yellow silk tie, and went down the line, speaking in relaxed tones to each of the assembled guests with agents leading and trailing him. He pumped the hands and said, "Thank you for everything." The official photographer took a picture of them smiling into the camera.

Susan whispered, "Is this where we get ours?"

"Afraid not. You'll get your photo tomorrow," Roberts whispered back.

She poked him in the ribs. "Tomorrow, huh?"

Abbey stared, fixated, at the waiting people. Roberts nudged Susan and tilted his head discretely toward her daughter. She only shrugged. POTUS continued meeting and greeting the well-wishers, so Roberts directed Susan and Abbey around the corner and onto the great hall's podium.

He knelt in front of Abbey. "Did you see something back there?"

Abbey showed that deadpan expression again. "The man the president talked to isn't very nice."

"Which one?" Roberts strained to recall them all.

"The fat one with glasses."

Abbey's powers were again confirmed. The man she'd picked out, Jake Smiley, was a local businessman with a bad reputation—twice indicted, never convicted, on real estate, wire and mail fraud charges. How had he finagled his way into a personal meeting and photograph with the president? Large contributors gained access, that's how.

The elevated podium stood almost eight feet above the floor. In an emergency, the armored lectern provided safe cover for the president until evacuated to a hard room. Red, white, and blue decorations hung everywhere—from the fifty American flags flanking each wall to the bunting around the podium's base. The giant, overhead screen ensured everyone a front-row seat.

Susan moved to the edge of the podium and took in the view. The massive arena stood empty except for several uniformed men and women walking dogs between the seats and down the aisles.

"Where did the delegates go?" she asked.

"Bomb sweep," Roberts replied. "We let the delegates take a long lunch break and come back at two o'clock. See those guys, there?" He pointed toward another group of uniformed men and women unloading equipment from long black cases at each door of the grand hall. "Secret Service mag teams."

Her eyes pinched. "Mag?"

"Magnetometers. After the bomb sweep, they'll run everyone through the mags before letting them come back in."

The sound of the president's people preceded him as he walked around the corner onto the stage. Roberts moved his team near the far edge. POTUS glanced their way—he had a curious look, possibly wondering about the woman and child who followed him everywhere. A sound tech introduced himself to the president while adjusting the mic. The president stood with both hands on the lectern's sides as the man requested him to count down from ten. POTUS complied while the tech made the necessary adjustments to the equipment and locked the memory.

The sound tech said, "Thank you, Mr. President."

"No problem," the president said. He turned to the chief of staff. "When's the vice president coming over?"

"In about half an hour, sir."

Roberts gently took Susan's arm and Abbey's hand and made for the door ahead of POTUS.

Taking one last glance around, POTUS strolled back toward the motorcade.

Just as they got to the back stairs, Roberts spied someone walking to his left rear. He flinched at the sudden appearance.

Bishop said, "I'll see you later," then disappeared around a corner.

Roberts blew out a breath. *Damn, the guy came from nowhere and disappeared into nowhere.*

The motorcade left the American Airlines Center and headed to the president's friend's home for lunch. The house was located in North Dallas near Preston and Northwest Highway, a part of town where the home lots were more expensive than many of the Georgian mansions with their sweeping drives and lush gardens. As the motorcade weaved through the exclusive neighborhood, weariness enveloped Roberts. He massaged the back of his neck, should have slept longer.

He didn't bother getting out of the spare limo when they arrived. No use—they weren't going in. The ranch-style brick home was a late 1980s vintage. Boston ivy covered the outside, only the door, roof and windows still visible. Another large tent erected at the front hid the limo from view. The host greeted the president, and only the special agent in charge of the Presidential Protective Division accompanied them inside.

An agent made a chow run. Nothing fancy—burgers and soft drinks, with fries optional. The drivers rolled down the windows and turned off the vehicles. Keeping the car's engines from overheating meant no air-conditioning. They unloaded a cooler with chilled bottles of water, and everybody grabbed one.

"I can't believe it's so hot." Susan fanned herself and Abbey, their hair matting from sweat.

Roberts wiped perspiration from his face, squinted at the blazing sun, and didn't reply. There was no breeze to relieve the oppressive heat, and summer locusts in the trees and distant traffic were the only sounds. Agents inside the vehicles removed their jackets—only the ones standing post around the residence needed to look the part and sweat like hell.

With the arrival of the takeout food, their spirits lifted. Roberts, Susan, and Abbey relocated from the spare to the follow-up's back seat to eat while he showed them the weapons, radios, and other specialized equipment.

The vehicle's radio came to life: "Follow-up, this is Hercules Two."

The shift leader in the front passenger seat lifted the mic and answered, "Hercules Two, this is follow-up, go ahead."

"Sir, we have suspicious activity on top of building 153."

The shift leader thumbed through the counter-sniper survey and found building 153. He and Roberts leaned forward, staring out the windshield, searching in that direction.

Susan touched Roberts arm. "Who is Hercules Two?"

"Counter-sniper," Roberts replied.

"What kind of suspicious activity?" the shift leader asked.

The voice answered, "We have three non-Anglo males assembling some kind of tube device which they've just leaned over the side of the high rise. Appears it's pointed directly toward the residence."

Roberts didn't like the sound of that. Had he inadvertently put Susan and Abbey in harm's way? Did Sayed have other accomplices?

The shift leader glanced at Roberts before speaking into the mic. "George, did you copy Hercules Two's transmission?"

George was the first name of the detail's special agent in charge inside the residence with the president. The answer came back in a whisper over the follow-up radio.

"I copied. Is Huntsman up?"

"I'll check," the shift leader answered.

Roberts turned to Susan before she could ask. "Huntsman's the observation and escort helicopter."

The shift leader again spoke into the mic. "Huntsman… Huntsman, follow-up."

Another voice came on the radio. "Follow-up, this is counter-sniper response. We're en route to building 153."

Susan leaned over to whisper in his ear. "What's a counter-sniper response?"

"Counter-sniper response teams are agents and local police. They check out suspicious activity near the president."

After receiving no answer from Huntsman, the shift leader called them on his cell and asked their location. A few seconds later he hung up and grabbed the mic. "Hercules Two, this is follow-up."

"Go ahead, sir."

"Huntsman's down for a refuel—be back up in a minute. Direct the counter-sniper response unit to the suspect location."

"Roger, will do."

The special agent in charge of the detail exited the house and approached the follow-up. He squinted from the glare off the windshield and poked his head through the open passenger window, ignoring Roberts and his crew.

"Anything?" the SAIC asked the shift leader.

"Nope."

The SAIC took the mic. "Hercules Two—what do you see?"

Radio static broke the silence before they answered. "Subjects are erecting the tube-like device, and it's still pointed toward the residence. Unable to determine if it's a weapon."

The SAIC's eyes fixed on the distant building barely visible through the trees. "A missile?" he asked out loud. He keyed the mic. "Hercules Two, if we need it—do you have the shot?"

Roberts grimaced. From her expression, Susan didn't need this explained.

"I have it on two of the three, sir. One is working behind an air-conditioning unit out of sight."

Something kicked into Roberts' mind. Something unexpected—something he wouldn't have believed. He was no longer concerned about the president's safety. There were plenty of other agents to take care of that. His only thought was how to keep Susan and Abbey safe from whatever was out there. But there was nowhere to go. Remaining in the armored follow-up was the best he could offer. His chest tightened, waiting for the SAIC's decision.

At that moment Huntsman announced it was back en route.

Roberts read the thoughts of the special agent in charge, staring at the radio while he mulled over his options—he had few. He could wait for Huntsman or CS response to report in. If the guys on the roof finished assembling a weapon and fired it, then the president's life was at risk. The SAIC couldn't evacuate POTUS without bringing him outside into the kill zone. However, he could put him into the designated hard room of the host's residence and wait it out. Or the last option—order Hercules Two to take the shot.

Susan couldn't sit still, moving from one window to the other trying to see through the thick canopy of tree limbs to the building hundreds of yards away.

Roberts studied the SAIC's eyes as he weighed his choices. The sound of Huntsman's rotors overhead made the decision easier. Roberts scanned the treetops. *At last, air support.* The chopper passed to their right racing toward the suspect building. Moments later they called.

"Follow-up, this is Huntsman. Counter-Sniper Response agents are on the roof. They have all the suspects in custody."

The SAIC's grim expression broke and he let out a breath. Roberts hadn't noticed the tiny hand holding his sleeve until then. He glanced at Abbey; she had a tight grip on Susan's arm with her other hand.

"It's okay," he whispered.

She let go and sat back in the seat. Sweat trickled down her neck.

"Follow-up, this is CS Response."

The shift leader answered, "Good job, guys."

The voice on the radio had a ring of concern. "Call me on my cell."

The shift leader called the CS Response team. Moments into the conversation he laughed. "Okay, make our apologies, then."

When he hung up, he looked at the special agent in charge. "We've captured a group of Hispanic window washers putting together their scaffolding."

The SAIC grinned and strolled back toward the residence.

Roberts said a silent prayer of thanks.

Susan's eyes widened as she shot smoldering stares back and forth at Roberts and the shift leader. "They were only window washers!

They scared the wits out of us over window washers?" She sat back in the seat and crossed her arms. She didn't have a happy face.

Just before three o'clock, radio traffic indicated the president was preparing to depart. The wait in the heat had exhausted them—Abbey and Susan resembled wilted flowers.

Roberts had come to a turning point he didn't want to face. He wasn't sure how much longer he could expose Susan and Abbey to this kind of danger. His earlier thoughts about wanting to protect them above the president shocked him. How could he do his job and look out for them as well? Of course, if he dismissed Abbey and Susan, he had no job. He was just another suit with his head on a swivel looking for a face in a crowd. There had to be a happy medium. Some way he could do both jobs. He turned to Susan and she was eying him. Neither spoke, but a silent message was sent and received. *I trust you to do the right thing.* He'd never been in this kind of emotional tug of war before—he didn't like it.

FORTY-FOUR

Bishop sat in the parking lot of the Renaissance Hotel with the car running. He'd removed his jacket and let the air conditioner dry the sweat from his shirt as he reviewed the schedule. Since the Secret Service worked the president close, Bishop figured he could best serve as a perimeter lookout. Knowing the Service had special surveillance teams, he had identified himself to them the first day so he didn't distract them from their assignment.

Bishop's time in Delta doing covert ops in the Middle East prepared him well for this job. He knew the profile. He concentrated on people or vehicles that seemed out of place—the car that circled the area too many times, the person who didn't dress appropriately, and someone behaving nervously.

Bishop had a lot of acquaintances in the Mossad. He'd attended more than one school in Israel on anti-terrorism tactics. The Israelis laughed at American airport security and scoffed at America's idea of refusing to target specific groups of people because of political correctness. Age, race, and sex were used extensively by the Israelis to form their "human profile." Of course, they didn't officially call it profiling, but the effect was the same.

When Bishop's phone rang, he checked the number before answering—General Cook.

"Good afternoon, sir."

"Go secure," Cook said.

Bishop flicked the tiny switch on the side of his cell and a chirping sound echoed through the receiver. "Secure."

"What's the status?" Cook asked with a raspy voice.

"Running smooth. Nothing to report."

Cook didn't reply so Bishop said, "Anything on your end?"

Cook related the story about the accidental death of the CIA's asset.

"Any last bit of intel before he met his demise?"

"No."

Cook had a tired, disappointed sound. Not like him at all.

"So, how do you see it?" Cook asked.

Bishop had expected him to ask this sooner or later.

"If Sayed is going to strike, there's no better venue than the convention tonight when the president accepts the nomination. I recall that Sayed wanted a big audience when he made his move."

Cook grunted and there was silence on the line for what seemed like a long time.

Finally, Cook said, "I want to reconfirm with you that you have a go if necessary. Fuller signed the order."

"Thank you, sir. I understand."

As Bishop disconnected, he chuckled. General Cook was obsessed with operational security. Even on a secure line, he couldn't bring himself to say the words.

Kill order.

———

The motorcade arrived back at the Renaissance Hotel, and everyone understood that, in a few hours, they'd be leaving again for the American Airlines Center.

Susan and Abbey took up their positions in the cool lobby and Roberts fetched colas for them. They were exhausted from the heat and tension at the private residence, and he felt stupid for having them go.

Their presence there served no purpose but to wear them down and expose them to potential danger. They still had the most challenging part of the day ahead.

Just as Roberts flopped down beside Susan, he received a call on his radio.

"Roberts—O'Neal, what's your location?"

"I'm in the lobby."

"Copy, be there in two."

Moments later, Bridget hiked up. She gave Susan and Abbey a hard stare. Roberts made the introductions.

Bridget showed one of her quick smiles and said, "Can I speak to you a moment?"

She and Roberts strolled a few feet away from Susan and Abbey.

"What's up?"

Bridget related her efforts to interview the Frenchman, Bertrand.

Roberts scratched the underside of his neck, gazing at the floor for a couple of seconds. "Well, at least he's not dead like the English reporter."

"But he's ignoring our calls," she reminded him.

"What do you think, Bridget?"

"I say get the press agent involved. Probably has the guy's cell number in the press book."

"Good idea."

"And if he can't reach him—what then?" she asked.

Roberts shrugged. "If this guy is too busy to return our calls, then he gets no consideration as far as I'm concerned. Have the press agent keep an eye out for him and pull his creds the next time he sees him—that'll get his attention."

"He'll raise hell with State Department."

"Too bad. We've wasted more time on him than he deserves."

Bridget beamed. "My pleasure." She gave one last glance Susan's way before taking off.

Roberts probably should have gotten the press agent involved earlier, but who knew the French jerk would prove so elusive?

When Roberts moved closer to Susan, she asked, "What do a press agent and press book have to do with Secret Service?"

Roberts cleared his throat. "'Press agent,' in Secret Service lingo, refers to the agent who manages the press. Their mission is to keep reporters out of the way of the working shift while still allowing press access to the protectee. At big events like conventions, they keep a Press Book. It's a binder with photographs, employer information, and contact numbers on each credentialed reporter."

"Oh."

Roberts' thoughts drifted back to Bertrand. Anomalies like him happened with regularity. When some people leave home, they can go a little crazy. Bertrand fit the profile. Probably found a girlfriend, or possibly a boyfriend. Only bothered going back to his room to grab a shower and fresh clothes. No time or inclination to complicate his fun by returning phone calls.

Roberts, Susan, and Abbey broke off their surveillance long enough for a sandwich about six o'clock. Dick joined them as they finished, his restless manner putting Susan and Abbey on edge. Roberts read his expression. This was his last major event as an agent. It was like he wanted to soak up as many good vibes as possible before it all ended.

"Ace, we're leaving a little before seven. The VP's heading over around 6:15. He'll give his speech first and introduce POTUS. Director Carroll and the president's chief of staff are riding with you again."

Dick's shoulders sagged and he looked like he just finished a half marathon. Roberts knew the feeling. A convention was high speed, low drag. Late nights, early mornings, and enough stress to bring on a panic attack.

At exactly 6:40, the motorcade agent announced the vehicles were lined up and ready. Roberts and his group made their way down the now familiar back hall of the hotel and took their seats in the spare limo. The director and chief of staff joined them just before departure. The summer sun still blazed in the western sky, making the heat unbearable. With blaring sirens, the motorcade pulled onto the service road as the director and chief of staff exchanged ideas about the next day's activities.

The five-vehicle secure package pulled up to the same steps it had earlier that afternoon in the underground parking garage of the American Airlines Center. POTUS ran up the stairs almost before Roberts could get Susan and Abbey ahead of him. Abbey wasn't moving as fast this evening.

Roberts whispered to Susan, "How's she doing?"

Susan stroked Abbey's hair. "Tired—but she'll be all right."

Roberts hated the stuffy madhouse backstage. Dozens of agents, staffers, and official visitors rushed up and down the halls. Roberts couldn't stand in one spot without someone bumping into him.

The president and chief of staff huddled with a speechwriter in the holding room. Roberts looked around. *Not doing any good back here.* He took Susan's arm. "Let's go."

They found the service door leading to the arena floor and slipped into the chaos of the convention. The nomination process was just a big party nowadays for a president seeking a second term, but it still held the people spellbound. The merriment rolled in waves with cheers, horns, and whistles sounding from twenty-five hundred delegates wearing goofy hats, showing off campaign buttons, and holding up banners. Add to that the hundreds of reporters, guests, and observers who also attended, and you had the beginnings of a shit show ready for prime time.

The vice president had just received his introduction when Roberts, Susan, and Abbey waded into the thick, hot crowd. Roberts stared at the packed arena and then at Abbey. No way could she see everyone without help. He knelt in front of her.

"I'm going to carry you so you'll be tall enough to see the crowd. Is that okay?"

She nodded and he lifted her eye level while resting her on his left hip. He cradled her with his arm and walked up the first aisle with Susan bringing up the rear. While most people sat, others milled up and down the same aisle Roberts walked. After covering almost half the arena, Abbey suddenly tensed. Roberts felt the change and snapped his head toward her. She craned her neck, staring at someone down the line of seats to her left. Her arm tightened around his neck.

"What is it?" Roberts asked.

Searching the faces, she didn't answer.

He glanced in the same direction, then back at her. "Do you see something?"

Keeping her eyes fixed she said, "Take a couple of steps back."

Roberts backed up about four feet and stopped. Abbey leaned a little further to the left and stared at a tall man between two women.

"What's going on?" Susan asked.

Roberts eyed the man while Abbey studied him.

Susan touched Roberts shoulder, her warm breath floating across the back of his neck.

Roberts' gut twisted as Abbey watched the man. "Is that him?"

"I'm not sure. He has a dark aura, but something's different. I don't understand."

Roberts let Abbey slide to the floor.

The man wore a red, white, and blue cardboard top hat and held a large paper bag in his right hand. Bag had to have been searched when he came in. But what was in it?

"Wait here," Roberts whispered to Susan.

Roberts slowly moved down the row of people behind the man. He looked nothing like the photos of Sayed, but if Abbey had doubts, that was enough for Roberts.

The cheers and shouting for the VP's speech kept everyone distracted enough for Roberts to approach the suspect from behind, undetected. The crowd's attention stayed on the stage as the man in the cardboard top hat whispered something to the women on each side of him. He quickly reached into his bag and handed something to the woman on his right, then to the one on his left. Roberts spotted the sudden movement and roughly pushed past a couple of people, drawing curses and insults as the man and two women made their move.

Roberts reached over the guy's shoulder and grabbed for what they were raising.

"Hey! What the hell are you doing?" the man yelled, turning to Roberts.

Roberts gazed at what he held in his hands—a cloth banner. The woman on the guy's right wound up and threw a punch at Roberts, which he ducked.

"Police. Sorry, my mistake." Roberts released the banner and held his hands up in surrender as he moved away.

That didn't go well.

The guy was red-faced, mumbling something about *damn cops* as he stared Roberts down. The woman who'd tried to punch Roberts said something to the man, and he and the women held the banner high and cheered. It read *FOUR MORE YEARS.*

When Roberts made it back to Susan and Abbey, neither said a word, but Susan's nervousness had reemerged. She gnawed her lower lip, moving with the quick jerky movements he seen earlier.

Roberts lifted Abbey and said, "Not him."

As Roberts wormed his way up one side and down the other of the great hall, Abbey's rigid body became more relaxed. The place was too hot and crowded. Roberts pulled in a tired breath. Walking the whole room was going to take a while. Susan walked behind, occasionally stroking Abbey's hair when they stopped. Roberts was happy Abbey spotted no threats, but anxious at the same time. Sayed could be anywhere just waiting his chance. When he struck, it would be too late. Susan and Abbey would be on their own. Roberts kept asking himself, if it came down to it, whom would he chose to protect? Not the kind of question an agent should ever ask.

The vice president completed his remarks just as Roberts, Susan, and Abbey finished walking the arena and returned to the bottom of the elevated podium. Satisfied the hall held no danger, Roberts found a place near the service door and waited for the president's introduction. Abbey laid her head on his shoulder. She didn't appear that heavy when he first lifted her, but carrying her through the hot press of thousands of people exhausted Roberts. He was breathing hard, and his shirt was plastered to his back. He wiped his brow and shifted from one foot to the other, looking for a more comfortable stance. Just as he decided to lower Abbey to the floor, Susan spoke, but the noise drowned out her words.

"What?"

"I said looks like she's out."

"Huh?"

"Your junior Secret Service agent is asleep on duty." Susan raked the child's damp hair off her forehead.

Roberts scrutinized the horde of people in the massive complex.

They'd laid eyes on all of them and found nothing. "Let her sleep—we've done all we can."

With the introduction of POTUS, the place erupted into screams, applause, and the squawks of souvenir horns. The president confidently strolled onto the podium and shook hands with the VP while giving him a quick hug and whisper. They both smiled, clasping raised hands, and waved to the crowd. Everyone broke into another round of cheers and applause. The noise didn't affect Abbey in the least.

Someone touched Roberts' shoulder. He turned around and found Dick standing behind him.

Roberts leaned his way. "How's it going?"

"So far, so good," Dick yelled over the noise. "I need you at a special briefing after we get back to the hotel."

"Briefing?" Roberts asked.

"Yeah, here's the room number." Dick handed him a folded piece of paper. "Come by as soon as you drop the girls off."

Dick had a seldom-seen expression that Roberts couldn't read. It wasn't the devil smile, but something akin to mischief or thuggery. It worried Roberts. What was he up to?

"Okay, Dick."

The president spoke only briefly, outlining his administration's accomplishments the past four years and previewing what he wanted to achieve in the next four. Of course, the crowd went wild—everybody loves presidential promises.

Before POTUS finished, Roberts took Susan's arm and strolled out the service door and down the hall. Halfway to the garage stairs, the final cheer went up. The president had accepted the nomination of his party for another term.

Roberts, Abbey, and Susan waited beside the spare limo for the masses to emerge down the back stairs. The quiet of the underground garage stood in stark contrast to the loud noise of the arena above. If not for the silence, Roberts' might never have heard Abbey's soft whispers.

"Don't ever leave us, Michael... don't ever leave us... don't ever leave us, Michael." Abbey's cheek rested on his shoulder, and she repeated the chant over and over in his ear. The way she mumbled, she sounded asleep—like talking in a dream. Her hand softly stroked the back of his neck. *Was she asleep?*

He caught a glimpse of Susan. She leaned against the spare, arms folded, with a tired, bored expression. She'd not heard the whispers.

"Don't ever leave us, Michael," Abbey kept repeating.

Something about the whole thing made Roberts uncomfortable. As his radio announced POTUS heading for the limo, he shifted Abbey to Susan and opened the car door. Five minutes later the motorcade weaved its way back to the Renaissance Hotel—the convention had concluded without incident.

———

Roberts strolled into the hotel lobby and again read the folded piece of paper Dick had passed him. The room number indicated the president's floor. Odd, not usually the place for briefings. With POTUS in for the night and buttoned up, what was so important they needed to have a meeting? Roberts was relieved nothing happened at the convention, but also a little disappointed. His excellent master plan upon which he'd rested his professional reputation and career on ended with only a fizzle. The most excitement of the whole evening was Abbey picking out the wrong guy in the crowd.

Roberts knocked on the door and Dick answered—his jacket and tie removed and a drink in his hand. "Come on in, Ace."

Director Carroll sat in a chair, also with his jacket off and a drink on the rocks. The director didn't get up. "What will you have, Michael?" he asked.

Oh, God. What's all this about? "Nothing, Mr. Director—I'm fine."

"Bullshit," Dick exclaimed, walking to the bar. "Is bourbon okay?"

A tingle crept up Roberts' back. Dick and the director had been friends thirty years—Roberts had only met the man a few times, and never socially.

Roberts took a seat. "Yes, bourbon's fine."

Dick handed him his drink, then flopped into a chair.

Director Carroll took a sip of his and sat the glass on the end table. "So, where do you see this Sayed investigation going from here?"

Roberts shot a glance at Dick. He showed a slight grin.

"Well, Mr. Director, I haven't considered it, to tell you the truth. Agent Tortorziie told me earlier that once the president left Dallas—I was cut out of the investigation. So, I've just concentrated on this end."

The director turned to Dick with the hint of a smile. "At last, an honest man who doesn't know it all."

Dick raised his glass in a toast salute but didn't respond.

The director motioned at Roberts. "Michael, your drink's getting warm."

Roberts took a long gulp; it tasted good—*too good*. Carroll appeared to study him, taking his measure.

The director shifted and crossed his legs. "How's it working with the guy from P2OG?"

"P2OG?"

"Bishop," Dick said.

"Oh, he's fine—been a great help."

Carroll took another sip. "Think we should keep his group involved in the hunt?"

Roberts figured this was the real reason for the meeting. Secret Service, just like all federal law enforcement, jealously guarded their turf. Having a guy like Bishop hanging around might prove embarrassing, especially if he didn't follow the Secret Service rule book.

"Yes sir, I'd keep them on," Roberts said. "They appear to have access to better intelligence faster than we do. Could be an asset in the future."

The director kept his eyes on Roberts and nodded his approval at the answer. Carroll stood and Roberts and Dick also rose.

"Well, thanks for dropping by," Director Carroll said. "I enjoyed the visit." He shook hands with Roberts.

"Thank you, sir. Good night."

Dick walked to the bar to mix another round as Roberts left.

As Roberts meandered through the dark parking lot, he was still trying to figure out the purpose of the meeting. In retrospect it probably wasn't about keeping Bishop and P2OG on the case. From the director's tone, and the way he'd eyed Roberts, *he* was the real purpose of the meeting. The director was taking a personal interest in him. No doubt, all a part of Dick's doing.

When Roberts opened his car door, the whiskey and fatigue took hold. Exhaustion swept through his body. Thank God. Only one more event tomorrow. The last thing on the schedule—the foreign journalist's press conference at the Anatole.

FORTY-FIVE

Sayed rose early as usual. He always set his alarm for dawn. He typically prayed, meditated, then prayed again at sunrise. He had faithfully followed this routine of five prayers daily since childhood. This sunrise would be his last. Before noon he would enter paradise as a martyr, his name spoken with reverence in all Arab countries. Giving one's life for the Allah's glory and Islam was the most any Muslim could hope to achieve.

He caught a cab to the Anatole Hotel. At this hour, the police and Secret Service had just started setting up barricades, and the bulk of the security forces would arrive later before the president's visit. Each trip to the Anatole increased the danger of detection, but Sayed had to take the chance. He did not know how big the security ring would be, and if he were on the inside, he would have one less checkpoint to negotiate. If they suspected a serious threat, the ring could tighten.

Sayed carefully scanned the halls before entering his room. He turned on the bathroom light and leaned close to the mirror. Then he held up Bertrand's passport to the glass and ran a hand over his face. Not one wrinkle, line, or hair out of place—a perfect likeness.

If not for the new high explosive, the plan would never have been possible. The brother known as The Professor had worked at several munitions plants and the British Defense Ministry, making strides in organic chemistry and blast-related research for years. After retirement, he returned home to join the struggle and pass his most significant discovery to al-Qaeda—an explosive with five times the power in half the size of a standard device. Sayed had a quarter of a pound. More than enough. And since 99 percent of the device was plastic, it never alerted an airport scanner or magnetometer.

Sayed stripped the bed. After removing the sheets, he draped one on the floor. He then unpacked his suitcase, laying each item out for inspection. His confidence rose. They could not stop him now.

He undressed and stepped into the shower to begin the full ablution. The warm water flowed over his body and a sense of peace entered him. He had no fear. He would soon be in paradise.

With eyes closed and palms up, he first declared his intended purpose of worship and purity. Speaking in Arabic, his soft words did not escape the bathroom. He washed his entire body, including the nostrils and mouth. He mumbled the prayer as he ceremonially lifted his palms filled with water to his face three times. It was fitting he die on Friday, a holy day.

"Allah is great; Allah be praised." Sayed leaned both hands against the shower wall, enjoying the silky feel of the water. He closed his eyes and the memory rushed back. The real reason he was here. The reason he must be the martyr. Sayed was again with the sheikh, at his villa, the night of the storm.

———

"I've finished. I have them here."

That night at the reception, when he'd spoken those words to the sheikh, Sayed had put a series of events into motion that would change his life forever. Weeks earlier, the sheikh had given Sayed an assignment. The sheikh understood al-Qaeda couldn't rest on its laurels. They had to move forward or stagnate. Their previous attacks had met with great success, but more was needed to maintain al-Qaeda's relevance in the struggle. They needed to organize even greater attacks that would strike at the very fabric of the United States.

Sayed had spent every day and half the nights targeting American interests worldwide, working up a bold plan to strike soft targets in countries with ineffective police and intelligence organizations. Diplomatic missions, educational institutions, and industrial plants were all scouted and plans drawn up. The plans had been what the sheikh wanted most, and he gave this great responsibility to Sayed.

The sheikh whispered, "You have already completed your assessment?"

"Yes, Sheikh," Sayed said, patting the pocket on his robe.

A loud rumble of thunder sounded from the south and streaks of lighting raced across the dark sky.

The sheikh's eyes lit up in a way Sayed had seen only a few times. The excitement hardly contained. "Come, we will speak of this later this evening."

Sayed and Rasha mingled with the other guests, and the children disappeared into another room to play. Sayed was most pleased with himself. He was one of the sheikh's favorites. The plans he carried would ensure his continued status in the sheikh's ever-tightening circle of trusted advisors.

A loud clap of thunder outside shook the building just before the clouds released their contents. The deluge pounding on the roof made it difficult to hear inside. There were smiles all around, as the area around the villa was just finishing one of the worst droughts in decades. All rain was a blessing.

A light, simple meal was served. The women dined at a separate table. The sheikh spoke to the men of the struggle to come, assuring them even greater plans were in the works. His eyes drifted to Sayed.

After the meal, the sheikh approached Sayed. "We must talk." He took Sayed's elbow and guided him to the room he used as an office. Like all the rooms in the villa, the furnishings were simple and utilitarian. The sheikh was an austere man, never needing or desiring luxuries.

Another explosion of thunder caused Sayed to stare at the ceiling as he and the sheikh sat at the desk. Sayed laid out all the attacks he had so carefully planned. The sheik was fascinated. He examined every aspect of the raids, quizzing Sayed about the smallest details. Time passed and before Sayed realized it, most of the guests had departed. He attempted to excuse himself for the evening.

"My family, Sheikh. I must see them home. It is late—the girls, you know."

A flush crept across the sheikh's cheeks. Seeing the sheikh's response, a tingle swept up the back of Sayed's neck and across his face. *I should not have spoken that way.*

"Apologies," the sheikh said, "I have been thoughtless." He laid his hands on Sayed's plans. "But I would very much like you to remain and we finish this. Would you allow me to provide an escort to see your family home?"

Sayed was honored by the sheikh's generosity. "Of course."

"Then say your goodbyes, and I shall have them driven in my car. It is more comfortable than the others."

Sayed stood. "Thank you, I won't be long."

Sayed found Rasha in deep conversation with bin Laden's favorite wife—or at least the one who believed she was the favorite. Sayed motioned with his head and Rasha excused herself, joining him around the corner.

"My business with the sheikh isn't finished. He wishes me to remain a little longer. He's offered his vehicle for you and the children."

She moved closer and placed her hand on his chest. "Getting the sheikh to give up his car. Aren't you the special one, my husband?"

His hand squeezed hers. "I will not be long, promise."

Rasha smiled the mischievous smile and gave him a quick kiss before anyone noticed. "I will get the girls to bed and wait up for you." Her eyes had a sensual sparkle. "And if you are not too late, perhaps a special surprise as well."

Sayed embraced the twins and wished them a good night before returning to the sheikh's study. He and the sheikh picked up where they had left off, discussing the plan for the attack on the refinery in the UAE. The sheikh showed a particular interest in attacking countries that were puppets of the United States. Another muffled explosion sounded to the north. It appeared the storm was departing the area.

Moments later, the door to the study burst open. Nasser al-Bahri, the sheikh's bodyguard and Sayed's old boss, filled the threshold. He was out of breath and his wild expression brought a disturbing stillness to the small room.

He bowed. "Forgive the interruption, but we must leave now... we must all leave now!"

Before the Sheik or Sayed could answer, al-Bahri delivered the news. "Your vehicle was just hit in town. Whoever directed the attack may know of your whereabouts. We must go."

A numb sensation enveloped Sayed. He tried to speak, but no words passed his lips.

Bin Laden asked, "Sayed's family?"

Al-Bahri swallowed and gazed at Sayed. The bodyguard shook his head and a single tear formed in the corner of his eye.

———

Sayed leaned against the shower's tile wall, his tears mixing with the warm water flowing over him. Oh, the cruel irony. While he was planning attacks against the United States, they had taken away his reason to live. It was later determined a missile fired from a drone had targeted what was believed to be bin Laden's personal Land Rover.

Since that day, Sayed had a new reason to live—to cause as much damage and disruption to America as possible. He had begged for the opportunity to hijack a plane on 9/11, but the sheikh had vetoed the idea. Sayed had worked on significant parts of the plan, but most believed he was too important to the organization to waste on a one-time attack.

Sayed ran his wet hand over his scars. He had fought the best fight possible. After today, no more wounds, no more surgeries, no more pain.

Today he would show the world that even the invincible United States could not stop Islam. He would show everyone. He would avenge his family. Since the day they were murdered, joining them in paradise had been his greatest desire. They would welcome him as a martyr and defender of Islam, and he would at last be able to embrace them again.

Sayed completed the ritual, washing and drying himself. Back in the bedroom, he wrapped his naked body in a bedsheet and lay on the sheet he'd already spread across the floor. He stretched out on his back, turned his head in the direction of Mecca, and said the prayer of those who were about to die:

"There is no God but Allah, Muhammad (peace be upon him) is the messenger of Allah. I bear witness that there is no God but Allah, he alone, he has no partner, and I bear witness that Muhammad (peace be upon him) is His servant and messenger."

Sayed repeated the prayer over and over for half an hour. He ended with:

"Oh Allah, admit me into paradise, and protect me from the torment of the grave, and the torment of hell-fire; make my grave spacious and fill it with light. Oh Allah, do not deprive me of the reward, and do not cause me to go astray after this."

———

When the alarm sounded, Roberts reached out, silenced the thing, and rolled back over. Exhaustion—too much stress. He'd done more tossing and turning than sleeping during the night. He twisted to the edge of the bed and dragged himself up.

Roberts showered and mentally recalled the morning's itinerary. He'd almost convinced himself they had somehow beaten Sayed. Police and Secret Service beefed up, bomb squads reinforced, and DHS guys behind every corner. Why did he still have this uneasy feeling?

Roberts ate an apple and sipped coffee on his way to Susan's. Dick called and suggested they not ride in the motorcade. He thought it better to drive to the hotel in advance and wait for the president in the press conference room. Roberts had no problem with that. He just wanted this last event to be over and see the president wheels up and flying home.

When Susan met him at the door, she looked refreshed and rested —a far cry from the washed-out woman he'd left last night.

"Good morning." She gave him a quick kiss.

"You're chipper today," he said.

"Oh, I slept like you wouldn't believe. I feel great."

He followed her into the living room.

"Like some coffee? Help yourself. I'll get Abbey going." Susan disappeared down the hall.

A dull headache forced Roberts to the coffee pot. He poured himself a cup, massaged his temple, and wandered back into the living room. The girls soon emerged, and he stood. Abbey appeared rested and happy—a good sign, perhaps.

"Ready?"

"We're ready," Susan said.

They arrived at the Anatole a few minutes after eight. The place buzzed with activity even at this early hour. Police and hotel staff directed guests and reporters to the press conference room. Roberts called Dick on the radio and requested him to meet them in the lobby. While they waited, Roberts' phone rang.

"Agent Roberts?" the familiar voice asked.

"Yes, this is Roberts."

"Sergeant Brown, remember me?"

"Yes, sergeant, you're Detective Howard's supervisor, right?"

"Good memory."

"How's he doing?"

"Fine, complaining about hospital food already."

Dick walked through the lobby and made eye contact with Roberts. "So, what's on your mind, Sergeant?"

"I don't know if it counts for a whole lot this late in the game, but Howard wanted me to tell you something. He insisted I should tell you, immediately."

"What?"

Brown paused and cleared his throat. "He wanted me to give you the description of a suspect he'd developed in his investigation—you know the English guy's murder."

"Right."

Roberts nodded a hello to Dick when he walked up. Dick had dark puffy rings under each eye.

"Where did he get this description?" Roberts asked.

"Some valet guys who saw the suspect the night the English guy was killed."

Roberts' feeling about Howard withholding information was confirmed. "I'm listening," Roberts said.

Brown went on to give him a basic description of the suspect.

Roberts rolled his neck and grimaced, only about half listening. This information was relevant several days ago, but, in a couple of hours, only held relevance for the Dallas Police Homicide Unit. Roberts shifted his weight, trying to find a position his lower back hurt the least. When Brown finished talking, Roberts's scratched his chin. "That's all."

"Yes, that's it," Brown said.

"And he got this description from someone at the Anatole?"

"Right, just before he got shot in the alley the other night."

"Okay, thanks for the info." Roberts hung up.

Susan glanced around the lobby. "I think we girls will make a quick stop in the powder room." She took Abbey's hand and walked away.

Roberts whispered to Dick, "That was Detective Howard's supervisor. Said Howard wanted to pass on the description of the guy who was a suspect in the English reporter's murder."

Dick cocked his head and his lips pursed. "I'm confused. I thought Howard killed the guys who murdered the English reporter."

"Yeah, me too—doesn't make sense," Roberts said.

"Where did he get the info?"

"Some interview he did here. Said the guy is white, in his fifties, has a mustache and goatee, and speaks with a foreign accent."

"What kind of foreign accent?"

"Didn't say."

"Not a lot of help."

"Yeah, I know."

Dick rubbed his eyes with thumb and index finger and released a sigh. "Got a call back from HQ about my request to reconfirm all the foreign reporter's credentials. They all checked out but one."

"Who?"

"The French guy, Bertrand."

"That's the one with food poisoning. We checked his room out the other day."

Dick leaned in closer. "Well, his magazine's lost contact with him. Doesn't return their phone calls or emails."

"He hasn't answered ours either," Roberts said. "Bridget investigated and he's still in the hotel as of yesterday—apparently doing fine. Still haven't caught him for an interview, though. I gave her permission to have the press agent pull his convention creds the next time he showed."

"Good idea," Dick said. "Something odd there. Whatever we do, let's keep him away from this POTUS event."

Susan and Abbey rejoined them, and Dick clapped his hands and smiled. "I think we've got it locked down about as tight as we can. Why don't you guys make your way to the press conference?"

Dick turned to Susan. "By the way, I've got the White House photographer on standby. Just before the press conference ends, slide around to the back hall and join him. As the president leaves, I'll have a staffer introduce you guys, and the photographer will snap a quick picture."

Susan tugged at Abbey's hand. "Did you hear that? We're going to meet the president. Isn't that exciting?"

Abbey flashed a broad smile.

Roberts couldn't wait for this morning to end. He still had a crick in his neck from Dick's couch, a headache from too little sleep, and now a knot in his lower back brought on by the ten pounds of equipment hooked around his belt. He stared at Dick. "Where will you be?"

Dick pulled his shirt sleeves a little farther out past the edge of his jacket and made sure the cufflinks were lined up. "At the arrival area. Don't worry, we've got this visit licked. A damn fly couldn't get in here without having a body cavity search."

FORTY-SIX

Roberts, Susan, and Abbey followed the rear hall toward the Desoto room, where the press conference was scheduled. The number of agents, police, bomb dogs, and staff made it a tight squeeze. They passed through the DPD checkpoint, and Roberts held up his badge to the DPD Intelligence Unit detectives and pointed to Susan and Abbey.

"They're with me," he said.

The Desoto rooms A & B were meeting rooms in the west wing of the hotel. Only Desoto room B had been opened for the press conference. Standing outside, Bishop waited near the mags.

"'Bout time you showed up," he said.

Roberts took a glance into the room. He was confident the real threat had passed last night with the conclusion of the convention. Sayed had made the smart choice. He'd bugged out and wait for another day. "Anything going on, yet?"

"Nothing much. Just got here myself. The bomb techs ran everyone out a while ago and did a complete sweep, examined everything twice. Checked the risers and all the cameras and other gear the press dragged in. Half a dozen agents posted after the sweep. Place looks like a dog show with all the canines."

"Yeah, guess we might have overdone it a little," Roberts mumbled.

A couple of foreign journalists eased around them, passing through the mags. Secret Service Uniform Division officers searched their bags, and then a dog sniffed them for confirmation.

The mag teams worked as fast as they could to clear everyone before the president showed up. After he arrived, everything stopped, and the room was sealed to all but security and senior staff.

"Any problems?" Roberts asked.

"Nothing so far," Bishop said.

"Okay, we're going in—see you later."

Roberts showed his credentials to the mag team sergeant and escorted Abbey and Susan into the room. As they stepped in, the camera crews set up the final bits of their equipment on the press riser to the right. Video cameras on tripods dotted the thing, their harried owners making last-minute adjustments. The armored lectern decorated with the presidential seal stood on another riser across the room from the cameras. Between the two risers, in front of the armored lectern, several dozen foreign journalists milled around the enclosed rope and stanchion area, talking among themselves. Standing near the video cameras, the Secret Service press agent made eye contact with Roberts and waved. Roberts waved back, and the agent paced over to them.

"Hey, Roberts," the agent said. "I called that journalist's cell phone, but he never answered. Didn't show up for the convention last night, or the reporters' party either. But I think I've just spotted him. Do you want to toss him, or shall I?"

Roberts had been looking over the press agent's shoulder at a journalist digging through his briefcase. Roberts jerked his head back to the press agent. "What?"

The agent held up his press book. "The French guy you're looking for, Bridget said you wanted his creds pulled."

Robert swiveled his head back to the crowd. "He's here?"

The agent nodded toward the group of reporters. "Yeah, one of the first to arrive. Guy works for a magazine in Paris. I got his photo here in the book." He thumbed through the pages while Roberts searched the crowd of reporters.

Abbey's small hand grabbed his and squeezed harder than Roberts thought possible. He glanced down, prepared to give her the standard wink or smile of assurance, but she wasn't looking his way. The big, blue eyes stared straight ahead; her face twisted into a terrified expression.

"It's him," Abbey's low voice was almost lost in the background noise of the hectic room.

Susan didn't hear her, distracted by the press agent still flipping pages.

Roberts squatted down in front of Abbey. "What did you just say?"

Her eyes never blinked, focused on the group of reporters chatting in front of the riser. "It's him, the man from Houston." A tear rolled down her cheek and her lower lip quivered.

Susan heard her that time. She snapped her head toward the reporters, then back to Roberts, her composure gone. Her voice cracked. "Michael!"

"Found it," the press agent said. "Is this him?" He handed the book to Roberts. On the page was the photo of a white male in his fifties; the well-trimmed mustache and goatee gave him a distinguished appearance. The name printed below the picture—Rene Bertrand.

A cold sensation creped down Roberts' spine. He studied the book's photo and the man standing thirty feet away. *Oh, my God!*

"Well, is that him?" The press agent sighed.

A sick feeling rolled through Roberts' gut and his chest tightened before he said, "Yes, thanks. I'll see to it from here."

He handed the book back to the agent. Roberts never took his eyes off the man with the mustache and goatee.

"Suit yourself." The press agent shrugged, closed the book, and returned to the press riser.

Roberts lifted Abbey and held her close. The rapid pounding of her heart accelerating his own. *Have to get them out.* Susan's face was ashen as her wild eyes took in the mass of journalists. She'd latched onto Roberts' arm with a death grip.

"Don't stare at him," Roberts whispered. He took Susan's hand and slowly walked to the open door where Bishop stood surveying three journalists with his hunter's eyes as they passed through the mags and had their bags searched and sniffed.

Roberts checked his watch. The room would be sealed in a few moments before the president's arrival.

Roberts led Susan and Abbey into the hall, motioning to Bishop to join them with a tilt of his head.

"Sayed's here—he's inside by the riser," Roberts said.

Bishop's eyes hardened as he turned back to the open door and glanced at the group of journalists. "What?"

"The guy in front, with the goatee and bright yellow tie holding the small green backpack—see him?"

The crowd briefly parted as people broke from conversation circles to join new ones, but not the man with the goatee. He stayed in his choice location, only a few feet from the riser. While he chatted with the other journalists, he never gave up his spot—closest to where the president would take questions.

Bishop blinked several times as he scrutinized the man. "You think he's posing as a foreign journalist?"

"Yes, I think it's him. And so does Abbey."

"Well, he didn't bring anything in," Bishop said, "they walked him through the mags and the dogs checked him and the backpack."

The echo of sirens filtered into the room as Roberts dialed Dick's cell phone. Roberts' earpiece buzzed with an announcement from the command post of the president's arrival at the Anatole Hotel. The phone almost went to voice mail before Dick answered.

"Crosby, here."

"Dick, we need you in the Desoto room, now."

"No can do, Ace. The president's here."

"So is Sayed. He's in the press conference."

A two-second pause before Dick asked, "What the hell did you just say?"

"Don't let the president come near this place; get over here fast."

"Are you sure?"

"One hundred percent," Roberts said.

"Be right there."

Roberts handed Abbey to Susan and she held her close. He turned to Bishop.

"Go back inside. Don't let him out of your sight. He may be working with someone. See if anybody passes him something."

Bishop nodded and strode back toward the Desoto Room. Abbey had stopped crying, but she still gulped in quick breaths.

"Are you positive that's him—no doubt in your mind?" Roberts asked.

Abbey's voice wobbled as she said, "It's him."

Roberts' thoughts went back to the previous night. Abbey thought she saw something at the convention. *No room for error this time.*

"What color is his aura?"

Abbey sniffed and wiped her nose. Her dark blue eyes looked like sparkling sapphires. "His aura's black, Michael, black as night."

Roberts knew what he had to do. "Okay then. You two get as far from this place as possible." He pulled his car keys out of his pocket and shoved them into Susan's hand. "Leave. Now."

Susan let Abbey slide from her arms to the floor. Tears streamed down their faces. "No, *you* take us, Michael—you go with us," Susan said, pulling one of his arms while Abbey cried and tugged at the other, saying, "Don't ever leave us."

He picked Abbey up, hugged them both, and kissed Abbey on the forehead before kissing Susan's lips. In a steady voice he said, "I can't go. I love you."

Susan's expression darkened and she nodded.

Abbey refused to listen—wasn't having any of it. Her face turned a scarlet red from panic and excitement. She shook her head and screamed, "No, Michael. He'll kill you. You won't kill him, he'll kill you!" She wrapped her arms around his neck and held tight.

Roberts couldn't wait. His emotions raw, he pulled her grip from his neck. Abbey's reaction was tearing him apart inside, but they needed to leave before it was too late. He shifted her over to Susan's arms and pushed them away while backing toward the open door. Abbey continued crying and screaming, leaning toward him with both arms extended.

Maybe the last time I'll see them.

Susan started to say something, but tears choked off the words. She hugged Abbey tighter before running down the hall. She glanced back once before sprinting out of sight around the corner.

Roberts met Dick racing down the other corridor toward him.

"Where's this guy?" Dick caught his breath, looking around. "How in the hell did he get in?"

Roberts led him through the door, back into the hum of excited reporter's voices waiting for the president and pointed the man out. He briefed him on what the press agent and Abbey told him. Bishop appeared in the doorway and moved to where they stood.

Dick had never shown a panicked expression before. It shook Roberts.

"Ace, if we get this wrong—it's our ass," Dick whispered.

"I know I'm right," Roberts said. "Where's the president?"

Dick fumbled with his sleeve mike before saying, "He's safe in the holding room, for now. They're waiting on me to give the okay to bring him in."

Bishop's hunter's eyes studied the man near the podium. "If that's him—where's the bomb? It's not in his bag or on his person—we doubled-checked everybody going in. He's clean."

Bishop's words flipped a switch in Roberts' memory. His memory about all the classified things Bishop had shared with him regarding Sayed and what the asset had told CIA.

An undetectable bomb. Sayed missing for two months. Spent time in a hospital. Gained weight. The attack would be at a time and place to guarantee maximum press coverage. No planned egress.

Of course, it was there all the time. Sayed was on a suicide mission. The bomb wasn't on his person—it was *in* his person. That's the reason dogs couldn't smell it, and magnetometers and airport scanners couldn't detect it.

Roberts stared at Bishop and Dick. "Guys, I think I know where it is." Roberts shared his new revelations with them. Dick's expression tightened and he shook his head.

"That's crazy talk."

Bishop spoke up. "Wait a minute. Maybe not so crazy. Everything Michael's saying makes sense. There's been more than one occasion where belly bombs were used in the Middle East. What we need to figure out is, if true, how will he detonate it? Most likely an electronic signal." Bishop gave a quick look around. "And we need to get these people out of here."

Dick also glanced at the crowd. "If he has a bomb in a room this size, he can kill us all."

Bishop said, "Somebody needs to get close enough to find out."

They all looked at each other.

"I'll go," Roberts said.

"Now hold on, Ace."

"Let him go," Bishop interrupted.

Dick's gaze met Bishop's before turning to Roberts. A fatherly-look raced across Dick's face before he fixed eyes back on Bishop. "Okay, you're the expert. Tell him what to look for."

Bishop leaned close. "He'll probably have the detonator in his hand, or if his hand is in his pocket—we need to know which pocket, understand?"

"Yes, anything else?" Roberts asked.

Bishop let a cold grin sweep across his lips. "Yeah, don't stare directly at him. It's already past the time for the president to arrive—they're getting impatient."

"Okay."

Roberts' hand shook as he removed his Secret Service lapel pin and convention credentials. He hid his earpiece under his collar and took a couple of deep breaths. He figured he'd be more scared, but oddly a relaxed confidence enveloped him.

I can do this.

The journalists' stares followed Roberts as he made his way toward them. He casually strolled to the riser and stood behind the armored lectern. Speaking into the mic, he said, "Ladies and gentleman, the president's running a little late. Please bear with us—only a few more minutes. Thank you."

As Roberts turned to leave, he glanced down at the reporters in the front row. Sayed stood patiently with the rest, but what was in his right hand drew Roberts' attention. He meandered to the rear of the room, making sure not to hurry.

"Well?" Dick asked.

"Had a notebook in his left hand and car keys in the right."

Bishop smiled and nodded.

Roberts nodded back. "And there was a key fob attached to the ring. He held it next to his abdomen. That's it, isn't it?"

Dick held the sleeve mic to his mouth and stared at Bishop. Dick's eyes still held a fair amount of doubt as he asked, "Can he detonate it with that?"

"You bet," Bishop said.

Dick took in a slow, deep breath and his shoulders tensed. He spoke into the mic. "Evacuate the president—now! Everyone in the press conference room hold fast."

The half dozen Secret Service agents in the room all snapped their heads in Dick's direction.

Bishop's whole demeanor changed, and his expression hardened. "I'll take care of it. That's my department—the reason I'm here." The hunter's eyes were gone. He set his jaw and the face of a killer stared at Sayed.

Dick grabbed his arm. "Hold on. What's your plan?"

Keeping his voice calm and low, Bishop said, "I'll walk up behind him and put a bullet in his brain before he can push the button."

Dick's jaw dropped and he shook his head. "No, we can't do it that way. This isn't a combat zone or some back alley in the Middle East. We need to take him alive—killing someone everybody believes is a journalist in a press conference is a no go." Dick's voice took on an excited quality and he spoke faster. "What if we're wrong? What if Abbey is mistaken?" He eyed Roberts. "I believe you and Abbey are on to something, but that's not good enough to murder someone in cold blood in front of a room full of people."

Bishop said, "If we try and do it your way, you know the odds."

Dick licked his lips and swallowed. "Yeah, I know."

"Okay, just as long as you know," Bishop said.

His voice had a tone of finality. Roberts got the feeling they were talking in code.

Dick waved Roberts closer. "Ace, I need you to do me a favor."

"Sure, name it."

"Don't ask any questions—just do as I say—okay?"

"Sure."

"Mr. Bishop and I will disarm Sayed."

"What?"

"Just listen. We're going to take him down, and get the detonator out of his reach."

Roberts searched Bishop's face for a reaction. Killer's eyes met his, never blinking. Roberts turned back to Dick. "What do you want me to do?"

"Bishop and I are going to walk up behind him and each of us will secure a hand, right?" He looked at Bishop for assurance.

Bishop nodded.

"Then we'll take him down and make sure he doesn't press any buttons on that damn fob."

Bishop nodded again.

Dick rested his hand on Roberts' shoulder. "What I need you to do is make sure everyone gets out of here safely."

"What? No! No!"

Dick's nostrils flared and his hand squeezed Roberts' shoulder tighter. "You heard me, Ace. I want you to stay by the door and evacuate everyone out of here."

"No, Dick, I can help you and Bishop take him down, I can—"

Dick shook his head and patted Roberts' shoulder. "Not in the plan. Stay by the door and get everyone out. If he gets away from us, don't let him out of this room alive."

Dick turned to Bishop. "You ready?"

Bishop unsnapped the holster under his jacket. "Yeah, I'll take the right hand. You take the left."

"Let's go," Dick said.

Dick and Bishop slowly walked toward the group of journalists, making their way behind them.

A helpless feeling washed over Roberts. He calculated all the options. If they failed to take him by surprise and he detonated the thing... The size of the explosive charge was unknown. No shrapnel concerns—except bone fragments. The room had high ceilings. That would affect the negative and positive pressure from the blast. If they stayed low and weren't in direct proximity...

No! No, this would work—it had to work.

Roberts stepped back to the door where the mag team stood. Every Secret Service agent and officer gazed at Dick, waiting for orders. Roberts eased beside the sergeant in charge of the team. "Sergeant," Roberts whispered.

The sergeant asked, "What's going on?"

"Without rushing, quietly get your people out of here, right now, and leave the doors blocked open."

Dick and Bishop had walked to the rear of the gaggle of journalists to get a better approach. Dick kept his voice low, speaking into his sleeve mic. "All personnel at the press conference, this is ATSAIC Crosby. There's a bomb in the room. Don't anyone move. I'm heading toward the individual I believe has it. When you see me jump him, evacuate everyone as fast as possible through the main entry doors."

The looks on the faces of agents posted around the room varied—a few furrowed foreheads, a couple of pinched eyes, and numerous confused expressions, but everyone held their positions. They watched Dick's every move.

The uniformed sergeant also heard the transmission. His mouth fell open and he gazed at Dick, then back to Roberts.

"Don't rush out," Roberts said. "You have plenty of time to leave without drawing attention. Go. Now."

The sergeant motioned with his head, and he and his team casually strolled toward the door. As he exited, he turned back and shot Roberts a look that said *nice knowing 'ya.*

Running footsteps in the hall caused Roberts to step outside into the corridor. A half dozen agents, pistols out, trotted toward the Desoto room. Roberts held up both hands with palms facing out. The lead agent halted, extending his arms to stop the others. They all had the same question on their faces: *How can we help?* Using hand signals, Roberts waved them back down the hall. They retreated, taking small steps.

Roberts moved back inside. Dick and Bishop were getting closer to Sayed. Wading through the crowd of foreign journalists, they approached him from his blind side. He'd not noticed them yet as he edged even closer to the lectern, his legs stretching the blue felt rope. Sirens blared outside as the presidential motorcade departed the hotel. The journalists turned their heads, bewildered. Excited whispers and mumblings about what was happening moved through the crowd. Sayed's expression changed, and his gaze darted from side to side. Thankfully, he didn't look directly behind him. Dick and Bishop were only a few feet away.

Roberts tried to think of something he could do to help them, but they were on their own. His hand drifted to the Sig Sauer .357 under his jacket. He unsnapped the holster.

Dick and Bishop were in position now, separated from Sayed by only one person. Bishop approached on his right and Dick on his left. Bishop glanced at Dick, nodded, and reached for Sayed's right hand. At the same time Dick grabbed for his left, pushing past the closest journalist, an obese, older man with a Berlin newspaper lanyard around his neck.

Dick's hand was two inches from Sayed's wrist. Roberts watched in horror as the journalist Dick had shoved past made a half turn to face him, his expression irritated. His sudden movement blocked Dick from grabbing Sayed's wrist.

"Do you mind?" the German said.

Bishop grabbed Sayed's right wrist, and Sayed turned to face him, his left arm free. The moment of surprise was lost. He swung and struck Bishop hard in the face.

A flurry of screams sounded from the agents. "There's a bomb in the room—get out!"

They herded the confused and frightened reporters toward Roberts. He stood by the double doors and waved as the horde of panicked journalists rushed past him and fled down the hall. He pushed them through the door and yelled, "Run!" Screams overrode the cacophony of pounding feet as everyone tried to pass through the doors at once.

The rush of reporters almost knocked Bishop and Sayed off their feet. Quick as a cat, Sayed twisted his wrist—breaking Bishop's tenuous grip.

In an attempt to grab Sayed, Dick reached over the now-terrified

German reporter as he fled. Sayed scrambled among the journalists rushing out, and Dick lost his grip on Sayed's sleeve.

Sayed ducked under the rope separating the reporter pen and presidential riser.

Bishop pushed through the crowd toward him.

The German reporter, red-faced and panicked, dashed toward Roberts.

Dick and Roberts both pulled their guns.

Bishop lunged and caught Sayed's foot as he jumped onto the riser, dragging Bishop up with him. They fell out of sight behind the armored lectern.

Roberts untangled the last reporters forming a bottleneck trying to exit the door.

The German reporter stumbled and dropped to one knee in front of Roberts, his chest heaving.

Roberts rushed forward, yanking him to his feet and half-carrying him toward the door.

Sayed jumped up before Bishop got to his feet. In one fluid motion, he caught Bishop in the temple with a perfect round-house kick, hurling him behind the lectern.

Dick fired his .357, and Sayed twisted from the impact, staggering back before turning his gaze toward Roberts as he pushed the last reporter through the door. When their eyes met, Roberts aimed his semiautomatic and tried to get Sayed in his sights. The angle was all wrong. He was shielded behind the armored lectern. Roberts fired twice. The first round glanced off the lectern, and the second grazed Sayed's head.

Dick kept his pistol on target. He was right in front of Sayed—not five feet.

Dick fired as Sayed leaped toward him—the fob still in his hand.

In mid-flight, Sayed screamed something in Arabic.

Roberts never heard the explosion, only sensed a bright, orange flash and searing heat on his skin. The concussion reminded him of being upended by a defensive end after jumping to catch a long pass. He recalled tumbling in the air but not landing. Roberts' chest hurt, and he gasped for air. He coughed and took a couple of painful breaths. He forced his eyes open, but could see little.

The ceiling tiles had disintegrated, and a dense, white cloud hung thick in the air like fog. Roberts squinted, examining the area. A weird burnt odor drifted past his nose. He was seated but leaning back against a wall. *There wasn't a wall behind me a second ago.* A loud buzzing roared through his head. He struggled to rise, but an agent kneeling at his side held him down. The man's mouth moved in slow motion, but his words were just a jumble of mysterious sounds. Several people rushed past and someone yelled something, pointing toward the presidential riser. The loud buzzing continued as more people ran into the milky cloud. *Dick! Bishop!*

Roberts placed his palms on the floor and tried to get up again—his last memory before dropping back to the floor.

FORTY-SEVEN

Roberts jolted awake, bathed in sweat again. He wiped sleep from his eyes and stared at the digital clock—1:43.

The same dream.

It played over and over in his mind like a movie he couldn't turn off. He rested his hands on his chest and took a few deep breaths. His heart pounded, and he felt ants crawling all over his body. How long before the dream stopped, or would it ever stop? He rubbed his eyes, trying to erase the memory. The vision of Sayed leaping from the riser, Dick firing his pistol, the bright orange flash.

Roberts turned to Susan, her sleeping nude body silhouetted by the night light. *Night light—hadn't used one since he was a kid.* But Susan insisted on keeping one in every room.

He watched her a long time. The curve of her hips still excited him. How long had it been—eight or ten weeks? He'd lost track of time. His sleeping problems and headaches made him edgy and short-tempered. But the touch of her hand could calm him. He loved her and she loved him. He couldn't imagine life without her and Abbey. Roberts had almost asked her to marry him several times but backed out at the last minute. He wanted her with him, but he'd not yet been able to accept the fact she would always have strange ideas. *Sprits, ghosts, psychic shadows*. She must believe in that stuff, but it was so far removed from his beliefs that...

Didn't matter. It was time to commit.

After the incident, there were congressional hearings. Roberts gave his testimony weeks ago. Allowing the president to get that close to a suicide bomber meant the whole stinking thing had gone wrong. The Secret Service needed a distraction from all the questions. Headquarters probably figured elevating someone to hero status was the fastest way to deflect criticism, and Roberts had been chosen, and Dick, posthumously.

Receiving the Medal of Valor should have been a wonderful experience. Roberts hated it. He still blamed himself for everything. A dozen times a day, he went over all his mistakes. Now everyone looked up to him as some kind of *super-agent*. He wasn't worthy of their praise or respect. *He'd failed.*

With Dick's death, Roberts got promoted to PI Squad Supervisor. No more need to transfer. His old nemesis, Special Agent in Charge Gonzales, had been transferred to the Detroit field office. The director had no patience for a SAIC on the wrong side of a good plan. Dick also probably had a hand in that during their last meeting.

Bishop had disappeared. He had been seriously injured during the blast and transported to Parkland hospital with Roberts. According to the story, falling behind the armored lectern before the explosion saved him. The day after the explosion, a military air ambulance showed up. Markings indicated it was assigned to Fort Sam Houston. A full bird colonel with the medical corps marched in and presented documents from the national security advisor officially transferring Bishop to an undisclosed military hospital.

Bishop's doctor at Parkland protested that he was too injured to transport. He didn't win that argument. The last anyone saw of Bishop, a uniform doctor and trauma nurse were attending him in the chopper as it flew south—probably San Antonio. Roberts lost track of him after that.

Roberts slipped on his boxers and tip-toed to the bedroom door. He'd woken Susan up so many times the last two months with his bad dreams; she needed one good night's rest. He unlocked the door and staggered down the hall, following the glow of the nightlight. What had triggered the dream? Something always did. *Of course, the two pieces of mail yesterday.*

He made his way to the kitchen and reached for the Scotch bottle in the cabinet over the sink, pouring three fingers. He took a sip. The warning from the Secret Service shrink came back to him. Everyone talked to the shrink after an on-duty traumatic incident.

"Don't let alcohol become a problem," the guy had told him.

Too late for that. The doc had written prescriptions for anti-anxiety and sleeping meds, telling Roberts he had a touch of PTSD. He'd filled neither prescription. He could handle this without drugs. Roberts chuckled at an old memory from childhood. During his teen years, Roberts' dad used to say, *"Remember boys, alcohol is a drug."*

Roberts wandered back into the living room and flopped down on the sofa. He opened his briefcase and shuffled through the papers, looking for the correspondence. The short report had originated from the Secret Service Interpol liaison in Paris. Two five-by-seven color photos were included with the account. The first photograph showed a badly decomposed body crumpled in some kind of ditch, half-covered with wet debris—the real Rene Bertrand's remains. According to autopsy records, he died due to two bullets fired point-blank into the back of his head. The second picture was Bertrand's employee photo from the *La Voix* magazine.

Roberts took another pull of Scotch and studied it a long time. The face looked exactly like Sayed's. What were the chances, a million to one, that two people could look so much alike? All it took was someone who closely resembled Sayed, a few nips and tucks, a change of color for hair and eyes. Probably true what they say: *Everyone has a double.*

"An audacious and daring plan." That's what the Secret Service Director said when giving testimony regarding the attack. Roberts sat back and took another sip. Nothing like that had ever been tried before. And since it failed, no one would ever try it again. He took another drink.

The loss of Dick still hit Roberts the hardest. He missed having him around. Having someone to confide in and advise him. Having Dick there to deliver his old verbal jabs and watching him always preening and grooming. Doing his old job gave Roberts no satisfaction. Getting promoted had been the only thing he'd cared about for years. Now, he didn't care about anything career-related. He could use Dick's advice right about now, which led him to open the second letter.

Roberts slipped the note from the envelope posted from Jordan five days earlier, its return address the U.S. Embassy. He read it for the fifth time and concentrated on each word, letting it sink in.

Michael, I'm doing well—been back at work less than a week. Try not to let the events of that day play on your mind too much. There's nothing any of us can do to change what happened. Just let it go. We could play the blame game the rest of our lives and it wouldn't change a thing. The country and the Secret Service need to move on. So do we. Don't fight it—it's not a battle. We fight battles not only to win but also to gain experience for the next one. There will be many more for both of us.

No need writing me back. By the time you receive this I'll be long gone. I enjoyed working with you and wish you all the best.

Stay safe,

Bishop

Roberts grinned. Bishop had come in from the shadows and had now returned to them. Roberts dropped the letter and photos back inside the briefcase before closing it.

Bishop's words finally hit home—*move on.* They'd all done their best and learned lessons. The president had been saved. So, in that sense, he hadn't failed, right? He went back into the kitchen and held the drink over the sink, thinking. He poured the last finger of Scotch down the drain and stared into the empty glass. Something his dad used to say popped back into his head. During the war, most of his dad's best friends had been killed. The only way the old man could cope with their loss was to move on. *"Let the dead bury the dead,"* the old guy used to say.

It was also time for Roberts. From now on, no more nightmares. Stop blaming yourself. Start living again and enjoying life.

Roberts turned off the kitchen light and headed back to Susan's bedroom. He eased under the covers and stared into the darkness, trying to relax himself back to sleep. A moment later, a dim light flashed in the hall, just outside the door. Roberts' breath caught. In the flash he thought he saw the image of a child briefly appear. *Psychic shadow?*

Roberts cautiously rose and walked to the door. He glanced up and down the dark hall—nothing. The doctor told him to expect headaches and flashes of light across his vision. Not at all uncommon for people with severe concussions. They would pass with time after the brain injury completely healed. He strolled to the open door leading to Abbey's room. She lay on her back sound asleep. Her arm curled around her favorite stuffed animal, Max, a penguin. Roberts quietly slipped back into bed with Susan and released a long breath. He never thought he'd fall in love with a woman who already had a child. What kind of life could he expect when he and Susan married?

Somewhere deep in his subconscious a familiar, comforting voice answered.

"A good life, Ace."

If you enjoyed this story and would like to read more:

- Leave a review on your favorite book site
- Tell a friend about the book and Larry Enmon
- Ask your local library to put Larry Enmon's work on the shelf
- Recommend Fawkes Press books to your local bookstore

Great readers make great books possible!

FAWKES PRESS

WWW.FAWKESPRESS.COM / NEWSLETTER
WWW.LARRY-ENMON.COM

ACKNOWLEDGMENTS

This project has been in the works on and off for over a decade. I long ago lost count of the many alpha/beta readers who were kind enough to give their time to read and make valuable comments on improving it. I won't attempt to name you all because I'd surely leave someone out, but know that your contributions were most appreciated. The most recent readers made the most significant contributions in pulling this across the finish line. They are as follows: James Bowen – U.S. Secret Service Supervisory Special Agent (ret.), Samuel Simon – FBI Supervisory Special Agent (ret.), Special Agent Shane Zittermanis – U.S. Secret Service, Mary Simon, Natalie Enmon Mobley, Kelli Grant, Daryle McGinnis, Ann Barnhart Washburn, and Susan Davis.

I also wish to thank my editors, who are the real stars of the show. You make me look better through your wordsmithing than I deserve to, Leslie Lutz and TwylaBeth Walker Lambert.

A big shout-out to the DFW Writer's Workshop for reteaching me creative writing.

And a special thanks to Jodi Thompson and Fawkes Press, without whose faith in the manuscript and me this would never have come to fruition.

Paul Evans stared out the passenger's window at the black desert racing by at seventy miles an hour. With no moon, the only illumination came from the SUV's headlights. This area of Interstate 40, between Santa Rosa and Clines Corners, was the loneliest stretch of the covert escort mission. Personnel from the Office of Secure Transportation voted it the most boring. Miles of endless, dark freeway with a featureless landscape on all sides. Of course, driving it on a Tuesday, in the middle of the night, what could he expect? Paul checked the time to confirm they were still on schedule. They should be at Sandia in less than two hours.

It was his wife's thirtieth birthday. She'd be up later getting Katherine off to school. Paul planned to be home with the bouquet of roses by then. The last few months had been crazy. The higher tensions with China and Russia only increase the frequency of the missions. He took a swallow of water from his bottle and turned to the back seat, searching the rear floorboard.

"Are there any cashews left?"

"I dropped them back there somewhere," Steve answered, turning to help search.

Paul waved him away. "I'll look—you just drive," Paul said before moving a ballistics vest to find them sitting on top of an M-4 assault rifle. "Got 'em."

"What in the hell do you suppose that is," Steve mumbled, leaning closer to the windshield.

Paul pulled open the bag and grabbed a handful of nuts, popping one in his mouth as he directed his attention back to the front. The horizon ahead glowed bright orange like an early sunrise, but from the west. Distances were hard to gauge in the desert at night, but he made it at less than ten miles. "No idea—aliens?" he joked as the glow continued filling the night sky. He chewed slowly, a feeling of dread settling in his gut.

Steve grunted. "Well, this is New Mexico; anything's possible."

"Better call it in." Paul grabbed the mike to the encrypted radio. The eighteen-wheeler was only five miles behind and closing fast. If there was a road obstruction up ahead, it needed to be checked out before the eighteen-wheeler rolled up on it. "Convoy Commander, this is Scout."

The deep, slow, baritone voice answering had a sound of authority. "Scout, this is Convoy Commander—go ahead."

The laid-back Tennessee drawl made Paul grin. The commander had grown up in Oak Ridge. He'd never lose that down-home accent. Cornbread, field peas, and sweet iced tea defined him.

"Sir, we have an orange glow directly ahead of us that may be a fire. It appears to be on the primary route. Request permission to investigate."

A few seconds passed before the commander answered. "That's a roger, Scout. I haven't heard anything on the state police radio—we'll give 'em a call."

"Commander, we suggest you drop it down to fifty—repeat, five zero miles an hour. We'll check it out and advise when we're on the scene."

"Copy that, Scout, we're shutting it back to five zero miles—call us when you have something."

Paul popped the rest of the nuts in his mouth and dusted his hands on his tactical pants. "Okay, kick this thing in the butt, and let's see what's up there."

They had only minutes to determine the situation before the convoy would be on them. If there was an obstruction on the primary, a quick secondary route must be established and approved. The convoy could never be allowed to stop—never, except in specially secured areas.

Steve hit the gas to eighty-five. The orange glow took on a large eerie appearance. Paul grabbed the binoculars but couldn't make out anything except a larger version of what they were already seeing. The bizarre glowing shadows in the dark desert sky danced like ghosts in the heavens. In five years working for DOE, Paul had seen nothing like it. A feeling of apprehension again crept through his stomach. Within the next few miles, it became clear; the light was a massive fire. Red and yellow flames rose a hundred feet in the air as their SUV approached the inferno. The blaze lit up the dark road with a light as bright as day. A New Mexico State Police car blocked the freeway about two hundred yards from the conflagration. The car's red and blue lights flashed with the wall of flames in the background. Flares and orange safety cones blocked the freeway and were laid out in a pattern that directed all traffic off to a gravel service road to the right. A state trooper waved Pal and Steve to the side of the freeway toward the gravel road with his flashlight.

"Let's talk to this guy," Paul said. There were no other vehicles on the freeway this time of night, so Steve slowed to a crawl and stopped a few feet from the officer. Paul lowered his window, and the growl of the fire became louder. A petrochemical smell wafted past his nostrils. "What's happened," he shouted over the noise.

The trooper paced to their vehicle. He had a look of total exhaustion. With the window down, the heat warmed Paul's face. The officer's features came into view. He had a lot of Native American blood. He was short—barely five foot eight, but with broad, muscular shoulders and a thick chest. His most notable feature was a thin scar across the bridge of his nose.

The trooper continued waving his flashlight toward the orange cones as he wiped sweat from his brow. "You'll have to get off here—freeway's closed."

Paul dug into his pocket and held up his federal agent credentials. "We're OST escorting special cargo to Sandia. What's going on?"

The officer's forehead wrinkled as he bent down to the passenger's window and examined the credentials with his flashlight. He handed them back and nodded. "Oh yeah, they told us at roll call you might be coming through tonight." He turned and pointed to the fire. "Tanker truck flipped—just rolled up on it about five minutes ago. Waiting for some help."

Paul asked, "Any survivors?"

The trooper removed his cap and wiped his face with a handkerchief. Had to be at least ninety-five degrees out there.

The officer shook his head. "Don't know—I can't get any closer—doesn't look good."

Paul had to make a decision—and fast. The convoy would be there in minutes. He glanced at the GPS before asking, "How far is Highway Three?"

The trooper leaned both hands on top of the vehicle while he spoke through the passenger window. His eyes narrowed before pointing straight toward the fire. "Highway Three exit is about two miles up the freeway."

Paul hated delays. Always came at the times he had plans he didn't want messed up. "How can we get there? Any chance of staying on the service road and making it through?"

The officer shook his head. "None—you'd cook, and so would your cargo." He nodded to the improvised exit he'd formed with the orange cones. "You could get off here, and in about fifty yards, take the gravel road that heads north. In a few miles, you can take a left on another gravel road that intersects Highway Three. Just follow the signs—nothing to it."

Paul studied the blaze. "Fifty yards, huh? Will that put us too close to the fire?"

The trooper shook his head. "No, you'll be well away from it. I directed three vehicles there a couple of minutes ago—not many choices until we clear the freeway."

Steve checked the officer's directions on the vehicle's GPS. He tapped the screen. "Here it is." He leaned toward the trooper. "Will that road handle an eighteen-wheeler?"

The officer smiled. "Sure—no problem."

Paul fiddled with the knobs on the police scanner and encrypted car radio. "We haven't heard a word about this. Have you reported it?"

The trooper glanced at the radio on his belt. "I'm having trouble getting through to base from here—must be a dead zone or something, had to use my cell to call it in."

Paul looked at Steve, who gave him a quick nod and then back to the trooper. "Thanks for the info. I'm calling the other convoy vehicles. Wish we could stick around and help, but we have to scout ahead. When they get here, just direct them toward the gravel road—I'll make sure they know where to go. Don't bother trying to talk to them. They're ordered not to stop for anyone."

"Will do—good luck." The officer stepped back and gave a quick wave.

Steve backed up and drove across the tiny sliver of turf to access the freeway's service road, while Paul attempted to call the commander on the radio. After several tries, he realized his transmissions weren't going anywhere. "Great, now our radio's not working." He dialed the cell phone number for the commander and explained what he'd discovered.

"Yeah," the commander said, "we got through to the state police. They confirmed the fire—said they'd had several calls about it. I'll contact Albuquerque base and tell them we're deviating from the primary. We'll be right behind you, so get well out ahead of us and keep in touch. Let us know when you hit Highway Three."

The light from the fire was like a giant torch behind Paul and Steve as they drove down the lonely gravel road into the black night. Paul kept messing with the encrypted radio, switching channels and trying different encryption codes, attempting to bring it back online—nothing. He couldn't understand it. Worked fine until they stopped to talk to the officer. By the time they made the final left turn on the lonely, dark road toward Highway Three, they were deep in the boonies. The narrow stretch wove through thick trees and desert scrum on each side of the road. Only the glow of the burning tanker in the distance to their left gave them any light. The commander wouldn't like this—always hated tight areas with no visibility.

After about three miles, they came to a major road and a sign that read Highway Three. Paul let out a sigh of relief just as his phone rang —the Convoy Commander.

"Scout, we just made the turn onto the gravel road, and we're only a few miles behind you. This is the crappiest damn excuse for a road I've ever seen. How's it look up ahead?"

"You're clear to Highway Three, sir. We're turning on it now." Paul disconnected and looked at Steve. "Take a left here—we'll try and put a little distance between us. Want to make sure there are no more surprises—he sounds pissed." Paul calculated the time. He could still be home with the flowers before his wife left to take his daughter to school—if there were no other delays. Every time he planned a surprise for his family, something like this always came up.

Steve turned onto the hardtop just as the alert signal broke the silence. He and Paul looked at each other with the same thought—the convoy was under attack. The shrill beeping alarm and flashing red light on the SUV's console so distracted Paul that he grabbed the dead radio's mic. "Convoy Commander—this is Scout!"

"Forget it—it's still out," Steve yelled, making a U-turn and heading back down the dark narrow road they'd just left.

"Hurry!" Paul punched buttons on his phone. The commander's cell rang five times—then went to voice mail. Paul grabbed the ballistics vest from the back seat and slipped it over his head. His hands shook as he reached for the M-4 and chambered a round.

Steve's speed tested their nerves racing to the rescue. The SUV fishtailed in the loose gravel, and he had to let off the accelerator. When he rounded the only curve in the road, they both spotted it at the same time. The white, three-quarter-ton, dually pickup truck with a large camper shell straddled the dark narrow road.

"Where did that come from?" Steve yelled, slamming hard on the brakes. Paul was pushed forward as the SUV skidded to a stop and blinding dust overtook them. They were enveloped in a thick white cloud as Paul reached for the door handle. Through the swirling dust around the front windshield, the outline of a man popped up from behind the hood of the blocking vehicle.

Paul squinted. What tha—

The flash from the shoulder-fired rocket the man held lit up the night. Paul had always assumed before someone died, their last thoughts would be on friends or family. He was wrong. His were on the eighteen-wheeler they were escorting.

Filled with nuclear weapons.

And under attack.

FAWKES PRESS

CPSIA information can be obtained
at www.ICGtesting.com
Printed in the USA
LVHW090442120721
692445LV00001B/47

9 781945 419898